A FORBIDDEN GAME
BOOK 1

A GAME OF CHOICE

ALISHA WILLIAMS

A GAME OF CHOICE

ALISHA WILLIAMS

Book Cover Design: Pretty In Ink Creation

Photographer: Xram Ragde

Cover Model: Samuel Nogueira Cintra

To my SVU readers who's been dying for Lilly and Toby's story, this one is for you!

AUTHOR NOTE

Thank you for picking up A Game Of Choice. This is book one in the A Forbidden Game Duet. It is an MFM stepbrother and best friend hockey romance. This story follows the children, Lillianna and Tobias, from my why choose Silver Valley University series. While you don't need to read the previous series to understand this one, if you would like to ready Lillianna's parent's story, the first book is Hidden Secrets.

While this duet is not a dark romance, it may contain some potentially dark content. Expect the topic of mental health to play a big role in this duet.

CHAPTER ONE

LILLIANNA

August

I'M GOING TO DO IT. I'M GOING TO TELL HIM THAT I LOVE HIM.

Taking a deep, encouraging breath, I wipe my sweaty palms on my yellow sundress as I stand up and follow Toby outside the door he just left through a few minutes ago.

"Where are you going?" my best friend, Bianca, asks.

"I'm just going to get another drink," I lie, my eyes glued to the door and my heart pounding painfully in my chest.

I can't believe I'm doing this. One step at a time, my feet carry me out the door and down the front steps of the house where the party is being held at.

Biting my lip, my eyes scan the front lawn, looking for Toby.

"Hey there, *il mio cuore*," Bishop, Toby's best friend, says as he joins me at my side. "What're you doing out here?"

"Have you seen Toby?" I ask, not looking his way as I squint my eyes, scanning the treeline again.

"Ah, yeah. He just went that way. Said something about needing some air," Bishop answers, waving his hand to the left.

"Thanks," I say and start to head in that direction.

"Lilly, wait!" he calls out. I pause and look over my shoulder.

"What?" My brows furrow in question. He looks out at the forest then back to me, a worried look taking over his handsome features.

"Maybe you should just wait for him here. I'm sure he's not going to be long." He lets out a nervous chuckle, running a hand through his dark brown hair.

I give him a weird look. "Why are you acting so funny?"

He lets out a heavy sigh before shoving his hands in his pockets. The look of pity on his face has my belly swooping nervously. "Look, he was with a girl. I just don't want you walking in on anything, okay?"

A girl? Since when does Toby hang out with other girls? He's never shown interest in anyone before.

I'm sure Bishop is mistaken. He should know Toby better than that. I spin around, walking fast toward the trees, leaving Bishop and his stupid sympathetic look on the steps.

No. He has to be mistaken. There's no way Toby is out here with a girl. He came here with me tonight, just like he always does. He's been with me all night dancing and laughing. The way he touched me as we slow danced...you can't fake something like that.

He wants me. I want him. I have for as long as I can remember. And I'm finally going to tell him.

Once I get to the treeline, I pause for a moment, and that's when I hear murmuring voices coming from behind the shed next to the house.

Every step closer, I feel my legs growing heavy, my eyes

welling with tears. I pray Bishop is wrong, that Toby is just here with some friend, talking. That I won't walk into something that's going to shatter my heart.

But as I creep around the corner, I stop and watch as the blood in my ears pounds painfully.

"You know, I've been trying to get you to ask me out all year," Tiffany Watson, head cheerleader of Silver Valley High, runs her hand down Toby's arm. He looks down, watching her. I can't read the look on his face but he's not doing anything to stop her.

"Really?" He sounds uninterested and that lets me breathe just a little bit easier. But it doesn't settle the white hot jealousy filling my veins as I hold back angry tears.

"I guess my flirting game is off if you didn't even notice." She giggles, tucking her auburn hair behind her ear. "Any time I tried to get you alone, you're always with your little sister."

He shoots her a hard look. "I don't want to talk about her," his voice comes out in an almost growl. Hurt splinters through my chest at his anger toward just the thought of me. "I came out here to think." He looks up at the sky, shifting his body to lean back against the tree and causing Tiffany's hand to fall from his arm.

She steps closer to him, and all I want to do is scream at her, tell her to get away from him, or beg him to push her away.

When she cups his cheek, making him look down at her, I have to swallow back the bile that rises in my throat.

My hand falls to my belly as the tears I've been holding back finally break free. *Walk away, Toby, come back to the house. Come back to me. Please.*

"If you're looking to get your mind off something, I can help you with that." She leans up on her tiptoes and places her mouth to his.

And that's when my heart breaks.

I turn around and take off running. A deep sob rattles my

chest, tears streaming down my cheeks, making it harder to see in the dark.

Every few steps, I trip over my own feet. My mind is fuzzy, and I feel dizzy.

"Lilly!" someone shouts from behind me, but I don't stop. I head straight toward my car, needing to get out of here. "Lilly, wait!"

Hands grab me as I try to open my car door. It's locked, and my keys are back with Bianca in my purse. "Damn it!" I cry, kicking the car door and pounding on the window a few times weakly.

"Shhh." Strong arms wrap around me, and I turn in Bishop's hold. Burying my face into his chest, I let go and break down.

He holds me as I cry, not asking what's wrong. He knows what's wrong, and I hate him for it. But he's also one of my best friends, and I need him right now.

"I got you, *il mio cuore*," he murmurs, kissing the top of my head.

The kiss replays over and over in my mind. How did my night go from having an amazing time with Toby, to ending in pure devastation? I was going to tell him I love him.

I'm such a fool, a stupid sixteen year old girl clinging to the hope that what we had meant as much to him as it did to me.

"Take me home," I tell Bishop, pulling out of his arms and angrily wiping the tears from my face.

"Lilly..."

"Take me home!" I shout, abandoning my car and heading toward his.

"Shit," he curses, but then I hear his footsteps following me. He unlocks the car, and I yank open the passenger door before getting in.

Thankfully, he doesn't ask questions or try to get me to talk on the way home.

Leaning my head against the window, I look out into the darkness.

I feel so stupid and confused.

No one understands Toby's and my relationship. Since the moment we met back when we were just little kids, he's been my whole world.

He's not my best friend, not like Bishop or his sister, Bianca, or Jonas. Toby is my person, my soulmate. My protector. Hell, I don't even think there's a word in the English dictionary that could describe what he is to me.

Fucked up thing is...he's also my stepbrother. But never once did it ever feel like that. I knew deep in my heart that someday, we would be more. No one could have ever convinced me otherwise.

Until tonight.

I thought neither of us knew how to take that next step. I wanted to be the one to get over that hurdle so we could get past it and be with each other, like we've been wanting to for so long.

Does he really just see me as his little sister?

No. You don't look at your sister the way he looks at me; like he wants to consume me, like I'm his everything, his world.

But then how could he kiss her?! And after he knew what she's said to me, about our family?

I feel betrayed and broken. I'm a fool for thinking this was more.

We pull up into the driveway of our massive house. It's crazy to think that my mom and I lived in a small one bedroom apartment before meeting Theo and Toby.

"Lilly," Bishop starts, but I shake my head.

"Just...don't." I open the car door, about to step out when he grabs my arm, pulling me back.

I look over at him. There's pain in his eyes that I don't really understand. He opens his mouth to say something but thinks better of it and shakes his head, letting out a heavy sigh. He pulls me closer and kisses the top of my head, his lips lingering longer than they should. "I'm here for you, *il mio cuore*."

He's been calling me that for as long as I can remember, but I have no idea what it means. I really should look that up someday.

"Thanks," I murmur and pull out of his hold. "Night."

Getting out of his car, I head inside. The place is quiet, all my brothers are in bed by now, and God only knows what my parents are doing. They think I'm safe with Toby because they know he would never let anything happen to me. That's how protective he is. He would do anything to keep me safe.

I guess my heart isn't included in that, huh?

CHAPTER TWO

LILLIANNA

September

"I don't see why you boys can't just live here," my mom says as she looks at Toby with tears in her eyes. "You know Bishop is welcome to stay here too."

"I know, Mom." Toby laughs. "But we want the full college experience. Plus, with our hockey schedule, it would just be easier to live on campus."

"Fine," she sighs. "But you have to come home every Sunday for supper. I'm not taking no for an answer."

Full college experience? Since when? Toby has never shown interest in anything other than hockey, Bishop, and me. Now, all of a sudden, he's into parties? The idea of girls throwing themselves at him or Bishop makes my stomach sour.

They are my best friends, my people, and knowing that I won't see them every day makes it hard to hold back my tears.

My eyes are fixed on Toby as he talks to his dad. *Well, I guess our dad?* Theo is technically my stepdad.

My feelings for him still go beyond what you feel for a sibling. I love Toby more than words can describe.

Some people think our closeness is odd, but I've never cared. My whole family is different from what's deemed the social norm. Toby came into my life when I was three and he was six. We're not blood, we just grew up together.

I know he loves me. Even after what happened this summer. He tells me all the time. But I don't understand why he won't admit that it's something more, that he's *in love* with me. He can't act the way he does with me and not feel that. I just wish he would admit it and save me the heartbreak I've been feeling for weeks.

"Isaiah, Raiden!" Theo shouts to get my twin brothers' attention. "Come say goodbye to your brother."

Like I said, my family is different. My mom is in love with more than one person. Five, to be exact, and each of my dads passed on their DNA to one of us children. My dad, Jax, is Isaiah's bio-father, while Theo is Raiden's. They are five. Then there's Bennett, who's eleven and is fathered by our dad, Brody. And me? Our dad, Chase, helped make me.

But DNA doesn't matter in this family. They all love each and every one of us the same. The only reason why they found out whose DNA I have is so that my mom could give each of them a biological child.

I love my family, and even though people talk and stare, I wouldn't trade them for the world.

"You're gonna miss him, aren't you?" my other mom, Rain, says, coming to stand next to me. I look up at her, her green eyes shining down at me with understanding. I nod my head and look back at Toby, who's laughing with my little brothers as Bennett joins them.

Rain is my mom's partner. She's also the one in the family that I'm the closest to. I'm close with my mom too, but there's some things I feel more comfortable telling Rain.

Like this summer, when she found me crying my eyes out in my room after I saw Toby with that girl.

She ended up hanging around him and Bishop a lot during the past month, trying to find any chance she could to get Toby to leave his 'little sister' at home.

Even after that night, I couldn't bring myself to put distance between us. I know, it's pathetic. But I can't just throw years of my life away like that. He still doesn't know I saw him and Tiffany that first night, and I hope he never finds out.

Because while I wish we were more, losing him altogether would hurt way worse. I don't want things to be awkward between us.

But watching her dig her heels in, trying to get Toby's attention, was my own personal hell.

I spilled everything to Rain, and we sat, talking for hours. She didn't judge me or think I was gross for loving my stepbrother.

After that night, though, Toby slowly started to change. The last two weeks, he's started going out more with Bishop, leaving me behind. Not always, but most times.

We stopped cuddling like we used to. He stopped coming into my bed when he couldn't sleep at night.

I know things are changing between us and I hate it so much it hurts.

"Little Flower," Toby says, his gaze finding mine. My heart skips a beat at the nickname he hasn't called me in weeks. "You gonna come say goodbye, or what?" he asks with that side grin that takes my breath away.

All the adults and kids have disappeared, leaving Toby and me alone in the foyer. We stand there, only an inch between us. My eyes trace his face as if this is the last time I'll ever see him, and I need to remember every inch. He might only be moving across town, but I'm not going to see him every day. Things will probably never be the same again. That thought alone has tears forming in my eyes.

"Lills," Toby sighs. He brings his tattooed hand up, brushing the falling tears from my cheeks with his thumb. I wish he didn't do that; it makes my heart hurt more while loving his touch. "Don't cry, please. I hate seeing you cry."

"I'm sorry," I sniff. "It's just, I'm gonna miss you."

"I might be moving out of the house, but I'm not moving that far away," he reassures, pulling me into his arms as I wrap mine around him.

Every time he holds me like this, I break a little more inside.

"It's not that and you know it," I murmur against his chest as his strong arms hold me tight. We stand like that for a while, my hand fisting the back of his shirt, never wanting to let him go.

"I love you, Lilly," he whispers, kissing the top of my head, then breaks the little bubble that is us.

He quickly turns away, not giving me a chance to say it back, as he grabs his bag off the floor and heads out the open door. I stand in the doorway, watching him jog over to Bishop's new Jeep. He hops in the passenger seat as Bishop sticks his head out the top.

"See you later, *il mio cuore*. Be a good girl while we're gone," he teases, giving me a wink.

A smile finds my lips as I raise my hand with a soft laugh and flip him the finger. He gasps, his hand slapping against his chest like I wounded him. I just laugh and shake my head as he sits back down.

But the smile slips away as I watch the Jeep backing out of the driveway, my eyes finding Toby's again.

We stare at each other, a thousand unsaid words passing between us. When they are no longer in sight, I lean my head against the door frame and sigh, willing the tears to not return.

"How you doing, Lillypad?" Rain asks as she comes up behind me, putting her head on my shoulder.

"Not good," I admit.

"Don't give up on him, okay?"

"I won't." I don't think I could, even if I wanted to. And I don't.

I'm not sure what's going on inside that complicated mind of yours, Tobias Munro, but I plan on finding out, one way or another.

CHAPTER THREE

LILLIANNA

Two years later

The music is loud, my head is swimming, and I'm about to do something huge. I might regret it when I wake up, but drinking seems to have given me the courage that I've been needing for the past few weeks.

"Where are you going?" Bianca asks as I stand up from our place on the couch. I feel a rush of déjà vu hit me as I look down at my best friend. Only this time, I'm not going to try and confess my love to someone, more like the complete opposite.

"I just got to do something real quick. I'll be right back."

She gives me a funny look but takes a sip of her drink and goes about her conversation with Milly, one of our friends.

My eyes scan the crowd, looking for my boyfriend, Jonas

Well, I guess I should say soon-to-be-ex-boyfriend, because that's what I'm about to go do. Break up with my boyfriend of almost two years at the end of the year party.

Bianca, Jonas, and myself have been best friends almost as long as Toby, Bishop, and me.

The only difference is that Bianca and Jonas are in my grade, making it easy to form a friendship with them growing up. Plus, the fact that Bianca is Bishop's little sister, so she was always around.

How did Jonas and I go from best friends to dating when I was so madly head-over-heels for my stepbrother, you may ask?

The reason has a tinge of guilt bubbling up in my belly. See, after Toby went off to SVU and started to spend more and more time away, I got lonely. I was heartbroken and I felt like I needed someone to fill the void he'd left behind.

Jonas and I ended up hanging out alone one night because Bianca was sick. I'm not sure how it all happened, but the night ended with us kissing and him asking me to be his girlfriend.

I said yes because I did like Jonas. He's an amazing guy. Tall, black hair, a crooked smile that makes your belly flutter. He made me laugh, and I enjoyed being around him.

If I couldn't be with Toby, why not be with someone else, right?

Sadly, it's not that simple. It's been over a year and a half, and we still act more like best friends than two people in a relationship.

Hell, we hardly kiss. At best, we hold hands, hug, and cuddle. Very PG-13 for a couple of eighteen year olds.

I'm going into university in a few weeks, and I want to go into this new part of my life single, starting fresh. I owe that to the both of us.

And…well, maybe a part of my heart hopes that with me being in the same school as Toby, and not only seeing him on Sundays, maybe we could get that connection back like we once had.

Because I miss it. I miss him. I miss him so much it hurts my heart and soul. I think that's part of the reason why things never felt right with Jonas; because deep down, I really wanted to be with someone else. Someone I can't, and may never, have.

Not finding Jonas in the crowd of people in the living room or kitchen, I head out to the backyard. I spot him sitting with a group of his teammates.

Get this, he's a hockey player too. Guess I have a type. He ended up taking Toby's goalie position when Toby graduated.

"Hey." I put my hand on Jonas' shoulder.

He looks up at me, one of his bright, crooked smiles taking over his handsome face. "Hey, Babe. What's up? You and Bee still hanging out on the couch talking to the girls?"

By girls, he means the cheer team. Bee and I ended up joining this past year, mostly because my mom, Rain, was filling in for the coach who was off on maternity leave. Now Rain will be back to coach at SVU.

It's so weird having pretty much all my parents working for the school in some way. My dads, Brody and Chase, coach the football team. Theo is the new dean as of this year.

Mom has her own bookstore that she runs; one I've worked at for years now, but she fills in for Rain whenever needed.

Then there's Jax. He is now the coach of Toby's hockey team. Jax was set to go pro in the football world, but he ended up hurting his arm and retired from the sport. A few years later, he started playing for the local recreational hockey team. He ended up loving the game and it became his new passion.

He's been with the Silver Knights Hockey team for the past few years now.

"Can we talk?" I ask, not wanting to do some painful small talk.

"Ah, sure?" His brows furrow, and my belly churns.

I can't do this, can I? I don't want to break his heart. He's been nothing but amazing to me. But I also can't lead him on.

I'm not in love with him, I can't offer him anymore than what we've been doing, and that's not right.

"Lilly, what's going on?" he asks me as he pulls me over to the fence. I bite my lower lip, looking up at him with big, guilty eyes.

"I like you. A lot. You're my best friend. You're sweet, kind, and always there for me when I need you. But…"

His face softens into a sad smile. "But that's all you see us as, just friends?"

My heart pounds in my chest as I nod. "I'm sorry." Tears fill my eyes, and a cry breaks free when he pulls me into his arms.

"Shhh." He kisses the top of my head.

"Please, don't hate me," I murmur into his chest.

"I could never hate you, Lilly. And if we're being honest, as amazing as you are—and trust me, you are—I feel like we make better friends."

Relief fills me. "You promise you don't hate me?" I look up at him and wipe the tears from my eyes.

"Never. And we're still best friends." He kisses my forehead.

"You're the best."

"I know," he chuckles, shooting me a wink. "You okay?"

"Only if you are."

"I'm fine." He gives me a soft smile.

"Hey, Lilly!" Milly's voice has me looking over to see her standing by the back door. "Bee is looking for you. She's not feeling very well."

"Is she okay?" The rush of concern in Jonas' voice has me fighting back a smile.

So, there may have been another reason I wanted to end things with Jonas. I don't think the two of them realize it yet, but Bianca and Jonas are totally in love with each other. Honestly, I don't know why he asked me out and not Bee.

And Bee, being the best friend a girl could ask for, supported our relationship. It was only the past few months I've allowed myself to see their connection.

"I think so. She's out front getting air and waiting to get a ride home."

"Thanks, Milly," Jonas says before turning to me. "Come on, hot stuff, party is over. And we have a bestie to get home."

I giggle and follow him through the side gate, grateful that it went so well when I was preparing for the worst.

When Bianca comes into view, Jonas picks up his pace, wanting to get to her faster. He kneels down and puts his hand on her knee. "Hey, Bumblebee, you good?"

Bianca groans, "Too much beer. Why do I drink it? It's so nasty."

We both chuckle and Jonas gives her knee a squeeze but pauses, looking up at me like I might be upset about it. I just smile and shoot him a wink. He stares at me for a beat before scooping up our best friend.

"What are you doing?" Bianca asks as we start toward Jonas' truck.

"I'm taking you two home. I think you've had enough to drink."

"Put me down, you can't carry me like this," she protests, trying to get out of his arms.

"Why not?" he asks as we reach his truck. I rush ahead and open the passenger door.

"Because you have a girlfriend, right there." Jonas places her down on the seat and walks around the truck to his side.

"No he doesn't," I tell her as I slide in next to her, closing the door behind me.

"What?" she blinks over at me.

"That's where I went, to break up with Jonas." I grimace.

Her eyes widen, looking from me to Jonas, who gets in and starts up the truck. "But why?"

He shrugs. "We realized we're better off as friends." He looks over at us and smiles.

"Oh...I'm sorry?"

"Don't be." I put my head on her shoulder as we start down

the road. "Everyone should have the chance to be with someone who makes them their whole world. And that wasn't us."

"I wasn't going to say anything but, come on, you two hardly ever kissed," Bee slurs. "Did you ever fuck?"

"No!" Both Jonas and I shout. Then we shoot each other a look before diverting our attention to the road.

"So, you're both still virgins?"

"Looks like it," I sigh. "That's okay, we can be the Three Virgin Amigos."

"What makes you think I'm still one?" she tosses out there in a teasing tone.

Jonas snaps his attention down to her, giving her a glare that has me smiling hard. "Because I'm your bestie, bitch. You would have told me."

She lets out a deep sigh, putting her head on Jonas' shoulder. "True."

I see Jonas' shoulders relax a little bit, and I roll my eyes. I have no idea how I didn't see this before.

When we get to my house, Bianca is asleep. "I got her."

Jonas brings her into the pool house. It's, more or less, become mine since we spend all our time here. And with three younger brothers, a girl needs her space.

Taking a seat on the edge of the pool, I slip my feet into the cool water and lean back on my hands, looking up at the starry night sky. The alcohol has pretty much left my system, and I can't help but feel relieved at how well tonight went. I shouldn't be surprised, Jonas is just that good of a guy. He would have never made me feel guilty for ending things.

"Hey," he says, taking a seat next to me.

"Hey." I move my attention from the sky over to him. "If I ask you something, would you be honest with me?"

"Always." He nods.

"Do you have feelings for B?"

His eyes widen at my question and I note a slight blush

taking over his cheeks. I can tell he wants to deny it, but he doesn't. Taking a deep breath he nods. "I'm sorry, Lilly."

"Don't be." I give him a reassuring smile. "It's okay. I've kind of gotten the impression you did for a while now."

"Really?"

"Yup. It's partly why I don't feel so bad for dumping your ass." I grin wide.

He snorts out a laugh, shaking his head. "Like you don't have feelings for someone else too."

My smile drops, my stomach sinks, and I look away. "I don't know what you mean."

"Lilly, I know you love him." *Ugh, why does his voice have to be so understanding and sweet.*

"I shouldn't," my voice is barely a whisper as I blink back tears.

"Whatever happens in the future, you will always have me and Bee." He wraps his arm around my shoulder.

"Thank you." I lean into his touch, placing my head on his shoulder. We just sit for a little while, enjoying the warm summer air.

"I better get going." He helps me to my feet and looks behind me at the pool house, a worried look on his face. I can tell he wants to stay here and take care of Bianca.

"I got her," I laugh. "Go, before one of my dads finds you here late at night."

"Fuck," he curses. "Last thing I need is my new coach and dean kicking my ass."

"You're so dramatic," I giggle, shaking my head. "They love you."

"Not if they think I'm out here fucking their daughter." He cocks a brow.

"Yeah, good point." I nod. "Better get going."

I walk Jonas out to his truck and wave goodbye before heading inside the house to grab a few things I know Bee is going to need when she wakes up.

After I grab some bottles of water and some pain meds, I head toward the back door when something out of the corner of my eye has me pausing.

Looking over, I see Toby standing in the doorway of the kitchen. I swallow hard, my eyes raking over his tattooed body. The man doesn't have a damn shirt on. *Why is the world so cruel to me?*

When our eyes lock, I'm met with a pissed off, annoyed glare. That hurts. Things between us haven't been the same for a couple of years now.

We don't hang out anymore, hardly talk when he comes over for supper on Sundays, and… he's so distant, even when he's right next to me. He hates Jonas with a passion and loves to point it out when he can.

Thankfully, Bishop and I are still close as ever, texting all the time. Mostly, it's just him sending me stupid memes.

Not being able to handle him looking at me like that, I break eye contact and head out to the pool house.

I didn't realize I was holding my breath until I get outside and gasp for air.

He has a way of doing that, sucking the air out of my lungs and leaving me vulnerable.

My eyes sting with tears again because all I want to do is go back over there and hug him, tell him I love him, that I miss him, and demand he stop being such an asshole. Demand to know why he's changed so much. What happened between us for him to act like we weren't each other's whole world for most of our lives.

The cold shoulder didn't start until I started dating Jonas. Maybe now that I'm not, things will change.

I know something is going to change because I've sat back and done nothing for long enough. One way or another, I'm getting Toby back in my life. It's up to him what position he will play when I do.

CHAPTER FOUR

LILLIANNA

"I CAN'T BELIEVE MY SWEET BABY IS GOING AWAY TO UNIVERSITY." My mom hugs me so tight it's starting to hurt.

"I'm only going to be across town. I'll be home all the time. You're being a little overdramatic," I sigh, trying to squirm my way out of her hold.

"Ellie, baby, let the girl breathe," my dad, Brody, says, coming up behind her and kissing the top of her head. He gives me a wink, and I smile.

"Why do my babies keep leaving me?" she huffs, leaning back into Brody's arms.

"No one has left you," I laugh. "Toby has come home every Sunday for the past two years. He's never missed a day." The consistency makes me happy because it's the only time I get to see him these days, apart from holiday breaks when he stays

But then it also hurts because the fact is, I miss him like crazy, and even when he's here, he's not *here*.

It's a rare occasion when we hold a conversation. And that's only when he's drunk, the man can chat my ear off about everything and anything then.

Especially when it has anything to do with Jonas. He truly despises the guy, and I don't know why. Jonas is sweet, kind, and only ever treated me well.

I feel bad for Jonas because he's going to be on the same hockey team as Toby this year.

I've heard the stories of how Brody and the others were to my mom, and I hate that. I hate what they did to my mom, who is the sweetest, most loving person…well, ever.

Thankfully, that's in the past, but I don't want to see Toby become that kind of person. I'm not sure what he's like around everyone else, but with Jonas he really does resemble a bully. It's a big reason why I've avoided him anytime Jonas' name would get brought up.

It's hard to have your "brother" hate your boyfriend.

Ex-boyfriend now. But that doesn't change the fact that Jonas is still one of my best friends and he's not going anywhere if I can help it.

So, if Toby or the other team members, start giving him a hard time, I won't hesitate to get my dad involved. Perks of being the coaches' daughter, right? I just hope that Jonas doesn't get mad at me for it. But I'm not one to sit around and let that kind of shit happen. Hopefully, it doesn't come to that.

"I still think you should just live here," Mom's voice pulls me from my inner ramblings. "I don't see the point of going through all that trouble of moving when you don't have to."

"Because as much as I love you, Rain, and the dads, along with the three little turds, I'm eighteen. I want to enjoy life as an adult. To make memories with Bianca and Jonas. I want to live in the dorms, be close to campus, and just be a regular ol' college student."

"Fine," Mom pouts. "You're breaking my heart, just so you know."

I roll my eyes as she heads out to the car, helping Brody carry some boxes. Ever the dramatic one, she is. But I love her.

I turn to my dad, Chase. "You're a bad influence on her."

"I know," he chuckles. "I've turned her into a naughty, naughty girl."

"Ew, gross. No!" I cover my ears. "Dad, just no."

"Ah, Lillypad. You should know by now we have no shame in this family."

"And, Ace, you should know by now that I don't have any shame in regard to this family. But what I do have a lot of shame for is knowing anything, and I mean *anything*, about my parents' sex life."

"Sex? What is *sex*?" He scratches his chin. "Not sure that's a thing. And it's definitely not a thing you should look into. Or ever do. Never, ever." He gives me a pointed glare, making me roll my eyes even harder.

"What's this about sex?" Brody asks, stepping back into the house. He shoots me a death glare.

"Nothing. Nothing about sex." I groan, putting my face in my hands as I die of embarrassment. "Can we stop, *please*?"

"No sex. Ever. Or until you're, like, eighty." Brody crosses his arms and lifts his chin, pulling off the over-protective-dad-thing well.

"I'm not having sex, okay?" I let out a heavy sigh.

"Of course you're not," Chase adds. "Because that's not a thing. So how could you do something that doesn't exist?"

I hit him with an *are you kidding me* look. I'm eighteen, not eight. I've known what sex was since around the time I turned ten when I had a nightmare and walked in on all, and I mean all, of my parents going at it. It's an image that's forever engraved in my brain that I really wish I could wash out with soap.

Rain pulled me to the side and helped make it a little less traumatic, but then I was stuck with so many more questions I didn't want to ask. So, I made the mistake and used the internet. It just made everything so much worse.

"Also, now I can't get the image of a naked eighty-year-old lady out of my head, thank you very much." Chase gives Brody a deadpan look as he walks past him.

"Happy to help!" Brody shouts back, then turns to me. "How are you doing, kiddo?"

I give him a small smile. "Nervous? Excited? Both?"

"You're going to do great. You have your best friend and your *ex-boyfriend*," he makes sure to emphasize the ex part. "And you have Toby and Bishop. I think you're in pretty good hands. But, if you ever need anything, you know your dads and I are here for you."

"Right. The dean, hockey coach, and football coaches. That's totally going to win people over," I sigh.

He grins. "You're just like your mom with the dramatics."

"From what I heard, she only started acting like that after you all tied her down."

He nods. "Nah. You're a lot like your mom, more than you know. We put her through a lot, and we regret it every day. But she was strong, held her head high, and fought really damn hard. Just like you."

Pride fills me. I might be closer with Rain when it comes to things you don't normally tell a parent, but my mom really is my person. I trust her with my life. It was us against the world at one point. She's my hero, and I'd take the compliment of being like her any day.

"Alright. Car's packed. Let's get the boys ready, and then we can meet Lilly over at the dorms," Mom states, walking past us and into the kitchen. A second later, Theo shouts for the boys.

Brody and Chase leave, passing Rain who's on her way in and over to me. "Hey. Ready to go?"

"I think so? It's not like I have to go far if I forget anything," I laugh.

She smiles and laughs too. "Very true." She looks around for a second and then steps closer. "How are you doing with everything?"

"I'm scared." I nibble on my lower lip. "I miss him." Tears form in my eyes. "I hate this distance between us. I'm hoping now that Jonas and I aren't together, he will loosen up a bit."

"I don't know why he's acting this way. But there has to be a reason. He loves you, and I know he would act the same way with you as your dads would if something happened to your mom. I think he's just a young man, trying to find his way in the world and figure out who he is. He's just not sure how to do that yet. But you're going to be in the same school as him now. He can't avoid you as easily."

"I plan on making an effort to hang out with Bishop more. Even though Toby and I don't talk much, Bishop and I are still close; we text every day."

"That's good." Rain smiles. "And he is besties with Toby. Like I said, he can't avoid you forever."

"Ugh, this is so stupid. Most of my life, I don't think I went more than a day without seeing or talking to Toby. And now it's weeks, sometimes months, before I can even say hi to him without him avoiding eye contact and acting like he would rather be anywhere else."

"I can kick his ass if you want?" Rain smirks. "I'll make him cry."

That makes me burst out laughing. "I love you."

She pulls me into her arms. "I love you too. But really, I'm here whenever you want to talk. And when it comes to you and Toby, if it ever goes where you're hoping it would, I'm on your side."

My eyes sting with tears. "Thank you."

The boys come barreling into the room and out the door like the scene from *Jumanji*. The original, not the new ones.

Everyone parts ways to different cars, and I slip into mine.

It's a little yellow Bug. Mom and I used to watch *Once Upon*

A Time together, and when I saw Emma pulling up in her yellow Bug, I told my mom I wanted one when I was older.

On my sixteenth birthday it was waiting for me in the driveway. This car is my baby. I'm glad it's not a real baby because it would have been taken away from lack of care, due to the fact that I know nothing about cars. All I know is how to drive one and that they need gas to run.

As I pull away from the house, excitement fills me. This is it, the start of my new life.

Only thing is, will that new life include the most important person to me? I can't imagine not having him there by my side through all my big life moments.

I really hope things change. I guess there's only one way to find out.

Bickering voices as I approach my dorm room have a smile stretching across my lips. "If you don't stop fucking with my shit, I'm telling Mom," Bianca's familiar voice drifts out into the hall.

A loud snort joins after. "Really, B? Gonna tattle on me to mommy? You're in college, buttercup, so suck it up. It's only going to get worse."

Knowing that Bishop's here sends a thrill of excitement through me. I've missed him like crazy.

"Oh, thank god, you're here," Bianca sighs when she sees me step into the room. "This asshole won't stop touching my shit. Make him leave."

I giggle, shaking my head. "You know better than me that Ship doesn't listen to anyone."

"Hey, that's not true." Bishop says as he playfully glares at me. "I listened to that cop one time when he told me to stop pissing on that statue when I was drunk."

I roll my lips together, biting down to stop myself from laughing as I place the box in my hands on the empty bed on the other side of the room. I am not surprised at all by that, it sounds like something he would do.

"You're crazy." I roll my eyes and grin, moving back over to him.

"Only for you, sugar-tits." He winks, and my eyes go wide before an embarrassing snort leaves my lips.

"Ewww, don't talk about my friend's tits." Bianca shoots him a disgusted look.

"Ah, sorry to break it to you, sis, but she's my friend too."

"Don't remind me," she scoffs.

"She was my friend first, actually." Bishop chuckles. "How does it feel to know your bestie was mine before she was yours?"

"You might have become friends with her first, but I've been closer to her the last few years, so suck it." She flips him off before turning to her boxes sitting atop her bed.

I don't miss the flash of hurt that crosses his face, but it's gone in the next breath.

"But that's gonna change now." Bishop turns to me. "Can't believe you're finally here. Going to school with us old guys." He slings his arm over my shoulder, giving my elbow a little squeeze.

"You're not old." I raise a brow. "You're like, what, thirty?"

"Ha-ha," he says with a blank face before poking me in the side. "So funny." He starts to tickle me, and I'm instantly laughing.

"Stop!" I gasp out through a laugh. "I'm gonna pee myself if you don't."

"Lilly, that's just gross. Don't do that." But the asshole doesn't stop.

"What the fuck is going on?" a deep, gruff voice that I know all too well sounds from the doorway of our dorm.

Bishop's hands leave me like he was caught stealing from the cookie jar and he takes a huge step back. My eyes flick up to Toby standing in the doorway. His eyes are narrowed, glaring at the both of us, fists clenched at his side. Ugh, why does he have to be so damn good looking that it hurts? With his brown eyes and matching hair. And all those tattoos. I'm a sucker for tattoos.

"Well, my brother was flirting with your sister. So, thanks for saving me," Bianca throws out and I really want to slap a hand over my best friend's mouth right now.

"We were not flirting." I shoot a glare her way.

"Looked like it to me." She sends me a teasing grin. I know she's messing with me, but Toby doesn't seem to like the joke.

"What the fuck?" He glares daggers at his best friend.

"Oh, relax," Bishop chuckles, running a hand through his messy black hair. "I was just tickling her."

"Don't tickle my sister, man. It's fucking weird." Calling me his sister is like a punch to the gut, and a reminder that he really doesn't feel the same way about me that I do for him. He turns his attention to me. "What are you doing here?" Toby asks me, nostrils flaring.

Is he for real right now? "I live here now." I blink at him, not sure why he's so pissed.

His eyes widen slightly. "Here? As in this dorm or this room?"

"Both...." My brows furrow. "So what?"

"Fucking hell," he sighs, running a hand down his face.

"What? What am I missing?" I look between him and Bishop.

He steps out of the way and points to the door across the hall. "That's Bishop's room."

"Oh." I look over at Bishop. "So, we're neighbors?" I can't help but smile.

"Yup. And so is Toby." He grins, shooting his best friend a shit eating grin. "We're rooming together again this year."

My eyes snap back over to Toby. "Really?"

His jaw clenches. "Yup. So, if you could keep the sex with your boyfriend, Joan, down, that would be wonderful."

"His name is Jonas," I respond, not correcting him on the fact that Jonas isn't my boyfriend anymore.

"Don't care," he huffs. He looks to Bishop asking, "Do you need me anymore, or did you get all B's stuff?"

"What?" My brows furrow. "You came to help Bee move in? What about me?"

"Didn't know you were moving in today." He shrugs his shoulders. That's a lie. I know Theo told him.

"Nice," I huff out a laugh, shaking my head, about done with his bullshit today. "You're an asshole, you know that?" I slip past him and head toward the elevator to go back down and wait for our parents, trying not to be a baby and cry, but damn, when he's like this, it really hurts.

"I'm the asshole?" Toby follows after me. "What did I do?"

I whip around, getting in his face. "It's what you haven't done." I shake my head. "You changed, Toby. And not for the better. I don't know who you've become, but it's not the boy I've known most of my life. Whoever this is—" I wave my hand up and down at him, "—is an asshole. And you've been one for years now."

I leave him gaping at me as I step into the elevator. I stare at him, trying not to show how much this new version of him hurts me, as the doors close.

People grow up, they change, they grow apart. I just didn't think that would be us. But I have a feeling that maybe that's just the way things are right now.

I came to SVU with a plan to get my best friend back, to make him admit he loves me. But why?

Why should I wait around for someone who doesn't see my worth? It's one thing my moms taught me from a young age. Don't settle for less than what you deserve, and if the man you love doesn't see your worth, then he's not for you.

I see the way my dads and Rain treat my mom. It's like she hung the damn moon. I want someone to look at me like that.

I'm not sure what I did to make Toby change the way he was with me, but it hurts.

I'm in college now. I'm eighteen and young. These are supposed to be the best years of my life, and that's what I plan on doing. To work hard in school and have fun with my friends.

If Toby wants to smarten up and join me, awesome. But I need to realize that when it comes to what we feel for each other, we're not on the same page. He sees me as a little sister, I see him as…so much more.

But I need to try and move on and let him go. As much as that is going to kill me. I'd rather have him at least as a friend than nothing at all. I just need him to stop being such an asshole. When I'm not so pissed at him, I'll force him to sit his ass down and talk to me like an adult.

CHAPTER FIVE

LILLIANNA

It's been a few days since I moved into my dorm. Aside from the few minutes on moving day, I haven't seen Toby. Or Bishop, for that matter. He didn't even come to help me and our parents move my stuff in.

"I'm so excited!" Bianca squeals as we walk across campus toward the Hockey House, a dorm where the entire hockey team lives. With the exception of Toby and Bishop. I overheard my parents talking and he isn't living there because his grades are already bad as it is and living in a frat house would be too big of a distraction. Since Bishop goes wherever Toby goes, they're rooming together. In my dorm. Across the damn hall.

The first night in the dorm, I couldn't sleep. My mind wandered with stupid little things like if Toby was in his room with a girl. Would he have sex with her knowing I was across the

They've either gone home to sleep, or stayed at the Hockey House. He's likely trying to avoid me. I'm trying to not let it bother me, but it does.

"So, like, how drunk are we getting?" I ask my best friends as I spin to face them while walking backward. A grin plays on my lips as Bee gives me a matching one.

"White-girl wasted?" she suggests, wiggling her eyebrows.

A grin slips across my face. "Fuck, yeah." I high-five her, and we burst into giggles.

Jonas groans from where he's walking next to Bianca. "You two are going to be a handful tonight, I just know it."

"Awe, come on, Jonas. We're in college now! Live a little. We get to drink with the big kids." I laugh. We went to a few college parties last year, but it's like they knew we were in high school. It just felt weird.

"Also, we're going to be in your house, right?" Bianca asks. Jonas moved into the Hockey House the same day we moved into the dorm. "We could just crash in your room."

"Hell no." He shakes his head. "That house is full of horny hockey players and puck bunnies looking for an in. I don't want you two around them at all, let alone drunk and vulnerable."

"You really think they would fuck with us? Our brothers are on the team. And, ah, it would be kind of hard not to ever be around them, seeing how our brothers are on the team and her dad coaches it." Bianca hikes a thumb over at me. "And the fact that we're going to a party at the house they all live in, I'm sure we're bound to bump into one of them."

Jonas sighs, running a hand through his inky black hair. "Just no fucking my team members, okay? I don't want to get kicked off the team for kicking their asses before even getting to practice." He gives us a pointed look.

"No trouble from me," Bianca says. "Hockey players are not my type."

I cringe and Jonas flicks me a look, hurt flashing in his eyes for a moment.

As we get closer to the house, Bianca sees someone she knows and rushes over to say hi.

"Don't worry about it," I tell Jonas, stepping closer to him.

"Worry about what?" he asks me. I look up at him, raising a brow.

"What Bee said, before. You know, about hockey players not being her type."

He looks away, shrugging his shoulder. "Oh, that." He brushes it off like it doesn't matter. "What about it?"

I grin, rolling my eyes. "Hockey players might not be her type. But you want to know what is?" I ask playfully.

His eyes flick down to me, interest shining bright. "What?"

I grin. "You." I bump my shoulder into his arm. He grins, chuckling as he shakes his head.

"Still a hockey player, Lills."

"So? Sure, I know how you hockey players can be, the sport becomes your whole life. But there's so much more to you. You're kind, loyal, and you're a good listener."

"Lilly, is this going somewhere? You're pretty much describing a dog." He looks down at me with a blank look.

"Yes." I laugh. "What I'm trying to say is, she would be lucky to have you. I know I was. You're a good man, Jonas, and I know you would treat her right."

"This is weird, you know?" He rubs the back of his neck, giving me a lopsided grin.

"What is?"

"Us. Talking like this. As if we never dated."

"But did we really?" I ask, blinking up at him. "I know we said we labeled it that way, but could we call what we were doing *dating*? A relationship? Now, when I look back on it, we were just friends with the wrong title."

"Yeah. I think I agree." He nods, looking over at Bee.

"But you were my best friend before we ever became more. And it's what you're always going to be. So, I just want you happy. I want her happy."

His eyes flick back over to me. "What if she doesn't want me? Has she ever told you she did?"

"Well, no." I look toward Bee. "I mean, you don't really tell your best friend 'Hey, by the way, I have the hots for your boyfriend.'" I laugh.

"Okay, fair point," he chuckles.

"But, Jonas, I see the way she looks at you when she thinks no one is watching. It's a big reason why I wanted to end things before we came to school. Seeing her long for someone she thought she couldn't have sucked, mostly because I was the one causing it."

"So, she was pining after me?" His voice takes on an amused, hopeful tone.

"Jonas," I warn. "We shouldn't even be talking about this. She's my best friend. It goes against girl code."

"But so am I," he pouts.

"Ugh. This is so complicated." I want to be there for both my friends, but it's kind of hard when secrets are involved. *I hate secrets.*

"What's complicated?" Bianca asks, making Jonas and I jump.

"Ahh…" I blink up at him, mind going blank on what to say.

"The fact that Lilly has to live across the hall from the stepbrother she's in love with," Jonas blurts.

"Jonas!" I gasp, eyes widening. *Way to throw me under the bus.*

Bianca swings her gaze over to me. "Still? Babe, I thought you would have gotten over him by now."

You would think. But no, being away from him like this has only made me long for him more. "Don't give me that pitying look. I can't help it, okay? I'm trying to move on," I mutter, glaring over at Jonas who mouths. 'I'm sorry' from behind Bianca's back.

"New goal. We're going to have fun this year, mess around with some hot guys, and live a little. Help you forget all about him." She throws her arm over my shoulder, urging me to keep walking.

Jonas' eyes snap down to her fast, a dark jealousy taking over. Oh, he did not like hearing about her messing around with other guys.

"I'm not sleeping with random guys, Bee."

"I didn't say you had to. I said mess around. Flirt, kiss, go on some fun dates. This is college and we are not going to spend the best years of our lives pining after a boy."

Easy for her to say. And he's not just a boy to me. He was my everything. Maybe that's my problem. I made Toby my whole life. It was so easy to do it because it's what he wanted too.

Now, he's not that person to me anymore, and I don't know what I'm doing.

"Okay, fine. Drinking tonight, dancing with some cute boys, and just having fun."

"That's my girl." Bianca kisses my cheek.

Jonas' eyes go from her to me. It's his turn to glare. 'Sorry' I mouth back.

Sadly, until he mans the fuck up and tells her how he feels, Bee is going to do her own thing. I don't feel right trying to deter her from having fun just to make Jonas happy.

Jonas lets out a low growl as the house comes into view. "I'm going to get a fucking drink."

Something tells me tonight is going to be one interesting night.

The party is crowded, loud, everyone is drunk, and I'm having the time of my life. I've flirted with a few cute guys and even danced with one. For the most part, it's just been me, Bee, and Jonas.

We've been here for about an hour, and I've still yet to see Toby or Bishop. But I have seen a lot of their teammates, almost all of them with a puck bunny hanging off them, looking at them like they're God's gift to woman.

"I gotta go piss!" I scream to Bianca over the music.

"Very lady-like, Lills." Jonas snorts, eyes dancing with humor.

"When you gotta go, you gotta go." I giggle, very tipsy at this point.

"I'll come with you!" Bee shouts back, looping her arm through mine. "Watch this." She shoves her drink at Jonas.

We weave our way through the crowd, bumping into people and giggling up a storm. "This line is too long." Bianca pouts as we get to one of the bathrooms.

"Jonas said there's another one on the top floor," I tell her.

"Isn't that where more of the guys' rooms are? I thought it was off limits to the party?"

I shrug. "If anyone gives us shit, I'll tell them Jonas told us we could."

"Well, I'm about to pee myself, so I'll take the risk." She giggles as we head down to the end of the hall where the stairs lead upward. There're a few people who look our way, and I recognize them from the team. They don't say anything, so they must know who we are.

"Which door?" Bianca asks as we look at all the closed doors.

"Ahh...I don't know." I blink, my head feeling more than a little tipsy.

"You two looking for the bathroom?" a voice behind us has me squealing. I spin around and look up at a cute guy with shaggy blond hair.

"Yes?"

"You're cute." Bee giggles.

"And your Bishop's little sister," he chuckles.

"Ugh, don't remind me," she sighs.

He chuckles again. "Top floor is closed off, team members only. But I think we can make an exception for you two." He winks, making Bee giggle again. "Just make it quick, okay? Bathroom is at the end of the hall on the left."

"Thank you," I rush the words out, spinning to Bee. "Come on, let's go."

Grabbing her by the arm, I pull her down the hall. We can't help but giggle the whole way. But as I pass one of the rooms, I notice the door isn't fully closed. And then a moan drifts out, causing both Bianca and me to stop.

She looks at me, eyes wide as she bites her lips together. "Oh my god," she whispers, looking over at the cracked door. "Do you think they're fucking in there?"

Another moan has me wanting to break into giggles again. "Maybe?"

Her eyes light up with glee. "We should peek."

"No!" I laugh. "What if we see someone's butt."

She rolls her eyes. "Yeah, because butts are far more scandalous than seeing a penis."

I blink, not even thinking about that. *God, how drunk am I?* "I've never seen a penis before. And I don't want to see some random guy's." I scrunch up my nose. Okay, so I have seen penises before, in porn and online, but never in person.

"Don't be such a prude." She rolls her eyes. "We're in college now, do you know how much dick we're going to see at college parties?" She grabs my arm and pulls me toward the door

"I'm not looking," I whisper-yell at her.

"Fine, but I am." She grins at me, then tip-toes over to the door. She pauses, looking in. Then I see the smile on her face slowly melt away before her face goes pale and her eyes go comically wide.

She shakes her head and rushes over to me, grabbing my arm. "Nevermind. You don't want to see that anyways."

I pull my arm out of her grasp, my heart beating faster in alarm. "Bee, what did you see?"

She bites her lip, looking toward the door and back to me. "It doesn't matter. Come on, babe, let's go pee. Then we can go dance with some cute guys." She reaches for me again, but I pull out of her grasp. I look at her, my feet walking me backward toward the door.

I know in my gut, I don't want to see what's happening in that room, but it's like I can't help it.

"Lilly!" Bianca's tone is pleading, and now I have to know.

Stopping, I look toward the crack and peek in. I immediately wish I listened to her, that we did our business and went back downstairs. Because what I'm seeing makes me want to hurl everything I've drank tonight.

Toby sits on the edge of the bed, leaning back, his eyes shut in pure bliss. His fingers are laced through some blonde's hair as she kneels between his legs...with his cock in her mouth.

He lets out a low rumbling groan, lips parted as the girl bobs up and down, sucking him like he's her favorite lollipop.

My eyes sting as everything grows blurry. My stomach turns, and I slap my hand over my mouth, spin around, and run to the room I hope is the bathroom.

Thankfully, when I throw open the door, there's a toilet in there. I rush over to it and just make it before I heave everything up.

"Fuck," Bianca hisses, and I hear the door click behind me. "I'm so fucking sorry you had to see that. I tried to warn you."

I groan, flush the toilet, and place my head against the seat. I don't say anything, knowing if I try, I'll break. Just like my heart is doing right now.

I'm utterly gutted. I feel like someone shoved their hand in my chest and ripped my heart out, squeezing it tightly between their fingers until it burst.

A part of me knew he's been with girls. Why wouldn't he be? He's good looking and a solid hockey player. I know puck bunnies throw themselves at him; I've seen them do it at his games.

But I've made myself oblivious, lying to myself, convincing myself that he's still a virgin. But seeing it with my own eyes, I can't play dumb anymore.

God, it hurts so much.

"You want to go home?" she asks, rubbing my back.

"No." I shake my head. "No." I get up and go over to the sink to rinse out my mouth. "What I want to do is get white-girl wasted. I want to drink so much, I black the fuck out."

I'm not thinking right. I'm letting the pain of what I just saw fuel my shitty choices.

"I don't know, Lills." She looks at me with concern.

"Not enough to hurt myself, but enough to forget about tonight until tomorrow morning." I give her a pleading look, still trying to hold back the tears. "I don't need to remember that. Ever."

She chews on her bottom lip for a moment before nodding. "Alright. Let's go get drunk. And dance!"

"I'd say make out with some cute boys, but..." I look over at the toilet and shake my head.

"Come on." She laughs.

We pee, wash our hands and leave the bathroom, heading back down the hall. As if I can't help myself, my eyes find the door. Only it's shut now.

Is he in there fucking her? Or did he finish and now they're at the party?

Doesn't matter. Because I'm about to be too drunk to care.

We head back down to the party and over to where all the drinks are. We grab a few coolers from the ice bucket, crack them open, and chug them. I pray that the nausea from what I've seen goes away so I can keep drinking. The idea of that image being engraved in my mind has me drinking a little faster.

"There you both are. What took you so long?" Jonas asks,

joining us. I drink the last mouthful and sigh, wiping my mouth off with the back of my hand and burp.

Jonas looks at me with an amused grin, but I wipe it clean off when I tell him, "Just saw some puck bunny choking on my stepbrother's cock. And now I need to get shit-faced so I can erase that image from my mind," I tell him, giving him a fake-as-fuck smile before I turn around and grab a bottle of tequila.

"Body shots!" I shout, and it's followed by a round of rowdy cheers.

"Lilly," Jonas says warily.

I turn to him. "I'm getting blackout drunk. So, you can go about your night and have fun, or you can babysit my ass and make sure I don't hurt myself. But either way, I'm doing this."

He groans, scrubbing his face with his hands. "You're lucky, you're my best friend."

"Love you too, babe." I lean up and kiss him on his cheek before turning to Bee. "Let's do this!"

I know I'm not being smart, but I'm too heartbroken and already too tipsy to care. I know I'm going to hate myself in the morning, but all I can think about right now is forgetting. Forgetting Toby and my stupid love for him. Forgetting the fact that he will never want me in the way I want him, and most of all forgetting about him being with that girl. The way he moaned, enjoying everything she was doing with her mouth.

Because in this moment, no matter how dramatic it might seem, I feel like if I don't I might just die of a shattered heart.

CHAPTER SIX

TOBIAS

I SNEER AT THE MAN STARING BACK AT ME IN THE MIRROR. I'M disgusted with myself. All I want to do is go home and scrub my dick clean.

I never learn. Every time I hook up with a chick, I always end up hating myself. And then thoughts of *her* consume me, taking up every inch of my mind. Then I find myself doing whatever I can to forget.

Only I don't want to forget about her, not really. I love Lilly with every fucking inch of my being. I would die for her, kill for her. But it's wrong. So fucking wrong. She can't be mine. I can never have her.

It doesn't stop me from seeing her when I close my eyes, though. Or thinking of her when my hand is wrapped around my cock. Or when it's down another girl's throat.

I'm sick. So fucked up. Because I shouldn't be thinking about her, not when I'm with another girl. She's so much better than any of them and doesn't deserve to be associated with my messed up fantasies.

When I came to this party, I didn't plan on hooking up with anyone. I never do. I never *want* to. But then Bishop was talking about Lilly and Bianca and how things will be different with them here this year. My mind got stuck on Lilly, on how she will be right across the hall from me.

Where her boyfriend will fucking visit. The thoughts of them fucking so damn close to me filled me with rage. Having to listen to her scream *his* name while he's balls fucking deep in her was too much. So I drank... and drank and drank. So when Ruby, a puck bunny who's had her eye on me all last year, offered to take my mind off things, I stupidly agreed.

It felt nice at the moment, but after I came down her throat and she pulled back, licking her lips while giving me a sultry smile, I felt sick. I felt like I was betraying Lilly and my feelings for her. And it's fucked up. Because I shouldn't care, because I shouldn't have these feelings for my *stepsister*.

But she's not my stepsister, at least, not to me. She's never been that to me.

Fifteen years ago, my dad took me to a park. At that park was a little blonde girl with a smile and laugh you couldn't help but be enchanted by. She was only three, and I was six. From that moment, I knew I wanted to be there for her, be her friend, and to protect her at all costs.

Then our parents started dating and she became my person. I hated doing anything without her, always needing to be near her. And when I wasn't, I worried.

When Lilly was three, someone attempted to kidnap her. Thankfully, her father, Chase, got to her in time before anything happened. But Lilly told me about that day, and I remember crying angry tears because I wasn't there to keep her safe.

How could I have been? I was six. There wasn't any way I could have helped her, aside from screaming for help.

But I didn't see it like that back then. And from that moment on, I vowed to protect her. At the time, it was just a little boy making a big promise.

Over time, things changed. We got older and that protectiveness I felt over her, that obsessiveness that fueled me, wasn't something a big brother felt for a little sister.

No, it was something much more. And for as long as I could, I gave into that feeling. I soaked up every laugh, smile, hug, and cuddle she gave me. When we became teenagers, I started sleeping in her bed when I couldn't sleep. Her being in my arms was the only thing that settled me. I didn't care how wrong it was.

But then people started talking and I started to see just how wrong my feelings for her were.

Everywhere I turned, people reminded me that she was my sister. They asked why I *always* brought my sister along with me, that it was weird. The thing is, none of them blamed it on me, they always made Lilly out to be the sick one.

Your sister is sick, look at her staring at you like that.

She's acting like you're her boyfriend, how sad is that?

How pathetic, she can't get anyone else, so she goes after her own brother.

I can't count the number of times I've gotten into fist fights with people who opened their mouths and went too far.

I was torn between keeping my distance to protect her from their nasty words and staying close so that no one would mess with her.

Something big happened my senior year of high school and changed everything. It changed me, and not for the better. I tried so hard to stay the man I was before, but as time went on, it got harder and harder.

I became bitter, more angry. At first, the fighting stayed on the rink. But then I was at risk of losing it all because I found any reason to rip my gloves off and get in a fight. I was the goalie, for fuck's sake, people fight to protect me, and there I was putting myself at risk.

My dad sat me down and told me if I didn't stop, I'd lose everything I'd worked so hard for.

So, when I graduated, I told myself I would distance myself from Lilly. She'd have a clean slate. When I was here, she was still in high school. She had her friends, and I had mine.

As much as it hurt, I came to SVU and put everything I had into hockey, making it my whole life. At first, it worked. I hardly ever let a puck in.

Then, she started dating Jonas, bringing him to my fucking games, and it was so damn hard to concentrate when all I had to do was look up in the stands, and see her laughing and smiling at him.

"Get a hold of yourself," I growl at my reflection. I need to drink. To forget about what I just did and how gross it made me feel.

I leave the bathroom in an overall shitty mood. I join my teammates out back and we sit around the fire, drinking while reliving games from last year. Just for a moment, I'm able to forget about every thing.

That is until some drunk football player named Brandon Cole comes stumbling over. "Hey, Munro."

I look over my shoulder at Bishop, brows furrowed, and we both look over at the guy.

"Yeah?"

"Dude, you never told us how hot your little sister is." He chuckles, and the hairs on the back of my neck stand up.

"What the fuck?" I snarl, getting to my feet. "Why the fuck would you say that?" It's so random and out of the blue.

"And you too, Grant." He grins at Bishop. "They're both smokin'." He and his buddy start cackling like hyenas.

Unlike me, Bishop is quick to nip this in the bud as Bianca's actual brother. "Don't fucking talk about how hot my sister is to me, man. That's weird. Stay the fuck away from her too." He shakes his head, taking a drink of his beer.

"I don't think it's us you need to worry about," Brandon says.

"What the fuck are you talking about?" I ask, taking a step forward, my shitty mood making me extra on-edge tonight.

"Seeing how they're giving the whole party a strip tease in there, you have the football and hockey teams drooling over them."

My eyes snap to Bishop, and he's out of his seat in a flash, taking off toward the house.

I knew having Lilly here was going to be an adjustment. The idea of seeing her every day both settles my soul and fucks with my heart.

Not to mention, seeing her all over her boyfriend is going to make it really fucking hard to keep myself from punching him in his stupid face.

Is she not here with him tonight? Why would she get drunk and do something like this?

As we get into the house, we're blocked by a wall of people. "What the hell?" Bishop hisses, brows furrowing.

They're all cheering, going wild for whatever show the girls are putting on and my blood boils.

"Damn, that blonde one is fine!" one of the guys toward the back shouts to his friend next to him. "I wouldn't mind getting a private show from her." They both laugh. My lip curls, and so does my fist. Bishop grabs my arm, pulling me back.

"They're not worth it, man. Come on. We need to see what the hell is going on." Tearing my eyes away from the fuckers, I nod, and we start to push our way through, not giving a single fuck about being polite.

It feels like it's never fucking ending and when we break from the crowd, I'm met with a version of Lilly I've never seen before.

She and Bianca are standing on the kitchen island in nothing but jeans and their bras. I should go over there and get her down, but I pause, letting myself take her in. *All Night Longer* by Sammy Adams is blasting through the speakers, and the girls are screaming out the lyrics, big smiles on their faces as they laugh in between verses.

She looks like she's having a good time or, by the way her eyes are glassed over, maybe too good of a time is more accurate.

I shouldn't, but my eyes get caught on her breasts. Fuck, she's wearing a thin lacy bra. I can see her nipples pressed up against the fabric and the knowledge that everyone here is seeing my girl like this, has me snapping out of my frozen state.

"Where the fuck is Jonas?!" I bark, and like magic, he fucking appears next to me.

"I'll grab Bee," he shouts over the music before heading over to the girls. He grabs Bianca's arm, forcing her to lower herself before he tosses her over his shoulder.

"What the fuck?" I look at Bishop. *Why is Jonas looking after Bianca and not his fucking girlfriend?*

"I'll grab Lilly." Bishop takes a step forward, but I pull him back.

"I got her." The idea of him touching her when she's half-naked like this sends a jealous surge through me.

"Lilly!" I shout, but her eyes are closed as she continues to dance and sing. She doesn't even know her best friend isn't beside her anymore. I'm pissed at her for pulling this kind of stunt, because it's not like her at all, and all these motherfuckers are getting an eyeful of my girl.

Not your girl, Toby, you've made sure of that.

I tap her leg, getting her attention. She finally opens her eyes and looks down at me. The smile on her face slips into an expression of anger. I deserve that. I was an asshole to her the other day. I didn't mean to be. I never *meant* to be. This distance between us has been killing me. But I'm afraid that if we go back to being that close, or even friends in any capacity, I'm not going to be able to control myself when it comes to her.

And I need to because the last thing she needs is me.

"Come on, Lilly. Party's over."

"Go away," she huffs, crossing her arms. It pushes her breasts up, not helping her case with the ogling idiots.

"Lilly, you're drunk. Let me take you back to your dorm."

"I'm having fun. And you're ruining it." She looks to the side, brows furrowing. "Where did Bee go?"

"Jonas took her home," I say through gritted teeth, pissed that he left his fucking girlfriend here. Who does that?

"What? Oh, come on," she whines.

"Time for you to go home too." I go to grab her legs, but she kicks at me.

"Don't touch me!" she shouts, and then squeals as she loses her balance, eyes going wide.

"Fuck!" I dive forward, but thankfully, Bishop is there to catch her.

"Come on, party girl, it's time to get you home," he chuckles.

My fists clench, nostrils flaring, and anger fills me as I watch her wrap her arms around Bishop's neck. "My hero," she mumbles, closing her eyes. "Yeah, I'm tired and I don't feel so good. I wanna go home."

I follow after them as Bishop leads us outside. "Bring her to my car," I tell him, taking a few steps in front of them.

"No. I don't want him to bring me home. Ship, *you* bring me home," she slurs.

I stop and look back, jaw tense. "I'll meet you there," he tells me, and I want to tell him fuck no. To demand he hand her over to me.

But the way she's looking at me, it's a fucking punch to the gut. I've never seen such disdain from her in my life. I knew she was pissed with how I've been acting, but does she really hate me?

She should. You just let some chick suck you off while you thought of her. And I fucking hate myself for it.

"Fine," I grind out, jogging to my car. I don't leave until I see Bishop's Jeep pulling out.

"I got her." I open the passenger door to the Jeep.

"Go away," she grumbles. Her eyes are closed, her head resting against the seat.

"Come on, Lilly. Please don't be like this," I sigh.

"I don't like you," she slurs. "You're mean."

"I'm not being mean right now. I just want to help you. To get you to bed safely."

"Ha." She laughs, her head rolling to the side. Her eyes crack open just a little bit so that she can see me. "You didn't seem to care much about me the past two years, so why do you care now?"

My heart clenches. "I've been an asshole, okay. I'm sorry, but right now is not the time to kiss and make up."

Her brows jump. "Kiss?"

My brows furrow. "Not what I meant." I don't give her time to argue anymore as I reach over and unclip her seatbelt.

"Wrap your arms around me," I tell her as I scoop her up into my arms. She's light and fits easily in my arms.

She snuggles into me, putting her face in the crook of my neck. "Mmmhmm. You smell good." She runs her nose along my neck. Goosebumps break out all over and my cock twitches. Fucking hell, now is not the time for that.

"Thanks," I grunt. And damn it, she smells good too. She smells like my Lilly. Warm vanilla and sugar.

"You got this? I'm going to make sure Bee is okay. You know

how she can get when she's drunk too much. Probably fighting with Jonas if she's not puking her guts out."

I nod my head. I don't want his help. I've always protected Lilly, and I'm perfectly capable of doing it now. *Unlike the last two years.*

By the time we get to the elevators, Lilly is asleep in my arms. On the ride up, I watch her. The way her long blonde lashes fan across her cheeks, down to the freckles scattered over her nose and under her eyes. Her lips are plump and pink, and I've dreamt of kissing them so many times.

The elevator doors open, and I'm walking down the hall toward her dorm when she starts to wiggle.

"Toby. Bathroom. Now." She slaps a hand over her mouth. Fuck. I rush us two doors down to the communal bathroom, pushing the door open with my foot. "Put me down!" She demands, and I do. She takes off running to the first stall and a second later, sounds of her puking fill the bathroom.

I close my eyes and take a deep breath. This two year streak of keeping my distance? Yeah, that's breaking tonight, because there's no way I can't take care of her tonight. I'd be too worried about her and wouldn't be able to sleep knowing she's like this.

She's pissed at me right now, but I don't care. I go into the stall, and the sight of her like this hurts to see.

"Go away," she moans as I gather her hair up and hold it back for her.

"Nope." I kneel beside her and rub her back with my other hand.

"Why?" Her forehead is resting on her arm, which is slung along the toilet seat. Poor girl looks rough. I still think she's the most gorgeous girl I've ever laid eyes on, though.

"Because I care about you, and I'm not going to just leave you here when you're sick and drunk."

"I'm not drunk... okay, maybe a little. But it's only because I needed to forget."

My brows furrow. "Forget about what?"

She looks up at me, her bright blue eyes making my heart beat just a bit faster. She bites her lower lip for a moment before shaking her head. "Doesn't matter."

Not wanting to pry and piss her off even more, I just nod. "So, not that I don't enjoy holding your hair back for you. But shouldn't this be a job for your boyfriend?" I try really hard not to grind out that last word.

"Nope," she sighs heavily. "I don't have one."

Wait. What? "Since when?"

"Since the night I saw you in the kitchen. When you looked at me like you'd rather have been anywhere else but in the same room with me." She blinks, and fuck, my heart cracks when I see her eyes fill with tears. That was also the night I went to my room and jacked off to the thought of being inside her. *God, I'm fucked up.*

"So, you've been single for weeks. How come I didn't know?" I've been stressing about the fact that I'd have to see her and Jonas eating each other's faces and making me want to gouge my eyes out. Or his.

Jonas isn't a bad guy. From what I've seen, he's nice, good to his friends, and everyone talks highly of him. But I've hated him since the moment he started dating Lilly. Petty, I know, but knowing that another man was touching her, kissing her. God, the idea of them fucking... It made me sick. It made me fucking murderous. It's also a big reason why I've put distance between Lilly and me. In this case, I knew I couldn't be the bigger person for her, but I also didn't want to get in the way of her happiness.

But hearing the fact that they're not together anymore? It fills me with so much fucking joy it's sad.

"Because," she scoffs, shaking her head, but groans like she regrets the movement. "We don't talk anymore, remember? Unless you're shit-faced like me, you're not a real chatter."

I can't help but smile. It's true. When I've been drinking, my guard is down. I'm surprised I haven't spilled to her how much I want her.

Lilly catches the smile. "Oh, please. Of course, you'd be happy about it. You've always hated Jonas. And I don't know why, he was nothing but good to me."

"I hated him because he was dating you. Now he's not. So, I guess he's not so bad."

"Really? You're not even going to ask why we broke up? Maybe I'm drinking because I'm heart-broken and need to numb the pain."

Oh shit. I didn't even think about that. My face softens. "I'm sorry, Flower, are you okay? Did he hurt you, do you need me to kick his ass?"

"Don't call me that," her voice cracks, tears filling her eyes. "And no, I don't. I'm fine. Jonas and I are friends. We just realized we were better that way. He's not the one I'm drinking to forget."

"Oh." *What does she mean by that?*

I'm about to ask her when she groans and turns her head back to the bowl. I grimace, keeping her hair out of the way and rubbing her back. "That's it. Let it out. I got you."

"I wish you didn't," she cries, and my brows furrow.

"Why?"

"Because it hurts too much to have you this close." She wipes her eyes. "But it doesn't matter. Now, I'm single, so I'm gonna have fun."

"What do you mean by that?" I scowl.

She flushes and starts to stand, stumbling while she does. I stand with her, ready to catch her, but she storms out of the stall and over to the sink. "God, I look like hot garbage," she groans.

"Don't talk about yourself like that." My words come out on a growl.

She glares at me. "Do your eyes work?" She waves her hand at the mirror. "I look like a raccoon."

My lip twitches. "An adorable raccoon," I correct.

"Stop." She glares at me. "You're not allowed to make fun of me."

"I'm not." I chuckle. "Lilly, you look fine. Perfect, even."

She glares harder. "Liar."

"Nope. But let's get back to what you were saying before. What do you mean by now that you're single, you're going to have fun?"

She shrugs, ducking her head under the water to rinse her mouth. She spits and then answers me. "I've only ever dated one guy. I want to see what else is out there. Go on some dates, meet some nice guys." She pauses as our eyes lock in the mirror. With each passing second, I can feel the rage boiling inside me.

She's not allowed to date, to be with other guys. She's fucking mine!

Only, she's not.

"Who knows? Maybe I'll find Mr. Right. Someone who will love me. Someone who will make me their person. Someone who will treat me right. You know?"

I want to scream, *Me! I'm that guy.* But I don't.

"Come on." I clear my throat. "Let's get you to bed."

She nods and starts toward the door, stumbling and swaying as she goes. I let out a heavy sigh, the sight is just sad. "Let me," I grumble, and she squeaks as I scoop her up.

"You need to stop doing that," she scolds.

"Never." I grin down at her. She blinks up at me with a look in her eyes I can't quite figure out, but then she's biting her lip and looking away.

"Brothers don't carry sisters like this, Toby," she mutters, and the grin slips from my face.

I've been reminded all my life that Lilly is my stepsister, but never from her.

We stop at her dorm room door, and I let her down. She's about to go inside when she hears horrible sounds of puking from behind the door.

"Oh, god," she groans. "I love Bee, but if I have to listen to her getting sick, I'll be joining her."

"Come sleep in my room."

"What?" She looks up at me. "No."

"You can take Bishop's bed. I'll make him sleep in yours. That way he can deal with pukey in there," I chuckle.

There it is, that smile I've been dying to see. "Okay. You think he's going to be okay with that?"

"Since when hasn't Bishop stayed with Bee when she was sick?"

"Good point." She nods. "But I need a change of clothes."

My eyes flick down, remembering that she's only in jeans and a bra. *Fuck.* I clear my throat and go across the hall. Grabbing my key, I open my door and nod my head toward the door. "Just wait in here. I'll go grab you some things, okay?"

"Okay," she whispers.

She slips inside the room, and I knock on her door. Bishop answers a second later. "Where's Lilly?"

"She's gonna be sleeping in your bed tonight. She can't listen to–" Bianca pukes again, and I wrinkle my nose. "That. So you're sleeping in her bed."

I don't like the idea of him sleeping in her bed or her sleeping in his. But a part of me needs to be near Lilly.

"Fine," he sighs.

"I just need to grab a few things." I slip in past him, eyes going to Bee. Poor girl looks like hell. "You okay, Bee?"

"Get fucked," she groans. "No more tequila."

"Yeah. Fair enough." I chuckle.

"How's Lilly? Where is she?"

"She's gonna sleep in mine and Bishop's room. And she's doing a hell of a lot better than you."

She glares at me. "I'm very pissed off at you."

"What? Why? What did I do?"

"You know what you did." She narrows her eyes at me.

"No... I really don't."

She shakes her head and groans. *Weird.* I try to ignore her dry heaving as I gather Lilly's change of pajamas and pillow. "Let me know if you need anything," Bishop offers before taking the bucket and leaving to clean it.

"Toby," Bianca says, stopping me as I get to the door.

"Yeah?" I look over to see her lying back on her bed.

"Don't forget to wash your dick," she sneers.

My brows jump. "What the fuck?"

She just closes her eyes, rolling over and giving me her back. *Why the hell would she say that?*

My gut sinks and my heart races. "Bee... Did you guys see something you shouldn't have?"

She says nothing for a few seconds too long. "Next time, close the damn door."

Fuck. Oh, fuck no. Please don't tell me Lilly saw that girl sucking me off. I feel like I'm going to be sick.

I leave the room with my skin crawling, but I come to a halt, just standing in the hallway. I don't even want to look at Lilly right now, knowing what she saw.

I'm not stupid. I've known exactly how Lilly has felt about me. I've seen the way she looks at me. And the thing is, I loved it. Because I knew one day, she would be mine.

Until life showed me just how wrong I was.

So knowing I've hurt her in so many ways, I hate myself even more. Opening my door, my eyes go right to Lilly. She's in Bishop's bed, already passed out.

I sigh, looking down at the bundle of clothes and pillow gripped in my hand. Bringing them over to the bed, I place them down. I'm about to go to my side of the room when Lilly speaks.

"Why don't you love me?" she murmurs ever so softly.

My head snaps in her direction. "I do love you."

"Not like a little sister. Love me... how... I... love you." It takes her a while to get the words out as she drifts in and out of sleep.

I shouldn't ask but I do. "And how do you love me?"

"With... my whole... heart... and soul..."

I'm frozen, standing there waiting for her to say something else, but she doesn't.

She falls back to sleep. I walk over to her and lean down, kissing her on the forehead. "I love you with my whole heart and soul too, Little Flower. That's why I won't be the reason the assholes of the world bring you down."

I leave her sleeping and go to the showers. I don't know how long I spend under the hot water, scrubbing myself clean, needing to get that girl off of me.

My dad told me I needed to get my anger out in other ways, to stop picking fights and causing problems. I can't risk getting kicked off the team, and after tonight, I know that I can't do anything else with another girl. Just thinking about it makes me sick.

The only thing I can think of is drinking, and that's a slippery slope I'm not sure I can go down.

By the time I'm out of the shower and changed, I know what I'm going to have to do. And Bishop is going to lose his shit.

CHAPTER SEVEN

LILLIANNA

When I wake up the next morning, I am not in my bed. I'm not even in my dorm room. Groaning, I sit up and look around. From the looks of it, I'm in the guys' room.

Sighing, I swing my legs off the bed and stand. I'm still in my jeans and bra. *No wonder I feel so uncomfortable.* "Shit."

At the end of my bed is a change of clothes and my pillow, with a note sitting on top of them.

Sorry I wasn't here when you woke up. Had to get my workout in with some of the guys since practice starts today. I left you some pain meds and a Gatorade on my bedside table. Hope you're not feeling too bad this morning.

– Toby

I smile, biting my lower lip as butterflies fill my belly. This is something the old Toby would have done. I miss it. I miss him.

Shaking my head, I put an end to the fuzzy feelings. I'm pissed at him. I might not remember coming home from the party last night, but I do remember what me and Bee walked in on.

Closing my eyes, I take a deep breath, willing that image to get out of my head.

The table next to the bed I slept in doesn't have what the note mentioned, so I'm going to guess this isn't Toby's bed. I should have known, it doesn't smell of him. It's got Bishop's cologne all over it. And yes, I know what kind of cologne they use, they've been wearing the same stuff for years.

Bishop's is more of a woodsy smell, while Toby's is more of a spice. So, I go over to the other bedside table.

I grab the Gatorade and meds, downing them both. But something else on the table top catches my eye. I look down at the photo of Toby and me. It was his sixteenth birthday, and all of his friends came over for a pool party. Our parents went all out.

Rain bought me my first bikini, and I was excited to wear it. I didn't care that there was going to be a bunch of guys there. Over that past winter, my boobs grew like crazy. I felt sexy, and I wanted to see if Toby would notice me in the way I'd been wanting him to.

And he did just that. He couldn't keep his eyes off me, and I loved every second of it. But his eyes weren't the only ones on me. So were his friends.

The way he kept punching his friends in the arms or pushing them in the pool for looking at me had me over the moon, thinking he was jealous.

And the best part was, when he told them to stop looking, he used my name, never calling me his sister. It was those small moments that gave me hope, proving he felt something more than just friendship.

This photo wasn't taken at the pool party, but after, when we all went to the arcade. Toby had a room full of friends there to see him, but spent the whole night playing games with me. Even Bishop called him out on it, saying I was hogging him too much.

I smile at the photo, a pang of sadness hitting me. I miss those days. I crave that friendship with Toby and Bishop again. I'm hoping that whatever crawled up Toby's ass these past few years crawls right back out, because I know there's got to be a reason why he's been treating me like this. I just don't know what it is, but this isn't him. I want the old Toby back. Even if it's just as friends. I would rather have him in my life in any way possible than to not have him at all.

Slipping my shirt over my bra, I head across the hall to Bee's and my room. "B?" I look at the lump in the bed.

"Go away. I'm busy dying," she groans from under the blankets.

"Hungover, huh?" I giggle, moving to sit on the edge of her bed.

"Where did you go last night? I got up to puke and Bishop was in your bed."

"Ah, yes. That would make sense why I was in his bed." I laugh. "You know I'm a sympathy puker, babe."

"I know." She moves the blanket away from her face and glares at me. "But I'd rather listen to you puke with me than Bishop bitching about having to clean up after me."

"Well, who else would have done it?" I laugh. "I love you, but it wouldn't have been me, and Bishop cares about you."

"I know," she grumbles. "He gets on my nerves, but the big idiot is a good big brother."

"The best." I nod.

"So, I'm guessing Toby took care of you?"

I shrug. "No idea. I don't remember much of last night." I grimace.

"Same," she moans. "My head is killing me."

"Surprisingly, I don't feel all that bad this morning. But based on the gross taste in my mouth, I did my fair share of puking last night too."

Most girls would be mortified of puking in front of someone they liked, but not me. Ever since we were kids, Toby would sit with me when I was sick, trying to get my mind off of it. Even if my mom or one of my dads was sitting there with me.

He was also the one to hold my hair back the first time I got drunk. He didn't help by cracking jokes while I emptied my stomach. Do you know how hard it is to laugh and puke at the same time?

"Lucky bitch." She brushes some of her black hair away from her face.

Vibration against my ass has my brows furrowing. I stand up and reach into my back pocket. It's my phone? "He couldn't have even taken my phone out of my pocket," I mutter and check to see who's calling.

"Who is it?"

"My mom," I tell her, pressing the answer button. "Hey, Mama, what's up?"

"Lilly," her voice is stern, and I know I'm about to get chewed out.

"Yes?" My eyes flick down to Bee's.

"Put it on speaker," Bee whispers. Ever the nosy one.

I press the speaker button, tossing the phone on the bed, and my mom starts again. "Would you care to explain why not one, but all of your fathers got emails today with links to photos and videos of you and Bee dancing on top of a table without your shirts on?"

Dread fills my stomach. "No," I whisper, my eyes widening in horror, Bee's doing the same.

"Well, you're going to anyway," my mom sighs, any anger she had fading away. "Lilly, what happened?"

"I don't remember," I groan. "The last thing I remember was seeing something that upset me and needing to drink to forget it."

"Are you okay? What did you see that got you so upset?" her voice is full of concern.

I bite my lower lip, scrambling to think of something. I can't tell my mom I saw my stepbrother, whom I'm in love with, get his dick sucked. So I panic and say. "I saw Jonas kissing another girl."

Bianca's eyes widen, and I cringe. "Oh, honey, I thought you two ended things on good terms."

"We did. I guess it was just a reminder that things are over. But it's okay, I'm okay."

"I'm glad you're okay, but, Lilly... it's all over social media. Theo has gotten many links on the school message boards taken down. But they're on Instagram too."

My belly turns as I bring up the app. It doesn't take long to see I've been tagged in a ton of posts. I read the captions. *'Coaches daughter is a bombshell.' 'Dean's daughter is a wild child.',* and then there's one that pisses me off the most. *'Like mother, like daughter. Both love the attention.'*

I click on the profile to see who it is. Just fucking great.

"It's fine," I sigh. "Just means I'll have to be more careful. But it's nothing new for Silver Valley. And the fact that all of my dads are some kind of faculty figure means that more eyes are on me. I'm sorry, Mom. I didn't mean for anything like this to happen. You know me." There's shuffling on the other side of the phone, and I wait for a response.

"Hey, Lills," my mom, Rain's, voice comes through the speaker.

"Hey."

"Your dads are talking your mom down from going full mama bear mode." She sighs. "Do you have any idea why they would have posted it? We can do a mass reporting, hopefully get it taken down."

"They're all being reposted from the original post. You remember that girl who had a very unhealthy obsession for Dad back when you all were in college?"

"Yes..." I can hear the disdain in my mom's voice.

"Well, It's her daughter, Katie, who posted the photo and video."

"You have got to be fucking kidding. God, this is fucking bullshit," Rain groans. "I swear, I will lose my shit if she does anything batshit crazy like her mom."

We finish up the conversation and I sigh, flopping back on Bianca's bed.

"What do we do? Do we try to get her to take them down?"

"If it's important to you, of course we will do whatever we can to get her to take them down."

"I don't get it, Lilly. How are you not more pissed? She shared photos of us."

I roll my head to look at her. "We're in college now. People take photos of everything and post it online. There's tons of photos of us on Instagram from parties in the past."

"Yeah, but we're in the background. No one knows nor cares that it's us. This was meant to point us out. And she sent links to your dads."

"No, it was meant to point me out. You just got dragged into it. I'm sorry." Guilt hits me hard.

"I'm not mad at you, I'm pissed at her. Do you think this has to do with Toby?"

My brows furrow, and I sit up again. "Why would it be?"

"You saw her post, she's obviously a puck bunny. And I know she had a thing for Toby in the past, wouldn't surprise me if she still does."

"But what does that have to do with me? I'm his sister, not his girlfriend." Even as I say the words, it feels wrong.

"She was always a snarky bitch to you in high school. She hated how close you and Toby were. Now you're attending the same school. Maybe she's not happy about it."

"School hasn't even started and I've only been seen with Toby last night. I don't know. Maybe she was just doing it to be a bitch. It is kind of her thing."

Katie Teller is a girl we grew up with. She never liked us, always had some kind of issues with Toby and me, then Bishop and Bianca by default for being our friends.

Kayla, Katie's mother, attended SVU with my mom and Rain. They were friends until my mama Rain saw just how crazy she was. She was obsessed with my dad, Chase, so much so that she got arrested for assault.

She was in jail for a few years, but got out and went to live with her parents. Everything was quiet for a while, but not too long after Katie graduated from high school, her grandparents died, and a big secret came out that was the talk of the town. The whole town thought that Katie was Kayla's sister, not her daughter.

Turns out, Kayla got pregnant when she was younger, but her parents took Katie in and raised her as their own because Kayla wasn't a fit parent. I'm not at all surprised.

Anyway, Katie stayed living with Kayla and... well, I wouldn't be surprised if Kayla poisoned Katie's mind when it came to our family.

"Again, how are you so chill about this?"

"I don't know, Bee," I sigh, getting up and going over to my side of the room to grab a change of clothes so I can go shower. "You know me. I've never let things get to me. What's the point? I don't care what people think of me, I never have. If she posts more shit, sure, I'll do something about it. But there's no point in getting worked up over something I can't change. It's not like there wasn't a crap-ton of people who didn't see that video happen live at the party. We're not naked. We have pants on. I don't know what to tell you, Bee." I shrug.

I've always been a go with the flow kind of person. I don't let things like what others think of me bother me. It's *my* life, as long as *I'm* happy, I don't care what others think.

When you grow up in a small town with a family like mine, people talk. I'm not stupid, I know some of the things they say.

My parents sat Toby and I down when we were old enough

and told us about their pasts, knowing damn well that this town was going to talk and that we would hear it. They wanted us to hear it from them firsthand.

I love my family, and I think their love is beautiful. So as much as it sucked to hear people talk bad about them, I didn't let it get to me.

"I need to shower. I feel gross." Grabbing my shower caddy, I leave the room and head down the hall to the bathroom. When I step through the door, I hear a shower running.

Quickly and quietly, I make my way to the last stall. With the bathroom being coed, I plan on using the one furthest away for as much privacy as possible.

I put my change of clothes in one of the lockers, grab my caddy, and step inside the stall. I strip out of my clothes and hang them on the hook with my towel.

My hand is on the tap, about to turn on the water, when I hear a deep, masculine moan echoing through the room. My body freezes, eyes going wide. *Is that what I think it was?*

Another noise rings through the bathroom, this time a grunt. And then a curse and holy shit, I think there's a guy masturbating in here.

A blush creeps onto my cheeks as the sounds of him pleasuring himself grow louder. And then he starts to speak. "Fucking hell," he moans, his breathing heavy. "That's it, baby girl, fucking choke on my cock." He grunts. "Look at you, taking me like a good girl. Now fucking swallow every fucking drop I give you."

Blood pounds in my ears as a fire starts in my lower belly. I shouldn't be getting aroused by the sounds of some stranger jacking off, but the way he's talking and how deep and husky his voice is, it's really sexy.

Wait. He's talking. Is he fucking someone? Oh, god. This was a really bad time to take a shower.

A few seconds later, he lets out a pained groan, indicating

he's reached his release, and my clit throbs with need as I think about him covering the tiles with his cum. *God, I'm so messed up.*

The water shuts off and the sounds of the curtain being pulled back lets me know whoever this is, is getting out.

Curiosity gets the better of me, and I slowly pull my curtain back to peek around it. I bite my lower lip when I'm met with a view of a full, naked ass as the person bends over, drying his muscled legs. It's a nice ass, all round and firm.

He stands at full height, and I see that his back is covered in tattoos, but he's far away enough that I can't really make out what any of them are.

Okay, so his body is hot. But what about his face?

I watch eagerly as the guy brings his towel up to dry his hair, turning around enough to give me a straight line of sight to his semi-hard dick. Damn, it's a nice dick, too. I swallow hard, arousal filling me as my gaze travels up to his toned abs, over his pecs before stopping at his face.

My heart stops, pussy pulses, and I struggle to breath, because that's not just any dick. Nope, it's Toby's dick. Toby is standing here in the bathroom, naked... and oh god, I just heard him jerking off.

I duck back into the shower, plastering myself to the wall as I struggle to breathe and keep quiet. Squeezing my eyes shut, I bite the inside of my cheek as I wait.

It feels like a lifetime before I hear his retreating footsteps and the bathroom door close.

"Holy fuck," I let out on the breath I was holding. "Holy shit, holy shit!" I scrub my face with my hands as I pace the small stall. I just listened to my stepbrother masturbate. Listened to him cum. And god, the dirty talk. The mouth on that man. Who was that man because he sure as hell isn't the Toby I know.

And how do I get him to talk to me like that?

"Fuck." I turn on the shower and stand under the hot water.

I'm in shock as I wash my body and hair, trying to figure out if that really just happened. I need to stop thinking about it, but it's impossible.

I'm turned on and my clit is begging for attention. I've imagined having sex with Toby so many times, his hands all over my body, his cock deep inside me and, god, if he said those things to me, I'd be coming so hard I'd see stars.

I need to take care of the ache between my legs or I'm going to be uncomfortable for the rest of the day. And I can't do it back in my room because Bianca is there. *If he can touch himself in the bathroom, why can't I, right?*

I peek my head back around the curtain, checking to make sure no one else is in here. When I don't see or hear anyone, I bite my lower lip and settle back against the wall.

Closing my eyes, I bring my fingers down over my pussy and bite back a moan as my middle finger brushes against the swollen bud.

I'm so wet I can feel it dripping down my thighs as I work myself slowly, adding pressure as the pleasure builds.

I think of Toby as I move my fingers faster, wishing it was him touching me. My breathing picks up as I imagine him in the shower with me, the water beating down over his sexy naked body.

He looks at me with his hunger, eyes locked with mine as he slowly kneels to the ground in front of me.

I picture him widening my legs, making room so he can bury his face between them before he starts to suck and lick at my center. He uses those dirty words, asking me if I like it, if I want more.

I tell him yes, I want more, need more. He sucks my clit as he fills me with two of his thick fingers.

A whimper slips from my lips as I use my own fingers to fuck myself, rubbing my clit before slipping them inside me and back out again.

In my mind, Toby is the one doing sinful things to my pussy

with his dirty tongue, working me into a frenzy as I grab a handful of his hair and grind against his sexy mouth.

The fire in my belly quickly burns hotter and hotter until I feel like I'm going to burst.

With my free hand, I brush it over my stiff nipple, the shock of pleasure through my body almost has me crumbling to the ground. My orgasm hits me hard, and I cry out. "Oh, god!" I sob, praying no one walks in as my pussy pulses around my fingers. My release drips down my hand. I don't think I've made myself cum that hard in a long time.

I've only ever used my hands and a small bullet vibrator. My fingers have never really done anything for me, and seeing how I'm still a virgin, I didn't feel right losing it to a toy. Pathetically, I've always hoped it would be Toby who got that honor.

But thinking about my fingers as Toby's just now? Yeah, that worked way better than mine ever did.

Coming down from my climax, I take a moment to steady my breathing. I groan, but not in pleasure. It's due to the realization that I just got off with Toby on my mind. It's not that I haven't before, he's always been the star of my solo shows, but I'm supposed to be trying to get over him, and this isn't helping.

It's like I have no control when it comes to him. And thinking about someone else while I get off just feels wrong.

I still can't get over the fact that it was Toby in here. I remember his face last night at the party, the sounds he made, and they didn't sound anything like they did just moments ago. Was he not enjoying himself last night as much as he was just now?

I rinse myself off and clean up before shutting off the water. Wrapping my towel around myself, I grab my dirty clothes and head out to the locker to change.

"Lilly?"

I jump and spin around to find Bishop standing near the entrance. My eyes widen as his eyes trail down my body.

"What are you doing here?" I squeak out.

His eyes lift back up to my face, and a cocky smirk spreads across his lips. "A pipe burst at the gym, so Toby and I came back here to shower." He cocks his head to the side. "He was just in here... at the same time as you...?" He raises a brow. I turn my head and quickly grab my clothes, dirty and clean, shoving them under one arm before grabbing my caddy, using my free hand to keep my towel in place.

"I'll just go change in my room," I say quickly and rush past him, making sure not to make eye contact.

"Don't leave on my account, *il mio cuore*." Bishop chuckles. I look back and find him stripping out of his clothes.

Fucking hockey boys and their no shame in stripping down in front of people.

And damn these coed bathrooms. I'm going to have to shower when they're at practice or class.

Spinning around, I rush out of here fast and practically sprint down the hall.

Coming to a halt at my door, I reach for the handle. "Lilly?" My head whips to the side to see Toby standing in his room, the door wide open. He's in only a pair of grey sweatpants and no damn shirt! This school is going to be the death of me.

His eyes widen when he sees I'm only in a towel. I watch as his mind works out what's going on. "Were you just in the shower?" The way he asks it, sounds like he's dreading my answer.

So, I'll be nice and not give him one. I go to open the door, but the clothes in my arms slip, falling to the ground. "Fuck!" I curse again. I'm panicking, freaking the fuck out right now.

And the universe feels like having another chuckle at my expense because when I bend down to pick up my clothes, my towel falls, joining them on the ground.

Oh, dear god, no! Not now, not here, not in this moment. A choked sound has me snapping straight up, and I look at Toby in utter horror, realizing I made the situation worse. He stands there, gaping at me, eyes stuck on my tits as I stand there fucking naked.

"Oh, god!" I shout in anguish, abandoning all my things to shove the door open. I jump over my things and inside my room, slamming the door shut.

"What the hell?" Bianca asks, and now it's her turn to gape at me as I lean back against the door, my heart thundering in my chest. "Babe, where the hell are your clothes?"

I look down, reminded that I'm still naked. "Damn it," I groan before sprinting across the room, diving into my bed and throwing my blanket over me to cover myself. "Kill me now, Bee. Please, just put me out of my misery."

Bee is full on laughing, and I really want to go over there and slap her, but I'd rather just die here of embarrassment.

"What the hell happened?" she asks through laughs.

"So much," I whine. "So, so much."

Whoever said that college was never a dull moment was right. But I don't think they meant this.

And classes haven't even started yet.

What a way to start the school year.

CHAPTER EIGHT

LILLIANNA

"Come on, Bee!" I'm vibrating with giddy excitement as I hit my bestie with a pillow.

"What the fuck, Lills!" she shrieks.

"Your alarm has gone off three times. Get your ass up. We have class in an hour!" Grinning, I pull the blanket down and slap her ass hard.

"Ouch! Why are you such a bitch?" She shoots up into a sitting position.

"You love me." I blow her a kiss. "Now, get your sexy ass up. Jonas is gonna meet us here soon. Said we can go get food and some coffee beforehand."

"Coffee," she groans. "Yeah, I'm gonna need that shit or I'm not going to make it through the day. I miss the summer already," she whines, flopping back down onto her back.

Leaving her to get her own ass up, I grab a change of clothes towel, and my toothbrush. The guys are at practice this morning, so I should be able to get in and out without any run-ins with Toby.

God, I can't get the image of him naked out of my head. I even had a dream last night about him. It started off where my little imagination session in the bathroom ended. That he picked me up, I wrapped my legs around his waist, and he fucked me hard against the wall until we were moaning each other's names.

I woke up in the middle of the night sweaty, horny, and pissed. Thankfully, when I finally managed to go back to sleep again, I didn't have any more dreams.

"I'm going to shower. Your ass better be up, out of bed, and dressed by the time I get back."

"Alright, mom," she huffs.

Laughing, I slip out of the room and down the hall to the bathroom.

"Hey there, Lills," Bishop greets me with a cocky grin as I step into the bathroom.

"What are you guys doing here?" I ask, eyes flicking between him and Toby. "I thought you had practice." Both of them are standing there with towels around their waists. In all the years I've been friends with these two, I've seen more of their bodies in the last two days than all the years before. I mean, sure, I've seen them in swim trunks, but this is different. And I saw every inch of Toby yesterday.

"We did. But the pipe still isn't fixed."

"Great," I grumble, walking past the two of them and down to the very last stall, making sure not to make eye contact with Toby.

"So, Lills, how was that shower yesterday?" Bishop chuckles.

Shoving my clean clothes into the locker I look over at them. "It was amazing, very *relaxing*," I sass back.

His brows jump, eyes flicking to Toby. Mine do too. He's watching me, looking like he wants to say something, but he doesn't.

Grabbing my toothbrush and toothpaste, I head over to the sink. "Are you excited for your first day?" Toby finally speaks. Pulling the tooth brush from my mouth, I spit and turn to him. "So now you're talking to me?" I raise a brow. "Is this two year cold-shouldering all of a sudden over?"

"Flower," he sighs, a pained look on his face.

"Don't you *Flower* me." I glare, waving my toothbrush at him. "You can't just start acting like you haven't been a complete ass to me for a long time."

"I know."

"And—what?" my brows furrow.

He steps closer and I wish he wouldn't because he's still in his towel. My eyes are going to start wandering, and I don't want to be caught ogling him. "I've been a complete asshole to you and there's no excuse. I've been going through some things, and I thought putting distance between us would protect you. But, in reality, it only ended up hurting you more. I'm so fucking sorry. And you have no reason to forgive me, but I'm going to do my best to earn your trust back. I miss you, Little Flower, and I want our friendship back."

I blink at him, mouth agape. He steps up closer to me, and I swear my heart is going to drop out my ass as he leaves a lingering kiss on my forehead before walking past me and out the bathroom.

"What the fuck…"

Bishop chuckles, shaking his head. "About fucking time."

"What was that?"

"That was Toby realizing that he's an asshole."

"I get that." I roll my eyes. "But why now?"

He shrugs. "I don't know, babe. He's my best friend, but there's a lot about him I don't understand."

"W—what are you doing?!" I gape at him as he pulls the towel from his waist.

"Getting dressed." He looks at me confused.

"Dude! This is not your locker room. I do not want to see

your dick." I slap a hand over my eyes, cheeks flushing because I totally did see his dick and fuck me, I think I saw a piercing.

"Sorry, babe," he laughs. "Kind of a habit, you know."

I groan, spinning around. "You know, living with my two guy best friends is going to be a lot harder than I thought."

"Haha, that's what she said," he jokes.

"Really?" I sigh.

"Sorry." He laughs again. "Come on, Lills. It's going to be awesome. I've missed you, you know?"

I bite my lower lip, my heart feeling all warm and fuzzy. "Is it safe to turn around?"

"Yup."

Spinning around, I keep my eyes on his face. "You're still in your boxers."

He rolls his eyes. "Don't be a prude, Lills."

"I'm not." I chew on my lip. His eyes track the motion for a second before lifting back to mine. "And I miss you too."

"It's gonna be awesome having you here. Just like old times."

"You think? Because it won't be if Toby doesn't change."

"He will. You're a hard one to keep away from." He winks.

I don't know about that. Seemed pretty easy for him to do these past two years.

Enough bitching about it, you can't change the past. You're in University now, it's time to live your life and enjoy new things. And not be dependent on another person.

But I can't help the excited and hopeful feelings that fill me at the thought of getting what Toby and I had back. Even if it's only friendship from him. I'll get over my crush one day.

Only it's not a crush, is it?

Bishop gets dressed and leaves, so I shower quick.

"What's he doing here?" Toby's voice startles me as I reach my dorm room.

"Who?"

His jaw ticks. *Okay, so now he's in a pissy mood?* I don't remember him having mood swings. "Joan."

My brows furrow for a moment, and then I sigh, understanding who he's talking about. "Jonas is one of my best friends."

"I thought you two broke up," his voice comes out annoyed.

I don't remember telling him that, but I'm sure it spilled out at some point the other night. "Just because we broke up, doesn't mean we can't still be friends."

"I don't like him," he mutters, leaning against the frame of his door.

"Come on, man, Jonas is a good guy. You need to get the stick out of your ass. He's on our team now, you're going to have to learn to get along with him," Bishop points out from inside their room.

"Doesn't mean I have to like him," Toby responds, glaring at my door.

"Okay then." I tuck a piece of my wet hair behind my ear and slip inside my room.

"Is the guard dog still out there?" Jonas asks with a chuckle. He's sitting on my bed, his phone in hand.

"Yup." I go over to my dresser and get out my hair dryer.

"He does know we're not together, right?"

"Yes."

"Then why does he still look at me like he wants to punch me in the face?"

I groan. "I don't know. I'm sure he will get over it in time."

"I think he likes you. And not like a little sister." That has me pausing.

"What?" I spin around, and Bianca groans.

"Dude, no, don't tell her that!"

"What?" Jonas looks between the two of us.

"He doesn't." I shake my head. Although the way he used to look at me had me thinking otherwise. But if he loved me as something more, he wouldn't have so easily pushed me out of his life.

"You sure? Because that man looks at you like you hung the

moon. And if anyone else looks your way, it's like he's trying to kill them with his death glare." Jonas chuckles.

"Stop!" Bee throws her pillow at him. "No giving our girl false hope or making her confused. She's on operation move-the-hell-on."

"He's always been like that. He's just overly protective. We're each other's person." I shrug and turn the hair dryer on, cutting the conversation off.

Guess I'm not the only one who sees it.

Nope, not going down that line of thinking. I've already let myself pine over him for too long.

Something he said to me a few months ago flutters back to the front of my mind. Toby was drinking, having a few with our dads, and he ended up hanging out in the back by the pool.

I was coming out of the pool house, when I saw him and stopped in my tracks. I just stood there and watched him. It had been a while since the last time I saw him, and I don't know, I just wanted that moment.

I guess he could see me watching him because he sat up and said in a drunken slur, "Little sisters don't look at their brothers that way, Lilly." Then he got up and walked back into the house, leaving me shocked as hell.

Because that was one of the only few times he's ever referred to me as his sister. And fuck if that didn't hurt.

"People are looking at us," Bianca whispers as we walk toward the campus cafe.

"I'm aware of that." But I don't pay the people around me any mind. I've been getting stares and whispers all day. No one has said anything to my face, no rude comments or name calling, so I've ignored them. Just as I'm going to do now.

"It doesn't bother you?"

"Nope." I smile up at her. "This is Silver Valley, Bee. Give it a few days and something else will happen that has everyone talking."

"True." She raises her brows.

"Don't worry, if someone says shit, I'll kick their asses," Jonas says from the other side of Bianca.

"You will not." She slaps his arm. "That would just draw more attention."

"Oh, come on, Bumblebee. You're telling me you wouldn't enjoy a fine, studly man like me to defend your honor?" he teases, lifting his arm up to show off his tattooed muscled bicep.

Bianca laughs, shaking her head, and I giggle. "You're nuts."

"Nope, but I have two of them." He winks, making Bee snort.

I grin because they have no idea how perfect they are for each other. All in good time, I hope.

When we get to the cafe, I'm not at all surprised to see it's busy. "Come on. Molly and Robin saved us some seats."

Jonas starts to follow us when someone calls out for him. "Hey, Walker!" I look over to see one of the hockey guys waving Jonas over.

Jonas looks at us, uncertain what to do. "Go," I tell him. "It's good for you to bond with the boys and what not." I wave him away.

"We're probably just going to talk about boys anyway," Bianca says, agreeing with me.

Jonas glares at her, and I push him in the direction of the guys. "Go." I laugh.

"Alright. I'll see you after class?"

"Yup. We can talk about everything that happened during our first day."

He nods and takes off toward the table. The guys get up,

doing this bro-hug thing, and I smile. It slips away when I see Toby watching me.

Ugh, why does my body heat up under his attention? I lick my lips, and I swear his eyes heat. The moment is broken when a beautiful girl with black hair sits in his lap.

Unable to watch the girl paw at him, I let Bee know I'm going to go grab something to eat.

"Ugh, I don't know what to get," I murmur to myself as I look at the menu board.

"I'd recommend the fries. In my opinion, they're perfect. Crispy on the outside, fluffy on the inside." I turn to the guy who's standing behind me in line. He grins and continues. "But don't get the gravy. It ruins them completely."

"Well, I can't let perfectly good fries be ruined, now can I?" I giggle.

"It would be a tragedy, for sure." He winks. Okay, this guy is cute and from the letterman jacket he's wearing, he's most likely on one of the teams. He's tall with black shaggy hair and striking green eyes.

"So mouth watering fries are a must, anything else that you would think could taste good together?"

He taps his finger on his chin as he looks at the menu board while I smile and wait. "The chicken tendies are the bomb," he finally decides.

I giggle. "I do love me a good tendie."

"See, that right there makes you perfect wife material." He winks again. "Hi, I'm Ryan Tucker, by the way."

He holds his hand out, and I take it. "Lilliana Tatum."

"Oh, shit. You're Coach Creed and Coach River's kid." His eyes widen.

I pull my hand from his and force a smile. "Yup. That's me. I'm sure you have probably seen the video by now."

"Video?" His brows furrow. "Ah, no. Your dads just talk about you a lot," he snickers. "They actually lectured the team today. Told us all that we were not allowed to pursue you."

"They did not." My eyes widen in horror.

"Yup." he chuckles.

"Oh, god," I groan, covering my face with my hands. "I'm going to kill them."

"They're good guys. But damn, Coach is scary."

"I'm so sorry about them." I'm mortified, and they will be getting yelled at.

"Don't be." He scratches the back of his head, and it's kind of adorable. "I should be heeding their warning, but now that I've met you, you seem like a pretty cool chick."

"Thank you." I laugh. "You're not so bad yourself."

"Thanks." He grins. "Any chance we could hang out sometime? I know some pretty good places around here with better food than this. Because honestly, the fries and tenders are the only things on that menu worth eating."

I bite my lower lip. *Do I want to go out with a guy so soon?* Jonas and I broke up not too long ago and school *just* started.

But it's not like I'm heartbroken or hung up on Jonas.

No, that would be another man. One you can't have.

And I did agree with Bianca, we would try to have some fun. And Ryan seems like a nice guy.

"You know what? Yeah, why not? I'd like that." I smile. "Give me your phone."

"Really?" he looks surprised. "Awesome." He takes his phone out and hands it to me. When I'm done adding my number I hand it back.

"Just text me whenever. I know you must have a crazy schedule with football and all."

"Yeah, your dads are beasts." He chuckles. "But it's worth it. We hardly lost any games last year."

Ryan says goodbye, leaving me to order my food. Once I have everything, I head toward the table where the girls are at, when I feel eyes on me. Looking over, I see Toby watching me. He looks pissed, his eyes moving to somewhere behind me. I look to see what he's looking at and find Ryan at the table with some of the other football players. He sees me looking and gives me a wink before going back to talk to his buddy.

My cheeks heat, and I turn away, my gaze finding Toby again. He's not happy. And some fucked up part of me likes that.

Could he really be jealous?

This is a dangerous game to play, and it's only going to end with a broken heart.

CHAPTER NINE

BISHOP

"What kind of name is Ryan Tucker? Who has a first name as a last name?" Toby bitches as we skate off the ice.

We've just spent the last hour at practice and anytime we had a free second, Toby's been complaining about some football player named Ryan who asked Lilly out yesterday.

"Dude, shut the fuck up," I groan, taking my helmet off and shaking out my sweaty hair.

He shoots me a glare. "What's your problem?"

I stop and look over at him. "You haven't shut up about Lilly agreeing to go out with that guy. It's just a date. What's the big deal?"

I know what the big deal is. It's this asshat who acts like he's not madly in love with our little blonde bestie. For the love of all that is holy, I wish he would get over himself, and just tell her how he feels. It would save everyone a lot of heartache and drama.

But no. He says it's because they are step-siblings and it would never work, but I know the real reason why. Toby has always cared way too much about what this town thought of his family. Any time they would whisper anything negative, he was always the first to defend them. Usually by using his fists.

The only reason why he won't make a move on Lilly is because he's afraid that people will talk about her, and he can't handle that. Talk about him, sure, his family, he could deal, but trash talk Lilly?

Yeah, no. I've seen him snap. I've seen him beat people until they're bleeding for the way they've talked about her in the past. Hell, I've been there right beside him, punching some drunk fucker in the face for making crass comments about her.

Next to Toby, Lilly is my best friend. Since I started going over to their house when I was seven, we've been the three amigos. But Lilly is three years younger than us, so as we got older, we had to adjust with the changes.

She was stuck in elementary school while we went to junior high. That's when she got closer with my sister and her now-ex, Jonas, came along.

So in school, they were her people; outside of school, we were. At least until she hit high school. She didn't want to have to choose between us, so my sister and Jonas started tagging along with us everywhere.

Not that I cared too much. I might give my sister a hard time, but I love the girl. She's one of my best friends, too.

"The big deal is she just broke up with Jonas a few weeks ago, and she's already agreeing to a date with some guy she met in the lunch line after being here for only a few days."

We hang behind, slowly walking to the locker room so the other guys don't hear us, Jonas included.

"Hey, I have an idea that could solve all your problems," I chirp.

He looks at me with eager interest. "Really? What?"

Grabbing his shoulders, I give him a little shake. "Tell the girl how you fucking feel."

His face drops. "You know I can't," he growls, shaking my hands off and walking toward the locker room.

"Then you can't get pissed off if she dates other people."

"Like fuck, I can't," he mutters.

The locker room is loud, the guys already stripping out of their gear. We go over to our lockers and do the same.

"Hey, Toby." Toby turns to see Jonas standing nearby, towel wrapped around his waist. "Good practice."

"Thanks," Toby grunts, raising a brow.

"Look. I wanted to talk, you got a minute?"

"I guess."

Jonas runs a hand through his wet hair. "I know you don't really like me. I'm assuming it has to do with me dating Lilly, but I want you to know that we're not together anymore. It was a mutual agreement. With us being a team and stuff, I want to make sure there's no bad blood between us."

"You two are really over?" Toby's brows furrow.

"Yeah." Jonas nods.

"Why did you guys break up?"

Jonas shrugs his shoulders. "She broke up with me, but it was a good thing. We both realized that we were only meant to be friends."

"Do you still love her?"

I roll my eyes. God, people see an overprotective brother, I see a man who's jealous as fuck.

"Ah, no." Jonas chuckles. "As a best friend, sure, but I don't think I ever loved her that way."

"Why the hell not?" Toby snaps. Jonas' eyes widen.

"Dude, chill." I look around, seeing we've gained an audience.

Toby clears his throat. "Fine. Whatever. We're cool."

"Awesome." He nods. "Well, see-ya."

Jonas heads back over to his locker to get dressed.

"Toby, man, what the hell has gotten into you?"

He sighs, stripping down and heading for the shower. Thankfully, they're fixed now. I hated walking home smelling like sweaty ass until we could shower at the dorm.

After we shower and get dressed, we head out to my Jeep. I don't miss the group of girls who linger outside the rink. Normally, I'd stay and talk to a few, but Toby is in a shitty mood as he storms right past, jumping in the front seat of the Jeep.

"I knew it was going to be a change having her here, but fuck, man, I don't know if I can do it."

"Do what?" I start the engine and pull out of the parking lot.

"Keep my anger in check. Any time I think about her with someone else, I want to rip someone's face off."

"You need to watch it, T. You remember what Jax said? You get into any fights, you're getting benched. And as good as Jonas is, we need you in that net."

When we first got here, Toby was dealing with some demons from his past. And being away from Lilly added to his frustrations. He started getting into fights on and off the ice. It was becoming an issue until we found a different way to burn it out of his system, only that started becoming an issue, and he had to stop. He's been struggling ever since.

And now with Lilly here, shit's only going to go downhill fast. Stubborn fucker could just solve a lot of it by telling Lilly how he feels. I'm not stupid, I know she feels the same way about him. She looks at him like he hung the moon.

"I know. I know. And that's why I think I should start going to the ring more." He looks over at me, waiting for my reaction.

"Toby," I sigh, shaking my head. "It's not that I'm against the rings, but last time you depended on them so much, your hands were always fucked up and you were in pain during games. It's a risk to your health."

"I'll keep it to once a week, at most. Saturday nights, if I need to blow off steam. I won't take on more than one fight. Just one. Enough to relieve some pent up energy and anger. That's it."

I can see the pain on his face. He's struggling. "Are you sure?"

"Yes. I can't…" He looks out the window, running a hand over his face. "I can't use girls to forget anymore. Not with Lilly here on campus. It makes me sick, it makes my skin crawl, being with anyone else." His fist clenches and unclenches. "I can't."

"I… alright." I nod as we pull into the dorms. "T."

He looks over at me. "Yeah?"

"Why don't you just tell her?"

His face darkens. "Don't start, Bishop. You know I can't. I won't do that to her. It's not even just about what people would say, it's the fact that I'm broken. She deserves better than someone with anger issues and who wakes up screaming from night terrors every night."

"You're too fucking hard on yourself, man. I think you should let Lilly decide for herself."

He shakes his head. "It's not happening, so just drop it."

We get out of the Jeep and head inside the dorm. We don't have any classes for another two hours, so relaxing after that hour of practice is needed.

Giggling filters through the hallway as we walk toward our dorm room. I grin over at Toby, who looks amused. I jog ahead a few steps and pause in the girls' open door. "What are you two giggling about?"

Lilly looks up from her phone, a smile taking over her pretty face. She's sitting on the edge of B's bed as my sister stands by her closet.

"Just something someone said." Lilly blushes, and I raise a brow.

"Oh, really. Who's this someone?"

"That would be Ryyyyaaann," Bianca sing-songs in a teasing tone. "They stayed up late texting. He's so corny, it's adorable."

Toby makes a disgruntled sound from behind me. This isn't gonna be good.

"Stop." Lilly laughs. "We're just texting."

"And going on a date this weekend," Bianca counters, holding up one of her dresses. "I think you should wear this."

Lilly's eyes widen. "Ah, no. That's a nice dress but it's more for a club. He's taking me to a movie. I'd rather be in something comfortable."

"That's no fun." Bianca pouts. "How are you gonna get laid in your granny get up?"

Lilly chokes out a laugh, shooting me a look. I don't think she knows Toby is behind me, but I can feel the man ready to explode as his eyes bore into my back.

"B!" Lilly scolds her.

"What?" my sister blinks innocently. "You agreed to make the most out of your college experience. To get out there. Make the best of our first year and being single. That included having a little fun." She wiggles her brows.

Lilly rolls her eyes. "Stop. Ryan seems like a nice guy. I don't think he's going to try to get in my pants on the first date."

Both my sister and I snort out a laugh. Lilly shoots a glaring look my way. "What?"

"He's a football player, babe. And you're fine as fuck. I think the chances of him at least trying something are high."

"I agree with the big dummy over there."

"You both suck." Lilly gets up and walks over to the door, staring me down as she starts to shut it in my face. "Be nice," she mutters before the door clicks shut.

Spinning around, I let out a sigh when I don't find Toby standing outside in the hall anymore. "Fuck," I groan.

Toby is laying in his bed, a look of pure fury on his face.

"What?" I sigh.

"Don't what me!" he snaps.

"Dude." I flop back into my bed. Here we go again.

"She cannot go out with him."

"Why not?" I turn my head to look at him. "If you're not going to stake your claim, then why can't she be with anyone else?"

"Because," he growls, looking seconds away from kicking my ass. "I know she's going to find someone someday, get married, and live happily ever after. But that won't be right now. When I graduate, she can date until her heart's content after I leave. Until then, I don't want to see her with any other guy."

"You weren't like this when she was dating Jonas. She was with him for two years."

"I was too. I hated the guy. The idea of him touching her, kissing her, fucking her," he growls the last part. "Makes me want to commit murder. But I knew deep down that it was just a high school thing. They were never going to be anything more after they graduated. I've seen the two of them together. I'm surprised they lasted that long. Jonas was a nice guy, I'll give him that. But the guys at this school?" He shakes his head. "No fucking way."

"Looks like you're going to have to get used to the idea, man. Because what are you going to do? Tell her she can't? And what are you going to say when she asks you why?"

His jaw ticks, and I can tell he's getting worked up.

"You need to help me."

I sit up, spinning around so my legs hang over the side of the bed. "And how do I do that?"

"You date her."

My brows shoot up. "I'm sorry, what?" I bark out a laugh.

He runs a hand through his hair. "Not really date her. Just hang out with her, make plans, use up her free time so she can't go out with anyone else."

"You're nuts. You have officially lost it, man." I shake my head. "And what about me? I should just not have a life?"

He shrugs. "Make plans with chicks when she's hanging out with Bee and Jonas."

He's dead serious. I groan in defeat. "Here's what I can offer.

I'll try to hang out with her more, because Lilly is one of my best friends, so it's no hardship to me. But I'm not going to tell her who she can and can't date."

"Maybe you *should* fake date her."

"Nope. Not happening. I won't risk my friendship with Lilly by playing with her emotions." Or mine because he has no fucking idea how much he's asking of me by doing this.

"Fine. We'll go with your idea."

"You're stupid, and I hate you so fucking much," I grumble, flopping back down on the bed again.

"I know. But you're also my best friend and you deal with my crazy ass."

He's right. I don't try to understand Toby. The man has been through some shit and is still here, still dealing with it. I do my best to be there for him and support him because he's more of a brother than a friend.

If this helps him keep his cool a little better, then I guess I'll have to at least try. Not going to lie, the idea of hanging out with Lilly more feels good.

"Are you going to try being friends with her like you said yesterday?"

"Yeah. I can't keep being an asshole to her. It hurts too much. And the pain on her face when I do." He shakes head. "I fucking hate myself for how I treated her the past few years. I fucking miss her, and it kills me."

"Time to get back what we had before?"

"Yeah. I fucking need it more than I thought I would."

Me too, man, me too.

CHAPTER TEN

LILLIANNA

"What are we doing here?" Bianca groans as we step in the school's hockey arena. People are mulling around, but overall it's empty in here. By the looks of it, all the puck bunnies are hanging out.

"Because, we have nothing to do and our bestie is practicing. Also, I miss my dad. I want to say hi." I shrug my shoulders as we walk toward the rink's entrance.

It's not completely a lie. As much as I don't want to admit it, in a way I'm not any better than the puck bunnies. Only in high school I wasn't there to see just any player.

I've seen Bishop and Toby in a few games since they've started at SVU but I haven't come to a practice yet.

The idea of seeing Toby all sweaty in his gear? Yeah, it's wrong, but it does something very sinful to my body.

Just because I'm trying to move on, doesn't mean I can't look. I'm not going to touch. Even though I really want to.

"Fine, but I'm studying while we're in there," Bianca informs me, pulling open the doors.

I roll my eyes. "Girl, we've been in classes for three days now. Three. We don't even have any work due."

"I might." She gives me a guilty smile. "I may have been distracted by a really cute guy who gave me his number before class in English Lit. And I may or may not have texted him, causing me to miss most of the class. So now I have to copy the notes Jill gave me."

"Girl!" My eyes widen and I laugh, slapping her arm. "No. We are not going to let boys get in the way of our education."

"I know," She groans as she walks up the steps of the bleachers. "But he's really cute."

"I'm sure he is." I giggle. Bee takes a seat near the players bench, but I go and hang out with my dad. "Hey, Dad."

He looks over at me, his black curly hair hanging over his left eye. "Hey, sweetie. What are you doing here?"

I take a seat next to him on the bench. "Just wanted to see you. It's been a few days."

"Almost a week. Your moms have been counting," he chuckles. "I've also had to tell Brody and Chase that we can't track you down just to say hello."

"Oh, god!" The words come out as a groan but end with me laughing. "I should go by and see them, shouldn't I?"

"Might be a good idea." He gives me a grin. "You know I can't hold those two back for too long."

"I don't know." I knock my shoulder into his. "You just gotta bat your pretty lashes at Brody, and he's putty in your hands."

My dads, Jax and Brody, are a couple, an adorable one at that. Brody might come off as a scary asshole, and yes, that is one of many things I've heard people call him. Yet when it comes to me, my mom, and Jax, he's nothing but a big teddy bear.

Jax shakes his head, a grin playing on his lips. "So, how are you doing?"

"Good. The first few days of classes have been exciting. Met a few new people. And I got myself a date."

His brows jump. "Oh, really?" Jax is the only one of the dads who won't go into overprotective-dad-mode when it comes to boys. He listens to what I have to say and gives me advice.

I nod. "His name is Ryan Tucker. He's on the football team. He's also funny, sweet, and… I don't know, I think it will be fun." I haven't really been on a date before. Sure, Jonas and I have gone out a few times, but we already had an established friendship, and knew everything about each other. This is going to be different.

My attention turns to the rink. More specifically, the man in the net. I always wished it would be him. That we would take that step from friendship to something more. That butterflies would fill my belly as we held hands, snuggling together while we watched a movie.

But that's not going to happen, no matter how much I wish. I really need to get Toby out of my head, I have a date with someone else.

"I know him," Jax confirms. "He's a good kid. But I'm surprised he asked you out. Your dads warned them off." He gives me a mischievous grin.

"I know." I shoot him a glare. "I'm going to be having words with them about it too."

"They're just looking out for you," he chuckles.

"Dad!" I gape at him. "No, that's not how you do that. Plus, I already have enough people talking about me for other reasons, I don't need more."

Not that the football guys have been giving me a hard time about it; I have yet to run into anyone else on the team. But still. I'm not a big fan of having the attention on me and having pretty much all my parents as faculty members at my university, I know it's going to come with its challenges.

The amusement on Jax's face falls. "How are you doing with that? Are people giving you a hard time?"

I shrug. "Not really. I mean, I get a few whispers here and there and the odd look, but it's college and people do stupid stuff all the time. Just last night I saw a video of some guy streaking across campus and taking a bath in the fountain in front of the library."

"Dear god." He shakes his head. "You kids these days scare me."

"Like you haven't done anything crazy?" I giggle. "I've heard some stories, you know."

He grins. "Yeah, okay, point taken."

"I'm just sorry you guys had to see me like that." I nibble on my lower lip, my eyes falling to my hands as I play with my sweater. "Sloppy drunk and half naked. Not what a girl wants their parents to see."

"I'm gonna be honest, we could have lived without seeing it." He wraps his arm around my shoulder. "And not because of what was in the video. We wish you could just have fun without people trying to use it against you. Chase is not happy about who posted it."

"How is he doing? Has Kayla ever tried anything since she's gotten out?"

"No." Jax shakes his head. "Although, last year, your moms were out and bumped into her. Rain may have accidentally tripped her, leaving her with a bloody nose and two black eyes."

"Good," I huff angrily. "She deserves worse. Her daughter isn't all that better."

"Let us know if she starts to give you any issues, okay? We would rather put a stop to things before anything bad happens."

"I will."

"Hey, Coach," a guy from the rink shouts. "Who's the sexy little thing sitting next to you? And does your wife know?" he chuckles.

My eyes widen in shock. *Is this guy for real?* "Fucking little shit," Jax snarls. He stands up, about to chew him out, no doubt, but before he gets the chance to, someone speed skates over to him and body checks him onto the ice.

I gasp, jolting to my feet as Bishop rips his helmet off and looms over the guy laying flat on the ice. "Watch your fucking mouth, Newburry," Bishop spits. "That's the fucking coach's daughter. And my best friend. Disrespect her like that again, and I'll fucking make you eat your own teeth, got it?"

Jax blows his whistle. "Alright, everyone, that's enough. Practice is over. Grant." He directs towards Bishop. "Next time, let me do my job. And Newburry, disrespect me or my family again, and you're off the team. I don't care how much money your daddy has, I can assure you, I have more," Jax snarls, shooting this dude with a murderous look and holy shit, I don't think I've ever seen him this mad before.

"Sorry, Coach," Newburry mumbles, skating off the ice with the other members.

"I don't fucking like him," Bishop states, stopping next to me and Jax. His hair drips with sweat, falling over his forehead. *Ugh, okay, maybe it's not just Toby I've appreciated.* Bishop is hot, I'm not blind. But he's also one of my best friends, my best friend's brother, and my other best friend's best friend. Yeah, let's just say it's complicated enough that I'm in love with my step-brother, I'm not going to throw my best friend into the mix too. I have enough issues to deal with as it is.

"Hey, Bianca," a guy who skates up to the box greets. I look over to see B's head snap up and her eyes widen.

"Clay?" she blinks. "You're on the hockey team?"

"Surprised you didn't know." he chuckles, running a gloved hand over his blond hair. Okay, he's cute. I get why Bee was distracted. "So, you gonna answer my text?" He gives her a flirty grin.

Oh no. Jonas skates over, stopping between Bishop and Clay. "What text?" he asks, looking between Bee and Clay.

"Ah…" Bee blushes. "Yeah?"

"Yes, you're going to answer my text, or yes, you're gonna agree to go out on that date with me this weekend?"

"Both," she squeaks, the red on her cheeks burning bright.

I do not miss the way Jonas' face clouds over, jealousy marring his handsome face. He shakes his head and skates away, shoulders tense. I want to say I wish he would just tell her how he feels, but again, I don't have a leg to stand on. Falling for someone who's close to you is hard, you don't want to risk what you have, but the longing for more is hard to deny. He's like me. He would rather only be friends than take the chance of not having them at all.

"Dude." Bishop's face scrunches up. "That's my sister." He points toward Bianca.

"I know." Clay chuckles. "And she's pretty cool. I want to get to know her."

Bianca makes her way down to the glass. "Bishop, shut it. I can go on a date with whoever I want." She glares at him.

Clay looks over to me. "You cool if we double date?"

"What?" my brows furrow.

Clay chuckles. "Ryan is my buddy. He mentioned you two going out this weekend. But it's cool if you don't want to."

Bianca looks over with pleading eyes. "Ah... yeah, sure, that would be fun."

"Cool." He nods, looking back over to Bianca. "I'll talk to you later." He winks and Bianca grins, biting her lower lip.

"And that's my cue to leave." Jax chuckles, giving me a hug and kissing me on the top of the head. "See you later, sweetie. Might want to see your dads sooner than later before they track you down. They're at the field from seven to eight tonight."

"Thanks, dad, I will. Love you."

"Love you too, sweetie."

"Well, that was an eventful practice." I turn to Bishop but he's not standing there alone anymore, Toby is there.

"You okay?" he asks, his eyes searching mine.

"Yeah, I'm fine. Why wouldn't I be?" I ask, head tilting to the side in curiosity.

"Newburry is a fucking creep." Toby shakes his head, looking to Bishop. "We need to keep an eye on him. As good of a player as he is, I'm not tolerating his sexual-harassment bullshit."

"Agreed." Bishop nods.

"Gotta say, that was the first I've ever been mistaken for one of my dads' side pieces," I gag. "And dude must be stupid. Who talks to their coach like that?"

"Someone who thinks their daddy's money can get them out of anything," Toby scoffs. "He's new. Transferred from another school in hopes of being seen by the reps for the NHL."

"Can't believe Theo let him in here," Bianca comments, joining me at my side.

"Sadly, if his grades are good enough and there's no reason not to let him transfer, there's nothing he could have really done without backlash," Bishop says.

I feel Toby's eyes on me and I try not to look, but I can see him out of the corner of my eye. Why does he have to be so sexy? Coming here was a bad idea.

"Want to go get something to eat before we head over to the football field?" Bianca asks, nudging my shoulder. "Maybe spend a bit of time with Ryan before practice."

My eyes find Toby's. His jaw clenches, gaze darkening. "You really think dating someone after you just got out of a two year relationship is a good idea?"

Brows jumping, my stomach drops. "Really?" I hate the way my voice cracks.

"I just don't want you to jump into anything you're not ready for."

I shake my head. "You don't get to walk back into my life after two years of treating me like I'm nothing and start commenting on how I should live my life. It's none of your business, you've made sure of that." Anger fills me as I look over to Bianca, who's glaring at Toby. "Come on. Let's get out of here."

"Keep your boy on a leash, big brother." She looks to Bishop, who shakes his head at his best friend.

I leave the two of them on the ice and head toward the exit.

"The fucking balls on that guy," Bianca growls as she loops her arms through mine. "It's not *his* life. You can do whatever you damn well please. Asshole comes back after years and thinks he can start up again with his overprotective crap. Yeah, not happening."

"Yeah," I murmur in agreement. We walk down the pathway toward a cute little café on campus. Bee keeps talking, but I'm not listening.

Normally, I'd be excited by the fact that Toby is jealous, only that didn't come off as jealousy, it sounded more like he was judging me.

When we get to the café, we head over to the counter, ordering a sandwich and a coffee. "I'll bring it over when it's ready," the lady at the counter tells me.

"Thanks," I say with a smile as Bianca and I turn to find a seat. "Bee. Do you think it's too soon for me to date? It's been a few weeks since Jonas and I broke up, and even though we were together for a few years, it never felt like anything more than just friends, you know?"

"No, I don't think it's too soon. What I do think is that Toby was being a dick. You're young, single, and deserve to enjoy yourself. You've had, what, one boyfriend in your life? You need to get out there and live a little. He can't just start inserting himself in your life again. And he sure as hell can't judge you on how you live your life whether he's in it or not. You're going on a date for frig's sake. Not sleeping with the whole football team."

Heat creeps up my cheeks and I look around to see people watching. "Bee, shh," I whisper-hiss. I love this girl but sometimes she has no sense of volume.

"Sorry," she sighs. "He just gets me so worked up. Do you remember how we used to sneak out to hang out with boys?" She rolls her eyes. "I swear, any time a guy looked your way, he would growl like a dog."

"He would not." I laugh, a smile forming on my lips at the thought. She's not wrong, though; Toby never let a guy talk to me for long, always giving them a dirty look, but I didn't care because I didn't want any of them.

And now, even though I still want him, I know I need to move on. I want what we had back, but within reason. Yet, I want to talk like we used to, hang out, laugh, smile, and just be with my best friend.

But things won't be exactly the same because interfering with who I go out with isn't something he can do now, I won't let him.

If he doesn't want me in that way, then it's not fair for him to stop me from finding someone who does.

The waitress brings us our food and we spend the rest of our time in the café talking about school and our double date this weekend.

I feel bad for Jonas but he has a better chance at being with Bianca then I do with Toby. He's just too stubborn to say anything.

At least Bianca isn't sitting around waiting for a boy. I need to take a page from her book. And that's exactly what this weekend is.

I'm excited. Ryan is really sweet, he makes me laugh, and is the only guy I've felt butterflies for, apart from Toby.

"Come on, babe. We better get going if we're going to catch your dads."

We pack up and head down to the football stadium. "Girl, next time, can we take a car? I'm all about getting my steps in but this campus is massive. This is enough cardio for the month," I groan, tired as hell from all this walking.

"Drama queen, much?" Bianca giggles, patting me on the back.

The guys are already out on the field when we get there. My dad, Brody, is barking orders while my dad, Chase, is looking at a clipboard.

I smile, excited to see them. I really am a daddy's girl, and I have no shame in it. They're amazing men who would burn the world down for me. I'm lucky to have them.

Putting my fingers in my mouth, I give a sharp whistle. Chase looks up and when he sees it's me, his face splits into a wide grin.

I giggle, taking off running. He tosses the clipboard to the ground and catches me when I get to him. "Hey, Lillypad," he murmurs against the top of my head, giving me a kiss.

"Hey, Dad."

"Missed you, short stuff." When we pull back from the hug, he tousles my hair.

"Dad," I groan, ducking out of his way, laughing as I fix my hair.

"What brings you two here?"

"Hey, Chase," Bianca says, doing a drive-by wave as she heads over to the bleachers to sit with the cheerleaders.

"Bye, Bee," he chuckles.

"Well, we're here for a few reasons. But one of them is to scold you and Brody for warning the damn football team away from me. Really?" I cross my arms and glare at him.

He has the decency to look guilty. "I'm sorry. But also, I'm not. I heard a few guys on the team talking about the video from the party. They weren't being overly gross about it, but they were saying how hot you were. And when I mentioned it to Brody... well, you know your dad."

"Yeah, like you didn't agree with him?" I roll my eyes.

"Just looking out for you, short stuff. These are a good group of guys for the most part, but they have new girls hanging off their arms every other day. I was one of them before. I know how they can be."

"Eww, no. I don't need to think about you being with other women." I shiver and he chuckles. "What about Ryan Tucker?"

"What about him?" His brows furrow.

"Is he like all the other guys?"

"Ah, not from what I've seen." He shrugs. "He had a girl-friend but I haven't seen her around this year."

"Good," I nod and walk past him and over toward the play-ers' bench.

"What do you mean 'good?'" I almost laugh at the slight panic in my dad's voice.

Ignoring him, I look for Ryan. I have no idea what his jersey number is, and they all have helmets on. "Which one is Ryan?"

"Why?" he asks with suspicion.

"Dad!" I flick my eyes over to him.

"Twenty-two," he mutters.

Searching for his number, I find him tossing the ball to another player. Biting my lower lip, I feel the flutters in my belly. He's got a good arm.

Brody is too distracted doing his job, and when I don't pay Chase any more mind, he joins him. I just stand here and watch the sexy football players because, why not?

After a few, Ryan looks my way, making my heart speed up a little bit. He pulls his helmet off and shakes out his sweaty black hair.

He looks over at his teammate and says something before he starts jogging over to me. "Hey, gorgeous," he greets, leaning in to place a small kiss on my cheek.

"Hey," I say softly, finding myself giddy.

"Tucker!" Brody barks. "Want to tell me why the hell you're kissing my daughter?"

My eyes widen. "Dad!" I hiss.

"Is he your boyfriend or something?" Brody asks, shooting Ryan a glare. *Or something.*

"No, he's not my boyfriend." I roll my eyes. "I'd tell you if he was."

"Good. So why the hell is he kissing you?"

Ryan chuckles, and the dude must have a huge set of balls because most people shrink away when Brody looks at them the way he's doing to Ryan right now.

"Sorry, Coach. I'm taking Lilly out this weekend."

"What?" Brody growls. "I thought I told the lot of you to stay away from her."

Dear god, take me now.

"You did, but Lilly is an adult and is capable of making her own decisions. But I can assure you, I will treat your daughter with nothing but respect and be the best gentlemen I can be."

I gape at Ryan in awed shock. *Okay, not going to lie, that was hot.* "I'll see you this weekend. Text you after practice." He winks before looking back at my dad who I have no doubt is fuming right now. "And sir, she's gorgeous, I had to shoot my shot." He shrugs, chuckling before turning around and jogging back to his teammates.

"If the kid wasn't a hell of a player, I'd kick him off the team for that," Brody grumbles.

"Dad," I say in a warning tone. "Want to tell me why you did what you did?"

He wraps his arm around me, kissing my temple. "Nope. I did what any good father would do. And I don't regret it."

"Don't make a habit out of it, Dad." I sigh heavily. "Please. I don't want any more unwanted attention on me."

His face drops. "Shit, I'm sorry, kid. I didn't think."

"I know. And I'll forgive you… this time, but no more over-the-top dad things. You want me to go to RVU? Because I'll transfer," I bluff.

"You will not." He narrows his eyes. "Fine, I'll be good."

Chase snorts. "I'll believe that when I see it."

"No one asked you," Brody mutters to Chase.

"I'm gonna go catch up with Bee. I'll see you guys on Sunday for supper, okay?"

"Okay. Are you taking your car or getting a ride with Toby?"

I blink, not even knowing that was an option. "I'm not sure yet."

He nods. "I think it's about time you two make up. I don't know what the little shit's issue is, but it's not cool how he's treating his little sister."

The words are always a hot knife through my heart.

"He said he was going to stop being an ass."

"Good. He better."

As I walk over to Bee, I think about Sunday supper. This is going to be the first time in a long time that it's not going to be filled with awkward silence, at least between the two of us. Or that's what I'm hoping for. I guess it will be the real test to see if he actually meant what he said about wanting to be close again.

CHAPTER ELEVEN

TOBIAS

"Would you get away from the damn door?" Bishop says, tossing something at me.

"Fuck off," I grumble, shooting him a glare. I look down to see it's a pillow and pick it up, throwing it back at him. I hit him in the face, making him chuckle.

"You look pathetic, dude. You're looking out the fucking peephole like a stalker."

"So," I mumble.

"What do you see?"

"Nothing. Their door is closed." I sigh, turning around. "She said he was going to pick her up at eight, right?"

"Yes, she did. I texted her and asked, just like you wanted." He's grinning at me, and I hate it.

"Stop looking at me like that." I flip him off.

"I can't help it. It feels like the good old days." He sighs in a wistful way, being overly dramatic about the whole situation.

"What are you talking about?" I lean back against the door.

"The way you used to follow Lilly around like a little puppy, nipping at anyone's heels who got too close. It's been a while."

"I never followed her around." I roll my eyes. "It just so happens that she was always with us. Which I liked, so..." I shrug.

"Because you never gave her a choice," he snorts. "You've been her big bad watchdog since the moment she came into your life." He leans back, placing both arms behind his head, letting out a smug sigh. "Hey, don't get me wrong, I'm not complaining. Lilly is one of my best friends. I'm right there with you, wanting to make sure she is happy and whoever she goes out with is worthy of her."

"No one is." *Not even me.* Especially not me. "And didn't I ask you to hang out with her so she wouldn't go out on dates?"

He gives me a dry look. "Yeah, after she already agreed to go out with Ryan. What did you want me to do, try and talk her out of it? Like that would have gone over well. You know, my friendship with her suffered because of you. And I want that back. It's bad enough, I'm already risking it if she finds out what I'm doing for you. I'm not going to piss her off by prying into her business and making absurd requests. She's not stupid, man."

"I know she's not fucking stupid. She's one of the smartest people I've ever met," I snap at him, and the asshole breaks out into a fit of laughter.

"You are so fucking obsessed with her, it's fucking hilarious."

"I hate you," I growl. Walking over to him, I grab one of my pillows and start beating him with it. The fucker just laughs harder.

"Just admit it." He grabs me, pulling me down onto the bed before getting me in a chokehold. "I know you love her."

"I do," I grunt, elbowing him in the head. "You know I do."

"You're in love with her. Just tell her, for fuck's sake, and this can all be over."

"I can't," I seethe, getting out of his hold. I stand back up, huffing, brushing the hair out of my face. "You don't understand, and you don't have to. I love her, I'm in love with her, and I wish I could be with her more than anything, but it's not meant to be. The world sees her as my sister, and people fuck with my family as it is. You saw what one person did with just a video and a photo of her. She's here for four years, this school will fucking eat her alive if they found out she's fucking her stepbrother."

I hate that word. I'm not her *brother*. I've never felt like I was. There has always been something more between the two of us. I know she felt it. And a part of me hates it because I've hurt her by giving her false hope. I didn't do anything to make her think otherwise. But I also couldn't stay away. I needed her in my life. I craved her. She's the fucking blood that flows through my veins.

But the night of the end-of-the-year, everything changed for me. I went with Lilly and Bishop like I always did. Lilly and I were dancing, a few drinks in us. The way I held her... it wasn't how a brother should be touching their sister. People were watching and a part of me didn't care.

She looked so sexy, and I wanted to kiss her pink, pouty lips so damn much, to listen to her moan as I slipped my tongue in and over hers.

I was hard as she pressed up against me and that shook me out of my haze. I had to get out of there before I did something stupid, something that would ruin her.

I needed air, to be by myself, and to think. But then that chick, Tiffany, who had been trying to get my attention for years, followed me. I didn't want her there, I wanted to be alone.

And when she kissed me, for a moment I tried to like it, tried to see if she could take my mind off the one girl I couldn't have.

But it felt wrong, so I pushed her away.

When I went back to the party, Bianca said Lilly went outside to do something. I looked for her but couldn't find her.

That's when Bishop texted me, letting me know that he took her home. Worried about her, I rushed home and found her crying to Rain. I eavesdropped as she spilled everything to her. It was the first time I've ever had her feelings for me confirmed.

It made me so fucking happy, but at the same time, it crushed my soul because I knew things she didn't. I knew how people talked about our family. There's a good chance our family would be accepting of it, but Lilly has no plans to ever leave Silver Valley. If we were to become more, to confirm the whispers, I couldn't live with myself for putting her through that kind of ridicule on a daily basis. Mess with me, fine; say something about my family, I'll defend them. But Lilly? There's nothing I wouldn't do to protect her at any cost.

I've done it in the past, and I'm still paying for it to this day. But I don't regret it one fucking bit.

The distance I put between us, I thought it would help. Help me get over her, help her to move on. But the only thing I've done is hurt her and make myself fucking miserable.

I'm going to fix it. I just don't know how yet.

I hate the pitying look on Bishop's face. "Just this year. That's all I'm asking for. Then, once I'm gone, she's free to live her life however she wants to, whether I like it or not. We'll be gone, traveling for the first few years, then when we come back to settle down, maybe the idea of her moving on and being with someone else won't hurt so bad." I'm lying to myself because I know damn well it will kill me to see her belong to someone else.

I have this year to get back what we had, to enjoy her as much as I can. I'll keep in touch while I'm gone, but I want to leave here knowing she doesn't hate me.

"Hey!" A very excited voice says from the other side of my door. I'm over to the peephole in seconds, shoving my face up against the door. It's him, Ryan. Standing there in his stupid letterman jacket.

My eyes fall to Lilly, and the way she smiles up at him fucking guts me. She used to smile at me like that. Those are *my* fucking smiles, and he doesn't deserve them.

"Toby," Bishop says my name in a warning. I didn't even realize my hand was on the door handle before it is too late. I'm already opening it.

Lilly's eyes flick over to me and her smile slips just a little. "Toby?" Lilly questions.

Ryan looks over too and gives me a friendly smile. "Hey, You're Toby, Lilly's brother, right?"

I don't miss Lilly's reaction to the word 'brother' and I fucking hate it. At least when it's referring to her.

My tongue glides along my teeth before I answer. "*Step*brother." It's not any better. But it's the truth. I am her stepbrother.

"Right." He nods before holding out his hand. "I'm Ryan."

"I know." I don't shake his hand. Because if I do, I'll crush his fucking fingers, thinking about the possibility that they'll be on Lilly in some way tonight.

"Toby," Lilly hisses, glaring at me before looking at Ryan. "Sorry about him. He's not a people person."

Lie. I very much am a people person. Only she doesn't know that because she's only seen me as who I am when I'm around her. Back in the day, I was too focused on keeping her safe and happy, and since I've come to SVU, I've been nothing but a cold dick to her.

She doesn't know that I make friends with almost everyone I come in contact with, that people wave and greet me wherever I go.

Ryan knows this because, even though we're not friends, we run in the same circles.

To prove a point, his brows jerk up. "This guy? Not a people person?" he chuckles. "I find that hard to believe."

She bites her lower lip and looks at me. "Guess it's just me then," she mutters.

"Lilly," I sigh, taking a step towards her. I don't want her thinking of me like that when it comes to her.

She looks away and back to Ryan. "Just give me a second, I'll grab my purse and phone, then we can head out."

When she slips back into her room, leaving me alone in the hallway with Ryan, I step closer to him. "Listen here, Tucker," I growl. "Lay a fucking hand on her and I'll break all your fingers. Kind of hard to throw a ball with a broken hand. Kiss her and I'll break your face. Got it? Because you are not worthy of Lilly. Not even close. So don't even think for a moment you are."

This fucking asshole smiles. He *smiles* at me. And then he chuckles. "Well, might want to watch yourself there, Munro. You could say you're acting like a big brother, but for a moment, you almost sounded like a jealous ex. But don't worry. I have no plans on being anything but a gentleman to Lilly. Although, if she takes my hand, if *she* touches me or kisses me, I'm not going to pull away. She's an adult, not a child. So how about we let her make her own decisions?"

My blood boils as my anger rises rapidly. Fists clenching, nostrils flaring, I'm just about ready to raise my fist and punch his smug face when Lilly opens the door. "Ready." She smiles up at him.

Ryan tips his head at me, that smile still on his damn face, before bringing his attention back to Lilly. "Ladies first," he says, waving his hand out in front of him.

I watch as they walk down the hall, stopping at the elevators. When they step inside, Lilly looks over at me, biting her lip. Her eyes never leave mine as the door slowly closes.

I'm in my room within seconds, grabbing my phone and the keys to my car off my bedside table.

"Where are you going?" Bishop asks, jumping up from his bed.

"Out."

"What do you mean, out? Toby, where the hell are you going?"

I pause, looking over at him. "That guy is a fucking douchebag. You should have heard the way he just spoke to me. Cocksucking son of a bitch," I growl, shaking my head. "I don't trust him as far as I can throw him."

"So what, you're going to follow them?" Bishop gapes at me. "Man, that's next level stalker shit."

"Are you coming with me or not?" I spit, but I don't give him time to answer before I'm heading towards the door.

"Wait up!" he shouts, sounding all too fucking amused. "I'm coming."

I'll go to the movies, stay in the back, and just keep an eye on her. The only guy she's been with was Jonas, and as much as I hate to admit it, he's a good guy. He treated her well, from what I heard.

But I'm a guy, and I know how the male mind works when it comes to a good looking woman like Lilly.

I'm going to protect her like I always have.

At least that's what I'm going to keep telling myself because I'm a possessive, jealous dick. And right now, I don't even fucking care.

CHAPTER TWELVE

BISHOP

MY BEST FRIEND IS CRAZY. LIKE FULL-ON NEEDS-A-STRAIGHT-JACKET nuts. The dude has me sneaking around like I'm in some cheesy spy movie.

"There she is," Toby whispers, pointing to Lilly. She's standing by the entrance, Ryan's arm wrapped around her shoulder. "He's fucking touching her," Toby growls.

"Well, they are on a date," I point out. "But by all means, go on over there, and tell him to take his hands off her."

"Fuck you," Toby mutters, making me chuckle. "How are you not more upset that Clay is out on a date with your sister?"

Oh, fuck. How the hell did I forget that? "Fucking hell," I groan, watching as Bianca and Clay join Ryan and Lilly. "I was so focused on you freaking out about Lilly I completely forgot. Okay, yeah, it's a good thing we came. We need to make sure those fuckers keep their hands to themselves," I growl.

"Thank you," Toby sighs, waving an arm in the air. "That's what I've been trying to tell you."

Rolling my eyes, I nudge him forward. "Come on, we need to move."

Clay isn't a bad guy. I actually like him, he's one of my friends. But that's also my baby sister, and I don't really enjoy the fact that she's here on a date, with anyone.

I could be out, partying with a sexy little puck bunny, but I'm here with T, stalking our sisters on their dates. *What even is my life anymore?* I knew that the girls coming here was going to shake things up a little bit, but this is too much too soon.

But I still follow after Toby as we slowly walk towards the building. When they go inside, we buy our tickets.

"Where are they?" Toby asks, scanning the crowd.

"I don't know." I look around too, then spot them over by the concessions stand. "There." I point them out.

"Come on. We can slip into the back of the theater while they're waiting in line."

"I'll meet you in there, I've got to take a piss." He gives me a look, and I roll my eyes. "I'll be quick. I can't risk going during the movie, they might see me."

"Fine. But hurry." He takes off to the right towards the auditorium the movie is being played in, and I take off across the lobby to the bathrooms, keeping my eye on Lilly and my sister so they don't see me.

After I'm done, I wash my hands. "What are you doing?" I ask myself in the mirror. If this is how Toby is going to be when it comes to Lilly, this is going to be one hell of a year. Maybe me making plans with Lilly and using up her free time so she can't go out with other guys is the only way to keep him from going full-on caveman when it comes to her. "Never say I didn't do anything for you, man." I shake my head and make my way into the hall.

"Oh, sorry." I freeze, heart pounding as a tiny little thing bumps into me. "Bishop?"

Fucking hell. Of course, karma is laughing at me right now. "Lilly, what are you doing here?" I fake surprise, praying she can't see through my shitty acting.

"I'm here on a date... you knew that."

"I didn't know you were coming to the movies." I shrug.

"Yes, you did." She narrows her eyes. "I told you last night."

"Must have slipped my mind." I smile at her. *Play it cool, man.*

"Uh huh," she says slowly. *Am I sweating? I feel like I'm sweating.* "So, what are *you* doing here?" She asks me as we head out into the main lobby.

"I'm on a date too," I say the first thing that pops into my head and try not to laugh at the thought of Toby being my date. He's cute and all, but I don't swing that way.

"Oh, really? With who?"

Fuck. My eyes quickly scan the crowd, finding a group of girls. *Bingo.* "She's over there. What movie are you going to see?"

"The new horror movie, *The Chilling.*"

"Us too! Why don't I get my date and we can join you?"

She opens her mouth to say something but I take off, quickly heading towards the girls. Whelp, this night is turning out to be a lot more exciting than I thought it would. Oddly, it's kind of thrilling coming up with shit on the spot, seeing how far I can take this before Lilly calls me out on my bullshit.

"Hey, ladies." The girls look over at me, faces lighting up. I recognize a few puck bunnies. None I've slept with, so that's a good start. "Look, this might sound a little odd, but I need a date to see *The Chilling* with me. Would any of you lovely ladies like to join me? All I ask is you go with the flow and don't ask questions."

"Me!" A pretty redhead squeals eagerly. "I'd love to."

"Wonderful, right this way, my lady." I grin, holding my arm out.

"Later, girls." She giggles, leaving her friends behind, who look envious of her. I don't blame them. I've been with a good number of the puck bunnies since I've started at SVU, but there's never been a repeat night. I've never—and I mean never—gone on a date with any of them. I'm not one for dating or girlfriends.

I haven't found anyone that I connected with enough to want to see them more than once. I'm really hoping this doesn't bite me in the ass. "I just want to put this out there, this is a one-time thing. I hope you know that."

"Oh, for sure." She giggles. "But maybe if you want to get together tonight, you could come back to my dorm with me." She winks.

"Let's see where the night takes us." I wink back because, why not? If things don't go south, I could end the night having wild sex with a hot chick.

"What the hell are you doing here?" my sister asks, crossing her arms as she gives me a death glare.

"I'm here with my date. Ah—" Shit, I don't even know her name. I look down at her, and she giggles.

"Chloe."

"Date?" my sister's brows raise. Shit, she knows I don't date. Fuck, this may all go to hell.

"Hey, guys. Mind if we join you?" Jonas asks, joining our little group that's formed in the middle of the lobby.

"Jonas?" Both Lilly and my sister ask.

"What are you doing here?" Lilly asks.

"Same reason as you all." He wraps his arm around Isla, a puck bunny I slept with last year. "I'm on a date."

I expect a reaction from Lilly but when I look at her, I don't see anything but confusion. My sister, however, I can't quite place it, but she doesn't seem all too pleased to see her best friend here with a girl. *Interesting.* But now is not the time to go there.

"Hey, Chloe." Isla looks my fake date up and down. "Here with Bishop?"

If these two start a cat fight over me, I'm out. *Sorry, T, but I don't need that kind of drama.*

"Yup," Chloe confirms, wrapping her arm around my waist. I'm starting to regret this idea.

"Alright, let's go see a movie, shall we?"

Lilly and Bianca give each other a look. "You go ahead, I'm gonna talk to Bishop for a second," Ryan says to Lilly.

"Okay." She looks from him to me, back to him. "I'll get us some seats."

"Chloe, you mind finding us some too?"

"Sure," she says, looking Isla up and down, giving her a smirk before heading towards the auditorium.

"What's up?" I ask Ryan.

He chuckles, shaking his head. "Don't think I don't know what this is. Where is he?"

"Where's who?" I ask, playing stupid.

"You followed us here. Don't you think that's a little extreme on the 'big brother' part."

"Nope. My sister is here too. Just looking out for our girls." I shrug. "And I just so happen to have a date too."

"Right." He nods. Toby was right, this guy is a cocky fucker. My hand is itching to slap the smirk right off his face. "Look, Lilly is a nice girl, and I enjoy hanging out with her. Even if this doesn't go past the first date, I want to be friends with her. So, unless Lilly tells me herself to get lost, I'm not going anywhere."

"Good to know," I grind out.

He turns around and takes off towards the auditorium. Getting my phone out of my pocket, I send a quick text to Toby.

BIG DADDY B

> Change of plans. Got caught, had to come up with something on the spot. So, I'm here on a date now. You're on your own up there.

T MAN

> You're fucking kidding me, right? You just had to take a piss. Does she know I'm here?

BIG DADDY B

No. But just a heads up, Ryan does. Not sure if he's going to tell Lilly or not.

T MAN

Fuck!

BIG DADDY B

How about we never do this again?!

T MAN

"Middle finger emoji"

Shoving my phone back in my pocket, I head off to join my date. Fucking hell.

Well played, karma, well played.

CHAPTER THIRTEEN

LILLIANNA

Tonight did not go as I thought it would. Not that I didn't enjoy my time with Ryan, I did. The time we spent together before the movie was fun. We talked and laughed. I really enjoy hanging out with him. The movie was awesome, I screamed a few times, making Ryan chuckle.

But knowing that Bishop and my ex boyfriend were only a few seats down, had me second guessing everything. So there was no hand holding, no cuddling. And I'm okay with that. As excited as I was for this date, and while I don't regret it, the idea of getting all intimate like that with anyone… I'm just not ready for that. Not when there were a few times throughout the night that I wished it was Toby sitting next to me instead. All I could think about was how scary movies were our thing. How he would hold me tight any time I got freaked out.

It's not fair to Ryan to send him the wrong signals.

"That movie was awesome," Ryan says as we make our way into the lobby.

"It was," I agree. "Sorry if I hurt your ears." I giggle.

"Girl, you have a set of lungs on you, you know that?"

I bite my lip and grin. "Yeah. I love scary movies. The jump scares always get me. I love the thrill."

"Same." He nods, looking around. "Looks like we lost the others. Want to go get something to eat? I know it's kind of late but there's this really good diner that's open twenty-four-seven just down the block. They serve all day breakfast."

"Oh, pancakes!" My eyes light up, and my belly growls in approval at his suggestion.

"Pancakes it is." He chuckles. As we head out of the theater, I text Bee that we're leaving.

LILLY

> Are you okay if I head out to grab something to eat with Ryan?

WIFEY FOR LIFEY

Go for it, girl. And sorry about my stupid brother. I can't believe he pulled this shit. But it's Bishop and he's always like this with me and guys so I'm not all that surprised. Sorry he ruined our double date.

LILLY

> It's totally fine. I'm sure we will get a chance to all hang out again. Not including your brother and Jonas.

WIFEY FOR LIFEY

I can't believe he was there too. Did you know he had a date tonight?

LILLY

> Nope. It was just as much of a surprise to me as it was for you.

WIFEY FOR LIFEY

> He was such an ass. I don't think he likes Clay.
> I don't know why. Clay is a sweetheart, funny,
> and sexy. And they're on the same team. He's
> my best friend and his childish behavior fucking
> sucked. He's getting some colorful texts
> tonight, that's for sure.

> Anyways, you go have fun with that hottie and
> I'm going to a party with mine. Don't worry, I
> won't drink. I'll be a good girl. No more online
> photos in my bra.

Guilt hits me. It's my fault that happened in the first place. Thankfully, no one lingered on it too long, but now I can't help but wonder if Katie is going to pull something like that again. It's sad she's willing to stoop as low as her mother.

As for Jonas, I have a feeling about why he showed up here. From the look on his face when he found out about the date, he was jealous. He even tossed popcorn at them when Clay cuddled with Bianca. Bianca kept looking beside her, glaring at Jonas.

Bishop was no help. He kept laughing. Like what the hell is with these guys tonight?

LILLY

> Have fun and don't do anything I wouldn't do.

WIFEY FOR LIFEY

> So, act like a nun, got it ;P

LILLY

> Haha *Middle finger emoji* Bye, bitch

WIFEY FOR LIFEY

> Byeeeeeeee! Love you, bitch.

Grinning, I shake my head and slip my phone in my pocket. "Sorry about that. Bee and Clay are heading to a party. Just wanted to let them know where we were going."

"Oh, did you wanna go too?" Ryan asks, stopping when we reach the parking lot.

"Nah, I like a good party as much as the next person, but so far, I haven't had the best experience with SVU parties." I grin and he grimaces.

"Right. Fuck, I can't believe Katie did that."

"You know her?" I ask as we continue walking to his car.

"Oh, yeah. She's not just a puck bunny, she's also a cheerleader. Well, she was one. Got kicked off the team last year because she dropped a girl. The girl fell and broke her ankle."

"What? I hope she's okay. But stuff like that isn't uncommon in cheerleading."

"True, but Katie did it on purpose." He shakes his head. "That girl has a few screws loose."

We get into his car and once we're buckled up, I continue the conversation. "How did you know she did it on purpose?"

He licks his lips as we pull out of the parking lot. "My, ah, ex is on the cheerleading team. She overheard Katie telling the girl she dropped that if she flirted with the guy she likes again, she's going to do worse."

"Wow." I blink in surprise. "She really is crazy. But knowing who her mom is, I'm not surprised at all."

"You know about her mom?"

"Yeah." I shift in my seat. "She did bad things to my family. I don't really want to talk about it, though."

"I'm sorry," he whispers. "So, pancakes?" he says, offering a lighter subject.

"Pancakes." I look over at him with a grin.

The diner is packed with people. It seems to be a popular spot on a Saturday night, but seeing how it's in the middle of town, between a bar and the movies, it makes sense.

We order our pancakes, and I'm pleased that they end up being just as amazing as Ryan told me they were.

For the next hour, we talk, laugh, and get to know each other. Honestly, this is the best night I've had in a long time. This might not be who I wanted my first date with, but it's better than I could have hoped for.

That is until Ryan's body goes rigid. I follow his line of sight to see a group of girls walking in. And when the pretty blonde looks over, eyes locking with Ryan, I just know that this is the ex he was talking about.

They share this intense moment before a guy walks in behind the girls, wrapping his arm around the blonde's shoulder.

I look over at Ryan. It's not jealousy I see but hurt, which makes his whole body deflate.

"Ex?" I ask, offering him a comforting smile.

"What?" his eyes flick up to mine.

"I know that look. It's the look of someone who is hurting."

"Shit." He lets out a heavy sigh, running a hand through his hair. "I'm sorry, Lilly. I'm fucking up our date."

"No, you're not. I'm having a lot of fun. Really, I enjoy hanging out with you."

"I like hanging out with you too." He smiles, his mood lightening up a little bit, but I can still see the tension in his shoulders knowing she's in this building with us.

"But, I'm gonna be honest for the both of us, I don't think we should be anything more than friends."

His face drops. "What? Why?"

I raise a brow, grinning wider. "You're still in love with her."

He opens his mouth to protest but closes it and nods. "I don't want to be. She hurt me, bad. But we were together for a long time. It's not something that just goes away overnight, you know?"

"I know better than you think." I move my pancakes around on my plate. "I'm hung up on someone, too."

"Toby?" His voice comes out in a low whisper.

My eyes snap up to his. "What? No." I shake my head, my cheeks heating.

It's his turn to raise a brow and grin. "I see the way you two look at each other. I'm not sure what the history is there, but there's something. It's okay. I won't tell anyone anything. It's your business. But I have an idea."

I swallow, my belly twisting into knots. I hate when anyone knows my feelings for Toby because I never know how they're going to react, and I really don't want it getting back to Toby.

"What's your idea?"

"I think the only option is for you to become my new best friend." He sits back in his chair and shrugs.

"Oh, really?" I giggle, my smile taking up my whole face. "What makes you think that?"

"I'm awesome," he says with a smirk, and I snort. "And you're awesome." I nod in agreement. "So, I think it's only fair that we team up and be awesome together."

"I mean, you do have a valid point." I laugh.

After I take my last bite, he gets the bill and we leave. He drives me home and walks me to my door.

"I had a good time tonight, Lilly. Thanks for being an awesome chick and showing me that not all girls suck."

"You're welcome." I laugh, giving him a hug. "Thanks for the movie. I had fun too. Text me, okay? We'll hang out again soon."

"I'd like that." He leans in and kisses my forehead. "See you around, short stuff." He winks and turns around, heading for the elevator.

"I'm not short." I call back with a laugh. "I'm fun size."

He snorts out a laugh, and my cheeks heat as I realize how that sounds. "You're a wild one, Shorty!"

He winks again before the elevator door shuts. Shaking my head with a grin, I go to open my door when I feel someone watching me.

When I turn to look across the hall, I catch the movement just as Toby's door clicks shut. I stare at it for longer than I should. I want to go over there and ask him why he sent Bishop, because I don't believe for a second he was there on a date. Bishop doesn't date and definitely not with some random puck bunny. So he was either there to spy on me or his sister. Maybe both.

Was Toby there too? Did he see me sitting next to Ryan and get jealous? Because the way he was acting towards Ryan before the date, it sure seemed that way.

I'm only fooling myself, because it's not anything more than an older brother protecting his little sister. All these years, I've just convinced myself that it was something more.

Tonight showed me I'm not ready to date yet, but I do know I want to sometime soon. I want to be able to go out and enjoy being with someone without thinking of him. To laugh, smile, and not wish I was holding hands with someone else.

Toby says he wants our friendship back and that he's going to do what he can to prove he's sorry.

I should tell him no, to keep him out of my life, but I must be some kind of masochist because the idea of not having him in my life at all, feels like all the air in my lungs is being sucked out. It might be pathetic, but I think I'd take anything he's willing to give, even if it's just being friends. No matter how much it's going to hurt me in the long run.

I just need to learn to live my life without him being my person. He can't be that for me anymore, it will kill me. I have no doubt about that.

CHAPTER FOURTEEN

LILLIANNA

"Do you think it's going to be like before?" Bianca asks me as I tidy up my side of the room before I leave. I didn't pack a bag because I'm only going home for two nights, and I have things back home. I should only need my purse, phone, and charger.

"What do you mean?" I pause making my bed and look over at her.

"With you and Toby. He said he was going to stop being an ass, but has that actually started yet?"

"Kinda?" I sit down on the edge of my bed. "I don't know. I mean, he's not going out of his way to avoid me. But with school, working out, and hockey practice, I haven't seen much of him anyway."

Other than when he came out of his room to try and intimi-date Ryan, and watching me like a creeper when I got home.

I have no idea where Toby and I stand right now, and I hate it. We're both going home tonight because our parents miss us, so we agreed to the whole weekend, and not just supper on Sunday. Both of our dads had insisted on Toby driving me even though I'm perfectly capable of taking my own car. When I brought this up to him, he said it's better to take one car to save the environment. *Yeah, okay.*

"I swear, Lills, if he's a royal dick to you this weekend and nothing changes, I am invoking my best friend card and kicking his ass."

I grin, loving how much my bestie has my back. "And I'll get popcorn to watch while you do it. Oh! And I'll video tape it so we can look back and watch it later."

"I knew you were meant to be mine," she says with a dreamy sigh.

There's a knock on the door and both our eyes swing to it. "Who do you think it is?" she whispers, flicking her gaze to me. "Oh my god, do you think it's the stick man from *The Chilling?*" she asks so seriously that it's kinda sad.

"You are nuts." I giggle. "It's noon, babe. I don't think the stick man would be walking around in broad daylight. Also, remind me never to let you watch another scary movie. You always get over the top after."

"It was based on a true story!" she hisses, wide eyed. "And a good chunk of it happened on a college campus, to a group of girls." She waves her hand between us. "Helloooo? Girls, college campus."

"Helloooo?" I copy before my expression deadpans and I say, "you're nuts." I'm about to tell her it's probably Toby being early, but there's another knock—no, this time it's a bang. And it won't stop.

Bee jumps out of bed and runs over to her closet, pulling out a bat. "Okay, you open the door, and I'll swing." She brings the bat to her shoulder, looking ready to strike any moment.

I roll my eyes. "Put the damn bat down."

"Be careful!" She follows behind me as I head for the door. The banging keeps going right up until the moment my hand touches the door knob.

Breaking into a nervous sweat, my belly flips, heart pounding. "Oh my god, we're going to die!" she whispers-shouts, looking like she's on the verge of a breakdown.

Slowly, I rise on my tip toes and bring my eye to the peephole. When I see nothing in the hall or in front of our door, I look over at Bee with furrowed brows. "There's no one out there. It was probably someone playing a prank or being a pain."

"No!" she hisses as I go for the knob again. "It's what they want you to think."

"Bee, you're being dramatic." I take a deep breath, telling myself we're just hyping ourselves up and there really is nothing out there.

Twisting the door knob, I swing the door open and... nothing.

"See." I step back to show her the empty doorway. She steps forward, bat still in her grasp. "There's not—"

"Wanna play a game?" A mechanical voice asks as a person dressed as Ghost Face steps into the doorway.

We scream and Bee brings the bat around, hitting the guy hard in the stomach. "Oh, fuck!" he grunts, curling in on himself as he crumbles to the ground.

Hysterical laughter sounds from the hallway as Toby steps into view. "Holy fuck, that was awesome. And I got it on video too. Fucking hell, man, I told you it was a bad idea."

Bending over, I rip the mask off the guy's face. "Bishop!" Bianca shouts. "What the fuck!"

"What the fuck, me?" he shouts. "What the fuck, you! You fucking hit me with a bat, you crazy shithead."

"Well, why the hell are you banging on our door with a damn mask on?!"

"Dumb-ass here thought it would be fun to play a prank on you." Toby grins, loving every second of this. Me? My heart is still racing like crazy. "He wanted to mess with you because he knows how scary movies get to you." He directs the last part to Bianca.

"You can be the one to tell mom she's not getting any grand-kids from me." Bishop groans.

"I hit you in the stomach." She rolls her eyes.

"No, you didn't. You hit me in the fucking nuts. I think one of my balls burst."

I shouldn't, because the man is in pain and you heard him— he thinks one of his balls exploded—but I can't help the laughter that bubbles out of me.

Toby grins at me, and I grin back.

"Also, you numb nuts, that's the wrong movie."

"What?" Bishop rolls over to glare at Toby.

"You said 'Wanna play a game?' and that's *Saw,* dumb ass. You're wearing a ghost face mask."

"Isn't that what he says?"

"No." I giggle. "He asks 'What's your favorite scary movie?'"

"Who cares? My balls hurt!"

"Ahh, poor baby. Want me to call up one of the puck bunnies to come and ice them for you?" Bianca grins down at her brother as if she didn't just attack him.

"I hate you," he hisses.

"Nah, you love me."

"Not right now, I don't."

"Come on, Lilly." Toby holds out his hand. "Let's get going."

I look at his hand for a second before placing mine in his. We lock eyes for a moment before he helps me step over Bishop. "Ah… should we just leave him there?"

"He'll be fine." Toby waves it off.

"Like fuck, I will be! How the fuck am I supposed to defend you on the ice when I can't even stand?"

"Oh, shit." Toby's face goes serious. "Give me a second," he says before bending down to help Bishop to his feet.

He wraps his arm around his back, holding him up. Bishop

groans in pain as he straightens. "Give me that," he growls, snatching the bat from his sister's hand.

It's that moment I remember, I almost forgot to grab my purse with my stuff in it. So I slip back into our room to grab it. Seconds later, I'm back in the hall where Toby left me.

"I really am sorry!" Bee calls after them as Toby helps Bishop hobble back over to their room.

"You can make it up to him by going down to the ice machine in the lobby and getting some ice for his balls." Toby calls back.

Bianca's nose scrunches up. "Eww." She looks at me. "Okay, yeah, no more scary movies. If I'm going to double date with you and Ryan again, how about we just avoid the movies all together?"

I didn't tell Bee that Ryan and I agreed to just be friends. I don't know why I didn't, but in a way it felt like I failed, or maybe I gave up too easily on trying to get over Toby. Or maybe I was just fooling myself and I never really did plan on trying to move on.

Because as much fun as I had with Ryan, Toby was on my mind for most of the time. And no one deserves to have their date thinking of someone else while they're out with them.

"Bianca," Bishop whines from within his room, and I giggle again. This man takes beatings on the ice, but I guess a hit to the nuts is game over?

"I'm going!" she calls back, rolling her eyes. "Later, babes, be good, have fun." She winks before heading toward the elevator.

"Ready?" Toby asks as he steps back out of his room, closing the door behind him.

I do the same to my room and nod.

The whole way down to his car, we don't say a word. I don't know what to say or how to start a conversation with him anymore. Before, I'd talk his ear off and he would listen for the most part. But a lot of the time we would have random chats about anything and everything.

That was years ago, though, and I'm not sure where we stand anymore.

"How was your date?" he asks as we drive toward our house.

"It was fun," I tell him, looking out the window, not able to look him in the eye, especially if this is the talk we're going to have.

"I don't like the guy," he grunts. "He's too cocky and very full of himself."

"He is not." I sigh. "Ryan is a nice guy, okay? He was nothing but a gentleman."

"So, is he your new boyfriend then?" His question is harsh.

"Maybe." I look his way. "What's it to you? I'm your sister, right? Why does it matter?" I shouldn't get him going, but he can't just act like this out of the blue again and expect me to be okay with it.

His nostrils flair. He won't look at me, but I can see his fingers tighten around the steering wheel, knuckles turning white.

"I care about you, Lilly. I don't want some asshole taking advantage of you."

"I'm a big girl, Toby. I can take care of myself. You don't need to worry about me."

His eyes turn to me, his gaze so intense, it has me pausing. "I will always worry about you, Lilly. Always."

"My babies!" Mamma yells, running out of the house as we walk up the sidewalk towards the front door. She practically tackles me.

"Mom," I grunt as she wraps her arms around me.

"I've missed you so much." She starts to kiss me all over my face, and I just stand there, eyes closed while trying not to laugh but failing miserably.

"Alright, Love," Theo laughs, prying my mother off me. "Let the girl breathe." He wraps his arms around her from behind, kissing her cheek, and then grins over at me.

"I missed you too, Mom, but it's only been a week. And we've texted at least once every day." I laugh.

"I know, but I'm used to seeing you everyday. When are you coming back to the store?"

"I'm not sure. I'll know more once I get into a steady routine. I've only been to a few of my classes once, so I'm not sure what my workload will be like."

"Hello, Toby. It's so wonderful to see you. Boy, have we missed you, son!" Toby says sarcastically from behind me.

Both my mom and Theo look over at him. Theo lets go of my mom to hug his son. "We're happy to see you too," he chuckles.

My mom wraps her arms around Toby and gives him a big squeeze. I let them be and head into the house.

I can hear my little brothers shouting from the living room. "What's going on in here?" I laugh when I see Bennett being mauled by the twins.

"Lilly, help!" Bennett shouts. "The little snots ganged up on me. I was playing Xbox first!"

"We want to play now!" Isaiah shouts, his black curly hair mimicking Jax's, his bio-dad.

"Yeah, you're hogging the game," Raiden adds and my god, he's like a mini Toby.

"Guys, leave Bennett alone. Can't you go play something else?"

"No!" They both shout at once as Raiden jumps on Bennett's back.

"What's going on in here?" Toby's voice sounds from behind me.

The twins freeze, then abandon Bennett and race over to Toby. "Toby!" they shout as they tackle him next.

"Thanks for nothing," Bennett mutters.

"What?" I laugh. "I didn't even get a chance to help."

He rolls his eyes, and I take the few steps over to him, pulling him in a hug. "How's it going?"

"Good." He shrugs, plopping back down on the couch and going back to playing his video games.

"How's school?"

"It's school. My gym teacher sucks. He makes us run laps."

"Oh no, the horror." I snort, and he shoots me a glare.

"Hey, Lilly!" Raiden shouts. "Guess what?"

I look over to see him on Toby's shoulders and snort out another laugh as Toby grins over at me, loving the attention from our little brothers.

"What?" I ask with a smirk.

"Bennett has a boyyyyyfriend."

"Shut the fuck up!" Bennett shouts and my eyes go wide, snapping down to my little brother.

"What's going on in here?" Brody asks, sounding just like Toby did as he steps into the living room.

"We were telling Lilly about Bennett's boyfriend," Isaiah snickers.

Bennett stands up, his fists clenched, nostrils flaring. "I don't have a boyfriend!"

"Do tooooo. We saw you kiss him by the pool last weekend." Isaiah and Raiden start laughing.

"Enough!" Brody's booming voice has the boys zipping their lips fast. "You leave your brother alone, understand me?"

"Yes, sir," they both mumble before running out of the room.

My heart hurts for Bennett. He looks like he's on the verge of crying, his face red, and nostrils still flaring.

"Bennett." Brody sees his struggle and takes a step forward.

"Leave me alone!" he yells, taking off in the other direction towards the stairs.

Toby and Brody look like they want to go after him but I step forward. "I got it, I'll go talk to him."

"Maybe I should." Brody runs a hand through his hair. "If anyone knows what he's going through, it's me and Jax."

"Yeah, but you're his dad. As much as parents wish their kids would talk to them about everything, sometimes there's things we just don't feel comfortable talking to you about. I got this, okay? Trust me."

He looks torn, but after a moment he sighs and nods his head.

I take off up the stairs and knock on Bennett's door. "Hey, Benny, it's me."

"Come in," he mutters.

Opening the door, I find him curled up on his bed, hugging his pillow. "Sorry, the boys can suck sometimes."

He huffs. "All the time."

I grin, taking a seat next to him on his bed. "Wanna talk about it?"

"No," he murmurs, then sighs again. "I messed everything up, Lilly."

"What do you mean?" I reach over and brush some of his brown hair from his forehead. Out of all my brothers, Bennett and I have always been closest. From the moment he was born, I was always there whenever I could be, next to my parents as I tried to help or hold him when I could. Being five when he was born meant I couldn't do much with him at the time, but I enjoyed just being around him.

"I kissed him," he admits in a small voice, tears filling his eyes. "And now he won't talk to me."

"Easton?" Easton is his best friend, someone he's known his whole life. When Bennett was ten, he told me he had his first crush. I was expecting it to be one of the little girls in his class, but then he told me it was a guy, his best friend.

The best thing about growing up in this family is we've never been afraid to express our sexuality. With three of our parents being bisexual and one a lesbian, it was just a part of our lives.

That's why when I started being attracted to girls, I didn't worry, didn't freak. I've never dated one but I'm not opposed to it. The person I want just so happens to be a guy. But if I met a girl I liked enough to pursue, I would without hesitation.

Bennett nods. "I thought he liked me. But… I thought wrong. And now he hates me. When I went to talk to him the next day at his locker, he told me that he wasn't a—" tears spill from his eyes, "a faggot."

My brows jump and my lips part. "What?" I hiss, anger boiling within me. "That little fucking shithead. Who even uses that kind of hurtful slur anymore?" I shake my head. "I'm sorry he's being like this. Sometimes people don't know how to deal with their emotions."

"I don't get it. He seemed fine seeing our dads together around the house. Never acted weird when he saw them kiss. So why would he use such a nasty word?"

"I don't know, Benny. But I want you to know that there's nothing wrong with liking boys, okay?"

"I know." He nods, wiping at his eyes.

"Have you thought about talking to our dads about it?"

He shakes his head. "I will. Just… not right now. I'm not ready."

"What about Mom?"

He shrugs. "She knows. I told her when I stupidly got excited, thinking that Easton might like me back. Now I look like an idiot."

"You're not an idiot. And if Easton can't see how amazing you are, then it's his loss. And if he's not into guys, then that's fine too. But he really didn't have the right to act the way he did. He's your best friend, and best friends don't treat each other like shit."

"Your best friend did," he murmurs, eyes growing dark.

Bennett and Toby's relationship hasn't been the same since

Toby started distancing himself from me. Bennett was just as close with Toby as he is with me, so seeing him treat his big sister like she was nothing… well, let's just say Bennett is a lot like our dad. He doesn't tolerate others treating the people he loves badly.

I sigh and flop down on the bed next to him, rolling to my side so I can look him in the face. "It's complicated. Toby and I, our relationship isn't like most."

"Can I ask you something? And I promise I won't tell anyone."

"Sure." I nod.

"Do you like… do you like Toby, as more than a friend?"

I blink a few times, the question taking me by surprise as I try to think of what to say. "Of course. He's our brother."

Bennett shakes his head. "No. He's my brother. But you two? I'm not a stupid kid, Lilly. You two never, and I mean never, have referred to each other as brother and sister."

I narrow my eyes. "You're too smart for your own good, kid."

He laughs, and my heart feels a bit better seeing him smile. "I know. I'm awesome."

I poke him in the side, making him laugh harder. "Smart-ass."

"So?"

Chewing on my lower lip, I wonder if I'm telling him too much. But one thing I know about Bennett is he wouldn't break my trust, so I tell him the truth because I can't lie to him. Not when he trusts me so openly, like he does. "I do. But he doesn't. He only sees me as his best friend, and that's okay." I shrug. "What I feel for him isn't exactly right."

"You might be family, but you're not blood. I don't see why it would be wrong. And if he doesn't see how amazing you are, then he's the one missing out," he repeats my words I just said to him. "Also, you can do so much better than him. Oh!" his face lights up. "Like Bishop. He's a good guy, I think you should ask him out."

"Whoa there, big guy." I laugh. "Hold your horses. Since when are you so interested in my dating life?"

"You deserve to be happy. And as much as I liked Jonas, you two didn't have that vibe. Also, do you know he looks at Bee like she hung the moon?"

"You saw it too?" I laugh. "Yeah, me and Jonas were only ever meant to be friends. I did enjoy the time I was with him. But you're right, we didn't have that vibe. I'll meet the right person for me someday."

"I know you will." He smiles. "And it won't be Toby until he pulls his head out of his ass. If you don't tell him to fuck off with the way he treats you, I will. And I'll kick his ass. I don't care if he's some big hockey goalie. He won't fight back because I'm his brother. So I have the upper hand." He grins wildly, making me burst out laughing.

"One, cut it out with the swearing. Brody will have your ass. And two, no beating up Toby. Things have been getting better... I think."

"Don't forgive him so easily, Lilly. I know you. You want to see the best in everyone and while I do love Toby, I don't like how he treats you. Make him work for it."

"You got it, dude." I lean forward and kiss his forehead. "Want to watch a movie?"

He nods. "Yeah, but I should probably clean my room first. Dad told me I'm grounded if I don't do it after I'm done playing."

"Yeah, it's pretty nasty in here." I scrunch up my nose. "Guys are so gross."

He rolls his eyes but there's a smile on his lips. "I love you, Lilly."

"I love you too, Benny."

I leave him to clean his room and head down to where Toby and Brody are talking in the living room with Chase.

"How did it go?"

"Good, I think. And just have patience, okay? He will come talk to you and Jax when he's ready."

"Okay," Brody sighs, but he doesn't sound too happy about it.

"I told him we were going to watch a movie. So, how about a family movie night?"

"Sounds like a plan." Brody nods.

As I head to my childhood room and sit down on the bed, I realize just how much I miss home, even though I'm just across town. So much has changed in such a short time. I just hope that things keep getting better.

And by that, I mean I hope Toby keeps his word and stops acting so cold. He seems like he's really trying.

I've asked him why he started to drift away, but all he would tell me is that he's just busy with hockey and school. Then I started dating Jonas and that's when he really started acting so cold. Like he couldn't stand being in the same room with me and Jonas. And because Jonas was always over for Sunday suppers, along with Bee and even Bishop, Toby avoided me.

I thought it was because he just hated Jonas for whatever reason, but after the night of the party, he seemed fine with Jonas. I've even seen them talking at their table in the lunchroom.

So, if he didn't hate Jonas, why did he treat me like that? And what's made him change his mind?

CHAPTER FIFTEEN

LILLIANNA

The rest of the night ends up being fun. We hung out and watched a movie. But by the halfway point of *The Greatest Showman*, all my little brothers fall asleep, so Brody and Jax take the twins up to bed as Bennett follows along half asleep with Rain behind him so he doesn't fall.

Mom disappeared a while ago with Chase. *I don't even want to know what they were doing.*

Now everyone else is upstairs, getting ready for bed, leaving Toby and I down in the movie room, alone.

"Want to watch another movie?" he asks me as the credits pop up on the screen.

"Sure." I shrug. "Which one?"

"How about *Scream*?" he grins, and I laugh.

"I mean, I wouldn't say no to sexy killer men in masks." I

He narrows his eyes. "You know what, never mind. What movies are there with ugly guys?" he grumbles as he pulls up Netflix.

"Toby." I laugh and reach for the remote. But he's quick, moving his arm so the remote's just out of reach. "Toby!" I huff and move to go lean over him to grab it.

But the asshole moves it too far over, and I end up falling on top of him, right in his lap. He grunts, and my eyes shoot up to his. I realize my hand is very close to his dick right now.

My eyes widen, and I quickly move to put some distance between us, but then he does something that surprises the hell out of me.

He grabs me by the hips and flips me so that I'm no longer laying on top of his lap, but sitting in it. My body heats as he wraps his arms around me and hands me the remote. "We can watch your sexy killer movie," he murmurs against my ear.

I'm stunned, not sure what to do. This isn't something new for us—we've cuddled, hell, we've slept in the same bed before. So why does this time feel so different than all the others?

I should move, take the seat next to him, but I don't. I can't. I missed him too damn much, I missed this part of our relationship, the closeness. So I don't move, I stay right where I am and, with shaky hands, I find the movie and press play.

It's a good thing I've seen this movie more than once because I'm not paying attention at all. The whole time, my heart beats wildly in my chest, my palms are sweating, hell, I'm sweating all over. It's wrong, I know it's wrong, but I also can't help the dull ache in my belly.

This means nothing to him, Lilly. Relax. Enjoy this moment while it lasts.

Yeah, easier said than done, especially when Toby starts rubbing his thumb back and forth slowly along my thigh.

Fucking hell, this man is killing me and he doesn't even know it.

Or does he, because when I risk looking up at him, just ever so slightly, I don't find him watching the movie. No, his eyes are on me.

"I've missed you, Little Flower," he whispers, his lips close to my ear. I have to repress the shiver that threatens to run through my body. "I'm so fucking sorry for how I've treated you these past few years."

I swallow the lump in my throat. "Then why did you do it?" I whisper, bringing my full attention to him.

His eyes fill with pain. "I don't know." He sighs. "I really don't. And I hate myself for it. Maybe I was getting a head start on how things would change once we get older, when we find lovers and start our lives with them. The way we were, we wouldn't be able to be that close anymore."

"Why not?" I ask, but I know why. The closeness we had, it wasn't normal for siblings, step or blood related.

"You know why," his voice is low, husky, and fuck, I want to kiss him. As if he can hear my thoughts, his eyes drop to my lips as he licks his.

This is what always confuses me. I don't want to let myself believe he has the same feelings for me because the last time I did that, he crushed my heart into a million pieces. But how can I not when he looks at me like he wants to devour me.

"I promise, I'm done putting space between us. We'll deal with life as it comes. I have hockey and school, I don't have time to entertain any other girl but you. Because you're who's most important to me, Lilly." He lets out a sad chuckle. "I almost feel sorry for the girl I end up with."

"Why's that?" I ask, voice shaking.

He looks at me, really looks at me, deep into my eyes. "Because they will never measure up to what we have."

My breathing is shaky, and I can't look away. The air between us crackles, the tension so thick it's almost suffocating.

I want him more in this moment than I've ever wanted him before.

Kiss me. Kiss me. Kiss me. I chant in my head, begging,

pleading for him to cross that line because I'm too terrified to be the one to make the first move. Not after the last time, I was ready and had my heart crushed.

But he doesn't and disappointment fills me. I'm used to it, so as hard as it is, I look away and start to move, needing to put some space between us.

I don't get far because his hand cradles the back of my head, and then his lips are crashing into mine.

I'm stunned for a moment, asking myself if this is really happening. But when a low, feral growl leaves his chest as his lips move against mine, I know this is real.

All my pent up feelings and longing for him bubble to the surface, and I let go, free falling into what I've been wanting to do for so long.

I kiss him back, whimpering as my lips part. He takes advantage of the movement and slides his tongue in and over mine.

He tastes of the peppermint and chocolate popcorn we were eating, and I find myself starving for more.

My core aches and my clit pulses with the desperate need for him to touch me.

Toby kisses me like I'm the air he needs to keep living, and I do the same because, in a way, he's always been that for me.

I'm moving before I realize it, changing my position so that I'm now straddling his lap. His hand tightens in my hair, holding my mouth to his as he continues to ravish me.

I bring my aching pussy down to meet his thick cock pressing against his jeans. The moan that he swallows from me is utterly embarrassing, but I can't help it. I'm beyond turned on. Every nerve inside me is lit up like a fucking Christmas tree. This is happening, it's finally fucking happening. I'm kissing and grinding against Toby.

A part of me knows that there's a good chance I'm going to regret this, but I can't find it in me to care right now.

All I can feel is his hand in my hair, gripping me tightly as his other hand moves to my ass. He groans as he slides his hand under the bottom of my shorts, his fingers meeting my bare ass.

He grabs a handful, squeezing tightly. The slight pain sends a jolt to my clit, causing me to grind down harder against his cock.

The room fills with our heavy breathing and mingling breaths. I don't know where he starts and I end; we are molded into one another. Someone could come down here and catch us like this at any second, but I can't—I won't—pull away.

I need this, *crave* this. I'm drowning on the high of his lips, a taste I will never get enough of.

With his hold on my ass, he pushes me down against his dick, getting a good rhythm as we rock together.

There's a fire in my belly that is burning brightly, the tightness growing and growing. When I take care of myself, the feeling is always a nice pleasurable feeling. But this... this is so much more. It's raw, needy, and slowly driving me mad. I move frantically now, grinding my throbbing clit against his cock faster.

And the sounds leaving him tells me he's enjoying this just as much as I am.

His touch is almost punishing, but I welcome it because it's Toby. When I'm with him, the whole world drifts away.

I'm going to cum, there's no doubt about that. And I want him to fall over that edge with me. I think he's close based on how his movements have become erratic like he's losing control.

With a tug of my hair, he pulls my mouth away from his, and I gasp, trying to get air into my lungs, filling them back up with the air he stole with his kisses. He puts his forehead to mine and our eyes lock. We pant heavily, harsh breaths pushing past swollen lips from our hungry kisses.

I continue to move against him, my hips rocking, chasing the orgasm that's just out of reach.

And then he says something that's my undoing. "Cum with me, Little Flower." His words come out in a desperate, gravelly plea.

I'm lost in his gaze, eyes wild, lips parted as I let go, allowing my orgasm to crash over me. He swallows my cry of pleasure in another kiss, my eyes still on his because I refuse to look away, shattering in his lap. I've never had an orgasm so intense. My vision goes fuzzy, and I feel dizzy, like I'm about to pass out.

His eyes finally close as he groans into my mouth. I feel it, his thick cock pulsing against my spasming pussy. The idea of me making him cum like this sends another burst of pleasure through me, prolonging my orgasm.

We break the kiss again as we both slowly come down from our climax. My heart hammers in my chest, my lungs scream for air, and my mind feels hazy and sluggish.

My eyes flutter closed as our foreheads meet again and I give myself this moment to soak in everything that just happened.

I'm so fucking happy, my heart so damn full. I can't believe this just happened. And god, it was amazing. *Would it be too much to ask him to fuck me now?*

I let out a little squeak as he picks me up and deposits me next to him on the couch before jumping to his feet. I blink up at him, confused as he stands there, running a hand through his sweaty hair.

He looks at me with this gutted look on his face.

My stomach drops as dread fills it, all the warm and fuzzy feelings evaporate. "Toby?" His name comes out in a low, shaky whisper.

"T-that." He lets out a shaky breath as he grips his hair and tugs on it. "That shouldn't have happened."

Mouth agape, I blink at him. "W-what?"

He shakes his head. "We shouldn't have done that."

"Why the hell not?" I ask, trying not to cry. I'm not just heart-broken again, I'm fucking pissed.

"Because," he hisses, his eyes wild. "You're my sister."

I let out a harsh laugh. This fucking guy really has the fucking nerve to say that. "Yeah? Since when? And news flash, buddy, brothers and sisters don't do what we just did."

He runs a hand over his face. "It shouldn't have happened. Please, can we just forget it?"

Fury flairs inside me. "Fuck you, Toby." His name comes out in a broken rasp as I jump to my feet. "Fuck you for acting like there isn't something between us. Fuck you for acting like I'm your whole world and letting me make you mine only for you to toss me to the side for two fucking years. And fuck you for coming back into my life, telling me you want things back to how they were, only to give me something I've wanted for so fucking long just for you to toss me aside again. Just... fuck you!"

I take off running up the stairs. I don't go to my room because I don't want anyone to hear me cry. Instead, I head for the pool house, locking the door behind me and collapsing onto the bed. Pulling the blanket up, I cuddle into it and let the tears flow.

I hate him in this moment. I hate him for making me feel so alive only to completely crush me after.

I always wanted to know if he had feelings for me like I did for him, and I guess I just got my answer. *Does he only want me for my body and not for my heart?*

Well, screw him, because it's not one or the other. If he doesn't want all of me, then the selfish asshole can have nothing.

CHAPTER SIXTEEN

TOBIAS

I HATE MYSELF RIGHT NOW. I'M SITTING ACROSS FROM LILLY AT THE kitchen table, having supper with my family. All I can think about was how it felt to have her lips on mine, the taste of her tongue, the feeling of her pussy grinding against my cock until we both came apart in each other's arms.

It was everything I've ever wanted and more. Only, it shouldn't have happened. It's not that I didn't want it to, because fuck, I want her so damn bad it kills me sometimes not being able to touch her. But I'm supposed to be trying to build back that trust with her, have her back in my life, and I think I fucked it all up again, already.

She won't look at me, avoiding eye contact as much as possible. When our eyes do meet, her glare is so cold it feels like a punch to the gut.

Is this how she felt when it was me on the other side of those looks?

Just another reason I hate myself. I was wrong, so fucking wrong, for treating her how I did the past two years. I thought that if I put some distance between us, it would be easier for us both to move on.

I was so damn wrong.

Last night started off great. We watched a movie with our family. She sat next to me on the couch the whole time. And when everyone went upstairs, I wanted her to myself. We should have just watched the movie and enjoyed being in each other's company. But then we started joking around and it felt like old times. I loved it. She was sitting in my lap, in my arms.

It wasn't anything we hadn't done before, and maybe that's the problem. How many sisters sit in their brother's lap and cuddle? None that I know of.

I tried to watch the movie, but it was so damn hard when the girl I've always wanted but couldn't have was sitting in my lap. My cock was semi-hard the whole time, and I spent more time trying to think of weird things to keep it from going full mast than watching the actual movie.

Then she looked up at me with those big blue eyes. I could get lost in them for days. We started talking, the sexual tension so thick it was undeniable.

The way she looked at me with her lips parted, and each of her breaths coming out unsteadily. It was like she was begging to be kissed.

And when I didn't close the distance between us, causing a look of disappointment to flash in her eyes, I knew I couldn't just let her leave.

So I did something I've been dying to do for so fucking long. I kissed her. And it was as if everything in the world felt right, perfect. Like kissing me was what she was meant to be doing.

I was hooked on the taste of her lips the moment mine met hers. Something inside me opened up, a hunger I've been burying deep down clawed its way to the surface.

The outside world faded to black until the only thing left was me, her, and our lips locked together.

When she moved to straddle my lap, I couldn't hold back. Feeling her hot little cunt against my cock... I was fucking done for.

It was like I wasn't in control of my body anymore. That I only existed to please her and to be pleasured by the girl from my dreams. My girl. My everything.

And when she parted her lips, letting out the sweetest cry, which I quickly swallowed as she came apart in my arms, I couldn't help but follow her over the edge.

But while we caught our breath, our reality came crashing down on me. Our parents, or siblings, could have walked in on us at any moment.

What we have, what we did might not feel wrong, but at the end of the day, it's not right to the rest of the world.

She deserves better than me. Someone she can walk around with and be proud of. Someone who can show her off to the world. Someone who won't have people whispering behind her back, calling her names, and treating her like a pariah.

She doesn't need a life that consists of constantly defending her relationship and watching her back as people glare at her and whisper nasty words.

I shouldn't have told her it was a mistake because I don't want her to think for a moment that's what she is to me. But the words just came out, and then I was calling her my sister, and fuck, I messed it all up.

She had every right to snap at me. She was right about one thing—I was, and still am, denying my feelings for her. To her, at least.

I didn't mean to make her feel used. I didn't toss her to the side like she meant nothing. I'm just... I don't even know how to feel or what to think anymore. My head and my heart are a fucking mess.

Last night, I hardly got any sleep. I ended up grabbing a

bottle of whiskey from the liquor cabinet and drowned myself in it. I'm not sure what time I ended up passing out, but I know I was drunk when I did. I didn't get up until late in the afternoon, and I felt like I got hit by a bus when I did. Good, I deserve to feel like shit after what I did.

Lilly avoided me for the rest of the day choosing to hang out with Bennett instead, who still isn't talking to me. It kills me because I love my little brother so damn much. We used to have such a good relationship until I went and fucked that up too. Because Lilly is his favorite person, and I don't blame him, she's mine too. He didn't like how I treated her and has been giving me the same treatment I was giving Lilly. I deserve it all.

"So, Lilly," Rain brings the conversation over to her as Brody and Chase bicker about the football team. "How was your date the other night?"

The fork that I've been using to mindlessly push potatoes around on my plate for the past five minutes pauses mid-air, and my eyes snap up to Lilly.

A slight blush takes over her cheeks at the question and my jaw grinds. "It was fun." She clears her throat.

Brody and Chase stop their conversation. "That little shit better have treated you like a prince would a damn princess," Brody grumbles. He looks over to Ellie. "Can you believe that little shit told me to my face he was taking my daughter out whether I liked it or not?"

"What?" My brows narrow. "Are you serious?"

"Oh, yeah." He shakes his head. "If he wasn't so damn good at football, I'd kick his ass off the team."

"Brody," Ellie says in a warning tone. "There are kids at the table."

"Baby, I love you, but it's not anything the kids haven't heard," he tells her with a smirk.

Ellie puts her fork down and glares at her partner. "That doesn't matter. We need to be watching how we talk around the kids. You used to swear like a sailor, and look how Toby turned out."

"Hey." I give my mom a look. "I came out just fine." Ellie is one of the best people I've ever met. She took me in and loved me like her own when I was six and she started dating my dad. My mom passed away when I was three from cancer and, while I don't remember much of her, I know she was a good person. My dad told me that Ellie was exactly who my mom would have wanted as a mother figure in my life. And that's what she's been to me ever since; a mom.

Lilly snorts at what I just said and my eyes snap over to hers. "What's so funny?"

"Nothing." She doesn't meet my eyes before looking back at Rain. "Anyways. The date was amazing," she answers, laying it on thick now that she knows it's going to piss me off. "Ryan was a gentleman. I really enjoyed hanging out with him, and can't wait to go on another date." She looks at me out of the corner of her eyes. It's subtle, but I see it. "He walked me to my door and made sure I got in safe."

"That's good," Jax says. "He seems like a good guy."

And now it's my turn to snort. This gets Lilly's attention. "And what do you find so funny?" She glares at me.

"Ryan Tucker is a cocky little prick." I stare her down. "Brody isn't the only one he felt like he could talk to like that. Thought he had the right to tell me how I should feel about him taking you out."

"You shouldn't feel anything," she snaps. "I'm just your sister after all, right?"

My nostrils flair and it's taking everything in me not to blow up at the table.

"And your protective big brother act is getting old." She stands up and leans over to get in my face. "I can do what I want. Date who I want. And fuck who I please."

"Lilly!" Ellie gasps.

"Nope!" Chase shouts. "La-la-la. I can't hear you."

"Dear god," Brody groans.

"Come on, guys, let's just sit down and have a nice meal," my dad, the sweetest man of them all, suggests trying to de-escalate the situation.

And while all that happens, Lilly and I are locked in a heated stare down.

"What is going on?" Raiden asks.

"No idea. Adults are weird," Isaiah adds.

"I'm not hungry anymore." Lilly is the first to look away as she straightens up and leaves the table.

"Lilly," Ellie starts, but Rain stops her.

I'm pissed, the idea of her fucking anyone is the only thing I took from what she said.

"Why do you have to be so mean?" Bennett sneers, snapping me out of my own mind. I look over at him to see him down-right livid with me. "You don't deserve to be her friend," he states before taking off after Lilly.

"I'm so confused," Chase mumbles.

"It's okay, buddy. Don't think too much about it. Your brain might explode." Rain pats him on the head like a dog, and Chase flashes his teeth at her like one, making Rain laugh.

Adults really are weird.

"What the hell was that, Munro?" Jax barks after he calls the end of practice. It was the worst practice I've had since I started playing hockey. My mind is somewhere else, or should I say, on someone else.

It's been almost a week since Lilly ran out of the family

supper. It's the last time I saw her with the exception of glimpses of her coming and going from her room.

She's back to being pissed at me, and I don't blame her. Only thing is, I hate it. I wanted to mend our relationship, but I ended up fucking it up worse than before.

I shouldn't have kissed her, even though it's been on my mind, every second of every day. And I've shamefully jacked off more than once to the image of her grinding on my cock. I'm not proud of it, but fuck.

With each passing day that she doesn't answer my texts and continues to avoid me, I grow more and more restless. I've been distracted in all my classes and now it's affecting my game.

"You let every single fucking puck fly past you into that damn net."

"Sorry, Coach," I grind out. I'm not in a good mood, and I'm seconds away from losing it on a man who's like a father figure to me.

"Two weeks, Munro, we have two weeks before our first game. If this shit happens again, Walker will be taking your spot. Do you understand?"

"Yes, sir."

"Dude, what was that?" Bishop asks as I join him off the ice and head down to the locker room.

"Fuck off," I mutter, not in the mood to talk to anyone right now.

"Seriously, man. You were shit."

"I said, fuck off!" I snap shoving him and sending him into the wall with a loud thud.

He glares at me, wiping his sweaty hair away from his face. "Fuck you, man. I get it, you're pissed about whatever's going on between you and Lilly. But that doesn't mean you get to take it out on me."

I'm breathing heavily, chest heaving. The pent-up anger inside me is demanding to be set loose. It's been a while since I've gotten to release any. I've been doing my damn best at keeping my cool and staying out of trouble, but if I don't go to the club soon, like we've planned, I'm not sure when or how I'm going to snap.

There are demons lurking within me that I need to purge. My dad tried to get me help as I got older, thinking putting me in things like martial arts would help, and it did for the most part. But because I couldn't use it outside of classes, it soon became pointless.

The only time I ever felt at ease and the demon backed off was when I was with Lilly. It's partly why I selfishly kept her so close. That and I just needed to be with her.

"I know." I run a hand through my hair and grasp at it, tugging hard enough to feel a sting before I let go. "I'm sorry. Just, fuck." I scrub my face with my hand. "Last weekend, I fucked up, bad. Like, really bad."

"I assumed as much." He gives me a smirk that I want to wipe right off his face. "You plan on telling me how you managed to do that?"

I look around, afraid Jax or someone else is lurking nearby. "Not here."

He nods and we head into the locker room.

Once we're showered and out, we head to Bishop's Jeep, hockey bags in hand.

"Hey, Toby!" A voice that has my blood boiling calls out to me just as Katie steps in front of us, a few other puck bunnies lingering behind her. "How was practice?"

I've never liked Katie. She always came on too strong and never took the hint that I wasn't interested in her. Mostly because of what her mother did to my family. At first, I didn't want to judge her on her mother's past, because I don't believe that a child should pay for their parent's mistakes. But Katie showed signs of being just like her mom. She's my age, and I've unfortunately shared a few classes with her, so I know how she is with our fellow students.

But it's what she did to Lilly the weekend before school

started that has her on my permanent shit list. She fucked with Lilly, and now I officially despise her.

"Go away, Katie," I mutter, moving to step past her. The girl has the nerve to look hurt.

"Why are you being so mean?" she pouts, crossing her arms, refusing to get out of my way as she moves with me, blocking my path.

I grind my teeth and take a deep breath. I'm already on edge, and she's not helping at all. "I know what you did to Lilly, and I don't appreciate people messing with the people I care about."

"Oh, come on." She rolls her eyes. "It was a selfie. Why is everyone taking it as a personal attack on little miss perfect?"

My brows jump. "A selfie? The only part of you that was in that photo was your damn ear, so cut the crap. Not to mention, the caption you added sure wasn't something you would put on a selfie... unless you were trashing yourself? Not to mention, there was a video too."

"Okay, fine, but still. Lilly has always acted like she was better than everyone else, so what if I enjoyed seeing her fall off her high horse, showing the world she's no better than the rest of us."

I take a step forward, nostrils flaring. "Lilly has never acted like she was better than anyone else. She's kind, caring, and an amazing person to be friends with. But do you want to know what I think? I think she is a better person, someone who is a hell of a lot better than you. How about you gain a little self-respect and stop trying to bring others down because you hate yourself."

She gapes at me and I finally sidestep her, heading towards Bishop's Jeep. "Dude." Bishop chuckles. "That was savage."

That may end up biting me in the ass, but I don't care right now. People like Katie will keep pushing until someone pushes back. And the fact that she keeps trying to get me to fuck her is a fucking joke. I would never touch her.

"She needed to hear it," I reply, tossing my bag into the back seat. Bishop does the same thing and we both get into the car.

"Alright, spill." He turns to look at me. "You've been nothing but a grumpy ass since your family weekend, which I'm hurt you didn't bring me along for. But I forgive you because I know you needed some Lilly time."

"I wish I did bring you," I sigh, my head falling back against the headrest. "Maybe I wouldn't have fucked up so bad."

"Oh, come on, it couldn't have been that bad."

Bishop and I hardly keep any secrets; we've got a friendship similar to mine and Lilly's. He's like a brother to me, someone I trust with my life. And normally, I wouldn't talk about something so personal, especially involving Lilly, but I trust him. I turn my head to look at him. "After the rest of the family went upstairs to bed, we stayed in the movie room to watch another movie. Long story short, she ended up in my lap, I couldn't help it and kissed her. One thing led to another and well…"

His eyes go comically wide. If it was any other news I was telling him about I'd probably laugh. "Don't tell me you guys fucked?"

"No, but it was pretty damn close. She rubbed herself against me until we both… you know."

"Came? Toby, you're a big boy, if you can't talk about sexual things you shouldn't be doing them." He grins.

I glare at him. "Fuck you."

"Well, from what you're saying, you should be saying fuck Lilly."

"Dear god." I sigh, closing my eyes.

"Okay, okay. I'm sorry. So, what happened after?"

I grimace. "That's where I fucked up. I told her it was a mistake."

"Fucking hell, man." He shakes his head and moves to sit in his seat properly, starting up the Jeep.

"And now she hates me."

"I don't blame her. You can't do that shit. Playing with her heart like that... it's fucked up."

"I know," I growl as we pull out of the parking lot. "I didn't mean to. It's just, fuck, she was in my lap, her body was molded to mine. And her lips, fucking hell, her lips were heaven. It's everything I dreamed about and more."

"Unless you've changed your mind about being with her, you can't do that shit again." He sounds pissed, and he looks it too. "You're my best friend, but so is Lilly. I love you, man, but I'm not going to let you toy with her heart and hurt her."

"I don't want to do that!" I shout.

"Then don't fucking touch her like that again." He shouts back. "I don't even think getting the friendship back you had before is a good idea. Not when there's deeper emotions at play. But I understand you can't just cut her from your life. So, keep it as just friends. If anything, start acting like her brother and not a jealous ex."

I don't say anything, hating his words. I don't want to act like her brother. I'm not her fucking brother. I might not be able to be her lover, but I can still be her person, right?

Fuck, I'm selfish. I know that. But I'm not ready to let her go just yet. I don't know if I could survive that. The past two years have been my own personal hell.

"You know I can't do that."

"Then at least keep your fucking hands to yourself."

"I will." Or at least I'll try. It's easier said than done. When I'm around her it takes everything in me not to push her up against the nearest surface and fucking consume her.

"You better. Now, about your shitty mood. Club, tomorrow night. I'll get you in the line-up."

"Thanks," I sigh.

"Oh, and I have a date with Lilly on Sunday." He turns to grin at me and every muscle in my body tenses.

"I'm sorry, what?" I ask, eerily calm.

"Well, not a date." He chuckles. "She invited me to family

supper, and I know you're going to your grandparents' restaurant for your pop's birthday, so I thought why not? I haven't hung out with my girl in a while, and I need me some Lilly time."

I hate it when he says it like that. She's not his girl, but he's been calling her that since we were teenagers. She always laughs about it. But it's when he calls her *il mio cuore* that really pisses me off. Lilly may never have taken the time to look up the meaning, but I did. She's not his fucking heart, she's *mine*.

He might not know this, but I've seen the way he used to look at her. Even though he always said Lilly was like his little sister, I knew it was bullshit. I made it my life's mission to be aware of my surroundings, especially when it came to Lilly. And I saw how he looked at her when he thought no one else could see him. I asked him once, and he laughed it off like it was the funniest thing in the world.

It's been a while since he showed any signs, mostly since he started sleeping around in high school. But now, I'm regretting asking him to spend more time with her.

Mostly because I'm jealous that he can and I can't. Maybe if I could I would be able to get Lilly to stop hating me.

CHAPTER SEVENTEEN

LILLIANNA

For the past week, I've been in a sour mood. I just can't get past that night. We shared such a life changing moment, and then he has the balls to tell me that it shouldn't have happened and to just forget about it?

Does he honestly think I could do that? There's no way in hell I can pretend I didn't grind on top of him until we both came.

I was sure that what we did was proof that he liked me more than just friends, but maybe it was just something physical for him. Is that why he thought it could be so easy to act like nothing happened?

I'm pissed at him. He's been texting me, trying to get me to talk to him, but I've deleted all of his messages without even reading them. I debated blocking him, but I couldn't do it.

The thing is, I don't want Toby out of my life. On the other hand, I'm not ready to let him back in again either. Not after what he did. My mind is a mess and I don't know what to think or what I should do.

"Come on, bitch," Bianca says, snatching the book that I'm reading out of my hand and placing it on my bedside table.

"I was reading that," I mutter.

She rolls her eyes. "I know. It's all you've been doing this week if you're not in class or doing school work. But it's Saturday night and we are not spending it in our room, all gloom and doom. So, get up and get dressed. We're going out."

"Going where? I'm not in the partying mood." I sigh, sitting up on the bed and crossing my legs.

"Good thing we're not going to a party." She goes over to my closet and starts to look through it.

"Then where are we going?"

"Clay told me about this underground club thing that the students go to. They bet on fights and stuff. He said something about the students using it to let off steam and to make a bit of money. Some of the RVU students go too, but he said they just go to fight."

"So, we're going to what? A fight club?" My brows furrow.

She pulls out a pair of my fancy ripped jeans and tosses them to me. "Put these on. And yeah, pretty much. There's a bar and a dance floor too, but it's mostly for the fights."

Digging through my dresser, she grabs one of my bralette crop tops and tosses that to me as well. "This too. Girl, you're going to have Ryan drooling." She wiggles her eyebrows.

"Ryan? He's coming too?"

She nods. " He and Clay invited us."

"I don't know, Bee."

"Come on, please?" she pleads. "You've been a grumpy bitch, and I miss my sunshine and rainbow bestie. I know your brother can be an overbearing asshole, but so is mine. Don't let him get to you. We can test out our new fake IDs and have some fun."

"What if we get caught?"

She gives me a mischievous grin. "Then rich daddy, Brody, can bail you out of jail."

I narrow my eyes. "We're eighteen, Bee."

"So, what? Do you think we're the only underage people going? I don't even think they will card us because the fighting isn't exactly legal as it is. Come on, live a little."

"Fine," I sigh. Anything beats sitting here and thinking about Toby.

"Yay!" she squeals. "You're the best. Come on, get dressed, so we can go meet up with the guys."

An hour later, we're standing in a dingy looking club. Okay, it's not too bad, but it's dark, there's a lot of people here, and the music is loud.

"This is so cool!" Bianca yells with excitement, eyes wide as she takes in everything.

"You okay?" Ryan says in my ear so I can hear him over the music.

I smile up at him and nod. He wraps his arm around my shoulder and leads me through the room, following after Clay as we find a place to sit.

Ever since our date, and agreeing to just stay friends, we've grown closer. I think it's safe to say, he's joined my top five best friends list. He's funny, a good listener, and I just enjoy being around him.

I do feel bad about not telling Bianca that we're not dating, but by the way Clay acts, I don't think Ryan has told him either. Maybe he feels the same way I do and doesn't want to admit to our friends that our date was a failure because we're still hung up on other people. Even though it's the truth, whether we want it to be or not.

We've been hanging out every day. He has walked me to classes and eats lunch with us. Clay and Bianca have pretty much become a couple, although she hasn't said that they were official. She made it clear that they were just having fun and she still wants to enjoy the year like we planned, even though I've abandoned that mission by shacking up with Ryan. Her words, not mine.

But even if there was no Ryan, I don't think I could do it. The idea of dating, meeting other guys, it's just not something I'm ready for right now. I don't want to end up using them the same way I did Jonas, to forget about Toby. It's not fair to anyone if I'm hung up on another person.

I'm not opposed to dancing and having fun at a party, but it wouldn't go past that.

I want to make sure I'm over Toby before I put myself out there again. That way, when I do have sex, it'll be with someone I care about enough to give that piece of myself to.

We find a table and the guys order us some drinks. Bee and Clay don't even stay for one whole drink before they're taking off onto the dance floor, leaving Ryan and me at the table.

"You okay?" Ryan asks, trying to look me in the eye.

"Shit, sorry, did I zone out again?"

"Maybe just a little." He gives me a kind smile.

I shake my head. "Okay, no more shitty mood. We're here to hang out and enjoy our night."

"Are you sure you don't want to talk about it?"

Ryan was one of the first people to point out how I was in a bad mood all week and when he asked me about it, I didn't feel right telling him the personal details. He knew about Toby, but I guess that's pretty much obvious to everyone but the ones involved. Honestly, I don't want to talk to anyone about it, if anything, I'd like to forget it even happened.

"It's nothing. I'll get over it. How about another drink?" I hold up my glass.

He chuckles. "Don't you think you should drink that one first?"

I grin, wiggling my eyebrows before bringing the glass to my lips and downing the contents in three gulps. "All gone!" I gasp out and cough a little bit.

"Damn, girl." He laughs. "You're crazy."

"Maybe just a little bit tonight." I wasn't going to drink originally, I haven't felt like it since the party at the beginning of the year, but I could really use something to help me forget about Toby, even if it's just for a few hours. I know drinking isn't the right way to cope, but I know my worries will be washed away soon. I try not to let things out of my control ruin my life and I'm not about to let my broken heart do that now.

Over the next hour, we get a few more drinks and catch up with Bee and Clay before hitting the dance floor.

I've got a good buzz going on when the announcement stating that the fights will be starting in five minutes blares over the speakers.

"I got to pee!" I yell into B's ear over the music.

"Me too!"

We head to the bathroom, weaving our way through the crowd.

It takes longer than normal because we don't shut up or stop laughing the whole time we're doing our business.

As we finally stumble out of the bathroom, I see someone familiar. "Bishop?" I question out loud, but I only get a quick glimpse of him before he disappears into the crowd.

I shake my head. Maybe I've had a little bit too much to drink.

"Come on!" Bee pulls at my arm. "The fight is going to start. I want to see some sexy guys beat the shit out of each other."

"Okay, okay." I giggle, stumbling after her.

The announcer introduces the first two fighters and the guys guide us closer to the ring, wanting to get a good view. From what Clay said, they've been here a few times and he has some money on one of the fights tonight.

Two men step into the ring and the moment they get the green light to start, I'm invested right away. The guy with the shaved head seems a little too cocky for his own good. He's got a big mouth and a sly grin, but the guy with the short jet black hair dodges every kick and punch thrown at him.

He's got this concentrated look on his face, like he's trying to memorize each of his opponent's movements. It doesn't take long before the black haired guy has the other man on the ground and is announced as the winner.

"Okay, that was pretty cool." I giggle. I see the appeal of it. There's an electric thrill that I get while watching, wondering who's gonna make the next hit, where it's gonna land, and who's gonna come out on top.

I mean, I can't begin to understand why anyone would want to possibly have the crap beaten out of them, but I could see how some guys might be enticed by the high of being claimed as the victor.

We stand there and watch two more fights. Both are just as brutal as the last. I'm about to suggest we leave when I see Bishop again. "I knew I saw him!" I shout, pointing across the ring at Bishop as he steps inside the ropes.

"What the hell?" I look over at Bianca, who's staring at her brother with big eyes. "Please, don't tell me he's fighting! Is he crazy, does he have a death wish?"

"I wouldn't underestimate your brother." Clay chuckles. "I've seen him fight here a few times, and he's good."

"That's it, I'm going to kill him," Bianca grumbles.

"I don't think he's here to fight, though."

"Then why is he in there?" she waves her hand towards her brother, who is standing within the ropes of the ring.

"If he's here, he's most likely here to support—"

I don't hear the rest of what is said as my heart practically leaps out of my chest, my feet freezing me in my spot. I now know why Bishop is here, and I can't believe it. Toby steps into the ring, shirtless with his knuckles wrapped. The crowd goes insane as Toby puts his forehead to Bishop's. They exchange a few words before Toby steps into the middle of the ring.

Another guy joins Toby, looking like he wants nothing more than to beat his ass into the ground.

Fuck. Am I hyperventilating? I think I am. *Okay, Lilly, relax, breathe, you do not need to pass out right now.*

But, holy shit, Toby is about to fight. Fear for him races through my veins like a poison. Flashes of the last few fights push their way to the forefront of my mind and the idea of Toby getting hurt like the others makes me feel like I'm going to puke. Or it could be the five drinks I had. Maybe both.

I shouldn't, but I'm too drunk to care as my eyes trail down over Toby's body. I've seen him without a shirt on before, but those tattoos, they're new. He got them after he started attending SVU, it's why I didn't recognize it was him at first in the bathroom that day.

He's too damn sexy for his own good. *Or my own good?* Fuck, I don't know, but either way I can't take my eyes off him. All I can think about is getting in that ring, pinning him to the ground, and running my tongue along every line of his inked skin and right down to his…. *Okay, I'm drunk. And horny and shit.* The loud ringing of a bell signifies the start of the fight.

Shaking myself out of my dirty thoughts, I focus on Toby as he moves around the ring. There's no cocky grin, no calculating stare. He looks at his opponent like he wants to kill him, and the way he attacks him… I'm starting to get worried it might end up that way.

Toby punches and jabs, almost always making contact with his opponent. He doesn't even give the other guy the chance to get a shot in before Toby is punching him in the face or stomach again.

The sounds of grunting and flesh thumping against flesh

mixes with the cheering of the crowd. Blood and spit spray with each hit Toby makes.

Toby is a beast. One I find myself enchanted with. I've never seen him like this. He's wild, deadly, and unhinged.

I'm embarrassingly wet watching this. Or more like watching him. He looks like a god right now. His muscles ripple with each movement, his body covered in sweat. There's a bead right on the tip of his nose that I want to lick off.

My pussy throbs as I remember those deadly hands gripping my hips as he pushed me down to grind my core against his thick, very big cock, until we both shattered.

Toby shouts something as the other guy sways on his feet, looking pissed that this fight is about to be over. Toby calls him names and taunts him as the guy gives Toby what he wants. He snarls at Toby before charging him.

And that's when Toby gives him a satisfied grin before bringing his fist up and ramming it into the guy's face.

The crowd loses it as the guy hits the ground with a loud thud. Toby is the winner. But he doesn't boast like the others did, doesn't raise his hands in victory. He stands there, chest heaving, sweat dripping from his brow, and blood staining his fists. I shouldn't find it so attractive but seeing Toby like this does something to me. Something very naughty, and with my brain being clouded by alcohol, I'm not thinking straight.

I should leave before Toby sees me here, but I can't look away. And it's too late anyway because Toby's eyes dart over in my direction like he can sense I'm here.

My body heats, my heart pounds, and my lips part as I pant out shallow, sharp breaths. The whole room disappears and the only ones left are him and me.

He licks his lips, eyes darkening with promises he shouldn't be making because he always runs away, that's what he does.

Toby takes a step forward and a whimper leaves my lips, my core tightening with need. He can't hear me, not over the roar of the crowd, but the way his nostrils flair and hands clench as if he's holding himself back makes me think otherwise.

He says what we did in the movie room shouldn't have happened, but I call bullshit, because the way he's looking at me right now... he wants more of me. And I'm drunk enough to give it all to him. Hell, I'd get on my knees and beg for it. Maybe do something else while I'm down there.

Get a hold of yourself, woman! You're supposed to be the level-headed one.

Who am I kidding, I lose any common sense when it comes to this man. He owns my heart and that scares me. Because I keep telling myself I need to move on, to find someone else, or at the very least, stop thinking about him in ways I shouldn't be.

But then I have a moment of weakness, like right now. I break eye contact with him to tell Bee I'm going to use the bathroom. Lies, I'm going to the room I saw Bishop disappear into earlier.

I'm drunk, about to make some dumb choices, and I don't seem to care too much about that. I do know I'm going to hate myself in the morning, though.

Weaving my way through the crowd, I finally break free and dip into the hallway. I look around like I'm some sneaky ninja and run down the hall. Of course, I almost trip over my damn feet and have to grab onto the wall to keep my face from hitting the ground. "That was close." I giggle before ducking into the room.

"Oh." It's a locker room. "Eww." A smelly one, at that.

I'm only in the room for a few seconds before I'm joined by Bishop and Toby.

"Heeeey!" I greet them, smiling so wide it hurts. "Fancy meeting you here."

"What are you doing here, Lilly?" Toby asks, a growl vibrating in his chest.

I giggle. "You sound like a bear. Rawr." I make a clawing motion at him. Bishop snorts a laugh, doing nothing to hide his grin. "A very sexy bear." I lower my voice and bring up my arms like I'm showing off my muscles. "A big, strong, I'm-gonna-beat-you-up bear."

"Fucking hell, she's smashed." Bishop laughs, shaking his head.

"If anyone was doing the smashing it was Toby's fist in that dude's face. He's gonna feel that in the morning." I giggle. I lick my lips, allowing myself the moment to take him in up close. He looks lethal, and I'm ready to climb him like a tree. "If you want something else to smash, I mean…." I grin slowly and bite my bottom lip.

RIP a hungover, sober Lilly when she remembers making an idiot out of herself.

"I asked you, Lilly, what are you doing here?"

"Clay and Ryan brought us." I shrug. "Didn't expect to find *you* here. Although, it was a very nice surprise." I let my eyes roam over his body again, stopping at the V above the waistband of his shorts, and lick my lips again. *Very nice, indeed.*

"You're here with Ryan?" He spits my friend's name with venom. My eyes flick up at the hardness in his tone.

"Yes." I blink, not aware of the fact that I'm poking the bear. A very sexy bear.

"Bishop, take Lilly home before I do something I'll regret. I'm still on the high of the fight, and my mind isn't in the right place," he snarls, body vibrating like he's holding himself back.

"Where is it?" I blink at him. I really am drunk.

"Lilly," he growls again, making my pussy pulse.

"Oh, do that again," I say in a breathy tone. "My pussy liked that."

Bishop groans, trying really hard not to laugh. Toby's chest heaves, his nostrils flaring and it makes me think he's about to push me up against the locker and fuck me. *Oh, please! I'd very much like that.*

"Bishop." The way Toby says his name makes a shiver run through my body too. Drunk Lilly really likes this Toby.

"Come on, Shorty, let's go." Bishop steps forward and tosses me over his shoulder.

"But I didn't get to climb him like a tree," I whine, a pout forming on my lips.

Toby curses and Bishop laughs harder as he carries me out of the room.

"Put me down!" I demand, beating my tiny hands against his insanely muscular back.

"No can do, *il mio cuore*. You're drunk as a skunk, and Toby will rearrange my face if I don't get you home safely."

"He's so grumpy," I mutter.

"He's not in the best mood, no." Bishop sighs.

"I can go back there and make his mood better." I perk up at the idea.

"Enough out of you." He chuckles and brings a hand down hard on my ass.

I let out an involuntary moan that has his body stiffening and his steps faltering. "You're killing me, smalls," he mumbles to himself.

I bite my lower lip, my cheeks flaming. I feel floaty, and I have a loose tongue. Now I'm starting to remember why I don't drink. Bianca thinks it's funny as hell, and it can be, but tonight? Maybe not so much.

"What are you doing with my best friend?" I hear my bestest bestie ask. I can't see her though, still hanging upside down over Bishop's shoulder.

"She's drunk, and I'm getting her home before she gets herself in trouble," Bishop answers.

"And I'm going to puke if you don't put me down!" I warn.

He puts me down on my feet and I huff, spinning around to find Ryan, Clay, and Bianca standing there.

Ryan looks at Bishop and then down at me. "Do you want me to drive you home?"

Bishop steps forward, pushing me partially behind him. "I said I'd take her home. I think you've done enough."

"What does that mean?" Ryan's brows furrow. "I didn't do shit."

"You brought her to a place like this. And what the fuck, Clay? Bringing my baby sister here too?" He glares at Bianca. "You're coming home with me too. Say goodbye."

"Bishop," Bianca starts. She must see something on his face because she sighs heavily and says goodbye to Clay.

"You sure you're okay?" Ryan asks me, not paying any attention to Bishop.

"Of course, she's fucking okay," Bishop snarls. "Lilly is always safe in my care. I'd rather fucking die than let anything bad happen to her. Can't say the same about you, can I? Seeing how you're bringing her to a shady place like this."

I blink up at the tall, dark-haired, tattooed man before me. I didn't know he cared that much about me. My heart does this funny little thing but maybe it's the alcohol telling me I've had enough for the night.

"Lilly is an adult." Ryan shakes his head. "Don't you think it's a little ridiculous how you and her brother keep hovering over her like she's a porcelain doll? She's perfectly capable of making her own choices. I wouldn't have let anything bad happen to her. It's full of college students, not drug dealers and crime lords."

"Yes, college guys that are known for slipping drugs into girls' drinks. While they do their damn best here not to let that happen, it could." Bishop sounds beyond pissed.

"And it can happen at any club or any party. I bought all her drinks, she was fine. And Clay bought Bianca's. Both of them are fine."

"You—" he points to Clay, "—are going to stop dating my sister." He points to Ryan next. "And if you knew what was good for you, you would stay away from Lilly."

"Hey, now," I slur, the last drink I had finally hitting me. "I like Ryan. He's nice and funny and treats me good. So leave him alone, you big bully."

Bishop glares down at me, but I just glare back up at him. At least I think I did... because, at that moment, everything goes black.

"Alright, we're done here, you can hardly stay on your feet."

"Lies," I mumble. "What happened to the lights?" I feel a pair of warm arms wrap around me before my feet leave the ground. "Am I flying?"

"No." Bishop laughs.

"Oh," I pout, not having the strength to open my eyes. "You're warm and soft." I snuggle into him. He just laughs again. I swear I feel something warm and soft press against my forehead before I lose consciousness.

The next time I open my eyes, it's to the sound of shouting. Sitting up, I blink my eyes open and groan as my head pounds like someone's beating it with a drum.

I'm in my room, that much I know. Looking over at B's bed, I find her sleeping soundly, a snore coming from her lips.

"Must have been a dream," I murmur to myself, but then I hear the voices again. Brows furrowing, I get up from my bed and make my way over to the door on shaky legs.

Opening the door, I hear someone yelling again but it's coming from across the hall, from Toby and Bishop's room.

"What the..."

In only my sleep top and shorts—I pray it was Bianca who changed me, not Bishop—I slowly make my way over to their room. Testing the door, I find it unlocked. "Well, that's not safe."

Note to self, give the guys an earful on locking their door before someone slips in and kills them in their sleep or something.

"Lilly!" Toby screams my name with pure agony, making my whole world stop.

"Toby?" I ask in a panicked voice.

"Lilly, no, please!" he cries out again. I creep closer and my belly drops. He's fast asleep. And he's not dreaming. No, he's stuck in one of his night terrors.

My eyes tear up, my heart aching for him.

After Toby left for SVU, he would sometimes come home on the weekends to sleep over. On his first night back, I heard him calling out my name so I rushed to his room, only to find him asleep.

He said it in the same way he just did now, begging me not to do something and sounding like he was in utter pain while doing it.

I didn't know what to do. I tried to wake him up, calling out his name and shaking his shoulder. I was going to go get my parents when he reached out and pulled me into his arms. He immediately settled down, cuddling me tighter to him.

I didn't try to leave, being in his arms at a time like that meant everything to me. It meant my presence brought him comfort. Plus, I didn't want to hear him in pain like that anymore.

So, I slept in his arms that night and every night he visited since. But I'd always wake up before him and slip out of the room before he woke up.

I almost forgot about it until tonight. I didn't hear him any of the other nights since I moved in across the hall, but it's clear that they haven't gone away.

My eyes go to Bishop, but he's fast asleep... with earplugs in? I guess this isn't new for them and my heart breaks all over again.

I could try to wake him up, shake him out of his nightmare, but the way he whimpers my name... I can't.

Biting my lower lip, I creep across the room and pull back the covers. "Shhh," I whisper, brushing the sweaty hair on his forehead back. "I'm here."

He mumbles something unintelligible, and as soon as I lower myself onto the bed, his arms snake out, wrapping around me to pull me into his chest. I go willingly because when it comes to Toby, I'm weak.

I hate it sometimes, that I allow someone to have this much power over me. But it's Toby, and I can't explain it. He's my person.

"Sleep," I murmur against his chest as I close my eyes. I'm not sure what his nightmares consist of; I've never asked him about them because I didn't want him finding out about the nighttime visits. But I hope that whatever they are, I can help by doing this and soothing the ache they create within him.

And I do it over and over again even if it kills me to have him touch me like this, knowing he isn't mine and never will be.

CHAPTER EIGHTEEN

LILLIANNA

I HAVE NO RECOLLECTION OF LAST NIGHT OR HOW I ENDED UP IN Toby's room, let alone his bed. Thankfully, I woke up before he did, so I quickly left and went back to my own room. Grabbing everything I needed, I snuck right back out to get ready for the day.

For a small second, I wondered if something more happened between us, but I know Toby, and he would never have slept with me while I was drunk.

Now, I'm showered and dressed, but still feeling like death— yay for being hungover!— while I work on some school assignments.

There's a knock at my door.

"Hey, Shorty," Bishop greets me with a bashful smile after I open my dorm door.

Glaring at him, I blink my eyes, wishing I was still fast

asleep. But it's noon and I have family supper tonight. I usually go a few hours early to hang out with the family, but I didn't feel like driving, so I texted Bishop to see if he would take me.

"Well, don't you just look like the welcome wagon," he chuckles.

"I feel like death," I mutter, stepping away so that I can grab my purse. My hair is still wet, tossed up into a messy bun, and I'm wearing a baggie hoodie and a pair of sweats. I didn't feel well enough to put in the time and effort into looking nice today.

"You look like it, too." His grin grows wider.

I shoot him another glare over my shoulder and flip him off. "Asshole."

"Where's Bee?"

"Gone out with Clay. Lucky bitch isn't hung over."

"I thought I told her to stay away from him," Bishop grumbles.

I push him out of the doorway so I can close and lock the door. "Well, this is Bee we're talking about. You can't tell her what to do. It's never worked before."

"Would work if I broke the fucker's legs?" he questions as we walk to the elevator.

Rolling my eyes, I reply with, "Dramatic, much? Just because you don't want your sister dating someone, doesn't mean you can go around inflicting violence on anyone who goes near her."

"Says who?" he asks, looking over at me as we step into the elevator.

"Such a caveman." I sigh heavily.

"She's my sister, I just want what's best for her."

"And I love that you're such a good big brother, I do. But we both know Bee, the more you fight her on this, the harder she's going to push back. Until Clay does something that warrants your aggressiveness, back off, okay?" I give him a serious look.

"Fine." He narrows his eyes at me. "But you! You better listen to me."

We step out and head through the lobby.

"Listen to you about what?"

"Staying away from Ryan."

My brows jump. "Ah, since when did you warn me off, Ryan? And I love you, Bishop, I do, but you can't tell me to do shit. I get enough of that from Toby, I don't need it from you too."

"Fine," he huffs, sounding defeated. "Don't you remember? I said it last night at the club."

My face heats and I bite my lower lip as we get to his Jeep. Getting in, I buckle up and look over at him. "I think I drank too much last night. I don't remember anything after Toby won his fight." The fight I remember clear as day because there's no way I could ever forget the way he looked up there, chest heaving and his body covered in sweat and blood. I also remember being embarrassingly turned on.

Bishop barks out a laugh. "That's a shame, because fuck, I love drunk Lilly. I need to hang out with you more when you're drinking."

"Oh, god." I look over at him with unease. "What don't I remember?"

We head out of the parking lot and down the street towards my parents' place. "I don't know if I should tell you." He chuckles.

"Was it that bad?" I ask, anxious nerves swarming my belly.

"Bad? I don't know, you might think so, but you sure were funny as hell."

"Tell me." I punch him in the arm.

"Hey, now. Violence is no way to get me to do anything." He laughs harder but I quickly shut him up when I reach between his legs and grab his balls.

"Tell me or I pop these fuckers like balloons," I growl.

Instead of telling me, the Jeep goes silent because I'm touching Bishop's junk. I've never done that before. Also, I think I feel his dick... and fuck me, is he getting hard?

My eyes flick up to his as my body flushes with heat. He

looks at me for a moment, then back to the road, but his whole body is tense.

Let go, Lilly, fucking let go.

I hold on longer than I should, and I pray that a sinkhole will open up in the road and take me away from this awkward situation.

He swallows hard and clears his throat. "Spare my jewels and I'll tell you." His voice comes out thicker than normal.

Snatching my hand back, I sit upright in my seat and look out the window, eyes wide in horror.

He clears his throat again. "After the fight, you went back into the locker room. Toby, of course, followed after and… well, let's just say he wasn't too happy to find you in a place like that. Might I add, I also wasn't too happy that you and Bee were there. I let the guys know too. That's when I warned you both to stay away from them."

"Okay, that doesn't sound too bad," I say, not able to look his way as my eyes lower to where I'm playing with the cuff of my sweater.

His voice goes back to being amused when he says, "When you were in the locker room, let's just say you were a little… frisky with Toby."

Now my eyes snap over to his, a newfound horror rushing through me. "What do you mean *frisky*?!"

He grins over at me, and I want to slap it off his handsome face. "You didn't touch him, but the things you were saying…" He shakes his head and looks back over at the road. "I've never heard you talk like that."

"Oh, god!" I groan into my hands, covering my face in shame. "Please, no more. If you say one more detail, I'm going to throw myself from this Jeep."

"You will not!" He growls, and I peek over at him.

He's not looking at me, though. His eyes are on the road, brows furrowed. "I wasn't being serious," I mumble.

"I don't like hearing you talk like that."

"Like what?"

"Anything to do with harming yourself. Joke or not."

"Okay." I look away, nibbling on my lower lip. This is new. Bishop has always been protective when it came to Bianca and me. He would threaten a guy once in a while, but Bianca jokes like this all the time. His response is to just roll his eyes and call her a drama queen.

So, why is he reacting like this when I'm talking the same way?

"What do you want to do?" I ask Bishop when we get into my parents' place.

"I'm open for anything. I love coming here. You guys are always doing fun things."

"We could play video games, shoot pool, or go swimming."

"Yes," he says, grinning over at me as we stop in the kitchen.

"Yes?" I giggle. "Yes to which one?"

He shrugs and opens the fridge. "All of them."

"Okay, then." I laugh again.

Mom and Mama Rain are out at the grocery store with the twins. Toby and Theo went on some guys' day with Theo's dad for his birthday. His grandma was going to throw a big party, but his grandpa didn't want the big fuss, so they chose to go golfing and have dinner at the country club instead.

It's so weird that we're members of a friggin' country club. Sometimes I forget we even have money. Other than the luxury of the house, we don't live like we do. We don't buy expensive clothes or electronics. My mom came from little and even though my dad, Brody, came into a lot of money after the death of my grandfather, Mom made sure that we grew up to be humble and to work for things in life. It's why I got a job with her when I was old enough to work. And so will the boys when it comes time.

It's not like we don't spend any of it. Once a year we go on an elaborate vacation somewhere amazing. And all of our educations, cars, and future houses are paid for.

"Is anyone home?" Bishop asks.

"Some of my dads should be around here somewhere with Bennett," I say, finding the house oddly quiet.

Shouting from outside in the backyard has me looking up at Bishop with a curious expression.

"Let's go check it out." He chuckles before jogging towards the back door.

When we get outside, I find my dads playing basketball. Chase has Bennett on his shoulders and both of them are laughing as a red-faced Brody glares at them. Jax looks done with the lot of them.

"What's going on?" I ask, looking between them.

They all look my way. "This asshole here is cheating."

"Am not." Chase grins. "You're just a sore loser."

"You put our kid on your shoulders so he could get it in the net."

"I don't know what you're talking about. I did no such thing."

I bite my lower lip, trying to hide my grin. Chase lives to rile up Brody.

Brody steps forward, clenching his fists. "He's on your damn shoulders! And you want to tell me you didn't do it?"

Chase quickly puts a grinning Bennett down. "I think you need your eyes checked, man, there's no one on my shoulders."

"You little–"

"Dad." I burst into giggles. "Stop. You're doing exactly what he wants by getting all worked up." I look over to Chase. "And you. Stop getting him going. You're being an asshole."

His brows raise. "Hey there, potty mouth, don't make me wash it out with soap."

I roll my eyes. "I'm an adult, I swear now, get over it."

"Lies. Lies. Lies." He shrugs.

I look over at Brody and Jax. I'm gonna help them out with this one. "Sex," I say and watch as Chase's face drops.

"What?"

"Sex," I repeat and it's all I say.

"No. Nope. Don't you start." He shakes his head.

"Sex, sex, sex."

"My ears are bleeding," he shouts as he covers his ears and runs away.

"Ah, what the heck is that about?" Bishop asks, an amused grin on his face.

I smirk back. "Chase refuses to acknowledge I'm an adult and therefore can and will do adult things. And when it comes to me and sex? Yeah, he loses it." I giggle.

"Your family is so weird. I love it." He grins wider.

"Hey, who are you calling weird?" Jax asks with a smile on his lips.

"Not you, Coach." Bishop chuckles.

"You're like family, Bishop, just call me Jax." He shakes his head and walks inside with Brody.

"Hey, B-Man." Bishop greets my little brother with some bro handshake.

"Hey, Bishop. Glad you came over. Toby isn't going to be here tonight, though." He says Toby's name with a bit of disappointment. It hurts my heart that he's got this distance with Toby.

I've tried to talk to Bennett about it. Just because Toby and I don't have the same closeness as before doesn't mean he has to let it get in the way of their relationship. But he told me if Toby is going to treat me like I don't exist, he's going to give him the same treatment. I love my little brother and his strong love for me. But I don't want to be the reason he loses any more time with Toby. So, I need that asshole to stop being, well, an asshole, so we can work on being friends again.

But it's kind of hard when he dry humps me and then tells me it's a mistake.

Ugh, no. No more thinking of that.

"I know that, dude. I'm here to hang out with your sister. And you." He winks at Bennett and Bennett grins, shaking his head.

"Come on. I want to show you the new game Dad got me!" Bennett runs inside the house.

"You coming, Shorty?"

I smile. "Yeah."

"Dude! That was epic!" Bennett shouts as Bishop kills the boss in the game they're playing.

Bishop grins down at him. "I know, I'm awesome."

Bennett just smiles and shakes his head. "Bennett!" my dad, Brody, shouts. "Go do some homework before supper."

"Ah, man," he mutters. "Thanks for playing," he tells Bishop, tossing the controller on the couch.

"Any time."

"Really?" Bennett looks up at him with bright eyes.

"Yeah, of course. I'll get this one to start inviting me over more," he jokes, hooking a thumb at me.

"Awesome," Bennett says before running off. "Bye!"

"Later, dude!" Bishop shouts back with a chuckle.

I cross my arms from my seat on the couch, across from where he's sitting on the chair. He looks over at me and laughs. "What?"

I raise a brow. "You make it seem like I never invite you over here. You know you're always welcome. Like my dad said, you're practically family."

He nods his head and sighs, running a hand through his dark hair. "I know. And I miss it. I love hanging out here. Don't get me wrong, I love my own family, but it's always loud over there and my mom kind of scares me," he snickers.

"Your mom is a doll." I roll my eyes but smile too.

"Yeah, to you. She loves you. Do you know how many times she asked me when I was going to stop messing around and make you my wife?" He shakes his head with a huff.

My brows jump and my belly swoops. "I'm sorry, what?"

He looks at me, eyes going wide before looking away and... do I see a blush on his cheeks? *Interesting.* "Nothing. She just likes you enough that she's trying to make you a part of the family any way she can. I'm sure if my sister liked girls, she would try to get her to lock you down too."

I don't miss the way he won't keep eye contact.

"How about we go for a swim?" I suggest, standing up.

"Sure. I could swim."

We head out to the pool house, and Bishop follows me in. "So, this is what it looks like in here now; I heard you and Bee took it over after we left for SVU." He looks around the bedroom-like space that I have decked out in everything book related.

"It's my getaway from all of the testosterone inside the main house." I head over to the little dresser in here that I use to keep my swimsuits and a change of clothes. I grab a bikini out of the top drawer before squatting to grab a pair of guy's trunks from the bottom drawer. "Here, these should fit." I toss them at him.

"Thanks," he says, catching them.

He hangs them over the desk chair, and grabs at the hem of his shirt, pulling it off over his head. My eyes widen as I take in his naked, tattooed chest.

Ah... What is he doing? Is he about to change right here in front of me? What is it with this man randomly wanting to get naked? My body heats as my eyes drop to his shorts as he goes to take them off.

"Bishop!" I shout and his eyes snap up to mine. I blink at him in shock. His lips part and he looks down at his body before looking back up at me as realization of what he was about to do dawns on his face. "Shit, sorry, Lills." He laughs. "It's just a habit."

I narrow my eyes. "You just want me to see you naked, don't you?" I accuse him in a joking manner.

But this is Bishop we're talking about, and I should have known how he was going to play this. He turns to face me, a slow wicked grin taking over his face. "You know what, you got me, Lilly. I've been wanting to, dreaming about stripping down, and having you see me naked."

"Bishop," I say in a warning tone, but he just grins wider, his hands going to his shorts.

"What? It's true." He starts to pull his shorts down, his eyes daring me to look away. But for some reason, I can't. "I've been dying to show you my big, fat—" He pops the button on his shorts and pushes them down enough that I can see the trimmed dark hair above his junk, and holy shit, I think he's going to call my bluff. "Cock."

"I'm going to change in the bathroom," I squeak, clutching my bikini to my chest as I spin around and take off running into the bathroom.

I slam the door shut as the fucker starts laughing. Closing my eyes, I take a few deep breaths, willing my heart to relax.

I'm not blind, I've always thought Bishop was cute, and as we got older, I knew he was hot. He has an athletically toned body and clearly works out at the gym. He got his tattoos before going off to SVU, unlike Toby, so I've spent more than a time or two admiring them.

I used to think that if I wasn't so hung up on Toby, I could have ended up having a crush on Bishop. It wouldn't be all that hard to do. He's a good guy, cares about his family, is an amazing friend, and... well, like I said, he's hot.

But never did I think he would just flash me his dick. I know we're close friends, but not that close.

Shaking my head from wherever my thoughts were about to go, I quickly change into my bikini. It's a cute one I got over the summer. It's white with cherries and a red trim. The top is more like a bra and I love how my breasts look in it.

Would Bishop like it?

Why would I even care?

"What has gotten into you, Lilly?" I mutter to myself as I grab a hair tie. Bundling my hair up on top of my head, I give myself a once-over in the mirror.

"Ready?" I ask, opening the bathroom door.

He turns around to look at me. "Hey, Lills, I'm sorry about —" his words are cut off as his eyes hungrily roam my body.

I bite my lower lip without thinking, my body flushing at the attention he's giving me. *And why do I like it so much?*

"Fuck," I hear him curse under his breath before he clears his throat and runs a hand through his hair. "You look…" His eyes narrow as he stares at something on my belly before his eyes widen. "Shit, when did you get your belly button done?"

I look down at the cute ring dangling from my navel. "Oh, over the summer." I grin up at him. "Isn't it cute? I think I want to get my nipples done next."

He lets out a choking sound and I'm so close to laughing at the way his eyes practically bug out of his head.

"Nipples. Ah, yeah. That would be… fucking hell." He spins around on his heel and takes off out of the pool house.

I beam with victory. *Two can play this game, Mr. Grant.*

CHAPTER NINETEEN

BISHOP

WHAT THE HELL AM I DOING? I WAS JUST PLAYING SOME FUCKED UP game of chicken with my childhood best friend. I would have done it too. I would have pulled my damn dick out because, well, it's just who I am. I'm very comfortable with my body and... well, a dick is just a dick. I mean, I don't go flashing it around to random unexpecting girls because that's creepy and a good way to get arrested, but I'm a hockey player, stripping down to nothing in front of a group of guys in the locker room is an everyday occurrence.

But the way she looked at me... fucking hell. Her eyes were wide, cheeks flushed a bright pink. I expected her to give me some kind of sassy remark or tell me to fuck off, maybe give me the finger. I didn't think she would keep looking.

The competitive person in me wanted to see how far I could

push her until I won, but she lasted longer than I expected. I was seconds away from flashing her.

Then, when she ran inside the bathroom, all I could think about was her looking at my dick.

What's with me lately? Am I that sex deprived that I'm thinking about my best friend in a sexual way?

Because I was. I had to get out of there because the thoughts that ran through my mind when I saw her step out in that fucking cherry bikini were downright sinful.

Since when has Lilly become such a… woman? She's a tiny little thing—that's why I sometimes call her Shorty—with skin so creamy and untouched. Her body is like an hourglass. Big hips, tiny belly, and her tits, fucking hell.

And then I saw the belly button piercing and my thoughts got dirtier. I've seen girls with their belly button pierced before, but never did I find myself wanting to know what it feels like as I slowly lick my way down to her—

Lilly steps out of the pool house, drawing my attention like I'm under some sort of spell. I watch as she makes her way to the deep end, her hips swaying with every step, and fuck me, her ass looks so damn good in those bottoms.

Stop it, Bishop, that's your best friend's girl.

Only, she's not. He's made it clear that even though he has feelings for her, he won't be doing anything about them.

If you don't count their little dry humping session they had last week.

Still, it's wrong. What kind of friend am I, having these thoughts about someone my best friend loves?

I can't help it. It's hard not to. I thought I buried my attraction for Lilly deep down a long time ago and it went away, but maybe I've just been playing one big game of denial.

I enjoy spending time with Lilly. The past two years have sucked because of her rift with Toby, and it put a strain on our friendship. We used to hang out all the time, then it was hardly ever.

I'd come with Toby for suppers, but it got awkward with the tension between him and Lilly. I wanted to hang out with her, but I didn't want to ditch my friend, so I just stopped going.

When she asked me to come today, I couldn't say yes fast enough. I knew Toby wasn't going to be here, he told me about the thing with his grandad the day before so that meant time with just Lilly.

Now that I think about it, I don't think I've ever had time with just her. Toby always took up her spare time, and while it never bothered me then, I'm glad it's not the case now.

Toby wanted me to try and use up her free time now so that she doesn't have time to date. And yes, I did agree to it, but a part of me did it for myself. This is my chance to get our closeness back and to have that time with Lilly I never got growing up.

She's different. I've noticed she's not exactly the same Lilly that she was when I started SVU. Of course, she's not; she's grown since then. She's an adult now.

She was always a bubbly little thing, a bright smile and musical laugh. Now she's got a bit of a sassy side to her. She's still the caring, loving person she's always been, but she's not as… naïve as she used to be. Not saying she was gullible or anything, but I saw the way she looked at Toby. I knew in her mind that she really did think something would become more between the two of them.

When Toby left and distanced himself from her, he crushed that hope right out of her. I knew what she was going to do at that party the summer night after high school, or at least, I had my suspicions.

It's why I felt like I should try to stop her. I saw Toby go off with that girl, or rather she followed him, but still, when the girl didn't come back after a few minutes, I assumed something more was happening.

My thoughts were confirmed when Lilly followed after them and came back crying.

It killed me to see her like that. All I wanted to do in that moment was take her face in my hands, look her deep in her eyes, and tell her to give up on Toby and give me a chance instead. To let me be the one who owns her heart and to promise her that I'd never hurt it.

But I didn't. Because even though my best friend was off doing whatever with that girl, I knew he still loved her.

I understand why Toby thinks he can't be with her, but I don't agree with it.

I also don't think it's fair that because he won't claim her, no one else can. It's not fair to Lilly. It's pretty selfish of him to want that.

The sound of the diving board snaps me out of the past. I look just in time to see Lilly dive into the water.

She glides under the surface like a damn mermaid and makes it all the way to where her feet can touch before she comes up for air.

Is it fucked up of me that I wish her hair was down so she could do one of those sexy water hair flips?

Still doesn't stop me from eyeing up her tits as water runs down the valley between them. Fucking hell, now I'm getting a boner. *Really, what the hell has gotten into me?*

"Are you coming in or not?" she asks, raising a brow with a smirk.

I grin and start running toward the pool. Her eyes widen and she tries to get away, but she's not fast enough. "Cannonball!" I scream before jumping in, making a big splash.

"Asshole!" she shouts as I break the surface.

"Oh, come on, *il mio cuore,* don't be a big baby." I laugh and slap the water, sending a big wave of it at her.

She gasps, closing her eyes, gaping at me. "Oh, you're going to get it!" she screams before launching herself at me. I laugh harder and when she gets right in front of me, I grab her by the waist and pick her up, tossing her a few feet in the air, making her splash back into the pool.

I'm full-on belly laughing when she comes back up with pure murder in her eyes. "You're dead."

"Oh, I'm so scared. Please, little munchkin, don't hurt me."

"Fucking jocks with your crazy strength and big arms," she mutters.

"You like my big arms?" I grin, raising one up to flex. "Made them myself." I kiss my muscles.

"You're such a dork." She giggles, and fuck, I like the sound of it.

"Yeah, but you love me anyways." I shoot her a wink.

"Someone has to." She grins back.

We spend the next little while just lazily swimming around, reminiscing about the past, the present, and the future.

"So, what do you want to do when you graduate?" I ask her, floating on my back as I look up at the clouds.

"I don't really know what I want to do, if I'm honest, but I'm leaning closer to maybe becoming a teacher. Something with little kids because teenagers freak me out. They're a whole breed of their own." She laughs. "Or maybe work full time with Mom at the bookstore. It's doing amazing."

I could see her working with kids; she's amazing with the ones she works with when she volunteers at the rec center. But she also loves that store. We used to spend hours there after she was done working because she would want to check out all the new books her mom would get in. Of course, she had to read the back of every one of them to make sure it was something she would want to read. More times than not, she would end up reading them all anyway.

"You're eighteen." I chuckle. "Still technically a teenager."

"Not the same," she scoffs. "It's between the ages of thirteen and sixteen you have to worry about. The internet has matured them and they know things they shouldn't. Making them into, like I said, a breed of their own."

"You're so weird." I laugh, repeating her earlier statement about me as I stand up.

"Takes one to know one," she teases, making me shake my head. "So, what will you be doing after you graduate?"

"Well, I want to do some traveling for a few years. See the world and all it has to offer, all that jazz. Then I plan on coming back here and opening up a restaurant."

That makes her brows jump. "Really? I didn't know you wanted to do that."

I shrug. "I always liked cooking. It was one of my favorite things to do with my mom every night. I've been taking business classes too."

"Color me impressed." She smiles. "I always thought your mind was set on going to the NHL."

"I mean, that's a dream I always had in the back of my mind, but when it comes down to it, it's not for me. I'm not looking for hockey to be my life for the next seven to ten years. Life is short and I don't want to look back in thirty years and regret that I lost the best years of my life. It would be hard to fall in love and start a family when all my time would be practicing, playing, and traveling."

"Never thought of it that way," she comments, floating on her back while looking up at the sky. I just stand there, skimming my fingers along the surface of the water, watching her.

My eyes travel over her body like I have no control over them. So, I move them up to her face, that way it's less creepy.

Did she always have that big freckle under her eye? It's cute.

Right, be less creepy.

"I want this year to go by slow," she murmurs, breaking the silence.

I blink a few times, pulling my eyes away from traveling down to her lips. "Why's that?"

"Because in a few years, you and Toby will leave." When she's right in front of me, she dunks herself under the water before standing back up. Wiping the water from her face, she blinks, her eyes finding mine. "And I'm not ready to lose you for good."

What is going on with my heart right now? It's beating way too fast, and it feels like someone has their hand fisted around it, squeezing it tightly.

I step forward before I even know what I'm doing. Towering over her, I look down and into her stunning blue eyes that widen in wonder. Her lips part, and fuck me, I have the urge to see what they taste like. Lifting my hand up, I tuck a piece of her hair that's fallen from her hair tie behind her ear. "You're never going to lose me. I'll always be here for you, *il mio cuore*. No matter where I am in this world, all you need to do is say the word, and I'll come running back to you."

The need to touch her, to be close to her hits me like a punch to the gut. And then I'm picking her up as she wraps her legs around my waist. I'm hard, and the way her eyes grow wide, I know she can feel it. Her arms snake around my shoulders, bringing her face so damn close to mine. We just look at each other, frozen in the moment.

Our breaths mingle, hers coming in quicker than mine. I'm going to do something so fucking stupid that could ruin everything.

"Lilly, Bishop! Supper is ready!" Rain calls from the back door.

My eyes widen, and just like that, I'm snapped out of the moment. I pick Lilly up and toss her back into the water like she's a damn hot potato.

She yelps and goes under but I'm already rushing out of the pool, needing to put space between us. God, what is wrong with me? I just dunked the girl.

"Bishop Grant, you're an asshole!" she yells. "I'm going to kick your ass!"

I chuckle and look down at her adorable drowned rat look and angry scowls.

"You got to catch me first, Shorty."

She flips me off and I laugh harder. "There's my feisty girl."

We get dressed and join everyone for supper. The longer we

sit there, the more I'm throwing myself back into the box of denial. Or at least trying to, because every time my eyes meet with Lilly's across the table, I can't stop thinking about how I was so damn close to kissing her.

"Lilly," Rain says. "I got a call from Mike, the rec center director. He said they're looking for some skate instructors this year. The ones they had last year have all graduated and moved away. I said I'd ask you and see if you're interested."

The smile that lights up Lilly's face makes my heart thump harder. *Fuck me.*

"I'd love to! Oh, that would be so much fun."

"Awesome. I'll call him back and let him know. It starts next week, Sunday nights from six to seven. It would be right after dinner, is that alright?"

"Yup, works for me."

"Also, if you know anyone else who might want to volunteer, let me know."

"I'll do it," I say before I can stop myself.

Lilly and Rain's eyes turn to me. "You will?" Lilly asks.

I shrug. "I have Sundays free. And who better to teach kids to skate than a hockey player? Plus, we can ride together, I'll drive." I wink.

Okay, so maybe I'm looking for an excuse to spend more time with Lilly, sue me. With school and hockey, it's not as easy as I thought it would be.

"Good point. Thanks, Bishop."

"You should see if Toby would be up for it," Ellie suggests.

The smile on Lilly's face drops. "Oh, ah… I don't know if this would be his thing," she stammers, moving her food around while keeping her eyes cast down to her plate.

"Wouldn't hurt to ask. If Bishop is willing, maybe he will be too." Ellie keeps going, not picking up on her daughter's body language. But I see the way Rain is watching her. I have a feeling that the fiery redhead knows more than Lilly's other parents.

"Maybe."

Once supper is finished, it's time for us to head back to school, but Bennett wants to show her something he made for school before we leave, so I wait downstairs outside by the front door.

"Hey." I look over and see Rain stepping outside.

"Hey." I give her a friendly smile.

"So...." She gives me a look. I swallow hard. Not going to lie, she kind of scares me sometimes.

"So?"

"I saw you two in the pool, you know," she states, crossing her arms as she raises a brow.

My stomach drops. "It wasn't what it looked like."

She snorts a laugh. "Don't treat me like I'm stupid, boy. Look, that girl is my whole world, alongside her brothers, of course. I love Toby like he's mine, but sometimes I want to slap that boy. All I'm saying is my baby girl has had enough heartache to last her a lifetime as it is, don't add to it."

My eyes widen. "I wouldn't."

"Really? Because what I saw out there... that has the potential for heartache if you're not careful. Don't start something with her if you can't follow through. Don't lead her on. Don't crush her. Or her dads and I will be the ones to crush you." I can tell she means every word too.

"I..." My eyes flick to the door and back to hers. "I don't think she feels the same way."

"I think Lilly is stuck in a place where she doesn't know what to feel and who she's allowed to feel it for. But if she has the chance to get out of that isolated tower she put herself in, I want that for her. So, if you manage to bring her down from it, don't be the reason she goes back up, if you know what I mean."

"I think?" I blink at her. "Okay, dumb jock here. Are you okay with her feelings for Toby?" I ask and she nods. "And you would be alright if something happened between us?" She nods again. *Interesting.* "What if it's all three of us?" She shrugs. "And if we add another—"

"Alright, going to stop you there, smart-ass." She holds up a hand. "Just treat my girl well, or there will be hell to pay."

"Sorry that it took me so long," Lilly apologizes while stepping out the front door. She looks between Rain and me. "Everything okay here?"

"Perfect." I smile. "Ready to go?"

"Yup." She gives her mom, Rain, a hug before heading towards the Jeep. I look back over my shoulder as I follow after Lilly, and Rain gives me the *I'm watching you* gesture.

Yeah, she scares me, alright.

"Today was awesome," Lilly says as we drive back to school.

"It was." I grin over at her. "A lot better than hanging out with a bunch of rowdy hockey dudes."

"Awe, you think I'm better than your teammates?" she gushes playfully, putting a hand over her heart. "I'll be sure to let each and every one of them know that."

I chuckle, shaking my head.

I left thinking I was going to just hang out with my best friend, and came back more confused than ever. But one thing I do know is, the crush I worked so hard to push down? Yeah, that shit is coming back ten-fold.

I like my best friend.

I like my sister's best friend.

I like my best friend's girl.

Fuck. My. Life.

CHAPTER TWENTY

LILLIANNA

Today, saying my mind was a hot mess would be an understatement.

Ever since last night, all I can think about is that almost-kiss with Bishop. At least, I think he was about to kiss me. Maybe I was just making things up in my head.

But the way he looked at me before Rain interrupted, I can't get it out of my head.

What does it mean if I wanted him to kiss me? Because at that moment, I wasn't pulling away, and I don't think I would have if he followed through.

I'm overthinking this. I don't like him. He doesn't like me. We're only friends. I'm just making up things to feel better about Toby's rejection.

Speaking of Toby, while Bianca, Jonas, and I walk through

campus to grab a coffee, I spot him. He's sitting at one of the tables with a few of the guys from the team. And Bishop.

Girls are trying to get their attention, running their hands up and down their arms as they chat away. They don't seem to be paying attention to them as they speak with their teammates.

An uneasy feeling settles over me at the sight. I've always hated girls flirting and touching Toby, that's nothing new. But why do I not only hate the blonde next to Toby, but also the redhead next to Bishop?

"Girl, are you even paying attention?" my best friend asks, crossing her arms.

"What? Sorry." I blink over at her and realize it's our turn in line to order.

"Order your drink before I get you the nastiest thing on the menu for ignoring me," she huffs.

My cheeks heat as I look at the cute barista, who's giving me a small grin. "Ah, I'll have a large caramel frappuccino with whipped cream and toffee pieces on top, please."

He nods, types in my order, and tells me my total. I pay and turn to my best friend.

"I don't know why they keep trying," Bianca comments.

"Who is trying what?" I ask, and look over to see what she's talking about. My belly turns at the sight of the girl practically shoving her tits in Toby's face. "Oh."

"Why don't you have any girls all over you?" Bianca asks Jonas with a raised brow.

"Who said I don't?" he grins down at her. "You're not with me all the time. You're too busy with your new boyfriend, Bumblebee."

"His name is Clay, and he's not my boyfriend." She glares at him. "We're just messing around."

Jonas grinds his jaw but he doesn't say anything. I know he's trying really hard not to be an asshole and do what Bishop did by demanding that she stay away from him. But Jonas is still being a dummy and not telling Bee how he feels, so he has only himself to blame.

Just like you haven't told Toby how you feel. You only have yourself to blame, seeing him with other girls.

Only I pretty much did tell him, didn't I? Not with words, but I don't go grinding on just anyone until I'm cumming on their lap. He would have to be daft not to know.

"But I do agree. It's pointless because, from what I heard, he hardly ever hooks up with any of the puck bunnies," Jonas says.

Was the girl from the party a puck bunny? Or was she just some lucky girl for the night?

Nope, I'm not bringing that image up, not after I worked so hard to erase it from my mind.

"I also heard that they have this stupid bet," Bianca scoffs. "How sad?"

"Bet?" I ask, brows furrowed.

Bianca rolls her eyes. "It's like the more he closes himself off to them, the more they try. He's like untouchable in a way, a rare catch. So they've been trying to see who can get the furthest with him. Tiffany from the cheer team said none of them have made it into his bed though. That's like the golden ticket they're all working for. And guess who's determined to win it?" She gives me a knowing look, and I feel like I could puke.

"Katie?" I ask, even though I already know.

"Mhhmm. But she has no chance in hell. Doesn't stop her from trying though. You would think she would have given up after Toby chewed her out the other day."

"He did?" My pulse quickens. "What about?"

"You," Jonas answers. "From what I heard, she tried to justify what she did, you know… posting that video and photo of you two online."

"I wish I could have seen her face when he knocked her down a few pegs." Bianca giggles.

My eyes find Toby. He's watching me. The girl tries to get his attention, but he pushes her away gently before saying some-thing to his friends. Then he gets up and heads over to me.

"Hey," his voice comes out slow, hesitant.

"Hi," my response is similar.

"Order for a caramel frappuccino?" the barista calls out.

I turn to him and take my order. "Thanks." I smile and he grins back.

"No problem," he says and winks before turning to take another order.

A low annoyed growl sounds from next to me and I look over to see Toby glaring at the guy.

I raise a brow. "You good?"

"Can we talk?" Toby asks. "Alone."

Bianca giggles again. "We will be over there," she tells me, pointing to a table.

"Depends. Are you going to dry hump me and pretend like it didn't mean anything?" I ask, crossing my arm and taking a sip of my drink.

"Lilly," he says my name like it causes him pain. "I'm sorry about that, okay? I'm so fucking sorry. You would know that if you would just answer my calls or read my texts."

"Okay, so you're sorry it happened. Got it. I'm going to take a page from your book and pretend it didn't happen too." *Lies.* Because there's no way I could convince myself of that, but he doesn't need to know.

He looks around before grabbing my arm and pulling me down the small hallway. "What are you doing?" I huff. He doesn't say anything as he pushes the back exit door open, which leads us out to an alley. "Toby, what the hell?"

I gasp as he pushes me up against the wall, caging me in. My heart pounds in my chest as he looms over me.

"I was wrong to say it didn't mean anything to me, because fuck, it meant the world. It was everything I've ever wanted and more. You're everything I want, Little Flower, and I don't want you to think for a moment that I don't want you."

"You want me?" I whisper, my head swimming with confusion. "Then why did you want to just forget it?"

"Because even though I want you, I shouldn't."

"Why not?" My brow furrows.

"Because, it's wrong."

"No, it's not," I argue, getting pissed off. "You want me, I want you, it's as simple as that."

He lets out a pained groan, putting his forehead to the brick above me.

"But it's not. You're my sister, Lilly. It's *wrong*."

That causes a surge of anger to fill me. "Oh, that's fucking bullshit!" I snap. "You know damn well we've never been like that with each other, not even from the moment we met. So don't go spewing that shit to me. I want you, Toby. I've wanted you for so fucking long, it's killing me. When you left for SVU and started acting like I meant nothing to you, something inside me fucking died. But I still had this fucked up hope that someday you would see me as something more. That you would come back to me and things would be like they used to be." I shove at his chest a little in frustration.

"And then that night we watched the movie, you gave me everything I've been pathetically hoping for, only to then rip it all away and make a fool out of me. Now you want to tell me you want me but can't have me because of some bullshit reason." I shake my head, tears spilling from my eyes. He brings his thumb up to brush them away, whispering my name, but I shake him off.

"No. I'm done. I might love you and wish we could be together, but I'm done. I won't sit around and wait for you to want me back, because apparently you do, but I'm not worth the risk in your eyes. I can't keep letting you hurt me. Maybe we can be friends someday, but right now, I need to let myself move on. I deserve to be happy; I deserve to be with someone who loves me. And if that can't be you, then I'll find someone else."

With every ounce of strength I have in me, I slip out from under his arms and head towards the door.

"Fuck!" he roars, and I hear him hit something before cursing. But I don't look back and he doesn't call my name. That hurts. Really, really bad.

My lip quivers and my eyes sting as I make my way back into the café. I will not cry, I will not break. I've done that enough. As much as I love Toby, I won't keep hurting myself over wanting him.

When I get to the seating area, I see that the hockey guys and the puck bunnies are gone. "What's wrong?" Bishop's voice makes me jump. I look over to see him walking towards me

"Oh, nothing." I give him a smile, but I know my eyes give it away. "Nothing that matters."

He looks in the direction I just came from and back to me. He saw me leave with Toby, I'm sure of it.

But he doesn't say anything, and I'm grateful for that because I might just break down if he does.

"So, what are you doing after school tomorrow?"

I blink up at him. "Ahh, nothing really? Just some school work. Was going to go to the library to do it, and maybe study a little bit."

"Awesome. What time?"

"Six?"

He grins, reaches down and scoops up some of the whip cream from my drink and boops it on my nose. I laugh as he grins wide, sucking the rest from his finger. "I'll meet you there at six."

I blink in shock as he spins around on his heel and takes off towards the front door. He pauses before he leaves. "Until then, *il mio cuore.*" He winks, and then he's gone out the door.

"What a loser." Bianca laughs.

"He is not." I look over to her, a little frazzled from everything that just happened in the last five minutes.

My eyes cross as I look down at the whipped cream on my

nose and grin. Wiping it off, I lick it from my finger and shake my head.

That sick feeling in my belly? Yeah, it's slightly better. Just a bit, but it's enough to keep the tears away. And I have to thank my goofy best friend for that.

One thing I'm grateful for is that Bishop doesn't pick sides. Sure, he hasn't seen me much since he's come to school, mostly just texting, but he's been busy. Hockey is his life. And it gets even more insane when the games start.

I'm just glad that we're attending the same school and have this chance to be close again.

But just how close?

"I don't like that he's stealing you away again," Bee pouts.

"He is not." I laugh.

"Is too! You hung out with him all day yesterday and now you're going to hang out with him after school tomorrow. When do I get my Lilly time?"

I grin, raising my brows. "Babe, we share a room and we have five classes together a week."

"Still. It's not enough."

Jonas shakes his head, a grin of his own on his lips. "You should just date each other, then you can spend all the time in the world together."

"Oh, don't think I wouldn't, but I don't like the V. I'm all about the D." She wiggles her eyebrows. "But if I was, you would be my top pick." She winks at me.

"And you would be mine." I giggle.

"All about the D, huh? Who's D?" Jonas growls, leaning forward. God, he's so obvious yet my bestie doesn't see how he looks at her. Ugh. And the messed up thing is, she likes him too! How is she so blind?

"None of your business," she huffs, jutting out her chin.

And then Jonas does something I'm shocked by, but I also want to raise my hands in the air and shout, FINALLY!

He leans forward, his body halfway over the table and grips

Bianca's cheeks between his fingers. "Listen here, little bumble-bee. The only dick you should be all about is mine," he growls. "And any others you think about, I'll fucking chop off. So, pass along the message to your little Clay."

My eyes widen and Bianca's practically bug out of her head. He lets go of her face but keeps his right there in front of hers. "This is me, telling you, Bianca Grant, you are mine. Get that through your pretty little head." With a softness that his voice doesn't convey, he kisses her forehead before getting up and walking out of the café, leaving us gaping in shock.

We both sit there, watching the door for a few beats before I huff out a surprised laugh. I look over at Bianca, a grin stretching over my face.

"Did that just happen?" Lips parted, she slowly looks my way. "Please, tell me that just happened."

Biting my lower lip, I nod my head. "Oh, that totally just happened."

We stare at each other for another second before we both burst into girly squeals.

"Wait!" she looks at me in horror. "Oh my god, no. He's your ex."

"Babe, no." I laugh. "We were never really a thing. We hardly kissed, never had sex, and I'm pretty sure he's had a thing for you the whole time. I'm more than okay with it, trust me."

"Really?" she whispers, looking unsure.

"Do you like him?"

She gives me a hesitant nod. "I do."

"Then I say go for it. If he can make you happy, that's all I care about."

"I can't believe he just said that. I didn't know."

"How could you not?" I giggle. "Girl, he's been ready to murder any guy who has even looked your way and don't get me started on Clay. I'm surprised that man is still able to play hockey."

"Shit. Clay. What do I do about him?"

"Are you together?"

She shakes her head. "No, we've fooled around a bit, but nothing more than intense make outs and over the clothes petting."

"Then I say you need to have a chat with Clay."

"Yeah," she sighs. "Fucking hell, what do I do about Jonas now? We're best friends. I don't think I can just go from friends to dating overnight."

"Can't help you there, babe. Turns out I suck when it comes to guys. Maybe take it slow?"

"Yeah, slow. I can do slow. I think it would be best to go slow. Because, girl, that was intense." She laughs. "And nah, you're not that bad with guys, you have Ryan. He's amazing."

"He is." I give her a guilty look. "But we're nothing more than just friends."

"Really? Well, shit, I thought you two would get together for sure."

"Don't get me wrong, I totally would have, but…"

"You're still hung up on a certain someone?" She gives me a sympathetic look.

Thinking of Toby, my eyes threaten to tear up again. Even though my heart is slowly dying, I need to remember that I deserve more than to be jerked around. "Not for long. My mission is to forget all about him, at least in a-more-than-friends way."

"You know what they say, if you want to get over someone, get under someone else." She giggles, wiggling her eyebrows.

"No," I deadpan. "I'm not giving up my virginity as a fuck you to the guy who doesn't want me."

She cringes. "Yeah, bad idea."

"I think I'm just going to focus on friends and school. If someone comes along and sweeps me off my feet, then awesome. But I'll be okay in the meantime."

"That's right. You got me, babe. And my stupid brother." She rolls her eyes.

"Bee, he's awesome, leave him alone."

"Eww, don't defend him," she teases. "It's like he's got you under that charm of his that all the girls seem to fall for." She narrows her eyes at me. "He does, doesn't he?"

Does he? Because the thoughts I've had about him since yesterday don't scream *best friends vibes.*

But this is Bishop, there's no way he would feel that way about me. I've seen the girls he hooks up with, and I'm not like them.

And I wouldn't want to just be a hookup anyways, it would ruin our friendship.

"Oh, yes. Bee, he's won my heart, and I'll be throwing my panties at him the next time I see him."

"You suck." She glares and I laugh.

"But you love me."

CHAPTER TWENTY-ONE

LILLIANNA

"Come on!" I huff at Bianca, who is deep in her closet and still not dressed. "We're going to be late. I'm giving you five more minutes, but then I'm leaving your ass to book it across campus on your own."

"I'm hurrying! You can't rush perfection."

I roll my eyes, grinning from my spot on the edge of my bed. I'm already showered, dressed, and ready for the day; all by eight in the morning, for a nine AM class.

"No, but perfection can be late on her own to class. I actually want to learn."

"Yeah, yeah. Some best friend you are."

"Oh, hush." I laugh.

There's a knock at the door. "Can you get that?" Bianca asks, sticking her head out of the closet.

"Yeah." I giggle and get up to answer it.

"Good morning, Shorty," Bishop greets me as I open the door.

My brows lift and a smile finds my lips as butterflies fill my belly. "Hi. What are you doing here? Don't you have practice?"

"Just got done not too long ago. Stopped at the coffee shop on the way back and thought I'd bring you one," he explains, holding out a coffee cup. "I know you normally get caramel frappuccino but they didn't have any of the caramel mix, so I got you a sugar cookie latte because I also know you drink these things like crack when they come in season."

I gasp, eyes lighting up. "Oh my god, they started selling them!"

He gives me a bright grin. "Yup. Starting today. Good thing it's early because I remember that one year we went too late and they were already sold out of the sugar cookie mix and you cried like a baby all day."

"I did not." I giggle.

"Suuuure." He winks.

I take a sip and close my eyes, moaning at how delicious it is. "Damn, that's good," I sigh happily.

When I open my eyes, I find Bishop staring at me with a dark look. My pulse picks up, and I swallow hard.

"Okay, I'm ready. Who's at the door?"

I blink a few times and step back. "Bishop."

She looks at the coffee and then to her brother. "Where the hell is mine, asshole?"

"I'm sorry, who are you?" he asks, giving her a bemused look and I giggle, biting my lower lip at their antics.

"Haha, very fucking funny, jackass. Just for that, I'm going to drive down to that sandwich shop you love so much, buy a big old meatball sandwich, and eat it right in front of you."

"Oh, that's just cruel, baby sis. You know I'm banned from that place!"

"You are?" I ask. "Why?"

Bianca starts laughing. "Our cousin bet him a hundred bucks

that he couldn't eat three whole sandwiches in under ten minutes."

"And I won that bet." He points at her.

"Yeah, but you then threw up all over the table. It was nasty, and you had to give the money to the owner to pay to have the booth cleaned out."

"Oh my god. Gross." I cringe.

"Okay, enough making me look bad in front of the pretty lady," he grumbles.

Bianca's brows jump and so does my heart.

"Bishop!" someone barks his name from behind him. I look over to see a very pissed off looking Toby standing in their doorway. He's glaring at Bishop, but then his eyes flick over to me and that warm and fuzzy feeling I just had is gone. His face drops and the anger is replaced with a suffering look. Good. I hope he feels like shit.

"Thank you, Ship. You're amazing." I give him a hug, because I always hug him. It's not weird at all. So why am I thinking about how big and warm he is and how good his arms feel wrapped around me?

I let go and take a step back, wondering what the hell is going on with me. "We still good for tonight?"

"Yup." I smile, nodding.

"Shoo. Go away. You're getting enough of my best friend's time; she's mine right now," Bianca says, pushing her brother out of the door and closing it.

"She's my best friend too!" he shouts through the door.

"Fuck off!"

"Bee." I snort a laugh. "You're pissing all over me right now."

"Good." She nods. "Then he will know who you really belong to."

"I can't even with you two." I shake my head with a grin and grab my bag.

When we open the door to leave, Bishop is still there. "What the hell? Ewww!" Bianca shouts as Bishop sticks his finger in her ear. "Did you just give me a wet willy?!"

He takes off into his room, cackling like a madman as he slams the door shut.

"I hate you!" she shouts, wiping at her ear with a horrified look on her face.

I can't help it, I burst into laughter. "Traitor!" she gasps.

"I'm sorry, but you both are too much sometimes," I reply between laughs.

"That's it, we're fighting!" she huffs and takes off down the hallway.

"Bee. I'm sorry!" I call after her as I follow, still laughing.

"Liar!"

Thankfully, we got to class on time. But I still had trouble paying attention. All I could do was look at the coffee cup on my desk and think about how sweet it was that he brought me one. He remembered not only one but two of my favorite drinks.

And he thought to get me one when he was getting his own.

Now, I'm sitting in my second class of the day, and he's blowing up my phone, texting me funny memes. Looking up, I see my professor writing something on the board so I take the chance to text back.

ME

I'm in class! You're making my phone go off like crazy.

SHIP

> But I'm bored!!! My professor is droning on and on about some dead dude and I'm seconds from joining him in his grave if this man doesn't stop.

I snort out a laugh then slap a hand over my mouth and look up to see my professor glaring at me.

I mouth sorry and slink down in my seat. Putting away my phone, I try to pay attention.

Buzz. A few seconds later. Buzz. And then another. Buzz. Rolling my eyes, I open his text again.

SHIP

> Where did you go? Don't abandon me when I'm on the brink of death!

ME

> You are such a drama queen. What class is it anyways?

SHIP

> Business Ethics.

My brows furrow.

ME

> What does that have to do with some dead guy?

SHIP

> That's what I'm asking myself! I have no idea. It's some dude he knew who died before they could follow through with some business idea they had together. Save me, Shorty!

I grin.

ME

> I wish I could, but I'm in the middle of a riveting lecture. No can do.

SHIP

> Fine, party pooper. I'll just die here of boredom, and you're going to go to my funeral, sob your pretty eyes out, and then throw yourself onto my grave, demanding to be buried with me out of guilt.

This has me grinning like an idiot.

Turning my phone off vibrate, I do my best not to look at it for the rest of class. My head is a mess, I have no idea what to do or where to go when it comes to things with me and Toby, but I'm going to try to stay busy to keep my mind off things the best I can.

Anytime I think of Toby, I want to cry and I feel sick. I don't understand why he thinks it's wrong to want me. We've never once felt like brother and sister.

I don't care about the technicality of it, so why does he?

Is he ashamed of me? What people would think about us being together?

Nope, not thinking about that right now, I refuse to cry in class.

I wish we never kissed, never did what we did that night of the movie, because I don't think we're ever going to be able to go back to the way things were before.

I miss my best friend and I want him back, even if it hurts my heart to only have him that way. But it's not going to happen.

One day at a time, Lilly, I remind myself.

"Come on!" Bianca pulls on my arm. "I'm starving."

"Yes, just a second!" I grumble as I try to quickly finish sending an email to one of my professors. "You know I can't type and walk at the same time."

She laughs. "Last time you did that, you walked into a pole."

"My forehead hurts just remembering it." I type the last few words and press send. "There, okay. We can go now."

"Finally! I can't believe you were going to let me starve to death."

"Your brother is right, you are overly dramatic." I giggle as we walk down the sidewalk toward the cafeteria.

"Oh, so I see. We're going with betrayal today. Awesome," she says sarcastically, nodding her head.

"You're too much." I giggle harder.

"Who's betraying who?" a familiar voice sounds from behind me.

Spinning around, I smile at Ryan. "Hey, you." I give him a hug and then step back. "I've missed you."

"I've missed you too." He grins, ruffling up my hair. I just grin and pat it down when he stops. "Sorry, I've been so MIA. Between school, practice, and games, I hardly have enough time to eat."

"I don't know how you sports guys do it," Bianca says. "If it messes with my time for a social life, I'm out."

"What can I say, ball is my life." He shrugs.

"Spoken like a true jock. At least you're not an asshole, like most," Bianca responds.

Ryan joins us as we continue to walk. "Your brother isn't an asshole. Same with Jonas," I point out, leaving Toby out of it because he's still on my shit list.

"Okay, wrong. My brother is one of the biggest assholes *ever.*"

"To you." I grin. "He's a sweet goofball with me."

She narrows her eyes. "I said what I said."

Grinning, I roll my eyes.

"And as for Jonas." Her cheeks go pink and if Ryan wasn't here right now, I'd tease her about it. But she did just break up with the guy's best friend, so I don't want to put my foot in my mouth. "He's an exception. He can be a pain, but deep down he's a good guy."

I groan when I see that the lunchroom is packed. "See! I told you we should have gotten here sooner."

"Oh my god, I'm sorry." I slap her on the arm.

"You two go find a table before any more people come, I'll get in line. What did you want?" Ryan asks as he moves toward the line.

"Pizza and a soda?" I suggest taking out a ten dollar bill.

"Same." Bianca does the same.

"You got it," he says taking our money.

"Thank you." I lean up and kiss him on the cheek.

When I turn around to look for a table, I feel like I'm being watched. My eyes scan the room, landing on Toby.

He's watching me, a harsh scowl on his face. He must have just seen me kiss Ryan. And he looks pissed.

A sick satisfaction fills me. *Good, be pissed.* He's the one choosing not to be with me, not the other way around.

Remind me why I was so eager to find out if Toby had feelings for me again?

You know what, never mind, I don't want to think about him right now.

Following Bee, we happen to find a table with enough room at the end.

"I've never seen it so packed in here," she comments, looking around.

"If it becomes a thing, we can just hit up one of the shops around campus." I'm not a big fan of crowds, but I can handle them okay if I know I have a way of leaving if it becomes too much.

When we go to parties, we hang out outside or in less

crowded places, at least until I've gotten a few drinks in me and the anxiety disappears for a while.

Bee and I talk for a bit, and I try really hard not to look over at Toby's table where he's sitting with his hockey buddies. But I can feel his eyes on me.

"Pizza for the pretty ladies," Ryan jests, taking a seat next to me and placing a tray down with our food and drinks.

"Don't call Bianca pretty," Jonas scolds, appearing out of nowhere and sitting next to Bee on the other side of the table.

"What? Why?" Bianca asks, raising a brow. "Do you want him to call me ugly then?"

Jonas growls. "Not if he wants his pretty face to stay pretty."

"Hey, now. I have done nothing to warrant you rearranging my face. Relax. And if you're done pissing all over the poor girl, I was just getting them food while they got us a table."

Bee and I lock eyes. We both bite our lips together to try and keep ourselves from giggling. Jonas has become this possessive caveman, and I can tell Bianca loves it. But knowing my girl, she's not going to give in that easily.

"He is not pissing all over me, because I am not his to piss on." Bee grabs her pizza and drink from the tray.

Jonas' scowl turns into a grin. "You keep telling yourself that, Bumblebee. But you are. Mine, I mean." When she starts to bring her pizza to her mouth, Jonas swoops in and steals a bite.

"Get your own food, butthead," she grumbles, shooting him a glare.

"Butthead?" Jonas grins, chewing his food. "That's a new one. What are we, five? Gonna call me a poopy-head next?"

"Fuck you," she mutters, but I see a smile forming on her lips.

I'm sure people will probably think I'm weird because I'm so okay with my ex and best friend ending up together. But the thing is, I really am.

They are perfect together. He was never meant to be anything more than a friend to me. Hell, he's more of a brother to me than Toby is.

Speaking of Toby, like I have no control over myself at the moment, my eyes drift over to find him, of course, watching me.

But he's not the only one. Bishop is sitting next to Toby, glaring over at us. What's his issue? Is he mad at me for something? We seemed fine this morning. Did I do something wrong between now and then? I can't think of anything. Is he mad I didn't text him back and put my phone away? If so, that's stupid.

Ryan wraps his arm around me, and my head whips to the side. "What are you doing?"

"Giving Toby something to be jealous over." He grins, then kisses me on the nose.

My brows jump. "Why would you want to help me make him jealous?"

"Because I think he's a fool. He has an amazing girl right in front of his eyes but he's too blind to see it. Or maybe he does see it and just won't do anything about it."

It's like he can read my mind. I'm not normally into playing games, but what Toby did hurt. And maybe I want him to feel a little bit of that pain too.

So, I lean into Ryan's side and look over at Bee. She's giving us a weird look because I already told her there's nothing going on between Ryan and me.

"Toby is watching," I admit, my cheeks going pink.

"Ahh, gotcha." She smirks.

"Don't get me started on Toby," Jonas sighs.

"He's not giving you a hard time, is he?" I ask him.

"Nah, he seems to be cool now that we're not together. Or at least, he doesn't look like he wants to rip my head off anymore." He swings his gaze over to Bee. "That would be your brother's job now."

"Why would my brother want to rip your head off?" Her brows scrunch in question.

He shrugs. "Probably has to do with the fact I told him I was going to court you."

Her eyes widen in shock. "What? You told him that?" Then her brows furrow again. "Court me? What are we, in the fifties?"

"I'm not stupid to think you're just going to start dating me right off the bat. It's gonna take time. We date and get to know each other outside a friend setting. And that's fine by me; you are worth the wait." He winks, then turns his attention back to me, but I don't miss the shock on B's face. *Ugh, they are so stinking cute.* "Anyways, back to Mr. Grumpy-ass. He's been a nightmare at practice. So damn moody, to the point that some of the guys have started tossing tampons in his locker," he snickers. "And by some guys, I mean me." Jonas grins.

I burst out laughing. "You didn't!"

"I did," he chuckles. "And then some of the guys followed my lead. But, I mean, he's been so fucking moody. And the anger he has... I've never seen him like that before, Lilly. I'm not sure what's going on with him, but there's something wrong."

Something in my gut doesn't feel right. Is there something more going on with Toby? There's a lot about him I don't know anymore. He clearly has become someone different since he started SVU. But is there something more than just growing up?

I haven't heard him have any night terrors since the night after I saw him fighting. And I'd know because every night, I've found myself standing by his door, listening, waiting for him to cry out my name like his world is ending. Because even though I'm pissed at him, I still care. And the idea of him hurting like that kills me. I don't know what the night terrors are about, but clearly, they have something to do with me.

Biting my lower lip, I look over to Toby's table again, but he's not there anymore. And neither is Bishop.

"So, what's everyone talking about?" I jump when Bishop takes the free chair on my other side. I blink up at him, and he grins down at me with a beaming smile. "Hey, *il mio cuore.*"

He brushes Ryan's arm off my shoulder and replaces it with

his own. I look over at Bianca in shock, and she's watching with an expression that is similar to mine.

"What do you want?" Bianca accuses.

"What? Can't I come sit with my bestie?"

"You haven't since we started the school year." She narrows her eyes. "So, why now?"

"I don't know if our girl here told you, but I've missed her like crazy the past two years, and with hockey being most of my life, I've neglected our friendship. And for that, I'm gravely sorry about and disappointed in myself. So, I've vowed to spend all my free time with her now."

Bianca snorts a laugh. "Oh, really?" she crosses her arms. "What? Did you make your way through all the puck bunnies and now you're bored?"

I feel Bishop's body stiffen. "No. Not that it's any of your business. I know it's hard for you to accept, but Lilly is one of my best friends and has been for the past thirteen years. She's not someone I'm just hanging out with because I'm bored. She is someone I want to spend time with because I actually like spending time with her. So, fuck you." He glares at his sister, and she actually looks shocked.

Me? I get this giddy feeling that rushes through me that I try really hard to shut down fast but fail.

"Got a problem with that?" he asks, but not his sister. He asks Ryan.

I look over at Ryan who shakes his head. "Why would you two being friends be an issue for me?"

"Because I know most guys wouldn't want their girl to be friends with other guys."

"Well, I'm not most guys. If I can't trust my girl to be around another guy and not cheat on me, then I shouldn't be with her, should I?" *Oh, I like Ryan.* Well, not in that way, but, you know what I mean.

Bishop snorts out a laugh. "I like the way you think, but

don't be so easy to trust every guy. A girl like Lilly? Yeah, they would be working to steal her away, not become her friend."

"Not me."

"Why?" Bishop questions.

Ryan gives me a look like he's asking to admit out loud we're not dating, and I nod. I don't want to make some big lie out of it just for the off chance I might make Toby jealous. So, I nod.

"Because... Lilly and I are only friends. And I'm not trying to get in her pants. So, I do believe guys and girls can be just friends. And I hope whoever is lucky enough to win Lilly's heart would see that she's an amazing, loyal girl, and they should trust her not to stray, instead of causing issues with our friendship."

Why do I get the feeling Ryan means a lot more with what he said than it sounded? Does he see something I don't?

"Fucking hell," Bishop sighs. "So you're not dating?" he asks me, and I shake my head. He looks up at Ryan. "Why did you have to go and make me like you?"

Ryan laughs. "I don't know, man. Sorry?"

Bishop sighs. "Don't be." Then he looks at me. "Look at you, making all these amazing friends. I feel left out."

"You don't have to." I grin up at him. "You have me. And we're studying tonight, remember?"

"I do." He grins. "And you left me hanging in our chat."

"I was in class!" I giggle. "I can't spend the whole class texting you."

"And why not? I'm amazing," Bishop says in mock offense.

"You're also impossible." I shake my head, grinning like a fool.

"Awe, thanks!" Bishop coos.

"You two make me want to puke," Bianca mutters. "Come on, Jonas, walk me to class before my lunch comes back up over these two besties."

"Yes, ma'am." Jonas grins, jumping to his feet.

"Bye, babe." I wiggle my fingers as they both round the table.

"You make me sick!" She gags. "But I love you too. You're making it up to me, by the way!"

"Anything your heart desires," I coo back to her.

"I'm holding you to that." She points at me, then looks down at her brother. "And you."

Bishop tilts his head back. "What about me?"

She quickly leans down and licks up his cheek before taking off in a fit of giggles.

"Oh, that's fucking nasty," Bishop groans, wiping off his face. "That little shit is going to pay."

"You two are fucking hilarious. It's like you hate each other but will burn the world for the other."

"Damn right," Bishop grumbles. "But not before I kick her ass."

"You would not." I giggle, and he narrows his eyes at me for calling him out.

"Bishop." My eyes snap up to see Toby standing nearby. But he won't make eye contact with me as he glares at Bishop. "We gotta go or we're going to be late for class."

"Shit," Bishop hisses and gets to his feet. "Tonight, you're mine. Don't forget it." He winks, taking off with Toby.

"Lilly," Ryan says my name, getting my attention.

"Yeah?"

"Why does Bishop call you his heart?"

My brows rise. "What? He doesn't."

Ryan smirks. "But he does. *Il mio cuore* means 'my heart' in Italian. My nonna is Italian and that's what he's calling you."

I blink at him a few times, trying to process what he said, then look away, staring blankly at the table. If what Ryan's saying is true, why would he call me that? Why would he call me his heart?

Speaking of hearts, mine is racing about a mile a minute as my belly flutters. I'm not even mad about it—no, quite the opposite. I love it.

Damn it. I shouldn't be falling for my best friend, Toby's best friend. It's too messy, and I'm just going to get my heart hurt all over again.

It's not the idea of wanting two men that worries me, my mom is with five partners after all. It's the possibility that I'll be crushed by both of them that terrifies me. Losing one best friend is hard enough, I don't think I could take it if I lost both of them.

CHAPTER TWENTY-TWO

BISHOP

I'VE NEVER BEEN THIS EXCITED TO SEE A GIRL BEFORE IN MY LIFE. OR should I say another girl, because this is the same feeling I used to get when I first started having feelings for Lilly way back when.

It's so odd to feel nervous and excited over a girl. I'm not shy when it comes to women. I've had my fair share. Some might call me a manwhore, but I've always treated any woman I've been with respectfully, never leading them on, and I was always upfront about what things would be like between us when I took them to bed.

Not that the puck bunnies cared, they still tried to become more than just a fun night together. Never happened, though. I've never had a girlfriend, never wanted one. I've enjoyed having fun, being free and young.

But now the idea of touching another girl makes me shiver in unease. I want one girl, that much is very clear now.

At lunch, seeing Ryan's arm around her, made me want to fucking rip it off her body and shove it up his ass. So when they admitted they were nothing more than just friends, I got way too damn happy about that.

I'm so damn confused, and I don't know what to do. I want Lilly, I'm not going to be like Toby and fool myself into thinking I don't. But the thing is, my best friend is in love with her.

I stayed back, kept my feelings to myself, and left Lilly alone because I was convinced that someday Toby would get his head out of his ass and make her his. Clearly, that isn't going to happen, because he's a fucking fool.

But does that mean because he won't be with her, I can? Wouldn't that be a big fuck you to the bro code?

It's wrong, I know it is, and if I was to try and do anything with Lilly, Toby would kill me.

But I can't just shut my feelings off for her again. Believe me, I have tried but the moment she texts me, or I see her, my heartbeat rises, and my belly swoops. It's thrilling and exciting but also terrifying.

I'm not going to do anything right now, I don't even know if Lilly sees me as anything more than a friend. But I will keep hanging out with her, growing our bond while hoping it will change into something more.

Maybe I'm setting myself up for disaster, or maybe, just maybe, I could get the girl of my dreams out of it. I do know that if I don't try, I'm going to regret it. I'll deal with Toby when the time comes. Do I feel like shit for possibly betraying my best friend? Yes. But he's made it clear he won't make a move on his feelings, so wouldn't he rather she be with someone who would treat her well, someone he trusted?

I could be playing stupid but let me, just for now.

Looking down at my phone, I check the time. She should be here in five minutes. Why does it feel like a lifetime?

Maybe I was too early, but I was eager to see her.

I just want to see her. Texting her in class and seeing her at lunch wasn't enough. A few hours alone with her? Yeah, I need that.

Toby, of course, wasn't very happy about it. Which is stupid, seeing how he's the one who told me to use up all of her free time so she couldn't date someone else.

Fuck, and here I am trying to date her myself. God, I really am a shitty friend. But also, aren't I a good friend for stepping back before and giving them a chance? It's not my fault he didn't take it.

And to be honest, I'm not very happy with Toby these days. He's been nothing but a moody asshole who keeps snapping at the team due to his own anger issues.

I get it, he's pissed, sad, and everything in between, but he's doing it to himself. And I don't think we should all have to suffer because of it.

I'm trying to be a good friend and help him by setting up fights, but if anything, it's just winding him up more. He won't hook up with another girl, meaning that's not an option to help burn off the extra energy, so he turned to drinking. When he's drunk too much, that's when the terrors kick in.

He's only had one since the school year started, and that was the night Lilly showed up at the club, wasted off her rocker, and got a little frisky with him in the locker room. Which, by the way, was fucking hilarious. I love drunk Lilly.

After I brought Lilly home, I texted Toby and found out he was staying for a few drinks. Two hours later he came stumbling into our dorm room drunk as hell. I had a feeling he was going to have a night terror, so I slept with my earplugs in.

When I woke up, it was just as Lilly came into the room. I pretended to stay asleep to see what she would do. When she crawled into his bed and he calmed down the instant her body was tucked into his, all I could think was *Toby is a damn fool.*

Lilly is kind, loving, loyal, and even after he's hurt her heart so many times, she still puts him first.

But who's going to put her first?

I get it, Toby has his reasons, he deems himself not worthy of being with her. His reasoning being his anger and the fact that she's his stepsister.

He wouldn't listen to me when I told him that it's not something Lilly would care about.

He's so fucking stuck in his head, he doesn't see he's causing her more pain by rejecting her than she would be in by having to deal with this shitty town and their big mouths.

He cares too much for her to the point he's his own downfall.

But me? Nah, Lilly is someone worth risking everything for, just to have the chance to be loved by her.

He might want to go the rest of his life regretting the chances he's missed, but I don't.

"Hey, you," Lilly's sweet musical voice has me standing up straight from my slumped position against the wall.

"You're here early." She smiles at me and fuck, I'm really a goner for this girl.

"Didn't want to risk being late and have you thinking I wasn't going to show up. Then who would you spend all your precious time with?"

"I mean, there is this cute guy I met at the coffee shop that asked me out; I could always call him up if you didn't show," she taunts, giving me a little smirk.

The amusement falls from my face as jealousy fills me. I narrow my eyes. "What's his name?"

"I'm joking." She giggles, adjusting the straps on her messenger bag.

"Better be," I mutter and follow after her into the library.

God, she looks edible tonight. Her hair looks to be curled then thrown up in a ponytail with two pieces of her bangs free. She has on a school sweater that's tucked into her tight-fitted jeans.

My eyes are glued to her ass and my cock twitches. How the

hell did I ever manage to hang out with her before and not pop a boner? I guess Toby being there helped.

I follow her deep into the library, stopping at a little quiet corner with some couches.

"What are you studying?" she asks me, pulling out some textbooks from her bag and placing them on the small table in front of her.

I hold up my textbook. I just grabbed the first one I could find and left. I didn't realize it was my trig textbook until I was halfway here. "Trigonometry. Gotta study, I suck ass at it." I don't, I'm actually pretty decent in this class.

Her brows jump. "I don't know how much help I'll be if you get stuck, but I can try my best." She holds up her textbook. "I have to work on a paper for my gender and sexuality class."

"Oh, fun." I nod, not having a clue what that is. "Alright then, *il mio cuore*, let's get to work." I wink.

Her cheeks break out into a light shade of pink. *Is she blushing?* She smiles softly and looks down at her textbook.

Did she finally figure out what I've been calling her all these years? I used to ask her why she didn't just Google it. She told me she liked how it sounded and wanted it to be a mystery.

If she does know what it means, what does she think about me calling her my heart? Because it's not a lie. Other than my family, she's the only one who has a place in it.

For the next half hour, Lilly works hard at whatever she's doing, and I just watch her. I'm trying not to be so obvious about it, but it's hard not to. She looks so sexy when she's deep in thought.

Her pencil is trapped between her teeth, her brow scrunched as her eyes skim across the pages of her textbook. And when it's time for her to write something, she mouths everything she writes down.

Grinning, I try not to chuckle at how adorable she is.

She looks up at me. "Are you done?"

"No." I lean back, placing my arms on the backrests of the couch and my right ankle on my thigh, still grinning at her.

She blinks a few times, that blush finding its way back to her cheeks. "Stop it."

"Stop what?" I ask, cocking my head to the side.

"You're staring at me."

"So?"

"It's weird." She narrows her eyes.

I chuckle. "You're cute."

That gets her brows jumping. "I-I am?"

I nod my head. "And adorable."

"You're fucking with me." She narrows her eyes again. "Get back to work." She points to my book.

She looks back down at her textbook, doing her best to pay attention as I get up and move to join her on the couch, needing to be closer to her.

"What are you doing?" she mumbles, not looking up from her book. I scoot closer to her until I'm right next to her face.

"Let's go do something fun."

"I'm working," she whispers.

"Pleeeeease," I beg. "I wanna do something fun."

"This is fun." She glances up at me, then quickly back down to her work.

Reaching over, I tuck the loose piece of bangs behind her ear, and a smug satisfaction fills me when she shivers just a little bit.

"Babe, you're one of my best friends, and I respect the shit out of you." I chuckle.

"Thanks," she grumbles, still looking down.

"But you're crazy if you think this is fun."

She sighs and closes her book. "Alright then, fine. You win. You're lucky I'm pretty much done. And by the way, you're the one who wanted to come here and study." She raises a brow.

"Wanna know a secret?" I ask her, making it sound like I got some juicy top-secret information.

"What?" She gives me a blank look, knowing me all too well.

I look around as if I'm making sure no one is watching, and lower my voice into a whisper. "I didn't actually want to come here to study."

"Oh, really?" She sounds amused now. "And why did you want to come here?"

I take a moment to just look at her, finding that damn sexy freckle under her eye, and having to resist the urge to brush my thumb over it.

Her lips part, her breaths coming out quicker. My cock twitches and I really fucking want to kiss her right now.

But I don't. This is new and so damn confusing, I don't want to scare her or make things awkward.

"I just wanted to spend time with you," I murmur.

"Oh," she whispers, her cheeks heating as she licks her lips. This girl is making it so damn hard. So, I get up and grab her books, shove them in her bag, and throw it over my shoulder.

Holding my hand out to her, I say, "Come on."

"Where are we going?" she asks, giving me a skeptical look.

"Come on, Shorty, do you trust me?"

"Yes," she says without hesitation, and I fucking love it.

She places her hand in mine. It's soft and warm as I lace my fingers through hers. "Come with me, my lady, and I shall provide you a night full of riveting fun."

CHAPTER TWENTY-THREE

LILLIANNA

By riveting fun, I think he meant illegal.

"Bishop, are you crazy!" I whisper-hiss as he pulls me along. We're ducked down, being careful not to be seen by anyone, as we make our way along the barn on the RVU campus.

"Yes. Why do you ask?" he chuckles back.

"If we get caught, we're going to get arrested," my voice is laced with a worrying undertone.

"Nah. We do this all the time." He dismisses my worry, like the crazy man he is.

"Do what? You still haven't told me why we're here."

I almost stumble into him when he suddenly comes to a stop. "Just wait here." He pins himself to the wall and inches himself away from me.

I sit there in a damn bush, wondering why the hell I followed this sexy, crazy, tattooed hockey player here. I fail to see how this is more fun than schoolwork.

Okay, that sounds kinda sad.

I'm not trying to be a wet blanket, it's just I really don't want to get in trouble with the law.

I watch as Bishop disappears around the corner. As the seconds tick by, I grow more and more worried. *Did he get caught? Did he get hurt?*

When he doesn't come back for a minute, I say fuck it and stand up, slowly heading for the corner. Just as I'm about to peek around it, Bishop appears, scaring the crap out of me. I open my mouth to scream, but Bishop's large palm covers my mouth. "Shhh," he whispers, grinning like a fool. "Come on."

He removes his hand and grabs mine, tugging me along. My eyes widen when I hear the sound of a... *is that a goat?*

There's a little fenced in pen with a white and black pygmy goat. "Oh my god!" I gasp, putting my hand to my mouth. I look up at Bishop in surprise. "It's a goat."

"I know," he chuckles. "Meet Raccoon. He's the RVU mascot."

"He's so cute," I gush. "And so tiny. Hello, baby." I crouch down, sticking my hand through the fence. He bleats out a hello and lets me pet him. "Not that I don't love this surprise, but did we sneak onto another school's campus only to come see a goat? We could have just gone to the zoo for that."

"Note to self, take you to the zoo," he laughs. "But we're not here to visit Raccoon. We're here to take him."

"What!" I hiss. "No, Bishop, we can't steal him!"

"It's kind of a thing we do every year. We normally don't take him until deeper into the season, but the fucking assholes thought it would be fun to beat the shit out of Rodney."

"Who's Rodney?"

"The guy in the knight get-up at all our games. Our mascot."

"They beat him up! Why?"

Bishop's face darkens. "Because he's smaller and weaker

than them. They love to make fun of him, mocking him during every game we play against RVU. All because he's, in their words, 'the opposite of a knight'. We've had beef with them over it for a while. Kicking their asses got old, so we've started stealing Raccoon. This year was the first year they've put their hands on Rodney, though. We're going to hold onto him until they make a video apologizing and calling themselves out for being bullying assholes, then we're going to post it all over social media."

I look back down at the cutie-pie. "What if they call the cops?"

"They won't. Rodney agreed not to press charges, so we could go through with our plan."

Standing back up, I cross my arms and narrow my eyes. "So you're going to stop that poor guy from pressing charges and getting his justice on a group of assholes who harmed him?"

"Retract them claws, kitty cat." He grins. "Only until after the video is posted. Then we all plan on taking Rodney to the police station and helping him stick it to these assholes. The guys on the RVU hockey team." Bishop shakes his head. "They're not good guys. They're the ones you warn your daughters away from and why you cover your drink at parties."

"Oh." Understanding dawns on me. "Holy shit. Okay, then, let's steal a goat." I look back down at Raccoon, who bleats in response, making me giggle.

"Now that's what I'm talking about!" Bishop whoops.

He opens up the gate and walks in, bends down, and picks up the tiny little baby.

"How do they not have any cameras watching over him?" I ask as we head back the way we came.

"Oh, they do. That's why I was gone for a few, I was covering the cameras."

I'm on high alert as we rush over to the Jeep. "Why is it so dead?"

"Everyone is probably at one of the crazy parties they throw."

"On a weeknight?" I ask, raising a brow.

"Every night." He shoots me a look over his shoulder. "This school is full of sour rich kids who are pissed they didn't make it into SVU."

Bishop opens the Jeep's door and I bend down, wrapping my arms around Raccoon's belly to lift him up. "Dear god, he's heavy," I grunt, getting him into the back seat. "What have you been eating, my dude?"

"He's a goat, so probably anything he can get into." Bishop chuckles. I climb into the back seat with the goat, and Bishop quickly gets into the front to get us out of here.

"I can't believe we stole a goat." I giggle, thrumming with excitement. "This is crazy."

Bishop looks at me in the rearview mirror, grinning. "Admit it though, it's fun and thrilling, isn't it?"

"Okay, yeah, a little bit." I grin back. "So, where are we going to keep him?"

"The hockey house. We have a big backyard, and it's the best place to stash him; no easy access for the fuckers to try to steal him back before we're ready."

I give Raccoon a scratch on the head. "I wish I could keep you, Raccoon." He licks me, making me laugh again.

Bishop snorts. "I wonder who thought up the idea to name a goat Raccoon."

"Really?" I ask in disbelief. "You don't see it?"

"See what?"

"Ship, look at his eyes." I laugh. "He has black patches under both of them like a Raccoon."

He looks over his shoulder, giving Raccoon a double take. "Well, I'll be damned, I've never noticed."

"It's okay. You can blame getting smashed into the boards one too many times." I pat his shoulder.

"Haha." I see him roll his eyes in the mirror. "You're such a brat."

"Yeah, but you love it," I tease.

He looks up at me. "Yeah, I do."

My heart races as we lock eyes for a moment, but that moment feels like an eternity. When Bishop looks away, I blink out of the haze in time to feel a warmth hitting me.

Looking down, I scream in horror. "Oh my god!"

Bishop pulls into the hockey house's driveway. "What!?" He slams on the brakes and looks back.

"He pissed and shit on me!" I look down at the tiny pebbles of goat shit and the wet patch that is soaking into my thigh. I'm frozen in horror as Raccoon turns around, bleats in my face, then starts to eat my hair!

Bishop gapes at me before bursting into hysterical laughter. "I fucking hate you," I snarl to the goat, throwing the Jeep door open and storming my way up to the front door.

"Lilly, come on!" Bishop shouts, still fucking laughing.

I raise a finger at him before bursting through the front door. A guy stands by the front door, talking on the phone. He looks over at me and blinks. "I gotta go." He hangs up the phone. "Ah, can I help you?"

"Where's your shower?" I demand, rage filling me. I smell like a damn barn.

"What?"

Jonas walks into the room and gapes at me. "Lilly, what the fuck?" he steps towards me then steps back. "God, why the hell do you stink?"

"Fuck you, very much," I snap at my best friend. "Your dumb-ass teammate thought it would be fun to steal a goat, and now I'm covered in piss and shit."

Jonas bites his lips together, trying not to laugh. I give him the death glare. "Raccoon is here!" the guy from before hollers excitedly.

Just then, Bishop walks in with the little shit. Literally. "Hey, guys," phone-guy shouts.

A group of guys come running towards the front door, and I die a little inside because I smell horrible. I think Raccoon took a chunk of my hair, and there's a bunch of sexy hockey players witnessing my dismay.

And what makes it worse? Toby walks in. His brows jump, eyes going from the goat to Bishop, who's standing there smug as fuck, and then over to me. His eyes widen for a moment before a lazy smirk takes over. "How was studying?"

I'm still mad at him, so I just glare. His face drops, and he lets out a heavy sigh. "Come on, you can use our shower."

I want to tell him to fuck off, but I really do need to shower, so I look over at Bishop, who smirks back. I glare at him and then follow Toby up the stairs.

"You can use my shower."

"Yours?" I ask as we step into a room.

He nods. "Even though I technically live in the dorm, mostly to appease Dad, I spend most of my nights here. Or at least I did, until this year." He points to one bed then another. "Mine, Bishop's." Opening a drawer, he grabs a towel. "Here," he says, not making eye contact with me as he passes it to me, and I head into the attached bathroom.

"Thanks," I murmur, trying to ignore the aching feeling in my chest. Closing the door, I lock it and strip out of my soiled clothes, tossing them into the empty trashcan and tying up the bag to deal with later.

He wants me. He told me so. I told him I wanted him back. Then he rejected me. It hurts every time I think about it.

Things with him are so messed up, so damn confusing, I don't know where we go from here.

I told him I was done and I am. I'm not waiting around for the day he decides to act on his feelings for me.

But it doesn't mean my feelings for him just went away. When I think about it, I don't think they ever truly will. The love

I have for him is one that's woven into my soul, dooming me for any other man.

That doesn't mean I won't find someone who will love me. Who doesn't care about what people think or how society tells us we should be.

Do I believe the reason he won't be with me is because he sees me as his sister? No. I think that's utter bullshit, even if that is the excuse he gave me. There's something more, something deeper.

I want to find out what that is, but not at the cost of my heart.

So, I'm at a standstill. And now Toby is no longer the only man who makes me feel something. What do I do about Bishop?

Is there even anything there on his part, or am I looking too hard into things?

We shared a moment more than once tonight. I swear he was going to kiss me back in the library, and when he didn't, I was disappointed.

Now, not only am I in love with Toby, but I'm almost positive I'm crushing on his best friend. *My* best friend.

"Why couldn't you just have loved a normal boy? One who wasn't your stepbrother or best friend," I mutter to myself, avoiding the mirror because I do not want to know what state my hair is in, and turn the shower on.

I can tell myself to get over him until the cows come home, but it still doesn't change the fact my heart does this weird little dance and my belly flutters like crazy when I see him. Because even though things have changed over the past few years, we have history and sometimes that never goes away.

Grabbing whatever body wash and shampoo that's in here, I scrub myself down and curse myself because now I smell like Toby. It's like the universe hates me right now.

Once I'm clean, I get out and wrap the towel around me. "Shit," I groan. I don't have anything to change into.

Biting my lower lip, I make sure the towel is tight around me and crack open the door, checking to see if Toby stayed.

I let out a sigh of relief when I see he didn't and step out. "He did say this was his room," I murmur to myself, looking at his bed and then over to Bishop's. I wonder if they have any clothes they left behind.

I go over to Bishop's side first, and search through the dresser, only managing to find a pair of black SVU sweats. I grab those and go over to Toby's side. He has more. A few pairs of socks, boxers, shirts, and sweats.

So, I grab a plain black T-shirt and quickly change. My skin prickles as I shiver, still cold from the fresh shower.

I could grab the blanket off the bed and wrap myself up in it but it's too chunky. I go over to the closet on Bishop's side, but there are only metal hangers in there. I know I'm wearing Toby's clothes as a last resort, but I don't want him to think more about it if he sees me in them.

But when I go to his closet, of course, there are a few hoodies hanging. "Damn it," I grumble, grabbing the forest green hoodie.

Sliding it on, I close my eyes and inhale like a weirdo. It smells like him and I hate that he smells so good.

Going back into the bathroom, I do my best to fix my hair so it doesn't look like I haven't brushed it in a year before heading back down to find Bishop.

"Where is everyone?" I ask myself when I step into an empty living room. I check the kitchen next and hear laughing coming from the backyard.

"Hey, there she is," Bishop cheers when I step out. He walks over to me and grins. "In a better mood?"

"No thanks to your nasty little friend," I grumble, pouting as I cross my arms.

"But he's so cute. You can't stay mad at him forever. I mean, look at him." All the guys are playing with the goat, running around and laughing like a bunch of kids. It's cute.

"Where did you find the clothes?"

I look back over to him. "Your's and Toby's room. Didn't know you had one here."

As I say Toby's name, I feel his eyes on me. We lock gazes, and I see heat in his as he looks me over in his hoodie.

A sick satisfaction fills me.

And then realization hits me, and I don't know how I didn't see it before. That was the room I saw Toby get his dick sucked in. And now I feel sick.

"You okay?" Bishop asks me. "You look a little pale."

I force a smile. "I'm fine."

"Wanna hang out here for a bit before we go back?"

"Yeah, why not?" I smile. He grins, scooping me up. "Hey, what the hell!" I laugh.

"You have no shoes on. I don't want you to hurt your feet," he states.

Oh, that's... kind of cute.

He brings me over to one of the chairs but instead of putting me down in one and taking another, he sits down, placing me in his lap.

I should get up and move. But I don't. I look up at him, a damn blush betraying me.

He looks down at me, winks, and goes back to whatever conversation he was having before I came down.

No one else seems to give the two of us a second glance, but I feel Toby's eyes on me. I don't look for him though, closing my eyes and just enjoying the cozy warmth.

Tonight, I was expecting to have a quiet night in the library and study, but instead, this wild man took me on a crazy adventure. One I do have to admit was fun and thrilling.

I needed tonight more than I thought I would. And I have my best friend to thank for it.

CHAPTER TWENTY-FOUR

LILLIANNA

IF I WASN'T SURE ABOUT MY CRUSH ON BISHOP BEFORE, I SURE AS hell am now. That man has come to my door every morning since that first morning with a coffee in hand just for me.

And most of those days he didn't have an early morning practice, meaning he's been getting up early and going all the way across campus to get my favorite coffee.

Sadly, I haven't been able to hang out with him again because our schedules have been crazy. I have to admit his going out of his way to do this for me has my heart soaring and my belly erupting with butterflies every time.

My heart hasn't let Toby go, but it seems to be making room for another, and I'm so damn afraid. Maybe it's my broken heart, but I haven't allowed myself to be convinced he has feelings for me. I need him to make the first move. Until then, I'll just enjoy what we've got going on.

He texts me so much I've had to shut my phone off. I love it, though. He stopped sitting at the hockey table and has started sitting with my friends and me.

Bianca is suspicious, but she doesn't seem to care all that much. It's cute to see them bicker all the time.

As for her and Jonas, she's still playing hard to get, but I think Jonas is loving it.

Things have changed a lot in such a short amount of time, and most of it is in a good way, but not all. Like the fact that I don't recognize Toby anymore, and it's starting to scare me. He seems sad, maybe even depressed.

He had another nightmare last night, and I couldn't just stand by knowing the pain he was in, so I crawled into bed with him. I cried silent tears when he pulled me tight into his arms, his face pressed into the crook of my neck. It felt right like I was meant to be there. Why can't he see that?

If I were anyone else and didn't grow up with a family like mine, I might feel guilty for having feelings for more than one person. But I don't. I know love has no bounds, and sometimes it's okay to open your heart to more than one. Only thing is, one of the people I opened my heart to won't take it, and the other doesn't even know I want to offer the other half to him.

It's Sunday again and we're all here for family supper—Toby, Bishop, and me. I can feel the strain in their relationship. I don't know what's going on with the two of them, but I hope it's not because of me. I'd hate myself if it was.

"Hey." I stand in the doorway of my mom's room.

Rain looks over at me in the mirror from where she's doing her hair. "Hey, you." She grins, putting her brush down. "Come here."

I go with a smile, wrapping my arms around her in a tight hug. "I needed this." Sometimes a girl just needs her mama. I wanted to find my mom, tell her all the things that have been weighing on me, but I can't, not when it comes to my feelings for

Toby. I don't want to cause any issues if nothing is even going to happen between us.

"Are you okay?" she asks, still hugging me.

"Not really," I sigh deeply.

She steps away and moves to her bed, patting the spot next to her. "Talk to me, babe."

Crisscrossing my legs, I sit next to her. "My heart, it's a mess right now," I admit.

"Toby?" she growls. She loves him, but she also doesn't like how he's been treating me. I expected her to be more mad, but for some reason she never is. If only she knew the things he's done.

I nod. "So movie night the other week, Toby and I stayed down in the basement to watch another movie."

"Yes." She nods.

"Long story short, we ended up making out." My cheeks burn so damn hot I'm surprised I don't burst into flames.

Her brows jump. "You kissed?" I nod, looking guilty. "And then what happened?"

I skip over the dry humping because I am not going into details with that. "He told me it was a mistake because I was his sister."

"That little shit," she hisses. "He might be like a son to me, and you're my daughter, but you two have never had a sibling relationship, and we all know it."

"That's pretty much what I've been telling him. But he still thinks it's wrong. I don't get it. Look at our family, it's not conventional, but it works for us. Does that mean he thinks how you, mom, and dads live your lives is wrong? Because I sure as hell don't."

"Because it's not," she states strongly.

"So, that kind of put us back to square one when it comes to the strain in our friendship. Just when I thought I'd get my old Toby back." My eyes tear up.

"Honey, Toby... he's grown up a lot over the past few years, and there's things you don't know. It's taken a toll on him. I don't agree with how he's been treating you—I want to wring his damn neck sometimes—but please don't give up on him. I'm not asking you to sit back and take his shit, but just... don't hate him for it."

I blink at her, stunned. "What do you mean he's been through stuff? What? When?" I ask urgently.

She shakes her head. "It's not my place to say anything. I'm sorry."

I want to yell, demand to know what's going on. But if she's saying something happened, is that why he's been so cold to me the past few years? Did whatever it was change him that much? And why didn't he tell me about it? Why didn't he come to me and let me help him? Didn't he know I'd be there for him no matter what?

"It's not just Toby," I admit, making a mental note to circle back to the Toby thing later.

She gives me a small, knowing grin. "Let me guess. The dark-haired, tattooed hockey player you almost kissed last week?"

My brows shoot up, eyes widening. "W-What? You saw that?" My cheeks go crimson. I shouldn't be surprised, the pool is in view of the back door.

She just shrugs. "Is it him we're talking about?"

Chewing on my lower lip, I nod. "I like him. A lot," I confess. "At first I wasn't sure, but things have been slowly changing over the past week. I can't stop thinking about him. When he texts me, I get all excited, and when I see him, my belly goes nuts." Not just with butterflies, but that heated feeling too. Not going to tell Mama that, though.

She gives me a genuinely excited smile. "I like this side of you," she laughs. "I've never seen you like this before."

I smile. "I like how he makes me feel," I whisper, and then my smile drops. "But I don't know what to do. I don't know if he feels the same way, and I don't want to mess up our friendship by reading this wrong and making the wrong move. And then there's Toby." I groan, flopping back on the bed. "It's so wrong."

"What about this do you think is wrong?"

"Everything. Having feelings for my stepbrother, having feelings for his best friend who is also *my* best friend. And…"

"Don't you say it, Lilly," she says in a warning. "If you tell me that having feelings for more than one person is wrong, I might have to beat your ass for the first time in your life."

That makes me giggle. "No. I wasn't going to say that. I'm just confused, I guess."

She nods. "First off, it's okay to love more than one person. Never feel ashamed of that. I know not everyone is able to live the life me, your mom, and dads do, but love really is a powerful thing. If they wanted you bad enough, they would learn to share."

"Thanks." I roll my eyes.

"If you're not ready to let Bishop know about your feelings for him, then wait a little while longer. But, babe, don't keep quiet forever, not if it's going to hurt you more than risking the chance of your friendship. I've seen how you hurt over Toby. I don't want to see that happen again over another boy. You deserve love. Take it. If they can't give you what you're worth, then they're not worthy of you."

"Thanks, Mama." I smile, sitting up and giving her a hug.

"I don't want to put my nose where it doesn't belong, but I wouldn't write off Bishop having feelings for you."

"Did he say something to you?" I ask, narrowing my eyes.

She says nothing, just gets up and walks toward the door. "Come on, let's go see if your mom needs help with supper."

"He said something, didn't he?!" I rush after her.

"I can't wait. We're having your mom's cheesy baked chicken."

She's deliberately avoiding the question. I smile, a surge of hope filling me.

When we get to the kitchen, Mom is peeling potatoes. "Hey, Mom." I give her a hug from behind.

"Hi, Lillypad. How was your week?"

"It was good." I grin, remembering what Bishop and I did. The goat is still at the hockey house. I've forgiven the little asshole, but I still won't go near him. I look around to make sure none of my dads are around. When I see the coast is clear, I grin over at them. "Did Jax say anything about what the hockey players did?"

Mom snorts. "You mean taking that damn goat again?" She grins, shaking her head. "Oh, yeah, your dad was ranting all about it. But he's going to pretend he knows nothing because of what that team did to that poor boy."

My heart drops at the mention of Rodney. I hope he presses charges against those monsters. I can't believe they would go as far as to physically harm him.

"Well, I helped Bishop take him." I giggle.

"You did what?" My mom spins and gapes at me. "Lillianna Tatum!"

"Nice going, kid," Rain laughs. "Was it fun?"

"Yeah." I grin back. "The thrill of getting caught... there's nothing like it."

"You are too much like your dads and mama." Mom shakes her head, but she's grinning as she goes back to prepping supper.

"And you say that like it's a bad thing." Rain rolls her eyes and wraps her arms around Mom. Mom closes her eyes and leans back into Rain's embrace as Rain kisses her neck.

"You two are grossly adorable." I sigh heavily. "I'm going to find the guys."

I want what my parents have. The kind of love that seeps into your soul, making you wild and crazy for your person. The kind of love that makes you unable to function without the other, like you're each other's air to breathe. That you would die if they weren't there.

It's not healthy at all, and yes, I did say I didn't want Toby to be my whole world. But if someone felt the same about me, then I'd make an exception. Because I grew up with that raw, powerful kind of love, I watched my dads and mama treat my mom like the world was made for her. And in return, she's loved them with everything she has.

When I find the guys, they're hanging out in the living room with my little brothers. Bennett is on the couch on the other side of the room, far away from Toby. Toby watches him with this crushed look on his face. It hurts. I hate this.

"Lilly!" Bennett jumps up from his spot and rushes over to me, hugging me tightly. "I missed you."

"Missed you too, bud. Come hang out with me?" It's not that I don't want to hang out with the twins, but they're screaming at the TV, deep into their game.

"Always." He grins up at me.

Bennett and I head down to the game room and play a few rounds of foosball before it's time for supper.

Speaking of supper, it's awkward, to say the least.

Both Toby and Bishop's attention stay on me the whole time. Brody is eyeing up the guys like he wants to kick their asses, and the twins are talking about gross boy stuff. Sometimes, I wish my mom had another kid after them, giving me a little sister. Too many boys in this house.

"You ready to go?" Bishop asks me, giving me a knowing look when we're done eating.

Toby eyes us suspiciously. I feel bad, but we didn't tell him about volunteering at the ice rink. With things still being strained between us, I want my full attention on the kids, not the boy who has my heart in knots.

"Yup."

"Where are you two going?" Toby asks.

"Just heading back to the dorm. Maybe watch a movie or something," Bishop replies.

"Since when did you two become besties?" Toby crosses his arms and narrows his eyes. But not at me, at Bishop.

"Are you kidding me?" Bishop asks him, his words coming out in a disbelieving growl. "I don't know, pretty much our whole lives? What is wrong with you, man? I can't hang out with her now because you're not with us? You know, we can be friends without you there. You're not the one that holds our friendship together."

"I didn't say I was," he snaps at Bishop. "I just don't get why you two are spending so much time together."

Bishop shakes his head and steps closer. "Don't start with me, Toby. I know you've been in a shitty mood, but it's one of your own making. When you're done being a miserable asshole, give me a call and we'll invite you to hang out." Bishop looks at me. "Come on, Lilly."

I chew my lower lip, uneasy nerves swarming my belly. I don't know what's going on between them, but I don't like seeing them fight. I don't think I ever have before.

With one last look at Toby, who watches me with those pain-filled, longing eyes he's been sporting the past few weeks, I follow after Bishop. Because what else would I do?

Bishop is right. Toby is his own reason for being unhappy. He's the one who rejected me.

Before, I would want to stay behind, trying to make him feel better, to ease his pain. But Bishop makes me want to put myself first. He makes me smile and laugh. When I'm with him, I'm happy. Not hurting, not in pain, but feeling good.

Whenever Toby decides to stop being his own worst enemy, I'll be there to talk. Until then, yeah, I'm putting myself first.

CHAPTER TWENTY-FIVE

LILLIANNA

"Maybe this isn't a good idea," I tell Bishop as I lace up my skates from my spot on the players' bench.

"Why not?" Bishop asks, lazily skating while he waits for me.

"Because I haven't been on skates in years." I finish tightening the laces up and stand.

"It's like riding a bike. It's also why I wanted to come here before lessons start, just in case you were a bit rusty." He gives me a playful grin that makes my body flush.

I brush it off, giving him a teasing glare. "Thanks."

"You're very welcome," he chuckles. "Now get your cute little ass out on the ice." He holds his hand out and I take it, cheeks blushing.

"Thanks," I murmur as he helps me out onto the ice.

I'm a little wobbly at first but it doesn't take me long before

"There you go. Like a pro. You know, if you practiced more, you could be as good as me," he taunts, looping around me.

"Yeah, sure." I laugh.

We spend a few minutes skating around, laughing, and talking.

Bishop comes to a stop, spraying me with ice. "Wanna race?" he asks, wiggling his brows.

"Asshole." I giggle and grin. "You're on." I know I'm going to lose, but I'm excited to try.

We skate over to one side, hands on the plexiglass. "On the count of three. One." My heart pounds, excitement filling my body. "Two." I get in position. "Go!" he shouts, and I swear I feel a gust of wind hit my face as the speed demon races down the rink.

I lose, badly. He makes it to the other end with a whoop as I'm just reaching the middle of the rink. I laugh at his little victory dance but as I get closer and closer to him, I forget how to stop. My eyes widen and I let out a scream, closing my eyes as I brace myself for the crash into the hard boards that is about to come.

Only what I crash into isn't as hard as I was expecting. Bishop wraps his arms around me with the force knocking us both to the ice with a grunt.

"I'm so sorry," I say in a rushed breath. I open my eyes to find myself on top of Bishop, looking down.

"Forgot how to stop?" he chuckles, his brown eyes sparkling with humor and something else.

I should move, roll off him, and get to my feet. But I don't. I stay there on top of him, his arms still wrapped around me, holding me to his body.

My eyes flick between his as my pulse picks up, my breaths coming out in little pants. He stares at me with such intensity, it makes me want to squirm.

I want him to kiss me so bad right now, and when he licks his lips, a low whimper escapes me. His chest heaves as a low rumbling sound emits from his throat.

"*Il mio cuore.*" His voice is deep and husky, making my core clench. "Tell me no. Because if you don't, I'm going to kiss these fucking tempting lips of yours."

I don't dare say anything, my ears ringing, my mind hazy. I feel like I'm going to pass out if he doesn't kiss me right now.

With a pained groan, he growls, "Fuck it." His large hand comes up, cradling the back of my head as he crashes his lips to mine.

His lips are soft and warm. They feel perfect against mine.

Everything around me goes still, and the only thing I can hear is the sound of my beating heart and our mixed moans of pleasure. I part my lips, letting him slip his tongue in and over mine.

Bishop is quick to take control, and I hand it over to him freely. He flips us, pinning me against the ice under him as he kisses me hungrily.

My hands thread through his soft silky strands, grabbing handfuls and pulling him tightly as I push my lips harder against him. I need him so badly in this moment, afraid that if there's even an inch of space, he will disappear.

I'm only in a hoodie and leggings, him in his hockey jacket and jeans, so I can feel his hard cock pressed against my pussy as he grinds down into me. The hardness against my clit makes me moan, tugging harder at his hair.

"Fucking hell, Lilly," Bishop growls, breathing heavily as he breaks the kiss. "What are you doing to me?" he asks, but doesn't give me a chance to answer—if I was even meant to at all—before he's kissing me again. I'm clawing at him, desperate for more. I'm about to flip us back over and grind against him when we hear the voices of other people entering the building.

He pulls away from me and looks down, his eyes glazed over with lust. "We'll talk about this later," he murmurs, and I nod, eyes widening in disbelief at what just happened.

His eyes search mine. "Just tell me one thing. Do you regret it?"

I shake my head, unable to find the words right now. He gives me a relieved look and presses his warm lips to my forehead before rolling off me.

I lay there for a moment, catching my breath and wondering if I'm dreaming. Bishop gets to his feet and holds his hand out to me. I take it, letting him pull me to mine. We crash together again, and he steadies me. "We've got to stop meeting like this," he chuckles.

"Why?" is all I ask, making him laugh harder.

"Oh, *il mio cuore.*" He shakes his head and moves back, letting me go "I, ah, need a moment," he says, scratching the back of his head and looks down.

I bite my lower lip when I see the bulge in his pants. "Might be a good idea. Don't want to freak out the kids." I giggle and he groans, putting his hands over his face.

"World's worst timing."

"I didn't mind it," I whisper, my whole body humming, my heart so damn full. But I still feel those nervous flutters, wondering if he's going to think it was a mistake.

He removes his hands from his face and gives me a look that has my belly fluttering. Gripping my face between his hands, he presses a firm kiss against my lips. "If we were anywhere else but here, that kiss wouldn't have ended so soon," he grumbles. "I'll be back," he tells me before turning around and skating off the ice.

Bringing my hand to my lips, I smile like an idiot. I'm so happy, I could cry. Because this time, I wasn't asked to forget about it, or told that it was a mistake. Bishop wants me, and he kissed me again like he couldn't get enough.

Right now, I don't care about anything else but Bishop and that kiss.

That is, until I skate over to go greet the parents and find a few of them talking to Toby.

What is he doing here?

TOBIAS

My life is slowly crashing down around me, and I only have myself to blame. All I feel is anger and hatred towards myself.

After talking to Lilly at the café a few days ago, I've been spiraling. I can't focus on my studies, and practice has been shit. Jax isn't happy with me and with the first game coming up, I'm at risk of being pulled before the season has even started.

Seeing Lilly makes my heart ache and seeing her with Ryan makes me fucking murderous. I've gotten into a few fights with the guys on the team, snapping at the drop of a hat. I hate it. I don't like feeling like this, but I can't seem to get all these strong emotions to go away enough for me to think. I can't fucking think. And when I do think, she's the one who takes up the space in my head.

I hurt her, and I'll never forgive myself for it. I just wish she could understand why we can't be together. I'm doing this for her own good. She'll see it one day… I hope. And it's not just protecting her from the people of this town, I'm protecting her from myself. I'm not good enough for her. But no one is, really.

It's not just my relationship with Lilly that's suffering. Bishop and I… I can feel a rift between us. I've snapped at him too, been a moody bastard.

I've hardly seen him the past week because he's been doing exactly what I asked him to do by using up all of Lilly's free time.

I fucking hate it. I thought it was a good idea at the time, but the more I see them together, the angrier I get, because I feel like I'm being replaced. I used to be the most important person in Lilly's life. I was the one who knew everything about her, who made her laugh and smile.

And then everything went to shit because I couldn't keep my anger in check. My parents had to do a lot of things to keep me from doing jail time. I thought I was doing the right thing by putting distance between Lilly and me, to protect her from the damage.

Now, I very well might have lost her forever. Why couldn't I just have kept my fucking hands and lips to myself? Why did I have to pull her into my lap that night? Why did I have to kiss her and change everything between us?

Because it's what my soul has been craving for years. It's what my heart has been aching for. It's everything I've dreamed about and more.

The look of pure devastation on her face when I asked her to just forget about it, that it shouldn't have happened, it's going to haunt me for life.

I didn't want to hurt her. The idea of anyone hurting her makes me physically ill. But I did. I hurt her and I can't take it back. I don't know how to make it right.

How do we go back to being friends, to having that closeness we had before?

We don't. We can't. Not unless it means being something more. And I won't do that to her. I won't shackle her to a broken man.

I've been drinking more often than not, and it scares me. Alcoholism isn't something that's in my bloodline, but Brody suffers from it. He's a recovering alcoholic and has been sober since I was seven. But I know it's something he still struggles with sometimes. Jax and Ellie are a big help with that and they've gone to the occasional meeting with him if he needs it.

I'm afraid that I might tumble down that same path. The pain is too much sometimes, and I just need something to take that pressure off. But when I drink, the night terrors come back.

I never wake up from them, but I know about them because Bishop has told me I have them.

All my life, I've tried to be the man my parents wanted me to be. Kind, caring, loving. But I've struggled with my anger, even before the incident. That night just unleashed the damage I knew I was capable of inflicting.

"Hey," Ellie walks into the living room, where I'm sitting on the couch, playing with my phone, not ready to go back to the dorm yet.

If I get bored, I'll go drinking and look for a fight. I don't want to do that tonight.

"Hey." I look up at her.

"How come you're here? I thought you would have gone with your sister and Bishop." I flinch slightly at the mention of Lilly being my sister. I might have given her that as an excuse for us not being together, but I didn't mean it. She will never be my sister, not in my eyes. She will always be so much fucking more.

"I didn't feel like going back to the dorms." I shrug.

"Dorms? They didn't go back to school." She looks at me with her brows slightly furrowed.

"Where did they go then?" I ask, my body going on high alert.

"To the community rink. It's their first week of volunteering to teach the little ones how to skate."

"What?" My brows furrow.

"You didn't know? I asked your sister to mention it to you. To see if you wanted to help them out because they were looking for more people."

"No," I grind out, jaw ticking as that familiar sense of rage fills me.

"I'm sure they didn't mean anything by it," Rain says, stepping into the room. "I think they've just wanted something they could do together, they seemed very excited about it."

"They could have asked Toby too. He's their friend." Ellie argues.

"Is he?" Rain asks, turning her attention to me, then back to Ellie. "I'm not sure if you've seen it, but Toby and Lilly haven't been as close as they used to."

"It's because Toby started school. Things change, people grow. It doesn't mean they're not still friends." Ellie's brows furrow.

Unease rushes through me as I get to my feet.

"If you'll excuse me, I gotta go," I mutter, stepping past them and heading to my car, fists clenched, body taut, and rage flowing through my veins.

So, they're doing shit behind my back? I can understand Lilly not wanting to be around me right now, but why is Bishop lying to me?

"Toby!" Rain yells my name, stopping next to me as I pull the door handle open.

"What?" I snarl out.

"Don't you get snippy with me," she warns. "I don't know what's going on with you lately, but you need to know, we're here for you. For anything, everything. You should know that by now."

I do. What they did for me, it's more than a lot of parents would do. "I know."

"I love you, you little shit. You're my son... but Lilly is my daughter. You've been hurting her and I don't appreciate it. Whatever has you holding back, let it go. Whatever is keeping you from loving Lilly like I damn well know you do, let that shit go. Because I can promise you, you're only going to end up hurting her more than whatever reason is in your head that has you believing you're doing what's best for her."

"You don't know anything," I say through clenched teeth, heart pounding.

"I know a lot more than you'd think. But I can't tell you what to do. It's your life, your choice. But Bishop and Lilly? Do not, and I repeat, do not come between their friendship. She needs him just as much as she needs you. She already lost one of you. Don't be the reason she loses someone else." She glares at me before spinning around on her heel and heading back into the house.

Getting into the car, I slam the door shut with a force that shakes the frame. I'm peeling out of the driveway and making my way to the rink in seconds.

When I get there, I see Bishop's Jeep.

Closing my eyes, I do something I never do. I put my head on the steering wheel and I cry.

I cry because I'm so fucking confused. I know my reasons for not allowing myself to be with Lilly don't make sense to anyone but me. But she doesn't know the things they've said. The things I've heard. The things I've had to fucking do to keep her safe.

I just want to keep her fucking safe!

But she hates me, and I hate myself. I feel like taking this fucking car and driving it off the nearest cliff. But that would only hurt her more, and I can't do that.

I don't know why I'm here. I'm not in any mindset to be teaching kids how to skate. But I get out of the car and make my way inside the building anyway.

When I get there, I find a bunch of kids, happy and excited as their parents help them lace up their skates.

A few of the parents know me, some are regulars at my grandparents' restaurant. I say hi, smile and chat a little, walking with one of the parents as we head towards the rink.

As if I have some kind of magical sense to know when she's near, I look up and there she is. She's dressed in a hoodie and leggings. She's in her skates, her cheeks pink from the cold air, or maybe from previously skating.

"Toby." she says with a confused whisper.

"Hey, sorry about that," Bishop says, skating over to Lilly as I walk towards them. He looks over at me with surprise. "Hey, man." He nods. "What are you doing here?"

"Why don't you tell me why you didn't bother to ask me to help out with this?" I wave my hand towards the rink and look at Lilly. "Mom told me you were supposed to ask me."

"I was," she admits, giving me a blank look.

"Then why didn't you?" I ask.

"Because." A flash of hurt flickers across her face as she steps off the ice and towards me. "Being around you hurts, Toby." Her voice cracks. "I hate this. I hate the distance. But you hurt me.

You rejected me. And no, I don't hate you. And no, I'm not cutting you from my life. And no, I didn't give up on the friendship we used to have, if that's something we can even get back. But it's going to take time. And this—" she points to her heart, "—is still too raw." Tears fill her eyes and my hands twitch to reach up and brush them away.

I want to pull her in my arms, tell her I love her, and make everything okay. But I can't because I'm the problem.

"Lilly." Her name comes out as an agonized rasp.

She closes her eyes tightly and shakes her head. "Not right now." She takes in a shaky breath. "I need to go get some things for the lesson. If you want to stay and help, we won't turn down an extra set of hands." She brushes past me, not bothering to put on her skate guards.

Spinning back around, I find Bishop watching me. "I changed my mind."

"What?" he asks, brows jumping.

"What I asked you to do, using up her free time. I changed my mind." Thing is, I'm jealous as fuck. He has the friendship with her that I used to. That I want back. He makes her smile and laugh. Those are *my* fucking smiles and laughs. I shouldn't feel like this, but right now, I don't like him. Even if this is my own doing.

He snorts out a laugh. "No." He shakes his head.

"What do you mean no? I don't need or want you to use up her time anymore. It was stupid of me to ask you to do that anyway. I thought it made sense at the time."

"You're right, it was stupid. But, Toby, I'm not hanging out with Lilly because you asked me to. I'm doing it because I *want* to. I was planning on strengthening our friendship before you asked. With me being away for school, I've missed her. I've missed hanging out with her."

"But you don't need to," I snarl.

He gets off the ice and steps closer to me, getting in my face. "I want to," he repeats, in a low, dangerous voice that has the hairs on the back of my neck standing up. "I know this isn't something you're used to. That all the years we've been friends, you were always there when I hung out with Lilly. You hate it, don't you? That we don't need you there in order for our friendship to work. But, Toby, that's what it is, *our* friendship. Mine and hers. Just because things between the two of you are strained doesn't mean my friendship with her has to suffer. I love you, Toby, you're like my brother. But I'm not going to give up being friends with an amazing person like Lilly because you're jealous and pissed off."

"I'm not jealous," I snap, body vibrating.

"You are, among a lot of other things. I'm not here to take your place in her heart, Toby. But I want to be there for her too."

"She's mine." My chest heaves.

"You keep saying that, but yet you still don't claim her. You keep hurting her, instead. She deserves better than that. So, until you get your head out of your fucking ass, I'll be there for her. I'll try to fix the damage you've done. Because it's not fair for her to love someone who won't love her back."

"I do!" my voice cracks.

"Then fucking be a man and take your fucking woman before someone else does!" he growls before turning around and heading in the direction Lilly went.

Closing my eyes, I struggle to take in deep breaths, to rein in my anger because there are kids here and I will never chance putting them at risk.

It's not easy, but I do it. I calm down and head to my car to grab my skates.

He is right. I am jealous. But it's also not right of me to ask him to stop being friends with her. She needs him too.

So, that means I need to at least try to get back in her good graces, right? Even if it's in small, baby steps.

CHAPTER TWENTY-SIX

LILLIANNA

I'M TRYING TO PAY ATTENTION TO THE KIDS ON THE ICE, BUT MY attention is divided in three ways; between the kids I'm teaching, the man who kissed me and shook up my whole world, and the man who broke my heart, but still holds a piece of it.

The guys are so damn cute with the kids. All the little boys look up to Toby and Bishop, wanting one of them to teach them because they know they're hockey players and want to be just like them when they grow up. The guys are so patient with them, and it's melting my heart.

In my group, there are a few adorable girls and the little blonde one is very determined to stay on her feet.

"You're all doing amazing." I beam as they move on wobbly legs, holding onto their skate supports.

"Look, Lilly, I'm doing it!" Ava, a sweet little redhead cheers

"That's awesome, Ava, but don't go too fast, okay?"

"Lilly," Breanna whines. "I keep falling."

I giggle under my breath as I go over to help her up. "There you go." I get her back up to a standing position and help her hold onto her support.

"Lilly!" Riley shouts, the little blonde is hell-bent on learning how to skate today.

I look over to see her moving without her support. It's slow, but she's going strong.

"Wahoo! Go, Riley." I clap then yelp as someone bumps into me, sending me on my ass. "Ugh."

"Shit, Lilly," Toby hisses, crouching down. "Are you okay?"

"I'm fine, but my ass hurts now." I sigh.

"Bad woooords," Rachel sings.

"I'll buy everyone hot cocoa after this lesson if you don't tell your parents." I grin.

"Deal!" she says excitedly. I'm not teaching kids how to lie or anything, it's not like I said bitch or fuck.

"Here." Toby holds out his hand, offering it to me. But when I just stare at it, he lets out a huff. "It's not going to bite you," he jokes. And I can't help it, a smile twitches on my lips.

Deciding I can't stay down here all night, I take his hand, letting him pull me to my feet. When I'm standing steady on my skates, I try to shake him off, but he doesn't let go. My eyes find his and everything inside me feels like it's on fire.

I miss him. I love him. I can't have him. I want to cry and scream all at once. "Thanks," I whisper, licking my lips.

His eyes drop, watching the motion, and I step away, spinning around to focus on the girls. "Alright, girls. You all did amazing! We have a few more minutes, then we need to go out and meet up with your parents."

"Are you going to be here next week?" Rachel asks me.

"Yup." I give her a big smile. "I'll bring cookies next time."

"Yay!" They all cheer.

"Are you doing okay?" Bishop asks me as we help all the

little ones off the ice and over to the benches so they can remove their skates. His eyes flick over to Toby and back to me. I look over to Toby too, seeing him laughing and talking to a few of the boys as he helps them unlace their skates.

Why does even the simplest of glances from him have some weird kind of emotion sweeping over me? The idea of not having him in my life, even after he broke my heart, makes me feel sick. But I can't even be in the same room as him without my brain and heart clashing together.

I know girls who would beg and plead for the person they love to give them a chance, I've seen it at parties more than I would have liked to.

As much as I want to, and I've thought about it, I need to stand my ground, be confident in my self-worth. I know I shouldn't have to beg someone to love me. That doesn't mean I don't still want him. I probably always will, in one way or another.

Turning my gaze back to Bishop, I give him a forced smile. "Of course. Why wouldn't I be?"

His eyes search mine for a moment. When he brings his hand up to tuck a piece of hair behind my ear, my heart goes nuts for a whole other reason. "Toby might be one of my best friends, but so are you. I don't like what he's done to you, so please, never for a moment think I'd be on his side when it comes to that stuff." He looks at me with pleading eyes.

My face softens. "I know. And thank you for that. I know stuff like this can be hard to deal with. But please, don't stop being friends with him just because of me."

"I'm not. But it doesn't mean I'm just going to sit back and watch him hurt you, Lilly. You don't deserve that." He frowns.

Tears sting my eyes. "Thank you," I whisper. "It's nice to hear that, you know?"

"What? That you're worth the world and more? Oh, *il mio cuore*. I'll tell you every damn day, if that's what you need."

My heart goes crazy, my lips part in surprise and for a

moment I forget where we are. Heat fills Bishop's eyes, and I want to ask him to kiss me again.

Then Toby clears his throat, snapping us out of the moment. "All the kids are good to go."

"What?" I blink out of the haze and look over to see the boys and girls are all out of their skates. "Oh, shoot. Sorry."

"It's fine." Toby gives me a small smile, then looks up at Bishop. "Do you mind taking them out to their parents? I'd like to talk to Lilly for a moment."

Bishop looks down at me. "You okay with that?"

I want to tell him no, but I nod instead. He doesn't look like he believes me, but he ushers the kids toward the lobby nonetheless.

Looking back at Toby, I have the urge to both run after Bishop, or to throw myself in Toby's arms and ask him to just hold me.

So, I just stand there, crossing my arms. "What do you want?"

"Please." He gives me this pained look. "This cold-shoulder and distance is killing me, Lilly. I miss you so fucking much it hurts. I'm so sorry… for everything. I hate that I'm hurting you. I hate that I can't give you what you deserve. But please, *please,* don't shut me out of your life for good."

"You're kidding me, right?" I blink at him in disbelief. "I stop talking to you for a few weeks and you think you're hurting?" I step closer to him, anger filling me. "Try two fucking years, Toby."

"I know." His voice cracks. "I know. And I'm so fucking sorry, Lilly. I know there aren't enough times I can tell you that to make this all better, but I am. Those two years… I was fucking miserable, too."

I don't know what to say. I feel like it's pointless.

"We keep going around in circles, it's not going to get us anywhere. You know how I feel about you." My cheeks heat.

"You know what I want. You tell me you feel the same way, but won't do anything about it. I don't know what you want from me."

"I want you." His nostrils flair.

"Then fucking take me," I shout, fling my arms in the air before letting them drop, smacking against my thighs.

He says nothing, his jaw tightening.

"That's what I thought," I huff out with a sarcastic laugh and turn to leave.

"Tell me one thing?" he asks, making me pause.

"What?" I turn back around.

"Are you dating Ryan? Is there something real between you two?"

Licking my lips, I don't say anything for a long moment, wondering if I should lie. But I don't want to. I don't want to play games. It's not who I am. "Not that it's any of your business, but no. Ryan and I are only friends. I like him; he's a good guy, but it wouldn't ever work."

"Are you telling me the truth?"

My eyes narrow. "Yes. I don't lie if asked a direct question, or skate around the truth like you do, Toby."

Turning away from him, I try to walk away with dignity but I still have my skates on and end up walking a little funny.

My heart is racing so damn fast and I'm trying so hard not to cry. Why is it that with everything else in my life, I try not to let the negative things get to me? I go with the flow and brush it off because life is short and it's not worth my energy, but when it comes to Toby, all of that goes out the window. I've never been someone who lets others get to me. He's not just anyone, though; he's under my skin, seeped into my bones.

"All the kids gone?" I ask Bishop when I find him standing alone in the lobby.

"Yup." He looks in the direction from which I just came, then back to me. "Everything okay?"

"Everything's fine." I go over and sit down on the bench to take off my skates and curse when I realize I left my boots back at the rink.

"Lilly." Toby's voice has me looking up. He has my boots in his hands. He brings them over to me and places them by my feet.

"Thanks," I murmur, keeping my eyes on the ground as I start to put my boots on.

"Of course." He lets out a sigh. "So, that was fun."

"It was." Bishop chuckles. "Who knew I liked little kids?"

"You like my little brothers," Toby points out.

"True. But they're like my brothers too."

I blink. Should I be thinking of Bishop like a brother too? *Nope, not going on that train of thought.*

"Do you two mind if I volunteer too?" Toby asks. "Seeing how you were supposed to ask me to help out anyway." He doesn't sound mad about it, though. Instead, he makes light of the fact we deliberately didn't tell him about volunteering.

"I don't see why not." I look up and give him a forced smile. "I know the rec center needs the help, and the kids seem to love you."

He nods. "They're good kids."

The idea of spending an hour with Toby every Sunday sends some sick thrill through me. Because even though I'm hurting and heart broken, I still love him. I still want to be around him even though I shouldn't. Maybe I'm a masochist. Sure feels like it sometimes.

"You coming next Saturday?" Toby asks me, referring to their first hockey game next week.

"Wouldn't miss it." This time the smile I give him is real. The one he gives me in return reminds me of *my* Toby. And fuck, I love that smile.

"Awesome." He nods, then looks at Bishop. "You wanna hang out at the hockey house tonight? It's your turn to help out with Raccoon."

"Fuck," Bishop chuckles. "Yeah, why not? I just have to take Lilly back first."

"You two go." I wave them off. "I'll text Bianca to come get me. I have to clean up everything anyways."

"You sure?" Bishop asks me, brows furrowing in concern.

"I'm sure." I give him a reassuring smile. "Go. Have fun. Spend some time with your teammates."

"Yeah, I hardly see you," Toby teases with a grin, but I see through his act. "You've been spending all your free time with this one." He nods his head in my direction, not making eye contact with me.

Bishop grins, but it's not a nice one. "Yeah. Just making up for the past two years."

There is clearly something going on, I just don't know what. I want to ask but I'm afraid to because if it's about me, I know I'll do what I can to take myself out of the equation so I don't come between their friendship. And well, I don't want to do that because the idea of losing Bishop so close to losing Toby, guts me.

"Go, go." I laugh it off. "I'll be fine."

"Are you sure?" Bishop asks me again.

"She said she was fine," Toby says in a tone I can't quite place.

Bishop's jaw ticks, and I sigh. "Bye." I turn and leave because I'm not sure what these two will do if I stay any longer.

Grabbing my headphones out of my hoodie pocket, I put some music on and spend the next hour cleaning up. By the time I'm ready to leave, it's nine.

I send Bee a text to see if she can come get me, but she sends one back telling me she's stuck at her house. Her grandparents showed up for a surprise visit and she has been trying to leave for the past two hours with no luck.

WIFEY FOR LIFEY

That woman doesn't stop talking. I love her, I really do. But If I have to hear about her BINGO buddies anymore, I'm going to pull my hair out. Although, the drama with old people be popping.

Biting my lips together, I snort out a laugh. God, I love that girl.

ME

Tell me all about it later. I'll text Jonas. Good luck and hope you're able to escape soon.

Pulling up Jonas' number, I call him instead of text. "Hey, Lills. What's up?"

"Any chance you could come get me from the rec center?" I ask, as the sounds of guys laughing in the background fills my ear.

"Yeah, sure. How come one of the guys didn't take you home before they came here?"

I sigh. "They wanted to hang out, but I still had to clean up. I told them I'd have Bee pick me up, but she's stuck with her grandparents. Things were getting tense between the three of us, so I sent them away."

"Ahh, yeah, I could see that."

"What do you mean?"

"They've been throwing backhanded insults at each other all night. I'm not the only one who's noticed either."

"Fuck." I sigh heavily. This is what I was afraid of.

"Oh, shit. Did you just swear? It must be really bad." Jonas chuckles.

"Sometimes I swear," I grumble, shutting some of the lights off in the building. "Are you coming or not?"

"Yes." He chuckles. "I'm already in my car."

We hang up and I finish closing the place down before going outside to wait for Jonas.

He pulls up five minutes later, parks the car and gets out, jogging over to me. "What are you doing?" I ask as he scoops me up in his arms, giving me a big hug.

"I've missed you," he murmurs against the side of my head. "And, it sounds like you could use a best friend hug."

I grin against his shoulders and drop my skate bag so I can wrap my arm around his waist. "Thanks," I sigh, settling into the hug. "I've missed you too. I'm sorry we haven't hung out much the past week."

"It's okay," he says, pulling back from the hug. "You're working on your crush with Bishop, and I'm making progress with his sister."

My eyes widen. "W-what? I don't have a crush on Bishop."

Jonas barks out a laugh. "Yeah, okay, babe." He pats me on the head, giving me a sympathetic look and bends over, grabbing my bag.

"I don't!" I insist as I follow him to the car.

He opens up his back door, tosses my bag in, and then opens the passenger door for me.

He gives me a look and tilts his head to the side.

I glare at him as I slide into the car. He closes the door behind me and walks around to his side.

"Okay, maybe I do," I mutter as we pull away from the rink. "Is it bad that I do? Even though I'm still hung up on Toby?"

"It's okay to like more than one person."

"I know that, but did it have to be my stepbrother and my best friend?" I groan, rubbing at my face. "I feel like I'm coming between them. I can see it, too. It's only been a month since school started and already I see a rift between them. And it all started when I came back into the picture."

"Don't." He shakes his head. "You are not to blame. I'm not sure what's going on between them exactly, but I have noticed Toby has been changing. He's always in a shitty mood and he snaps at people if they look at him wrong. He's a fucking goalie, but he's been getting into fights with his own teammates. Your dad looks ready to kick his ass, too."

My gut twists and my eyes fill with tears. It's hard to stay mad at Toby when my heart aches for him in more than one way. There's more going on with him, and maybe instead of pushing him away, I should try being there for him, to help him through whatever it is that's causing him so much stress.

I would hate myself if I found out there's something bigger going on with him and I abandoned him.

"Why does everything have to be so fucked up?" I sigh, leaning my head against the window.

"So, about that crush on Bishop." Jonas chuckles.

I close my eyes and smile. "I like him. A lot. He makes me laugh, smile, and feel so damn good about myself. He goes out of his way to bring me my favorite coffee every day. He makes sure to text me good morning and goodnight, but he also messages me all damn day." I open my eyes and look over at Jonas. "And tonight... we kissed."

His eyes widen, and he huffs out a surprised laugh. "Well, shit. How was it?"

My nose scrunches and there's a brief pause. "Why isn't this weird?"

"Why isn't *what* weird?" he asks, brows furrowing.

"Me and you, exes, talking about me kissing a different guy."

He chuckles. "Because we're best friends, Lilly, and always will be. Now, stop avoiding the question and spill like I'm Bee, because we both know you won't be gushing about this with her."

Guilt hits me. I know Bee wouldn't hate me if I ended up dating her brother; I think she would be happy because her brother has had shitty taste in women in the past. But I feel bad because I haven't told her about my feelings for Bishop yet.

They're still so new, and I'm still crazy confused about so much in my life right now. Before today, I didn't even know for sure if Bishop liked me back. I take a deep breath, pushing away all the worry and anxiety and, instead, just focus on answering his question.

"It was amazing." I can't help but smile. "We were racing and I lost, of course." I laugh. "I forgot how to stop and was ready to crash into the boards, but he stopped me. We fell to the ice, and I landed on top of him. Then… well, one thing led to another, and we kissed. It was everything and now I know I'm falling hard for him. I'm afraid it's all going to go to shit and he's going to reject me, like Toby did. Even though he didn't tonight, there's still time and—"

"Lilly, breathe. You're spiraling," Jonas interrupts, putting his hands on my knee and giving it a gentle squeeze. I suck in a breath, thankful for his help. "Look, I might not know Toby all that well, but I do know Bishop. I consider him a friend, and he doesn't seem like the kind of guy who would do all this for a girl he didn't like. Even a friend as awesome as you. You've been friends for years, right? Think about it, was he ever like this growing up?"

I do think about it. He's always been sweet, caring, and protective of me, but we were never like this. "No."

"I think you need to relax and see how things go, moving forward. But he likes you, Lilly. Only a fool or someone who was blind wouldn't be able to see it."

"Thanks, Jonas." I lean over and give my bestie a hug when we pull up to the dorm.

"Any time, Lills. You know I love you. You're my girl. Just not that way," he jokes, winking at me. I roll my eyes, grinning brightly at my supportive best friend.

"Goodnight."

The rest of the night, I try to pass the time by reading. Bee comes back an hour after I do and tells me all the old people drama.

We end up falling asleep around midnight, but I wake up around two, needing to use the bathroom.

Quickly, I head down the hall to do my thing and on my way back, I hear a noise from behind the guys' door.

Inching towards the door, I concentrate on listening. "Lilly," a ragged whimper sounds from behind the door, and my heart drops.

Worry fills me and I try the door handle, but it's locked. I rush back to my room to grab their spare key and my phone before going back over.

When I slip into their room, I find Toby tossing and turning in his bed. Sounds of distress come from him and my worry for him grows worse. "Toby," I whisper his name, and he replies by saying mine in a desperate plea.

At this moment, nothing else matters. I place my stuff on his bedside table and sit down next to him. "Shhh." I brush the sweaty hair away from his forehead. His brow pinches like he's in pain.

"Lilly," he murmurs. "Lilly."

"I'm here," I reassure, tears spilling down my cheeks. I feel helpless. He's in pain, and I want to take it away. What happened to make him have these night terrors, and what do they have to do with me?

I crawl into bed with him, and his arms wrap around me automatically, pulling me closely to him in a tight embrace.

Closing my eyes, I let him. Because even though this isn't a good time, even though this man confuses the hell out of me, I would still do anything for him. There's nowhere else in the world I'd rather be than in his arms like this.

"Sleep," I whisper, kissing him on the top of his pec. "I'm here."

He lets out a heavy sigh, like all the demons are being swept away now that I'm here.

Every second that passes, I'm painfully aware of how hard it is to be this close to him and know he's not mine.

"I love you," I whisper. "I'm here."

But right now, in the dead of night, in the pitch-dark room, I'll pretend that he's mine and I'm his. Because if this is all I can get, I'll take it.

CHAPTER TWENTY-SEVEN

TOBIAS

When I wake up, I know I'm not alone.

Blinking the sleep from my eyes, I take a moment to get my bearings. For a moment, I feared I fucked up big time and brought home a random puck bunny with me. The thought makes my stomach sink.

After the rink last night, Bishop and I went back to the hockey house. I thought we could hang out, but he avoided me as much as possible.

So, feeling bad for myself, I got wasted. Some of the puck bunnies were there and took every chance to flirt with me. I don't think I gave them any indication I was interested, but they're relentless.

When I look down, I don't see some random face. I see a familiar one, framed by blonde hair. I take a deep breath, staring at the dusting of freckles scattered over her nose and under her eyes. I've counted them a ton of times like a total creeper, and it's then that I know I didn't do anything stupid.

Because there's no way in hell I would have fucked Lilly last night and not remember it. The memory of being with her is something that would be tattooed into my mind forever.

She's sleeping softly, her head on my chest and my arm wrapped around her waist. In this moment, everything feels right in the world. I forget about the fact that she can't stand to be around me, that even looking at me hurts her. I forget about my past and my issues, which are preventing me from being with this amazing woman.

At this moment, it's just me and her. So, like a creep, I just watch her sleep. I don't care if I'm late for practice, hell, I don't care if I miss it completely.

It's like when your pet comes and cuddles with you. You're stuck there, unable to move for any reason because you would be a monster for disturbing their cuteness.

Only in this situation, I would be an idiot for fucking up this small bit of time I have with her. You would have to pry my cold, dead body away right now.

Bishop stayed at the hockey house last night, and I walked my drunk ass home, mumbling to myself like a crazy person about how horrible of a man I am.

I know I don't have the right to feel sorry for myself, but it's really fucking hard not to feel like a bag of shit and a crappy human with everything going on.

I smile down at my sleeping beauty. Her lips are parted, sending soft breaths of air skating across my chest. Her hand is on my abs, right above the waistline of my sleep shorts. I pray she doesn't move her hand any lower because it's not just morning wood that has me hard. I'm fucked up, I know it. But I can't stop thinking of that kiss and of her grinding against me until we both came apart.

I love this woman more than anything in this world. She is

my whole heart. And I've fucked it all up. She wants me and god, knowing that is everything.

But a part of me wishes the feelings were one-sided and she only thought of me as a friend; it might hurt a little less knowing I was the only one in pain.

I'm hurting her, and that's the last thing I ever wanted to do. Yet that's all I seem to be able to do.

At first, I told myself I was protecting her by keeping us apart. That I was giving her a chance at a normal life with a man who could give her the world. A life without any judgmental whispers and people turning her into a pariah. A chance to be with a man who doesn't have so many secrets, who's not fucked in the head like I am. Someone who doesn't have anger issues and could lose their shit at the drop of a hat.

Someone who isn't *me*.

But when I think of her with another man, it makes me fucking feral, like I want to beat them to a bloody pulp, proving to myself even more that I'm not good for her.

Lilly is so damn kind and loving; she's smart and funny. She's fucking everything, the whole package, and I'd just bring her down. I'd snuff out her light. Maybe not now, but eventually.

Right now, however, I'm going to be selfish and pretend for just a moment that Lilly is my girl. I mean, she is, she always will be, but not completely.

Slowly, my eyes take her in, committing everything to memory. Would it be weird to grab my phone and take a photo, so that I can look back on it later when life gets too hard?

Yeah, okay, that's fucking creepy; I won't do that.

We stay like this for a long time. Her sleeping, me watching and enjoying the small amount of time I'm not hurting.

After a while, my hand itches to touch her. Using my free hand, I reach up and run my thumb against her lower lip. On instinct, her tongue darts out, licking across where I'd just touched, then over the tip of my thumb.

My fucking cock twitches, and I hold back a groan as she

snuggles deeper into me. Looking over at the clock, I see that it's five thirty. I need to be at practice in a half hour.

This isn't the first time I've found Lilly in bed with me. Bishop has told me she's come in before during my nightmares and was able to settle me down.

She seems to be the only one who can do that. I know about the times she would come into my bed when I would sleep over at the house. A few times I'd wake up in the middle of the night and would assume it was because she just wanted things to be like old times. And just like now, I took the opportunity to hold her in the way my soul is aching to.

I'm not sure how I feel when it comes to her knowing about the nightmares, though.

I'm about to say fuck it and go back to sleep so this can last longer when Lilly moves again, and then her head pops up.

"Morning," the word comes out at the end of a sleepy yawn.

She looks up at me, recognition taking over her face as her eyes go wide. She goes to move away from me, but my arm wraps around her, holding her to me. I'm not ready for her to leave. I'm not ready to let this go, to let *her* go. I don't think I ever will be.

"Morning," I reply, and an adorable blush takes over her cheeks.

I won't draw attention to why she's in my arms, or even the fact that she is. I don't want to spook her, to put any pressure on her.

"What's your plan for today?" I ask casually.

"Oh." She blinks a few times, surprised by that question. "It's Monday, and my first class isn't until ten. So, I guess school, then studying."

I nod, reaching up to tuck some hair behind her ear. This, I've fucking missed this. It might be small, but god, it feels like old times. I didn't know how much I craved to have this again, even if it's just a casual conversation between us.

"Wanna come to practice?" I take the chance to ask because I need more time with her. It's been hell knowing she's across the hall and I never get to see her. I had plans to make things better between us when she came to school, but it all went to shit before I even got the chance to start earning her forgiveness. Maybe I can start now?

She chews on her lower lip, and I have to swallow back a hungry growl. Fuck, she's so damn sexy, all cute and sleepy.

And then she surprises the hell out of me. "Sure." I thought she would tell me no and leave. A swell of happiness fills me as I try really hard not to smile like a love sick fool. "Do I have enough time to shower and change?" She looks over at the time and curses. "Okay, not a shower, but I do need to change."

This time I do smile. "Go change, you can shower before your class if you think you have to, but I think you're perfect just like this."

That blush gets deeper, and my smile gets bigger. She says nothing, but nods and gets up.

Immediately, I miss the warmth of her body, the smell of her coconut shampoo dissipating the moment she's gone.

As I watch her slip out of my room, I feel like a piece of me goes with her.

Sighing heavily, I throw the blankets off and sit up. I groan as a throbbing pain starts up in my head. I really need to stop drinking but fuck, it helps dull… well, everything. It's too damn tempting to keep drinking.

Grabbing something for the pain, I wash the pill down with a bottle of water and quickly throw on some sweatpants, a T-shirt, and a hoodie from my floor. Then I grab clean clothes to change into after practice and stuff them into my duffle bag, along with my shower stuff.

When I'm done, I haul the bag over my shoulder and grab my phone before heading out into the hall, which is when Lilly steps out of her room. "Ready?" I ask her.

She smiles and nods. We stand there awkwardly for a

moment before I laugh. "Alright, Little Flower, lead the way," I say playfully, waving my arm in front of me.

Something flashes in her eyes but I can't make out what it is as we start walking down the hall toward the elevator.

When we get outside, I stop and ask. "Do you want to walk or drive?"

"Do we have time to walk?" she asks me, checking her phone.

"Yeah, I think we will be fine. And walking means stopping to get a sugar cookie latte," I taunt with a grin.

Her eyes light up and I know I've won the extra time with her. "Damn it, I can't say no to that. Alright, let's walk." She giggles and holy shit, my heart just stopped. Fuck… fuck! I want to hear that again, all the time, every fucking day.

We walk in silence for a little bit. It's still really early, so not many people are up. The campus looks like a ghost town. But thankfully the coffee shop opens up at five a.m. because of all the athletes who have early morning practice.

"So, how are classes going?" I ask her.

"Good. Harder than I thought. Although I'm not sure why I'm surprised because it's college. And it's nothing like high school." She laughs. "But I'm enjoying all my classes. Just sucks that I'm spending most of my free time studying." *And the rest of it with Bishop.*

I'm jealous and pissed off that he gets to see her all the time. The two of them are so close now, I feel like he's taking my place, and I fucking hate it. But it's my fault; I'm the dumbass who thought it would be a good idea to ask him to do it.

I thought that if he used up her free time she wouldn't have time to date. And sure, it worked because Ryan and her are only friends. Except now the two of them are so close, I can't help but worry it might become more.

Bishop isn't one to date, but if anyone could change his mind, it would be Lilly. Fuck, I can't think about that right now.

"I feel like I hardly see my friends unless they're with me

while we study. Bee has been bugging me to go out and party with her this weekend, but I'm not sure," she prattles on.

Parties mean drinking and guys hitting on her. That idea makes my fist clench. "Well, that's not a good idea." I laugh. "Don't want to be hung over for our first game."

"Shit." She giggles. "I almost forgot. And you're right. Nothing worse than feeling like death in an arena full of crazy hockey fans."

"Hey, they have a good reason to be crazy. We're fucking amazing." I grin.

She raises a brow. "From what Jonas says, your practices have been shit." *That little fucker.* He's not wrong though, I have been in a really bad place the past few weeks, but things are looking up now, and I feel great. And it's all because my best friend is talking to me again. All is right in the world. At least for now, and I'll take it.

"That's a little hiccup. I have a feeling things are going to get better. You'll see. Today will be good," I tell her with a wide grin.

She smiles and shakes her head. We arrive at the coffee shop and order. Lilly goes to pull out her card to pay, but I quickly tap mine.

"Thanks."

"Of course."

We get our coffees to go, continuing our walk to the arena.

"It's so weird being here, you know?" she muses, looking around the campus. "I feel like I blinked and now I'm eighteen, in college and like… an adult." She shivers in disgust, making both of us laugh.

"I know what you mean. Being an adult sucks."

"Right!" She looks at me with wide eyes. "I didn't sign up for this."

Grinning like a fool, my heart races. This! This is what I missed. I need my Little Flower.

"So, are you excited about your first game of the year?" she asks me.

"I am. I've been dying to kick RVU's asses. I fucking hate those guys." I shake my head. They're fucking grade-A assholes for what they did to Rodney, and I can't wait until they get what's coming to them.

I've been waiting for one of their team members to come to our hockey house so I can kick their asses, but they're all a bunch of pussies off the ice.

"You guys still have Raccoon. Did they contact you about him yet?"

I shake my head. "No, but they know we have him. Bishop sent them a selfie, but they haven't said anything back. We've made our demands, but I think they're at a standstill, wondering if a goat is worth the heap of shit they're going to get into. Doesn't matter if they don't do the trade, we still plan on getting justice for our boy."

"Good. I think bullies like them need a good dose of reality. It's scary that cruel people like that can be walking around the rest of the population, ready to focus all their wrath on an unsuspecting person. I'd understand if maybe they had a mental health disorder with legit reasons for their anger, but even people with bipolar disorder or borderline personality disorder don't bully people for the hell of it. Some people are just bad people."

"I agree. I can't speak for them, but I don't think it's any mental health issues that make them that way, just spoiled rich kids with too much of daddy's money and they let that power go to their heads."

"That's sad. We come from money, but Mom made sure to raise us to not depend on it."

"One of the things I admire her for." I nod. "She's an amazing mom. I'm glad to have her."

Lilly smiles up at me. "Me too."

We get to the rink and Lilly takes off towards the ice to talk to her dad while I head into the locker room.

"Good morning," I greet everyone as I burst into the room,

feeling really fucking good right now. There's a smile on my face that none of these fuckers are going to be able to wipe off.

The whole locker room goes quiet as everyone looks up at me. "Well, someone's in a good mood," Wilson chuckles.

"Damn right, I am. The sun is shining, the birds are chirping, and the world is just fucking fantastic," I reply, winking at him before heading over to my cubby. I'm a little late, so everyone is already geared up and ready to go.

"Alright, who is that man? Did the aliens take Munro and replace him with... that." Baker waves a hand at me.

"Haha." I laugh, pulling off my shirt.

"Hey, man," Bishop says, coming over to me. He's also in his gear. "You good?"

I scoff. "Hell yeah, I'm good. Why wouldn't I be?"

He raises his brows and I turn away to change into my practice gear. "Because for the past few weeks you've been in a rotten mood. And now, you're practically vibrating. What changed from your shitty mood last night to now?"

He's looking at me with suspicion, and I don't like it.

"Whatever it is, keep it coming. Bitchy Munro makes hockey practice suck!" Baker shouts as the rest of the guys head out.

"I woke up with the girl of my dreams sleeping in my arms." I give him a grin. "Best feeling in the fucking world."

His brows furrow. "Lilly slept in your bed?"

"Why, jealous?" I chuckle, a part of me hoping he is.

"No." He rolls his eyes. "I'm guessing you had another nightmare? You did drink a lot last night."

"Does it matter how she ended up there?" I snap. He goes to put a hand on my shoulder, but I jump back, not wanting to be touched.

His brows furrow even more. He looks around then back at me. "Look, man, I don't mean to pry, or push, or accuse you of anything. But... are you off your meds again? Because you've been pretty down for the past few weeks, and I thought it was because of everything happening with you and Lilly. But if you're off your meds again, it would explain a lot."

That pisses me off. "What? I can't be in a good mood without being accused of being off my meds? Fuck you, Bishop, I'm not going to let you ruin my good mood."

He lets out a harsh sigh as I sit down to lace up my skates. "I'm not trying to be an asshole, okay. It's just... I care about you, Toby. You're my best friend in the whole fucking world, and I don't want to see you hurting or suffering. But if you're off your meds, you need to go back on them. It's not healthy or safe."

"Fuck you. I don't need you telling me what to do. I'm a fucking adult, and I can take care of myself."

"Toby," he growls.

I just grin at him. "I'm fine, man. Everything is good. And my girl is waiting in the arena to watch me play, so if you'll excuse me."

I'm not letting him ruin my mood. This is the best I've felt in weeks. So what if I'm off my meds? I fucking hate them. They made me feel like a zombie, always wanting to sleep. And I never want to eat anything because I always felt sick.

I didn't mean to go off them. When Lilly started here, everything got shaken up. One missed day led to another and another and... well, it turned into weeks. But I don't need them. I'm fine. I feel fucking fine.

And now I'm going to go show my girl why I'm the best fucking goalie this team has ever had. Fuck everyone else.

CHAPTER TWENTY-EIGHT

LILLIANNA

WHEN I WOKE UP THIS MORNING, I WASN'T EXPECTING TO STILL BE IN Toby's bed. But then I remember that I forgot to set the alarm to wake myself up so I could be out of there before he woke up.

I'm glad I didn't though. Waking up in Toby's arms… felt good. Too good. And maybe that should be enough reason for me to take a step back and put some distance between us again. But I was seeing the old Toby in that moment, and I found myself wanting to hold onto it.

So when he invited me to practice, I agreed. I also wanted to see Bishop, so that was another reason why I agreed.

I was up anyway, and I knew there was no going back to sleep. Not that I needed it. Any night spent in Toby's arms, always guaranteed me an amazing night's rest. *How messed up is that?*

"Hey, Dad."

Jax looks up at me, and his face splits into a grin. "Hey, sweetheart. What on earth are you doing here so early?" He chuckles.

"Toby asked me to tag along, so I did." I shrug.

His brows jump. "Are you two getting along better?"

"I don't know," I sigh. "It's all very, very complicated. I just don't know where I stand with him right now."

His face softens, and he nods. "Just be patient with him. He'll come around."

I narrow my eyes. "Why is everyone telling me that? Is there something I don't know? Why are you all so adamant about the fact that this is some kind of phase Toby will grow out of?"

He looks at me for a second, like he's contemplating saying something, but then the guys all start making their way onto the ice.

"Dad?" I urge.

"We'll talk later, okay?" He kisses the side of my head and starts barking orders.

Huffing out a sigh, I find a seat in the stadium and get comfy. With my hands wrapped around my coffee and my knees tucked close to my chest, I watch as the guys warm up to start running their drills.

Toby comes out onto the ice a second later, decked out head to toe in his gear, with Bishop following after him.

For the next hour, my attention is split between Toby and Bishop. Toby blocks every shot sent his way, and I cheer like every one is the winning block. The whole team seems to be in better spirits, getting excited for their teammate.

And Bishop is like a fucking demon on the ice. He blocks and steals the puck, protecting his goalie like his life depends on it. Anything that does manage to get past Bishop or the other defenseman, Bowman, Toby blocks with the same intensity that Bishop uses to protect his goalie.

I'm on the edge of my seat the whole time, getting just as excited as the rest of the team.

By the time they're done, the whole room is vibrating with positive energy. "Now that's what I'm talking about!" Jax praises them. "I wanna see more of that on Saturday. Go hit the showers, I'll see you all tomorrow."

Licking my lips, I watch as Bishop slowly follows the others off the ice. He takes his helmet off, flicking his dark, sweaty hair out of his face. His eyes find mine, and he winks before disappearing with the others.

My whole body heats as my heart flutters. Damn it, I'm crushing on that boy hard. *How have I never noticed just how sexy he is?*

"Toby," Jax calls out, getting my attention. "Find me when you're done. We need to talk."

Toby takes his helmet off, his hair dripping with sweat and equally just as sexy as Bishop. *I'm hopeless.*

Toby flashes Jax a smile. "Sure thing, Coach." His eyes flick up to mine. "Told you I was awesome, Little Flower. That was all for you. Also, I hope you plan on attending every game now, because I think I just found my good luck charm." He chuckles as my eyes go wide.

Oh, hell. This can't be good. Being a hockey player's good luck charm comes with more responsibilities than I'd like to take on right now. Players and fans take it very seriously, to the point I may fear for my life if I don't do it.

Okay, not really, but I'd have some pretty pissed off people if I don't show up and they lose. I know they would very much blame it on me if Toby tells anyone I'm his good luck charm.

"Well," Jax starts, pausing to chuckle. "Guess I'll be seeing you more often."

I groan, getting up and walking the few steps down to him. "I'm not coming to every morning practice," I warn him.

"Wouldn't expect you to. Although, the guys may bug you.

It's the games that are important. But you know you don't actually have to. No one will force you."

"Nah, it's okay. I like watching them play. And it's kind of cool to be someone's good luck charm." Even if it's Toby's. "But, hey, if you lose the game on Saturday, I'm free!" I giggle as he glares at me.

"Lillianna Tatum, do not put those bad vibes out into the universe."

"What are you going to do?" I ask, raising a brow with a smirk.

"Can't ground you. You're too old for that. But you sure can babysit your brothers Friday night."

"Okay. But why?"

"Chase and Rain went rogue and got last minute tickets to go see the Backstreet Boys." He grins.

"Ahh, old people music." I nod in understanding, giggling when he gives me a look of horror.

"You take that back, young lady."

"Okay, fine. Not old people, just… vintage." I laugh harder when he pulls me into his arms and messes up my hair.

"Brat. So, babysit?"

"Yes." I grin as I fix my hair. "I miss the little snots. Well, the twins are snots, Bennett's a good kid."

Jax's face softens. "He is."

"Has he come to you or Brody yet?"

Jax sighs and takes a seat on the bench. "No. But I found him crying the other night. He was ripping up all the photos of him and Easton." Jax looks up at me with a stricken expression. "It's killing your dad and me that Bennett won't come to us. He's struggling with his sexuality, and we want to be there for him. He's hurting, but any time we try to bring it up, he shuts us down."

Tears sting the back of my eyes, and I give my dad a watery smile. "I'll talk to him again."

"Would you? He seems to do better after one of your talks."

"Of course. I hate that he's suffering. Maybe I can convince him to talk to you guys."

"Hopefully it's before your dad kicks Easton's ass."

"He wouldn't." I gape at him.

He gives me a blank look. "This is Brody we're talking about, what do you think?"

"Oh, god," I sigh.

"Yup. But don't worry about it. I'll tell your mom you said yes."

"I'll call her later."

As we leave the arena, Bishop is waiting by the front door but Toby is nowhere to be seen. "Where's Toby?" Jax asks.

"He took off. Why?"

Jax lets out a frustrated huff and shakes his head. "I told him to stay back. He's been dodging talking to us for weeks now."

"Why?" I ask.

They both look at me, then each other. "Just hockey stuff," Jax says, but I feel like he's not telling me the truth.

"Come on, Shorty, I'll take you back to the dorms." Bishop wraps his arm around my shoulder, steering me away from my dad.

I want to ask questions, but the feeling of his arm around me and his freshly showered smell distracts me.

Bishop Grant, what are you doing to me?

Friday, classes are over for the day, and I'm heading out of my dorm to leave for the house when Toby exits his room at the same time. "Where are you off to?" He leans against the frame of the door, one of those half grins on his face that make my belly heat.

Things have been different between us the past few days. He's in a way better mood and seems more like the Toby I grew up with. I should be keeping my distance because it still hurts to be around him, but I'm too captivated by seeing the old version of himself again.

We've been texting. Nothing like Bishop and me, but it's more than we have in years.

"Dad asked me to watch the boys tonight so they can all go out to the city," I tell him as I lock up my door.

"How come you didn't ask me to go with you?"

"Because I'm eighteen and I can babysit two little brats and a teenager on my own." I raise my brows, grinning at him.

He sticks out his lower lip and pouts. "I'm hurt, Little Flower. I wanna come too."

I chew the inside of my cheek at the use of that nickname. "Then come with me," I find myself saying.

"Really?" he looks so damn hopeful, I don't have the heart to change my mind.

"I mean, if you don't have anything better to do on a Friday night. Aren't the guys throwing a party?" I'm not going to tell him Bishop asked me if I wanted him to come along too. I turned him down because as much as I enjoy spending time with Bishop, I don't want to make myself his whole world. He should be enjoying his college years by going out, drinking, and having fun.

I am a little jealous, though. The idea of puck bunnies or other girls hanging around him and flirting with him makes my stomach drop. But I shouldn't be upset because he's not my boyfriend. He can do whatever he wants.

"I drank enough last weekend. I'm good. Just give me a second." I wait in the hall while he goes back into his room. A few seconds later, he comes back out, pulling a hoodie over his head. With his arms raised, I can see a bit of his lower belly and abs. Hell, that V…

"Lilly?" Toby's amused voice has my eyes snapping up to his.

Clearing my throat, I turn away and head down to the elevator. I'm glad he doesn't tease me about staring because I know that would ruin the night before it even started.

The ride there is spent talking about practice. He's chatting away, laughing, smiling, holding the conversation all on his own.

I don't remember the last time I've seen him like this. It's different. But it's helping to ease the awkwardness between us. If anything, it's like none of that even happened. At least, for him. Maybe, just for tonight, I can forget about it too and just enjoy a night with Toby and my brothers.

"Toby!" Raiden and Isaiah cheer, rushing towards the car as Toby exits.

When he hears them, he runs over to the twins, shouting, "Hey, little dudes!" He picks them both up and spins them around.

I follow after going over to my parents, who are standing by the front door watching Toby with an odd expression. "Hey."

"Hey, Lillypad. Thanks for watching the boys," Theo says, giving me a quick hug and kiss on top of my head. "We'll see you when we get back."

He heads over to Toby just as he puts the twins down. They go running back into the house, but I stand there and watch as Theo and Toby start having a heated discussion.

"Hey, sweetheart, why don't you come inside?" Mom suggests, wrapping her arm around my shoulder and urging me toward the front door.

"Oh-okay," I say hesitantly, my eyes still on Toby. He looks pissed, getting in his dad's face. "What's that about?"

"Oh, nothing, just boy stuff."

I love my mom, but is she for real right now? I'm not stupid, and I know when people are keeping things from me. However, now is not the time to be bringing that up.

"Hey, Benny," I greet my little brother when I find him sitting at the kitchen island eating an apple.

"Lilly!" My heart clenches when I see how happy he is to see me. He gives me a big hug, and I hold him tightly, hoping he always remembers I'm a safe place if he needs it.

"Hey, kiddo," Chase says, his blond hair styled back.

"Hey, Dad. Are you going to audition to be a part of the band or what?" I giggle at how decked out he is.

"Just looking good, baby girl." He winks. "Your mom loves it."

"Eww." I scrunch up my nose.

"Don't scar the kid, Chase." Brody slaps him on the shoulder lightly as he passes.

"Oh, you already have." I laugh. "No way that doesn't happen living with a poly family."

"What happened that made you scarred?" Bennett asks, looking at us.

"If you have to ask, you're lucky kid." I laugh. "Just... if you hear noises coming from their room, run the other way."

His face morphs into horror. "Oh, god." He shakes his head. "Gross!" He takes off running and Chase cackles.

"Sex is a perfectly normal and healthy thing, Bennett!"

"Oh, so you do know what that word means?" I laugh, crossing my arms and giving him a look.

His laughter stops, and he shoots me a glare. "Nope. Don't know the word. Not when it comes to you. It doesn't exist and neither does the action. Be good tonight, and no boys over."

I roll my eyes as he leaves to go join Mom and Rain by the front door.

"That man, I swear he will forever be a man child." Brody shakes his head.

"You all love it." I giggle. "And I know Mom wouldn't change it for the world." Chase wraps Mom up in his arms from behind, pulling her close, and peppering kisses all over her face. She giggles, smiling wide.

I want that. I want love like my parents have. Every one of their relationships is different but the one thing they all have in common is how madly in love they are with each other.

"Come on!" Jax shouts as he joins the others. "We gotta go or we're going to be late."

"Boys!" Rain shouts. "Come say goodbye."

The boys all run in like a herd of cats, jumping all over, laughing, and smiling at our parents as they wish them a good night and say their goodbyes.

Toby comes in, a smile on his face as if he wasn't just shouting at his dad, and Theo comes in after him. They share a look before Theo says goodbye to the boys.

"Alright," Toby starts when everyone leaves. "What do we wanna do?"

"Video games!" the twins shout at the same time.

"No," Bennett groans. "We always play video games. Can't we do something outside?"

"Pool!" they shout and beeline for the back.

"Are you okay with that?" I ask Bennett.

"Better than video games." He shrugs.

"Dude. Are you okay?" Toby chuckles. "Nothing is better than video games."

Bennett gives him a weird look then looks at me. "Do we still hate him?"

My eyes widen, and Toby's face drops, hurt morphing his handsome features. "Bennett," I hiss. "We never hated him. Ever."

"Okay, fine, are we still *mad* at him?" he huffs, crossing his arms.

My eyes flick over to Toby, he too seems to wait for my answer. "No," I finally confess after an intense moment. "We aren't."

"Okay," Bennett says wearily. He gives Toby a glare. "I'm still watching you, though."

Bennett heads outside, and I let out a heavy sigh. "Sorry about that."

"Don't be." Toby moves to stand next to me as we watch the boys go into the pool house to get changed, and I pray the little shits don't touch my stuff. "He's protective of his big sister. He loves you. You're his best friend, I get it. I hurt you, therefore, he was mad at me. He had every right. But I meant it when I said I want things to change between us. Asking you to forget what happened was wrong and mean. I could never, and would never, forget it. I don't want you to either, because that would mean it meant nothing when it did. It meant everything to me. But there's a lot of reasons, that I'm not going to go into right now, that led us to where we are. So can we start fresh? We will go as slow as you want. At least have a fun night with the goobers?"

"Deal." It's all I can say because this is not the right time to overthink things or get emotional.

Swimming was a bad idea because for the last hour, I've been trying to keep my eyes off Toby. It's hard, okay? He's so damn hot, and his tattoos are actually really cool, and well... they are even better because of the person they are on and, ugh!

"You got a little drool there," Bennett teases. My eyes snap away from Toby and over to him.

"Bennett!" I huff out a disbelieving laugh.

"I don't see how our parents haven't seen it yet." He shakes his head and goes back to reading his book.

"Rain knows." I sigh, my attention going to check on the

twins. Toby is playing with them, tossing them around in the pool.

"Rain knows a lot of things," Bennett replies. "I love the Dads and Mom, but… there's just something about Rain. It's like how I feel with you. I can tell her anything and I don't feel like I'm talking to a parent, but a friend."

"It's the same for me." I smile over at him. "But then she turns on mama mode when need be."

"Yeah." He nods. "She can be scary."

We both burst out laughing. "Want to order some pizza?" I ask.

"Yes!" he says excitedly, slamming his book shut. "Mom has been on this weird healthy food kick, and we're all dying over here."

"Well, damn, I'm glad I'm not here then." I laugh.

"I'm not." Hs face drops. "I miss you."

Getting up, I pull him to his feet and wrap my arms around him. "I'm always here for you. Just say the word, I will come running."

I tell Toby to get the boys out of the water and dressed before the pizza comes.

We end up eating out back at the deck table.

As we laugh and joke around, I feel happy, at home. Like for even just this moment everything is right in the world. I can't remember the last time just us kids spent time together.

"We need to do this more often," Toby comments as we head out to the grassy part of the backyard to play a game of tag. It's mainly to get the twins to run off their energy because we may have made ice cream sundaes after pizza and are now regretting it as the sugar rush hits them.

I look up at him to find him smiling. And shit, it's a nice sight. It's something I haven't seen much of before this week. "I agree." I smile back, my emotions at war.

A part of me wishes we could go back before that movie night and be oblivious to our feelings for one another, but the other part that always played the what-if game is happy to know the outcome, even if it's not what I've hoped for.

"Lilly's 'it' first!" Isaiah shouts.

"Hey." A laugh bubbles out of me. "Why me?"

"Because… girls first," he sing songs.

"Fine, then." I start racing after him. He screams and turns to run away from me.

We take turns tagging one another. Toby is never it for long because the man is a beast with his long legs and speed.

"God, I need to work out more," I tell Bennett as I struggle to breathe, putting my hands on my knees and sucking in deep lungfuls of air.

"You do." He laughs. "You're like an old lady."

"I feel like one too," I groan, standing up to find Toby running towards me. "Shit, he's 'it'. Run!"

Bennett and I break apart as I head for the playset, hiding behind it.

"Come out, Little Flower. There's no point in trying to run. I'm going to get you." He chuckles.

My heart pounds painfully in my chest. Mostly due to the running, but partly because of the man doing the chasing.

"T, I call a timeout," I say as I feel like I'm going to pass out.

"Well, that's not fair." Toby laughs again. "But fine. I grant you your timeout."

When I step out from behind the playset, I frown when I don't see Toby.

"Gotcha," a low, husky voice comes from behind me. I freeze, a full body shiver washes over me as my breathing labors. "Even if you need a timeout and a moment for yourself, I'll always find you, Lilly. I'll always get you."

What the hell does that mean?

I stand there frozen as Toby brushes past me and bends down to pick up one of the twins who's passed out on the grass. "Bedtime," he tells Isaiah and Bennett as he carries Raiden into the house. He pauses at the doorway and looks over at me.

I stare at him, more confused than ever. This man seems to have that power over me.

Is he going to give in to his feelings for me, or is he not and try to salvage some sort of a relationship with me?

That's the thing I hate the most, never knowing where I stand with this man. It's an emotional roller coaster.

One that, even if it is thrilling at times, I'd very much like to get off.

CHAPTER TWENTY-NINE

LILLIANNA

"This is so exciting," Bianca squeals, vibrating with energy as we weave our way through the crowd.

"I forgot how excited hockey fans get on game days," I murmur, holding my arms close to my body as I try to avoid touching as many people as I can.

"There's more people who come to our football games," Ryan huffs. I shoot him a grin over my shoulder, and he rolls his eyes. "Okay, fine, it's about the same."

"You jocks and your rivalries. You attend the same school. Show some spirit." I give him some jazz hands.

He snorts a laugh. "You're too much sometimes."

"Awe, thanks." We stop with the crowd, and I bat my eyelashes up at him.

"You're sure you two aren't dating?" Bianca asks, raising a brow as she looks at the both of us.

"No," we say at the same time. I look at Ryan, and we laugh.

"Could have fooled me," she says with a grin. "You're cute together."

"Sorry, Bee, but we're too hung up on other people. We're meant to be besties."

She narrows her eyes at Ryan. "I already have to fight my brother for her, don't make me fight you too."

Ryan raises his hands in surrender. "I'd never dream of taking your girl away from you."

"You know, being fought over is kind of a turn on," I sing-song, and we all laugh.

The sea of people starts moving again, and we follow along. It feels like forever before we finally make it to the arena seats. "I don't like to toss around my privilege, but sometimes having all your parents work for the school comes in handy." I laugh as we find our VIP seating. We're sitting right next to the penalty box, where all the best action happens, as Bennett likes to say. Best seats in the house to see everything up close and personal.

My parents and Bennett are already seated when we get there. "Hey," I greet my mom. "Where's the twins?"

It's Brody who answers. "They were being a nightmare so your grandparents have them for the night."

"They were not." Mom slaps his arms.

Brody gives her a blank look. "The little shits clogged every toilet in the house because they wanted to see if you could flush sand down them."

My brows raise. "What? Who even thinks to try that?" I ask laughing as I take a seat next to Mom.

She lets out a heavy sigh. "I have no idea. I love those boys with all my heart but, Lilly, I beg of you, please have all girls. You were an angel."

"A sassy little one," Chase adds, leaning forward so he can see me. "But I have to admit, you were pretty damn awesome."

"Were?" I fake offense. "I still am."

"Yeah, you are." Chase chuckles. He looks over at Ryan.

"Hey, Tucker."

"Hey, Coach." Ryan chuckles.

"Still not my daughter's boyfriend?" Chase asks, narrowing his eyes as I roll mine.

"Nope. But, trust me, if I was ready for a girlfriend, she would be my first choice." I'm not sure if he's being serious or if he's just messing with my dad, but Chase narrows his eyes anyways, and Brody growls.

"Oh, stop it, you two. Ryan is a nice guy. And he's a good friend to Lilly. Leave him be."

"I'm watching you, kid." Brody glares at him.

"They're really just big teddy bears." I giggle at Ryan, and he grins.

"Yeah, ones that will claw your eyes out," Brody grumbles.

Bennett gets up and wedges his way between Mom and me. "Our parents are a lot sometimes," he sighs.

"They are." I grin down at him. "But they mean well and love us fiercely."

He nods and puts his head on my shoulder.

We all talk amongst ourselves as the stadium becomes packed. Half of the crowd is dressed in silver, grey, and white SVU jerseys, while the other half is dressed in black and red RVU jerseys.

"I hope Wilson gives Buck a good beat down tonight," Ryan says as the team starts making their way out onto the ice.

My attention is immediately grabbed by both number thirteen, Bishop, and number thirty-five, Toby. Toby skates over towards the net while the others skate around warming up. Bishop starts slapping some pucks around, looking all sexy in his gear. Look, I've never been one for hockey. It's not the game for me, it's the men playing the game that I like.

"Why is that hot?" Bee whispers. Tearing my attention away from Bishop, I follow her gaze over to Toby to see him doing some stretches.

I bite the inside of my cheek as I watch. He looks like he's humping the ice and damn it, Bee is right, it's oddly arousing. Watching his legs spread wide, hips thrusting up and down on the ice as he stretches his muscles out has me thinking all the dirty thoughts. But then it dawns on me what she just said.

"Excuse me?" I glare over at her, and she giggles.

"Down, girl. The one I have my eye on is that one right there." She points to the jersey with the number twenty-six with the name Walker printed across it, Jonas' number.

"How's that going?"

From what I can tell, they're still playing this push and pull game. Bianca, for some reason, is playing hard to get, but Jonas seems to be loving the challenge.

"We kissed last night." She looks over at me with a blush.

"Aaaand…" I say excitedly. "How was it?"

"That man knows how to kiss." She groans, putting her face in her hands. I giggle hard at her reaction. "Why didn't you tell me he was such a good kisser?!"

"Okay, weird." I laugh. "And, well… we never really made out, it was mostly just pecks on the lips."

"Oh, girl, you were missing out." She grins.

My attention is captured by a bang on the glass. Jonas looks at Bee and gives her a wink, blowing her a kiss, making my friend blush a scarlet red.

"God, you two are so grossly cute." I laugh.

Bishop looks up from the ice, his eyes finding mine. He gives me a little head nod and a cocky smirk before going back to do his thing.

"So, when are you going to talk to me about your crush on my brother?"

My eyes go wide, and I look around to see if my parents are listening. Thankfully, they're not; they are busy talking with each other or watching the guys. "What do you mean?" It's my turn to blush as panic sets in. We're leaning over Ryan at this point to talk, but he just huffs out a laugh.

She gives me a knowing look. "Babe, I'm not blind. I see how he looks at you, it's not how a best friend looks at another. Plus, he's spending all of his free time with you. I haven't seen him flirt with another girl in weeks, and when you're not looking, he stares at you like a damn creeper."

My blush deepens and my belly flips. "Are you mad?" I whisper, praying like hell she isn't.

"No." She shakes his head. "I'd do the whole 'if you hurt my brother I'll hurt you speech,' but I'm not worried about that. But I swear to god if he hurts you, I'll do a repeat act with the baseball bat. No babies for him."

We both burst into giggles, and I'm so damn relieved she doesn't hate me. But that's what I love about Bianca, she's chill and easy going but also very protective over the ones she loves.

"I just ask you not to make out in front of me."

"I don't even know what we are." I sigh. "But I'll let you know when I do."

"What is this about a baseball bat?" Ryan asks, looking at us with an amused look.

"You had to be there." Bianca waves him off.

As if I can feel his eyes on me, I glance over to find Toby looking this way. I'm not sure if he's looking at me or Ryan, with the way he's standing ramrod straight.

Toby has been different. After the boys went to bed last night, we hung out and played cards. It was honestly the best time I've had in years with him. I was just so happy to be spending time with him, seeing my old friend back, I forgot all about my feelings for him. That was until I crawled into my bed and couldn't sleep for hours afterwards because all I could think about was him. Then Bishop, then the both of them.

Toby was blowing up my phone today with text messages after he dropped me off at the dorm before he went to the hockey house to meet up with the guys.

Some of them were bringing up random things we did as kids, putting a smile on my face and making me laugh. Others, were him updating me on everything he was doing.

It's not that the way he's acting is bad, it's just different and out of nowhere. I don't hate it, but I can't help but question it.

And from the look on his face right now, he might be back to the way he's been acting for weeks. The mood changes with him are not something I'm used to, and I don't know if I'm a fan.

"Oh my god!" I gasp as Bishop body checks someone into the boards. "Holy shit."

"That's my brother!" Bianca shouts, cheering along with the rest of the fans.

I forgot how brutal hockey can be. It's the middle of the second period, and I've seen one fight, along with a ton of body checks.

It was like a human game of bumper cars at one point.

Although, it's nice seeing RVU getting their ass kicked in more than one way, this game has been very satisfying to watch.

That body check made Bishop a target, and I forget all about the game, focusing on him. But it doesn't stop him, he dodges their advances and does a good job at providing defense for Toby. While Bishop is right wing, Jonas is left on the same line.

Is it odd that I think it's cute that all the guys in my life who are on this team have to work together as their own little unit?

The game goes on and I cheer with everyone when we get a goal and boo when the other team does the same. It's not often though because we're winning by two.

I'm guessing Toby has turned it around since practice because he's on fire tonight.

Bishop trades off, coming back to the players' bench.

And now comes my favorite part of the game.

I watch like a horny little bitch as Bishop takes off his helmet, and grabs his water bottle as he listens to whatever my dad has to say. I watch as he drinks deep, his throat bobbing with each swallow. His hair is soaked in sweat and god, he's sexy as hell. Wanna know what else is sexy? When he takes his water bottles and squirts the liquid on his face, then shakes out his hair. Fucking hell.

"I feel like that should be illegal," I find myself murmuring out loud. Ryan chuckles and Bee snorts a laugh. "What!" I blush like crazy. "It's hot!"

Then Jonas is doing the same, and I watch as Bee bites her lip. "Okay, I'll agree with you on that one." She looks like she's ready to jump over the seats and climb Jonas like a tree. Now it's my turn to giggle.

The game continues for a bit before the buzzer announces the end of the second period and all the guys skate off the ice to head back to the locker room.

The zamboni comes out, doing its thing.

"Oh, look!" Bee points up at the jumbotron.

"Awe," I coo as the kiss cam shows an older couple. They look at each other so lovingly before they kiss.

They move to another set of people whose eyes go wide, and they mouth something about being mother and son. The poor guy looks so embarrassed. The crowd laughs and they move onto the next.

But then, it's on Bee and Ryan. My eyes go wide as a laugh bubbles up. They look at each other in horror. "Sorry, dude, but I can't," Bee says.

Ryan turns to me. "Any chance you would take pity on me?" He looks at the screen, then at me again. "They won't move the camera."

I look too, my heart pounding in my chest as I feel all eyes on us. "Why not, it's just for fun." I laugh, and then I'm leaning in and pressing my lips to Ryan.

His lips are warm and soft, but I feel nothing. The crowd

cheers, but then banging on the glass startles me, making us jump apart.

My eyes snap to the ice. Toby has his hand on the glass, his lip peeled back in a snarl. There's a mix of pure anger and hurt in his eyes. What is he doing out here? I thought he went back with the team. And why does he think he can look so pissed? I shouldn't feel bad. We're not together, he made sure of that. But I do. I feel like I betrayed him in some way.

My shoulders slump, and I hold back tears as he continues to glare at me. And then he moves to Ryan.

"Fuck," he hisses. "Ah, I'm going to avoid you for a bit, if that's okay?" Ryan informs me. "Because I have a feeling if he sees me with you, he's going to murder me and hide my body so no one ever finds it."

Bishop shouts from across the ice, trying to get Toby's attention. With one last look at me, he skates over to Bishop. The two of them start shouting at each other until my dad appears behind them and intervenes.

My attention moves to Bishop as they disappear, worried I just ruined everything we've been building together. It was just a meaningless kiss. I wouldn't have done it in any other situation. Friends kiss friends on these things all the time.

I should have thought better, I should have waved off the camera and played it off in a joking manner.

"Well, that was interesting," Mom muses next to me. "I wonder why he got so upset?"

She looks at me, but I just shrug, unable to look her in the eye.

"I'm sure he was just being a protective big brother," Theo adds with a chuckle.

I cringe. I love that man but I really wish he didn't say that.

My gaze moves to Rain, and she gives me a sympathetic look. Did I just ruin whatever progress I made with Toby too?

I'm freaking out when I know I shouldn't be. We are nothing; I can date, kiss, and sleep with whoever I want.

But the person I want to do those things with isn't Ryan.

Why does such an innocent thing feel like the biggest betrayal?

I sit there for the rest of the game feeling horrible. Toby's game is off and it doesn't take long before the other team catches up. He's pissed after the next goal, shouting, and slamming his stick against the net, snapping it in two.

I gasp, never have I seen him this upset before. I've seen him get into fights on the ice, even though he shouldn't. But never something like this.

And it's all my fault. I hurt him.

But he hurt me first.

It's not an excuse. I'm not the kind of person who manipulates emotions to get revenge.

I shouldn't feel guilty though. I've done nothing wrong.

Then why does it feel like I did?

For a moment, I thought the game might end in a tie, but in the last thirty seconds, RVU scores one more time, and we lose.

My stomach sinks and I see our team all deflate. As the opposing team celebrates their victory, ours slink off the ice.

Not Toby though. He rips off his helmet and gloves, tossing them to the side, shouting to himself.

One of the guys from the other team shouts something at Toby. Toby's head snaps up, and I gasp when Toby charges for him.

"What is he doing!" my mom shouts as Toby and the guy start beating the shit out of each other.

My eyes are wide, my hands over my mouth in shock as I rise to my feet, watching in panic as I see the first drop of blood hit the ice.

Both teams jump in and it becomes a full out brawl. Everyone is taking swings at one another. I watch Bishop bury his fist into one guy's face before he hits him back, making Bishop's head snap to the side. A wicked grin takes over Bishop's face as he goes in for another hit.

Jax rushes onto the ice as the other coach and referees have to intervene, pulling players off one another.

"Fucking hell," Brody growls as he, Chase, and Theo get up and hurry out of the row of seats to join Jax on the ice.

I'm in tears, guilt smothering me as they finally get everyone to stop fighting and broken apart.

Jax is screaming at the team to get their asses to the locker room.

But the thing that surprises me the most is how Theo is shouting in Toby's face. I've never seen that man so angry in my life.

Toby stands there and takes it, his jaw clenched, eyes wild and face bloody.

I feel like I'm going to be sick when they finally exit off the ice. Just before Toby disappears out of sight, he looks up at me and my heart stops.

Everything in me is telling me to go after him, to make sure he's okay.

"Oh my god. That was wild," Bianca says, still a little shell shocked. "I'm going to go wait outside the locker room and make sure Jonas is okay. And if a puck bunny starts something with me, we're going to get a repeat of whatever that was. Ugh, why do boys have to be so stupid! Animals, the whole lot of them," Bianca growls, getting up and leaving.

"Are you okay?" Ryan asks, concern on his face.

Shaking my head, I blink away the tears, unable to speak, afraid I'll break further.

He goes to give me a hug but I lean away. He doesn't look hurt though, giving me a small smile.

I don't want him touching me right now. I know this isn't his fault, but I don't want to be anywhere near him.

"Excuse me," I say, my voice breaking as I get up and rush out of here, not stopping until I'm locking myself in a bathroom stall. Only then do I let the tears fall.

CHAPTER THIRTY

LILLIANNA

O<small>NE</small> <small>BY</small> <small>ONE</small> <small>EACH</small> <small>OF</small> <small>THE</small> <small>HOCKEY</small> <small>PLAYERS</small> <small>COME</small> <small>OUT</small> <small>OF</small> <small>THE</small> locker room with their heads hung low and their shoulders tight.

I could hear not only Jax handing them their asses but my other dads too. I know that fighting happens in hockey, but what happened out there tonight, the first game of the season, wasn't good.

And the amount of times Theo shouted that it makes SVU look bad is concerning. It doesn't look good. One by one, everyone leaves.

"Jonas." Bianca rushes over to him as he comes out of the locker room, Bishop's not far behind him.

"Are you okay?" I ask Bishop, assessing the damage.

"I'm fine, *il mio cuore.* Just a bloody lip, black eye, and a sore jaw." He gives me a forced smile, trying to play it off.

"Bishop," I reach up and run my thumb over the cut on his

lip. He hisses, and I go to move my hand back, afraid I hurt him, but he grabs my wrist and slowly brings it to his lips.

My pulse races as my breathing picks up. "I'm fine, baby," he murmurs, kissing my wrist again softly before letting it fall to my side.

I swallow hard, my eyes flick back towards the locker room. I've watched everyone, including my dads, leave, all except Toby.

"How is he?" I ask, tears welling in my eyes.

"Hey, none of this is your fault." Bishop cups my face.

"It is. I kissed Ryan after telling Toby we weren't dating. He thinks I lied to him," I insist.

"Doesn't matter if he does. You can kiss whoever the hell you want," he growls, stepping forward. "Although I'd prefer being one of the lucky fuckers."

He leans down and presses his lips to mine, making me whimper as my whole body flushes. He doesn't take it further, pulling back and putting his forehead to mine. "But, if you must know, I don't think he's doing very good in there."

"I gotta go see him."

Bishop gives me a hard look. "I don't think that's a good idea, Lilly. He's not in the best headspace right now. I don't want you to get hurt. We're in big shit. Disqualified for the next game."

Shocked, my eyes widen. "Toby would never hurt me. At least not physically. He has to be feeling like shit if he's the reason why you can't play the next game."

"Normally, I'd agree, but..." He shakes his head. "Just please, leave him to calm down on his own."

"Okay," I whisper, but my heart hurts, wanting to go check on him. No matter what's happened between Toby and me, he's still my person. The one who knows me best. The one who I've spent practically every moment of my life with. To the point I was aware of how unhealthy it was, but didn't care.

"I'll give you a ride home, okay?"

I nod. "I'll meet you outside. I was in such a rush to make sure everyone was okay, I forgot my hat back at my seat."

"I can wait for you right here." He furrows his brows.

"No. No, it's fine. I'll meet you out there." *Please just go.* I look over at Bee who's standing there with a pissy looking Jonas.

"Come on. We'll wait with you. You can fill us in on whatever this is," Bee tells her brother, giving us a pointed look.

He glares at his sister. He doesn't look convinced, but nods anyway. "Alright. I'll go warm up the Jeep and meet you out there." He kisses my forehead.

I give him a small smile and turn to head towards the rink. Rounding the corner, I wait for a few seconds, my heart thundering painfully in my chest. When I poke my head around the corner to see they're all gone, I rush back towards the locker room.

Wrinkling my nose as I step inside, I look around but don't see Toby in the locker room. I do however hear the shower running.

When I step further into the locker room where all the showers are, I see Toby stepping out of a shower.

I stop and watch from the shadows as he dries himself off, drying his hair with angry movements. My gaze shamefully trails down his body, and I swallow hard when I see his cock hanging between his legs. It's not hard but damn it, it's big.

Shaking my head, I look away. Right now is not the time to be ogling my stepbrother. It's a very serious moment.

But also, I'm not blind and his body is on full display. Kind of. Because he thinks he's alone and I kind of just walked in here when I shouldn't have.

Tucking my blonde waves behind my ear, I wait and watch as he gets dressed, throwing one of his clean jerseys on.

When I know it's safe, I step closer. "Hey," my voice comes out low, cracking with emotion.

His eyes snap up to mine. I almost don't continue closing the gap between us, gasping when I see his left eye turning an ugly shade of purple. "What are you doing in here?" His voice comes off harsh, but I don't let him scare me away.

"I wanted to make sure you were okay," I hate how my voice wavers, but I keep moving towards him.

"If I'm okay?" he huffs out a harsh laugh, tossing his bag to the side. "Are you joking? No, Lilly, I'm not fucking okay. Do you know how much it fucking hurt to see you kissing that asshole!" he shouts, his chest heaving. "To see another man's lips on yours?"

"He's not an asshole." I regret the words as soon as I say them.

His eyes flare with fire, and he takes a step closer. "Don't you fucking defend him to me, Lilly," he snarls.

"What do you want from me, Toby?" I ask, sounding defeated. "You want me to tell you we're only friends? Because we are."

"Sure as hell didn't look like it. You kiss all your friends like that?" he scoffs.

I shake my head. "No. It was the fucking kiss cam!" I throw my hands in the air, feeling the need to defend myself. "It was on him and Bee. She's got this thing with Jonas and didn't want to kiss him. So, instead of him being embarrassed, I did it. I didn't think it would be a big deal," I lean back against the lockers. "I don't know what else you want me to say."

"That you're fucking mine! That the only man you're kissing is me!" he screams, stepping closer.

Angry tears fill my eyes, and my heart cracks open. "That's what I want, Toby. It's what I've wanted for years. I want *you*! I love *you*! But you won't fucking take me!" I yell back, getting in his face until we're only an inch apart, so close that I can feel the hot air of his angry pants against my lips.

"You're mine, Little Flower," he growls so low, it's a deep rumble in his chest. "I'm done denying it, stopping myself from having you. You're my fucking girl. I don't care what anyone thinks. You are fucking *mine*."

I shouldn't give in. I shouldn't let him win. But in this moment, I'm weak... so fucking weak. He's saying all the things I've dreamt he'd say, and I don't have it in me to step away.

"If I'm yours, Toby," I whisper. "Then fucking take me."

There's this moment where everything goes still. The only thing I can hear is our heavy, harsh breathing as we not only look into each other's eyes but into our souls.

I know to the bottom of my core that everything is about to change. I'm just not sure if it's going to be for the better or worse.

With his lip peeled back, chest heaving, Toby let's out this feral sound from deep within his chest, and I know I'm fucked. There's no getting away, but I don't think I'd want to.

In a flash, his lips are on mine, fingers tangled in my hair in a painful grip. I don't care, it makes me moan as his lips move savagely against mine. He sucks and nips at my lips before sliding his tongue into my mouth.

My arms go around his neck, my own fingers grabbing a handful of his hair. I pull and he growls against my lips, kissing me harder.

Removing his hand from my hair, he grabs me by my thighs, lifting me up and pushing me back against the locker with force.

I whimper when I feel his thick cock press against my aching core. My body is on fire, a blaze engulfing me in its flame so sweetly.

"Fucking hell, Lilly," he groans against my lips, grinding his shaft against me. *Is this really happening right now? Or is he about to tell me we need to stop and it's a mistake?* "You drive me so damn crazy. Every single thing about you. From the way that you chew on your lip when you're nervous, to that addicting way you laugh. There's nothing about you that I don't love. That I'm not obsessed with. In my eyes, you are fucking perfect."

He kisses me again, making my mind go into a haze. I'm drunk off this feeling. Every part of me that's touching him is like a live wire.

I'm shamelessly grinding against him, saying *fuck you* to any logical thinking. Someone could walk in right now and I wouldn't care.

He rips his mouth away from mine again. I look at him, eyes half lidded, lips parted as I suck in shaky breaths. His eyes are wild, hungry, and lust filled for me.

Me. I'm making him feel this way. He loves me. He wants me.

He pins me against the locker with his hips, and grabs at my shirt. He pulls it up and over my head, tossing it to the side. "Fuuuuck," he groans, his eyes locked on my black lace bra. My cheeks heat. This is the first time he's seen me in my bra. Sure, my bikini covered less, but this is different. More intimate. He reaches behind me and unclasps my bra, freeing my breasts. He takes a moment to eye-fuck my tits before he leans down, sucking a nipple into his mouth.

"Oh, shit," I moan, closing my eyes as I arch into his touch. My hands grip at his hair harder, making him growl.

He sucks on my nipples a little before pulling back, letting go with a pop. "This is your one chance, Lilly." His voice is husky and full of restraint. "One chance to tell me no. To walk out of here. Because the moment my lips are back on this breathtaking body, I'm not holding back. I will fucking consume you."

The room is silent, except for our heavy breathing as I look him in the eye. His want for me shines too bright, and I've never felt more desired than in this moment.

This is my chance. To tell him to put me down, to say no. Not after the games he's been playing with my heart.

But I'm human, and I'm in love. And when someone is in a moment like this, finally getting the person they've been pining after for years, it's not so easy to say no. To step away from something that may never happen again. I don't know what this will mean for us after; I don't know if I'll truly be his, or if things will crash and burn.

What I do know is I want Toby. And I don't care how I get him.

So, I say nothing, giving him a small smile.

It slips away when he places me on my feet, my heart ready to drop down to my stomach as I wait for his rejection again.

Then my eyes widen as he drops to his knees before me. He pulls the zipper of my jeans down and then grips the waistband. In one harsh pull, he yanks them down my legs. I automatically step out of them, as well as my shoes, letting him toss them to the side.

He gets this smug look on his face to match his feral eyes as he grabs the thin strap of my g-string with both hands and pulls, hard, snapping it in half.

Oh my god, this is single-handedly the hottest moment of my life.

I'm breathing heavily, my legs shaking as I watch this sexy, tattooed hockey player on his knees for me.

"Just one taste," he murmurs, parting my thighs. I bite my lower lip as I watch his pupils go pitch black at the sight of my pussy. He adjusts my position so that I'm leaning back against the locker, my hips pressing forward with one leg over his shoulder so he has room to lower his head between my legs.

His eyes never leave mine, like he wants to make sure I'm watching him taste me. There's no way in hell I'd miss this. "This is a pretty pink pussy, Little Flower," his voice thick with arousal. "I think I'll keep it all to myself."

Dear god, this man and his mouth. I have a feeling this is just the tip of the iceberg with him.

Okay, I lied, that's the hottest thing to ever happen to me.

What else don't I know about Tobias Munro, because I'm starting to think it's a lot more than I thought.

This isn't the boy I grew up with, the one who was my whole world. No, Toby isn't a boy anymore, he is all man.

I suck in a breath when I feel his fingers part my pussy lips. I'm panting so hard I feel like I might pass out. But I can't, I don't want to miss anything.

Eyes still locked on mine, he opens his mouth, sticks out his tongue, and then he's licking me from ass to clit.

His tongue is hot and wet against my throbbing core. "Oh," I whimper, fingers curling into fists.

The moan that leaves his throat has arousal dripping onto his tongue, and he laps up every last drop.

He keeps his word, just having a taste. He doesn't feast on me, just a few licks but those licks feel far better than I was expecting. And just before he pulls away, he thrusts his tongue deep inside me, causing my hand to shoot out, grabbing a handful of his hair as I grind against his face.

He chuckles as he moves away. "When I taste you again, Little Flower, it will be somewhere I can feast on this messy cunt until you're soaking my beard in your juices."

I blink at him in shock, that heat on my cheeks burning bright.

He gets to his feet, ripping off his jersey. My eyes take in the ink on his chest, roaming down to his abs and right to that mouth watering V. His hands make quick work of his jeans, then he shoves them to the ground, boxers and all.

His thick cock slaps against his lower belly, making my thighs clench together and my belly burn with need. He's stunning, gorgeous, sexy as hell. Fuck me, this man is too perfect. I just want to run my tongue all over him, is that weird? I don't care, I very much want to taste every inch of his smooth inky skin.

Only I don't get the chance to do that because his mouth is on mine again, kissing me like a starving man as he lifts me again. I moan as I taste myself on his lips.

It hits me that we're not just kissing or just fooling around. We're about to have sex. In the SVU hockey team's locker room.

I ignore the weird smells and the coolness in the air. My heart is racing, my tummy a mess of nerves and need. I need to shut my brain off and not worry about what's going to happen afterwards. This is Toby. And I'm going to enjoy every bit of this. Maybe I'll regret it later, but I don't think that's possible. Not with him.

Toby's movements grow more frantic, harsher as he grips my thighs in a tight embrace. I feel the tip of his cock against my entrance, and my body tenses, panic filling me. I'm about to tell him to stop, to give me a moment to get myself ready.

I don't get that chance because he's pressing me roughly against the lockers as he slams into me.

I feel every pinch of pain as his thick cock stretches me, piercing through that little part of me I've kept intact just for him. This was always his to take.

I bite so hard on the inside of my cheek to keep the sobs of pain inside me that blood fills my mouth. My eyes squeeze shut, and I force myself to remember how to breathe.

It burns so damn bad, and I can feel a tear trickling down my cheek.

He moves his face into the crook of my neck and let's out a pained groan. "Lilly," he rasps. "You're so fucking tight. So fucking wet. Perfect is what you are. Mine and perfect."

My nails dig into his shoulders as he pulls out and thrusts back in a few times. I whimper, maybe from the pain, maybe from how his cock feels inside me.

He only takes a few thrusts to savor the moment before he's prying my fingers from his shoulders and pinning them above my head with one hand.

When he pulls back to look at me, I don't know if I should be turned on by the dark look in his eye or afraid. "Shhh," he soothes. "Don't cry." He leans forward, his tongue lapping up the tear that fell and moans.

I should be disturbed, but my pussy tightens around him, body flushing with heat. "Damn it, Lilly," he snarls. And then he's fucking me like a wild animal.

His thrusts are hard, forcing me against the locker. I ignore the uncomfortable feeling of the hard cool metal, the only thing I can do is look into his eyes, lips parted as I finally suck in that breath of air I've been needing.

"Years," he says with a panting growl. "Years of dreaming

about making you mine. Of my cock buried deep inside your incredible cunt." He leans in to suck and nip at my neck, and I allow my eyes to fall closed, letting my body feel every little thing he's doing to me.

The pain is gone, replaced with this burning pleasure in the pit of my belly. My clit is throbbing, and I want nothing more than to reach between my legs and relieve the pressure.

As if he can read my mind, his free hand snakes between us and my loud moan echos around the room. "Toby," I whimper as he works my clit with his thumb. I'm feeling so many different emotions, I can't think straight.

"God, the way you moan my name. It's even better than I imagined it would be when I touched myself, thinking of you on your fucking knees, gagging on my cock."

His words do amazing things to my body. It's all so new, so different. Who knew I didn't want a gentleman, but instead, a dirty-mouthed man who knows how to work his cock.

He shifts, changing the angle. It causes him to hit a spot I didn't know I had. "Oh, fuck!" I scream, my eyes rolling back as he adds more pressure to my clit, hitting that spot over and over.

My body is shaking in his arms, the pleasure almost too much to handle. I'm a sobbing mess now, chanting his name over and over again. It only seems to set him off. He tucks his face into my neck, grunting as he pounds into me.

He sucks and nips at my skin, and licks his hot tongue against my neck, no doubt leaving his mark on me that will be there as a reminder later.

I'm so close, that pressure in my belly is growing rapidly. This feels a little different, though. Not like the orgasms I've given myself.

This one is going to be explosive, I'm not sure I'm ready for that.

Doesn't matter because when Toby bites down on my neck with a snarling growl, I lose it.

My back arches off the locker, pressing my naked tits into his chest as my eyes roll back into my head. Stars burst behind my eyelids as my pussy clamps down around his cock, gripping him as I cum so hard that I almost pass out. And the sounds leaving me? Not anything I've ever made before.

The feeling is too much, and I kind of want to push him away because I don't think I can take it anymore. But it's also not enough. How can you need more and want less at the same time?

Toby moves his hand from between my legs and grips my ass as his hand around my wrists tighten.

"Lilly," he says my name like a prayer as he thrusts into me one more time. His whole body stiffens and then I feel it, his cock pulsing inside me. We didn't wear a condom, and he's cumming inside me. The thought has me whimpering, my walls gripping him tighter.

He lets go of my arms, letting them fall down to wrap around his neck. Pressing our foreheads together, it's just him and me, our heavy panting breaths mingling together.

Squeezing my eyes shut, I hold back the tears. I'm not sad or upset. It's just a lot of emotions racing through me, and I don't know how to handle them.

I'm naked… in Toby's arms. His cock is still buried deep inside me. This moment, it's everything, but I know the second I open my eyes and he pulls out of me, it's over.

He's my Toby. My best friend, my person, my everything. The world might see him as my stepbrother, but I just see him as mine.

I don't want this to be over. I want to stay like this forever.

CHAPTER THIRTY-ONE

TOBIAS

My whole world is wrapped around me right now, my cock still buried in her tight wet heat. This isn't how I thought my first time having sex would go, but fuck, it was everything.

As long as it was with her, it didn't matter where or when. The locker room was probably not the best place to do it considering anyone could have walked in. But I don't care.

I've never felt more alive. It's like every breath I've ever taken has been toxic. And being here with her, like this, is like inhaling crisp clean air. And fuck, it's never felt so good.

Part of me wonders if I open my eyes, will this have all been a dream? Will it just be me, alone in this locker room, sitting with the knowledge that I've fucked up the next few games for my team?

I know I reacted badly, but that fucker just had to go make a comment about me being pathetic, just like my family of whores.

I've been doing really good when it comes to letting comments like that roll off me. But I was already wound up so damn tight from seeing that Ryan-bastard's lips on my girl, adding in the fact we lost. It was too much, and I snapped. I sure as hell didn't think everyone on both teams would join in.

Lilly is warm in my arms, her naked body pressed against mine. I know we can't stay here, and every second that goes by we're at risk of someone walking in on us. The idea of someone seeing Lilly in this vulnerable state makes me protective.

"That was...." she lets out a low, airy laugh. "Unexpected but amazing."

I let out a chuckle. "Amazing? Nah, Little Flower. It was mind blowing, life changing, hands down the best thing to ever happen in my life."

She giggles and god, my heart explodes. This; I want this all day, every day. I want her. Need her.

"As much as I don't want to move, I think we have to," Lilly murmurs.

Opening my eyes, I move my head back from hers. Her face is flushed, hair wild, and lips puffy from my kisses. She looks like a goddess and my cock twitches inside her. Her eyes widen. Chuckling, I lean in and press a kiss to her lips, unable to get enough of her, and slowly pull out of her. She hisses, detaching her legs that were locked around my waist and I help her to her feet. Looking down, I get the smug satisfaction of watching my cum drip down her thighs before she cleans up. I'm not worried we didn't use a condom. I'm clean, seeing how she's my first and she's on birth control.

But when I look down at my dick, I see blood covering it. My whole body tenses and I just stare at the red coating my length, mixed with our cum.

"Toby?" Lilly's concerned voice breaks through the blood pounding in my ears.

Panic fills my chest and my horror-filled eyes meet hers. "I'm so fucking sorry. Lilly, fuck." I grab a handful of my hair. "I didn't mean to hurt you. Fuck. I was just so out of my mind with rage from losing, what that fucker said to me on the ice, and seeing you kiss Ryan. All I could think about was claiming you, making you mine. Proving to myself that you wanted me as much as I wanted you. I didn't realize my strength. Fuck. I'm a monster."

"Toby." She places her hand on my arm, but I jump back from her touch. I'm a monster. I'm a god damn monster. She shouldn't be anywhere near me. This, this is why I've stayed away. I'm no good for her. I'm no good for anyone. I'm broken and fucked up. A danger to anyone around me.

Her face flashes with hurt as she lowers her hand. "It's just a little blood. It's fine. You didn't hurt me. It was amazing. It felt good. So damn good. Toby, you're not a monster."

"But I hurt you," my voice cracks, tears filling my eyes. "There's blood."

"Well..." She laughs nervously. "I hear sometimes that happens when you lose your virginity."

I blink at her, mouth parted in shock. Sure as hell doesn't happen to guys, so that means... "Lilly." My breathing starts to pick up again. "Please don't tell me that was your first time."

Her cheeks turn bright pink, making me curse. "Then I don't know what to tell you. Because, ah... yeah, it was."

"What the fuck!" I shout, grabbing at my hair again, pacing back and forth. If someone walks in, they're going to see a naked man with a bloody dick and think I'm fucking nuts. And maybe I am. I don't feel exactly sane right now. "But you were with Jonas for two years."

"So?" She watches me, eyes staying on mine as she reaches down to grab her clothes. She gets dressed as she talks to me. "Jonas and I, we never did more than kiss a few times and hold hands. It never felt right. He wasn't the one I wanted to do those things with. It was you, Toby. I couldn't bring myself to do anything more. So, what we just did? It's what I've been waiting for." She laughs nervously again. "Maybe not in the hockey locker room, but at least it was with the right guy."

"How can you be so calm right now!" I growl, grabbing my own clothes. I can finish my meltdown clothed. "I just fucked you like a savage against the lockers, took your fucking virginity in a blink of an eye. You deserved better than that." I shake my head. "You deserve better than me."

"No," she states with force. "Don't. I know what you're doing right now, Toby, but stop it. Don't push me away, not after what we just did. I love *you*. I want to be with *you*. You told me I was yours."

There are so many things going through my mind that I can't think straight. I shake my head, over and over. She is mine, she will always be mine. But I can't be hers. I'm too broken, too fucked in the head. I can't and won't put her at risk of being hurt. If I hurt her, I would literally kill myself. "That was before I hurt you!" I shout. "I don't regret it, Lilly. I never could. You're everything to me. *That* was everything to me. But..."

"Stop it!" she shouts, tears streaming down her face. "Stop saying those things. I don't think you're a monster. What we did was everything to me too. So stop saying those things about yourself."

"But they're true! If you knew the things I've done, you would agree."

"Then tell me! I don't even know you anymore." Her crying makes me feel like trash. I'm upsetting her. I'm doing this to her. It's all I'm fucking good for.

"No." I shake my head, moving towards the exit.

"Tobias Munro, if you leave me here alone, if you walk out that door, we're done. You will lose me forever," she screams on a broken sob.

I look at her, eyes filled with pure agony, and give her a broken smile. "Maybe that's for the best. You deserve the world, Lilly, and all I can offer you is pain."

I turn around and shove the locker room door open.

"I hate you!" she screams before breaking into a sobbing mess.

I feel sick. I'm shaking with anger, with sorrow, with every fucked up sensation you can think of.

"Hey, man. What's wrong?" Jonas walks around the corner. "Bishop sent me to check on Lilly because he's tied up with your dad right now."

Rushing over to him, I grab his shoulders. "I'm trusting you, Walker. I'm trusting you to go in that locker room and take care of my girl. Because I can't." I hate how tears are spilling down my cheeks. I'm fucking weak. "Please, take care of her."

"Y-yeah, of course. What's going on? Is she okay?"

I don't answer him, I just take off. I need to get as far away from here as I can.

I'm on autopilot, unsure where I'm going until I reach my car. People are shouting my name from behind me, but I ignore them.

With shaking hands, I reach into my jeans and grab my car keys. Slamming the door shut, I put the keys in the ignition and start the car. I put it into drive, give it a rev, and take off. My eyes flick up to the rearview mirror to see Jax, Brody, Chase, and my dad standing there, watching me go.

If they knew what I just did to their daughter, they would kill me.

Going back to the dorm is out of the question—it's too close to Lilly—and the hockey house isn't an option. The team is not happy with me, not that I blame them. They have every right to be pissed. I fucked up big time tonight.

So I drive until I find the first shady motel. I'm crashing, the adrenaline dwindling down to the point that I just feel numb.

With nothing but the clothes on my body, I book a room for the night.

The room has a queen bed, a dresser with an older model TV on it, and a bedside table with a lamp.

It's good enough for me to sleep in. Tossing my keys, phone, and wallet on the dresser, I head for the bathroom. Thankfully, the towels are clean enough.

Stripping out of my clothes, I turn the hot water tap on so hot that it burns to the touch. I shower, scrubbing so hard my skin turns a bright shade of red. Or maybe it's from the heat of the water. I hardly register the pain. My eyes drop to my dick and a wave of nausea hits me hard. I swallow down the bile as I scrub the blood from my dick.

I hate myself for what I did. For causing her pain, making her cry. "Fuck!" I roar, smashing my fist so hard into the shower tile it cracks. Blood flows from the fresh cuts on my knuckles. Drip, drip, drip. I watch as the blood trickles down my fingers, falling into the porcelain tub before running down the drain.

After rinsing my hand the best I can, I get out and wrap it with one of the white towels, not caring if I'm ruining it.

Like a zombie, I get dressed again and crawl into the bed.

I'm sure there are a ton of people trying to get a hold of me right now, but I don't touch my phone. I just close my eyes, letting the numbness take over.

I'm drunk and in a pissy mood. That's why I'm going on this walk because at this point I'm just looking for a fight.

Bishop is keeping an eye on Lilly, it's the only reason I feel safe enough to leave her at the party.

Why did she have to dance with that guy? She came to the party with me.

God, I'm so fucking messed up. She's my stepsister, she has every right to flirt with guys. She's sixteen. I'm eighteen, going on nineteen. It's my last year before I head off to SVU and leave her behind. The thought makes my stomach roll. I don't like the idea of being away from Lilly for more than a day.

Sure, I'll be home every weekend for family supper, but she's going to be in school, living her life with her friends, meeting boys, and moving on.

While I'll be at SVU, playing hockey and trying not to drown without her.

I'm off my meds again. I know I shouldn't be but the side effects make me feel like a fucking zombie. I never have the energy to do anything, to go to school, to play hockey, nothing. And most of the time I feel too nauseous to eat anything.

My parents don't know I've stopped taking them, but I don't plan on staying off for long. I just need a break. Once hockey is done, I'll go back on them.

Why do I have to fucking be Bipolar anyways? Why can't I just be normal?

Lilly still doesn't know. It's been years since I was diagnosed.

When I found out, I begged my parents to keep it between us. I didn't want her to know. I hate lying to her, but I couldn't risk her thinking of me differently. To think I'm broken or damaged. I wasn't going to allow anything to come between us, even myself.

Plus, I've been fine with my meds. You can't even tell, not unless you're looking for it. And with her not being aware, she doesn't know the signs to look for.

That's one of the things I'm afraid of her finding out. If she knew, would she wonder if every choice I made was me, or because of my disorder controlling my actions?

My parents didn't like the idea of keeping it from her, but they ultimately agreed because it was my life, my choice.

My symptoms are mild for the most part. It's not like I'm out of control or anything.

And I know when to step back, to take a breath. Like tonight, I could have ripped the fucker off Lilly and beat him to a bloody pulp, but I didn't. I stayed in control.

But I had to leave, just to be safe.

"Fuck," I mutter as I stumble upon a group of people in the woods drinking. I'm about to turn around when one of the fuckers shouts.

"Hey, Munro. What are you doing out here?" It's Tod. I fucking hate that BVH scum. He and his buddies are from the town south of Silver Valley called Bridge View. It's what you might call the-wrong-side-of-the-tracks kind of town. But Tod Rodrick? Yeah, he's one of the biggest pieces of scum. He hit on Lilly one time, she turned him down. and he didn't like it. He tried to get in her face so I smashed in his. He's had it out for me ever since.

Every now and then, they venture their way to one of our parties, depending on who's throwing it and where. Lucky me, they're here now.

Planning on ignoring him, I keep walking away, but then he opens his fucking mouth again and I pause.

"Shouldn't you be back at the party fucking your little sister?" he laughs like a hyena. "Keep it in the family, isn't that your motto?"

His buddies start to laugh along with him.

My fingers curl into fists as my breathing starts to become labored. Closing my eyes, I try to take a deep breath. I will not let this fucker get the better of me.

"Your mother is such a whore," he scoffs. "Fucking a whole team of people. Has she gotten sick of them yet? I know my dad is looking for a new woman, think she would be interested? Seems like she would fuck anyone."

"Fuck you," I snarl, but don't turn around.

"Oh, seems like we hit a nerve. But come on, man, you know it's true. You and your two mommies and—fuck, I lost count— how many daddies? You sure those kids of hers are any of theirs? Wouldn't surprise me if she steps out, because if all of them can't keep her satisfied, I don't think anyone will."

As if he can't stand the fact I'm not reacting the way he wants me to, he amps up his insults. "Now, me? I'd go for that pretty little blonde daughter of hers. What's her name, Lilly?"

"Don't fucking say her name." I spin around, nostrils flaring. I'm going to fucking kill him.

I take a step forward but his buddies stand, blocking my path to him.

"She sure would be fun. I wonder what kind of sounds I could get from her as I fucked her raw. Would she scream? God, I hope so. I love it when they put up a fight. She looks like she would too. Kicking and screaming while I pinned her down, forcing her to take my fat cock. I'd lick the tears from her cheeks and fucking laugh as she begged me to stop. I wouldn't, though. I'd fuck her until I came into her ripped little cunt, then I'd take her ass. I'd make her bleed, Toby. I'd make her beg for her life, and then I'd take it. I'd slit her pretty throat before fucking her dead corpse. And you know what? I think I'd make you watch." He cackles like it's the funniest thing in the world. He's fucking sick. Fucked in the head. The things he's saying make me want to puke. I'm going to fucking kill him.

"You know what? Yeah, I think I'm gonna do that. Hold him, boys, she's back at the party, and I think I want to have a little bit of fun."

No fucking way. I'm not letting him get anywhere near my girl. I don't think, pure raw fury filling me. His friends step forward, stumbling over their feet from being so drunk. Thankfully, that works in my favor. I could take any one of these sacks of shit one-on-one, but three-on-one, I'm not too sure. I punch one in the face, and he goes down like a bag of rocks. The other one lets out a scream before he launches himself at me. Stepping to the side, he falls to the ground. I kick him in the gut before stomping the heel of my shoe into his face.

"You're dead, Munro," Tod spits, rage filling his face as he comes barreling towards me.

I give him a manic grin. *"Not if I fucking kill you first."* I grab a metal pipe from the pile of trash lying around and swing it up. It hits him in the face, busting his nose. Blood spurts out, and I use the momentary distraction to bring it down hard across his stomach.

He curses and grunts in pain. I drop the pipe, grabbing a handful of his hair as he bends over in pain. Over and over again, I punch him in the face.

My hand throbs, but I ignore it. His knees give out and he drops to *the ground. He's too intoxicated to defend himself, but I keep going. Straddling him, I keep swinging.*

"You will never fucking touch her!" I roar. "You will never hurt her. Never look at her again. You sick fuck."

I'm too lost in the moment, unable to stop. And I don't until I feel hands pulling me off. I hear Bishop yelling my name, telling me to stop. That I'm going to kill him. "That's the fucking point!" I shout in his face, chest heaving. I feel like a wild animal and probably look like one too.

He looks down at the bloody guy on the ground. "Fuck. Toby, what the hell!"

"He was going to hurt Lilly," is all I say. I can't go into details, I can't repeat the vile things he said.

Flashes of it fill my mind; him on top of her, him forcing her down and doing everything he said.

I lean over and throw up.

"We need to call the cops, man. He can't die."

"He can." I wipe my mouth with the back of my hand.

"You're eighteen! You're going to fucking go to jail," he snarls.

"Fuck. No. No, I can't go to jail. I can't leave Lilly!" I grab handfuls of my hair and start to pace. I'm spiraling, down down down. Fuck. Fuck! What have I done? No. I did the right thing. He would have hurt Lilly. He would have...

Over and over, images of his words play in my mind. I drop to my knees, begging them to stop.

"Lilly. No. Leave her alone. Lilly!"

I JOLT AWAKE IN THE SHITTY MOTEL BED, GASPING FOR AIR. SWEAT pours down my face, soaking my hair and the blankets. Scrambling from the bed, I rush to the bathroom, dropping to my knees just in time to heave everything in my stomach up.

It takes a while for the dream to stop feeling so real and for reality to kick back in. It's been a long time since I've woken up from one of my night terrors. Usually, I always have to suffer through them until my mind drifts onto something else, trapping me with those horrible thoughts.

They always feel so real, and it's always the same terror. I'm strapped in a chair, forced to watch while Tod pins Lilly down. He forces himself on her over and over again. Her eyes locked with mine, begging me for help, pleading with me to save her, but I can't.

Her screams of pain still echo in my head, causing me to puke again as tears spill from my eyes.

That night changed everything for the worst. Cops and an ambulance came to get Tod. I was arrested but let out on bail.

There was a court hearing, and in the end, I got off with a hefty fine. Tod and his family got rich, thanks to Brody doing whatever he could to get me out of that situation. Money helped, but so did my lawyer. He used the fact that I was off my meds, and I was having a manic episode, as our argument in court.

All of this was done quietly and out of the public eye. To this day, Lilly still has no idea what happened.

As for Tod's friends, they were paid off too. Not much damage was done to them, and they took the deal without another thought.

The worst part of it all was Tod was able to roam free. I told the judge everything he said about what he wanted to do to Lilly. But because it was just words and not actions, they didn't charge him with anything. Although we did get an order of protection on him. My parents didn't want him to be able to come anywhere near Lilly.

They were horrified, and after they found out why I lost it, they didn't hound me again. They agreed to keep everything from Lilly because it would only upset her and cause her to worry.

Two months into my first year of SVU, Tod was arrested and charged for brutally raping a girl.

I almost broke down when I found that out. It's part of the reason I put that distance between Lilly and me. I couldn't look at her without thinking of those awful images. I put all my time and energy into school and hockey. Even though I was on my meds, it wasn't enough. I needed the fight club. It kept me from going over the edge for good.

When I finally stumble out of the bathroom, I can see the sun streaming through the crack in the curtains. It's morning, and I'm sure my family has been going crazy not knowing where I am.

Grabbing my phone, wallet, and keys, I slip on my sneakers and head out to my car. When I check, I see I have a hundred missed text messages and forty calls from all my parents, Jonas, and Bishop.

Putting my phone down, I open the glove compartment and grab the bottle of pills. Opening it, I pop one in my mouth and swallow it whole. Then I bring up the contact of the one person I trust more than anyone and press call.

It rings only once before I hear a frantic voice on the other end. "Toby! Where are you? Are you okay?"

"No," my voice cracks. I close my eyes, tears streaming down my face and do something that I normally don't like to do. I ask for help. "I'm not okay. Dad, I need you. Please."

CHAPTER THIRTY-TWO

LILLIANNA

I'VE JUST FINISHED GETTING DRESSED WHEN JONAS STEPS INTO THE locker room. "Lilly?" His voice is cautious and soft.

Angrily, I wipe at my tears with the back of my sleeve. My body trembles as he steps into view. His eyes go wide when he sees how much of a mess I am.

"Are you okay?" he asks in a rush as he hurries over to me.

"I'm fine," my voice cracks. *Lie,* I'm not fine. I'm anything but fine. I'm pissed. So fucking pissed at Toby right now.

Something isn't right with him, and I hate that it took what just happened for me to see it. Whatever it is, I want answers.

He looked so scared, like he was so convinced that he hurt me. He was convinced that he was a monster and he looked horrified at what he did.

I'm hurt, so fucking hurt right now, that my chest aches, and

I feel sick. But I also can't help but feel for him. I don't under-stand why he's so convinced he's no good for me.

"Lills," Jonas says my name in a low, dangerous growl. "If he hurt you, I'll fucking kill him."

"He didn't." I shake my head. Because even if Toby thought he hurt me, I loved every moment of what we did. I don't care that I lost my virginity so roughly, or that my first time was in a locker room. The only thing that matters to me is that it was with him.

"You're crying. He had to have done something."

"Can we just forget about it, please?" I shake my head. "I don't want to talk about it."

He looks like he wants to argue but lets out a heavy sigh. "Come on." He wraps his arm around my shoulder, and I lean into his touch, trying not to cry again.

I'm a bundle of emotions right now. I'm pissed that he ran again. I'm sad because everything was so good, until it wasn't. And I'm hurting not just for myself, but for him too. And I'm confused. So damn fucking confused. This push and pull is giving me whiplash.

One moment, he's telling me he loves me and I'm his. For a second, I thought this was it, he's finally going to give in. I didn't plan on making it easy for him, he was going to have to work hard to earn my trust again, but I thought he was over all this bullshit.

Clearly, I was wrong. But I'm starting to think it's for a much bigger reason that I don't quite understand.

"Lilly!" Bishop rushes over to me and away from my dad when he sees me. I must look like a mess right now, my eyes red and swollen from crying. A wave of guilt hits me. I just fucked Toby when I'm crushing hard on Bishop, and he was waiting for me out here. I don't feel like I'm in the wrong or that I should feel bad about it, but I don't want to play with Bishop's emotions either. I should have talked to him about everything, seen where he and I stood before I slept with someone else.

It's not like I planned on any of that happening, though.

"Lilly, what happened?" Brody asks me, his eyes wild with concern. "Toby just took off like a bat out of hell. What did he do to you?"

Jax, Chase, and Brody all look pissed. Theo looks torn. My mom and Rain join us, and I stare them all down.

"What is going on with Toby?" I ask. "The man I've come to know the past few weeks, hell, the past two years, isn't the boy I grew up with. I get it, people change as they get older. But not like that." They all look at each other with guilty expressions. Instinct has my stomach turning. "You all know something that I don't!" I shout. "What is it? What's going on with him?"

So many different things come to mind. *Is he sick? Is he dying? What is it?* The questions in my head have me thinking the worst and it makes me start to panic.

My mom speaks, tears in her eyes. "It's not our place to tell you, Lillypad. It's Toby's life, Toby's health. He should be the one to tell you."

"His health?" My eyes widen. "Is he sick?"

"No." Theo clears his throat. "Not like that."

"Then like what!" my voice breaks as tears fall down my cheeks again. "Why would you all be in on a secret so serious and keep it from me?"

"He didn't want you to see him differently. It's... I think you need to talk to him about it, okay?" Rain suggests. She steps closer, putting her hands on my shoulders. "Remember when I told you not to give up on him, even after everything he's done?" I nod my head, sniffling. "It's because he doesn't always mean the things that he does."

"What does that even mean?" I ask helplessly.

"I'm telling her," Brody growls.

"No, you're not." Theo steps forward. "He is my son. And this is his medical history. If he does not want it disclosed to anyone, then he has the right."

"It's Lilly!" Chase snaps. "They're best friends. And he's kept this from her for years. Asked us to lie to our daughter. We did it because we thought it was best for her, but clearly it's doing more harm than good now!"

"Stop!" my mom cuts through everyone yelling. "Enough. We are not going to turn on each other." She looks at me. "Talk to him. Ask him. Make him tell you. And if he doesn't—" she looks up at Theo and back to me. "—then I will."

"Ellie." Theo looks so broken right now.

"You saw him tonight. He needs help. And I will not put our daughter at risk. Not to mention our son, Theo. Do you think getting into fistfights and high-tailing it out of here is good for him? Keeping this secret is doing him more harm than good and I will not stand by only to watch my kids crash and burn. Do you understand me?" My mom is a sweet woman, with a heart of gold. But when it comes to her kids, I've never seen her more fierce.

Theo nods and looks away. "I'm going to keep calling him."

"Is he okay?" I ask again, because I don't know what else to do.

"I don't know, baby." My mom cups my cheek, giving me a sad smile. "I'm hoping he is."

"What happened in there?" Jax asks me.

I chew on my lip as I think of an answer. "We fought. He was mad about the loss, and he thought I lied to him about Ryan." I'm sure as hell not telling them that my stepbrother fucked me like an animal in the hockey locker room, claiming my virginity as his own.

I'm tired, my head hurts, my stomach aches, and all I want to do is cry. "I want to go home."

"I'll take you," Bishop offers, putting his arm around me. Needing him so damn bad, I turn around and step into his embrace, letting him wrap his arms around me. I bite the inside of my cheeks to keep myself from breaking. *Not here.*

"Both of you come back to the house for the night, okay?"

Mom says, rubbing my back. I nod my head, not trusting myself to speak as tears sting the back of my eyes.

I forget Jonas and Bee are here until they are telling me goodbye and that they'll text me later.

"Come on, *il mio cuore.*" Bishop guides me to his Jeep, opening the door for me and helping me in.

The ride is quiet. I spend it with my eyes closed, silent tears falling with my head against the door. But Bishop? He has his hand on my thigh the whole way home, being the strength I so desperately need right now. If I wasn't falling for this man before, I sure as hell am now.

He's been my rock through this without me even realizing it.

We end up arriving around the same time my parents get home. Poor Bennett was in the car during the whole exchange, and he looks around with a worried, confused gaze. I'm sure he asked our parents what's going on and they told him what they could.

Bennett heads up to his room as my parents head into the kitchen.

"I'm going to stay in the pool house tonight." I let Bishop know.

He nods his head, scratching the back of his neck. "I'll take Toby's room."

"Could you… could you stay with me? I don't want to be alone tonight."

"Of course." He immediately wraps his arms around me, and I whimper, clinging to him like a life raft. "Come on, baby. I got you." He picks me up, wrapping my legs around his waist and my arms around his neck. I break apart in the safety of his arms while he carries me to the pool house.

He soothes me, rubbing a hand up and down my back as he whispers sweet things. I've been trying to be strong for so long now, but I can only handle so much pain before I break.

I don't want to hate Toby, I don't think I ever could. But I'm so mad at him. For hurting me, for keeping secrets, for not trusting me enough to tell me about something that seems really major in his life.

"I need to shower," my voice cracks. Bishop sits me on the bed.

"Are you sure? You could take one in the morning. You had a big day and should probably get some sleep."

My cheeks heat. I could lie to him or make up some kind of excuse, but there's been enough avoiding the truth for one day.

Taking a deep breath, I close my eyes. "Toby and I... we had sex in the locker room. I need to shower because I have cum and blood on me, and it's a reminder of everything that's happened tonight and I just..." I break down again, sobbing into my hands.

Bishop gets to his knees, wedges himself between my legs, and pulls me into his arms. "Shhh. Fuck, Lilly, it's okay. You're okay. Let's get you cleaned up, okay?"

He helps me to my feet, and my body responds as if on autopilot as I walk towards the bathroom. I don't bother closing the door as I start to strip out of my clothes. I don't even care that Bishop is there and can see me, I just want to clean my body of everything that has happened. I want to forget about the look in his eye as we broke together for very different reasons.

I want to forget about how my heart is in a million little pieces and the only thing that's keeping me from crumbling to the floor of the shower and losing my mind is that man in the next room.

Toby may have been my person for most of my life, but Bishop has always been by my side too. He was even there when Toby wasn't and continues to be there for me when he doesn't have to.

I'm selfish, and I won't turn him away. I need him right now, I need him tomorrow, and the day after.

Turning the water on hot, I get under the spray and just stand there, eyes closed, as the water beats down on me.

"I found you a change of clothes. I hope this is okay," Bishop says. "Lilly! Fuck, that's burning hot." Blinking my eyes open, I watch as he reaches in and turns it down to a comfortable warm. He looks at me, his brow furrowed. "Fuck, baby." He goes over to the shelf and grabs a towel, placing it on the sink before coming back over to me with a washcloth in hand.

As the water runs over my face, I stand there naked and watch as he strips down to only his boxers. Any other time I'd admire his body, but right now I don't feel anything.

His eyes focus on my face, not straying to my naked body as he gets in with me.

For the next little while, we say nothing as he washes my hair. I close my eyes, enjoying the feeling of his fingers against my scalp. "Turn around, baby." He turns my body so that he can rinse my hair.

After that, he guides me to sit down on the built-in bench, lathering some body wash on the washcloth. And then he does something that makes me fall in love with him.

He gets to his knees and starts to wash the dried blood and cum from my thighs. I don't deserve this man. He's so damn good to me. Bishop Grant isn't what everyone makes him out to be. Behind the fuckboy persona, he's a gentleman with a heart of gold.

Every brush of the cloth is careful and tentative. He makes sure to get everything and hands me the cloth before he gets any closer to my intimate spot.

"Thank you," I whisper, fresh tears filling my eyes, the numbness slowly leaving me the longer I'm with him.

He cups my face, water dripping down his. "Don't thank me, *il mio cuore*. I would do anything for you, Lilly. You have no idea just how far I'd go. If you're in pain, I'll do what I can to take it away. If someone hurt you, I'll do everything in my power to make them pay," he growls.

My heart beats faster. *Does he mean that he's going to do something to Toby?*

"Bishop."

"Yes?"

"Kiss me."

He blinks at me, droplets falling from his lashes. He must see my need for him in my eyes because he leans in and presses the softest of kisses to my lips. It's only a few seconds, but it's everything I need in this moment.

"This is the worst time to say something like this, but I feel like I need to tell you. I don't want you to think that I'm leading you on. I don't want you to think for a moment that I plan on hurting you," he confesses, his forehead resting against mine. After a couple of heartbeats, he leans back so he can look into my eyes. "I love you, Lilly. I have for a very long time. I will always be by your side, for whatever you need. If that's only as a friend, then I'll be the best friend you could ask for. If you want more, I'm all in, I'm all yours."

My lower lip wobbles as my heart fucking explodes. But my head is still a mess, and I don't know what to say right now. I don't know how to answer him in a way that would make any sense.

"Shh." He kisses my forehead. "Don't say anything right now. Think about it, okay?" I nod. "I'm going to go change while you finish up."

"Okay," I whisper. He kisses my forehead again before getting out of the shower.

I clean what he couldn't, hissing at the pain in my core. I feel sick when I see the red still on the cloth. *How am I still bleeding?* I thought it would have just been a little.

When Bishop comes back, I'm stepping out of the shower. He grabs the towel and wraps it around me. I want to cry with how fucking sweet he's being as he dries off my body and hair.

Something trickles down my leg, and I look down to see a pink drop. My gaze flicks up to his, seeing his reaction.

He's cool as a damn cucumber as he goes over to grab a pad from under the sink. Then he grabs my panties and comes back over. "Sit," he tells me, nodding to the toilet seat.

"You gotta stop," I reply, trying to say it in a lighthearted way, but it comes out broken, emotions fucking with my head.

"Stop what?" he asks as he grabs the washcloth and brings it over, wiping up my leg before tossing it in the sink. He grabs my panties and urges me to put my feet in the holes.

"Being so damn good to me. I don't deserve it."

He pauses and looks up at me. He gives me one of his signature grins that makes my heart skip a beat. "Get used to it, *il mio cuore*. I'm gonna be so damn good to you that you'll become spoiled. Because you know what, you do deserve it. You deserve the whole fucking world, Lilly. I can't give you that, but I sure as hell can try."

He leaves me stunned, lips parted in awe as he puts the pad into my panties and pulls them up my legs. "How do you know how to do thats?" I ask him as I stand up, letting him dress me.

I don't know why I'm so relaxed about this. This is a very intimate moment, and Bishop and I have only shared a kiss before tonight. But it feels right. I trust him, I feel safe with him. And right now, I need someone to take care of me for once.

"With a house full of women, my mom wanted to make sure I knew how to take care of my woman when the time came." He chuckles. This man doesn't stop, no he grabs my PJs and continues to dress me.

If it were any other time, any other situation, I'd jump him right now. Boyfriend goals is what he is, and he's not even my boyfriend.

I plan on changing that. Doesn't matter my feelings for Toby or how fucked up everything is. If Bishop is willing to be patient with me, and it seems like he is, then I'm not going to let him get away. I need him. I want him. So I'm going to fucking take him. He did offer himself to me.

"There," he says after I'm all dressed. "Let's get you to bed."

I'm about to start walking when he scoops me up in his arms. I can't help it, I laugh. "You're too much."

He chuckles. "Nah, baby, I'm not enough. But I'll keep

trying," he teases with a wink. He's wrong, though; he's more than enough.

He lays me down in the bed, tucking me in. "Do you need anything? Are you sore? I can grab you something for the pain. Water? I'll grab water. Fuck, did you eat?" He runs a hand through his still-wet hair. He's so damn adorable fawning all over me; my heart is so full.

"No." I pull back the blankets. "I only need you."

He pauses and my breath catches with the emotion that fills his face. "I'm here." He climbs into bed, laying down so I can cuddle on his chest.

I close my eyes and sigh, loving the feeling of my body against his.

"Bishop," I whisper as we lay there in silence.

"Yeah, baby," he murmurs, his fingers playing with my hair. It's relaxing and slowly starting to put me to sleep.

"About what you said in the shower."

"What about it?"

"Did you mean it?"

"Every word," he replies without missing a beat, making me smile.

"I like you. A lot. I—I want something more, if you're willing."

"Baby girl," his voice comes out husky, and I have to remind myself now is not the time. "I'd love to be something more with you."

"What about Toby?"

"What about him?" his voice grows hard. He's pissed at his best friend and rightfully so.

"I'm a mess when it comes to him, and I don't know when that's going to end, if it ever does. Is that something you're okay with? Knowing that I love another man while I'm with you?"

"I've known your feelings for Toby pretty much from the start. It's never stopped me from feeling the way I did about you. The way I still do. I knew that Toby was always going to be a factor, and I asked myself a long time ago if I was okay with that. And I am. So, if you find a way to make things work with Toby and you want to be with him too, I support that. If you choose not to become anything more, but can't seem to make those feelings go away, then that's fine too. I will not leave you for loving someone else. I will not deny myself you because your heart belongs to more than one person. I've seen the love your family has for one another. If they can make it work, then I know we can. We at least have to try, right?"

"Right," my voice cracks. "You're amazing, you know that?"

"Nah. You're the amazing one."

I giggle, burying my face into his chest. That was a lot to take in.

"Toby is my best friend. I love him too, although in a different way. But, Lilly, if there comes a time that Toby isn't okay with what we have, and he makes you choose, I'll step back. He was in your heart first, I wouldn't put you through the pain of having to make a decision."

"Stop it," I say firmly. "Toby doesn't get the right to tell me to pick. He'd be fucking lucky if he even stood a chance. I don't want to talk about him and all of that. Everything is so fucked up right now. But I will tell you, no, you won't step back. I want you, Bishop. You're mine," I growl, looking up at him. "If he can't accept that, then he won't get to be with me."

I know there's something deeper going on with him, and I will find out what it is. But he doesn't get to treat me the way he did, then start demanding and telling me how to live my life and what I have to do.

"Oh, yeah?" he chuckles. He leans in and presses a kiss to my lips. "I'm yours, am I?" I nod. "I kind of love the sound of that. And that growl, damn, baby, your possessiveness over me already is a major turn on."

I smile and his responding grin is so wide on his handsome face. "So, what does this mean?" I ask, biting my lower lip.

"Well, it means I'm yours and you're mine," he chuckles.

"So, like your girlfriend?" I know it's corny, but I need the label or I'll go out of my mind.

"Lillianna Tatum," he pauses, voice low, sending a shiver down my spine.

"Yes?" I breathe.

"Will you be my girlfriend?" His question makes me giddy and happy. It's everything I need after this shitty night.

"Yes."

He growls, his eyes flaring. I squeal as he flips me over, pins me to the bed, and kisses me until I'm a puddle under him.

I want him, I want more.

"No more," he whispers against my lips, both of our breaths coming out in heavy pants. "Sleep. I need to talk to him, to tell him about my feelings for you before anything goes further. If he wasn't such a bastard, I would have waited to make things official. But fuck it, you're mine whether he likes it or not. I'm just giving him this courtesy as his best friend."

"Okay," I agree. I'm a little disappointed, but it's for the better because I had sex for the first time tonight, and I don't want mine and Bishop's first time to be in the middle of an emotional breakdown on that same night.

How can nothing have gone right tonight but still ended with something so good? No, the way we confessed our feelings for one another wasn't in the most romantic way, but life is messy and unpredictable. You go with it or let it drag you down.

"Sleep," he tells me again. I curl up on my side as he tucks himself against my back. Because of Bishop, I'm able to fall asleep with nothing else but us on my mind. I know tomorrow I'll have to deal with the harsh reality that is my life, but for right now, it's just Bishop and me.

CHAPTER THIRTY-THREE

BISHOP

I'M AFRAID THAT IF I MOVE, SHE'S GOING TO DISAPPEAR. I'VE BEEN laying here, watching her sleep for about an hour like a creeper.

I can't help it, she's fucking gorgeous and, the kicker is she's mine. *Mine!* Part of me wants to hear her say it again so I can make sure I didn't make it up all in my head.

Last night was a nightmare. I wanted to ask Lilly to be my girlfriend after maybe a date or two. Spend time with her, show her how much I love being with her.

With the way the life in her was draining so quickly after my asshole of a best friend hurt her yet again, I knew I had to act quickly before she convinced herself that no one wanted her.

I love Toby, I do. And I know that he's for sure off his meds, there's no doubt in my mind about that, but he's hurt Lilly one too many times. There's only so much you can blame your mental health on before it's clear you need to do something about it.

He needs to get back on his meds and show that he's doing better before I even let him get anywhere near my girl.

I won't give him a chance to hurt her again. I know he doesn't mean to; he loves Lilly so hard that he's hurting himself because of it. He's so blinded by his own past and issues that he can't see the damage he's doing, even if it's unintentional.

He fucked her in that locker room then left like a bat out of hell. I don't know what was going through his mind to do that, but it was fucked up.

Lilly deserves so much better, and I'm going to make sure she gets it. If that means keeping my best friend away from her until he's better, then I will. I never thought it would come to this point, but if I have to choose between the two of them, I will pick Lilly every time.

"Are you done yet?" Lilly's sleepy voice murmurs as her eyes slowly blink open.

A smile twitches at my lips. I brush the hair from her face, letting my hand linger, rubbing her cheek with my thumb. I'm so in love with this woman it hurts. Like when I'm not with her, I ache to be. When I see her, my heart goes crazy and my body screams with need for her. But it's the good kind of pain. The pain I crave. "Done with what? Watching my beautiful girlfriend sleep? Nah, I could do this for hours."

She smiles and buries her face into the pillow. "You're being a creeper." Her voice is muffled.

"Yes, but I'm *your* creeper."

She turns her head to the side, looking at me. She gives me a shy smile. "You are, aren't you?" she whispers. "Did you really agree to be my boyfriend?"

"Damn right, I did, *il mio cuore*. I'll do it again too, but this time, I'm not asking. Lilly, you are my girlfriend. My girl. Mine. Understood?"

"Yes," she giggles, and the sound goes right to my cock.

"How is this not weird? I thought it might be a little awkward going from friends to more, but it feels…"

"Right?" She nods. "It's better than right. It's perfect." I lean in to kiss her lips. I'm happy she doesn't turn away because of morning breath or something. Something as silly as that would never keep me from my girl. *My girl—fuck, that sounds good.*

She hums softly, a little sigh leaving her chest. "Now all of those puck bunnies can fuck off," she mumbles against my lips, and I burst out laughing.

"Oh, really? You're sounding a little jealous there, Shorty."

She glares up at me, and it's fucking adorable. "Listen, I've seen those girls hanging off you. I don't like it. So, now that you're mine, I'll be more than happy to rub it in their faces."

"I like this side of you." I grin, pulling her closer so that she can feel just how turned on she's making me with all her possessiveness. "Feel free to piss on me any day to mark your territory."

Her eyes widen, and I struggle not to laugh. "You're a naughty little thing, aren't you? I wasn't talking about it like that. But I mean, if you wanna try—"

"No!" she shouts. "No, nope that's okay. Not to yuck on anyone's yum, but that's going to be a hell no for me. I might only be fresh off the virgin block and not know what I like in the bedroom yet, but I can tell you that's not it."

"I'm just fucking with you." I laugh. "You sure do look cute when you're all flustered and red-faced."

"You suck," she grumbles, sliding under the blankets.

"Hey, no hiding from me." I pull the blankets down. "Wanna go get something to eat? It's almost noon. We slept in late."

"I needed it though." She sighs, moving to sit up against the pillows. She still looks tired and the light isn't quite back in her eyes yet, but I'll keep working on it.

"How are you feeling?" I mean it in so many ways.

"Physically? A little sore but I'll be fine. Emotionally?" She shrugs. "I'm hurt, confused, and I really need to know what's going on with Toby. Do you know?"

I nod slowly, not wanting to lie to her. "I found out around senior year." Guilt hits me. That was a big moment in Toby's life, and I'm honestly surprised they were all able to keep something so major from Lilly. Toby shouldn't feel ashamed of having Bipolar disorder, it's not something he asked for. It doesn't change the fact that we all love him and want to see him healthy.

I've been beating myself up because I didn't see it sooner. I know he's been avoiding his parents, so I'm guessing they've been wanting to talk to him about it. I've been spending so much time with Lilly, I didn't see the warning signs of an impending episode sooner. I thought he was just beating himself up over everything with Lilly.

"And I'm guessing you're not going to tell me?"

"Unlike your parents, I don't plan on keeping it to myself. If he doesn't tell you today, I will."

"Really?" she asks, tears making her eyes glassy. I hate seeing her upset. It was so hard to keep it together last night, but I know she needed me, and I had to be there for her no matter what. But seeing that devastated look in her eyes, it crushes me.

"I don't agree with keeping you in the dark if it's only going to hurt you."

"I don't want to push or pry. I just feel..." She closes her eyes and the tears roll down her cheeks. "I thought we were closer than him keeping secrets. Why did he think he couldn't trust me?"

"It's not that, I can tell you that with absolute certainty. He was afraid of you looking at him differently and that you'd end up hating him. In his mind, that's the worst thing possible."

"So he treated me like I didn't exist for two years? I sure as hell did think of him differently after that. I don't hate him, but if he keeps pushing me, I just might. But I don't want to."

"Shh." I pull her into my arms. "Let's not think about that right now. Come on, eat first then worry, okay?"

She nods. We both slip into sweatpants and hoodies and head into the house.

Stepping into the kitchen, we both come to a halt. Toby is sitting at the island with all of the parents standing in various spots around him.

He looks over at us, mostly at Lilly, and his whole face crumbles. His eyes shine with tears and fuck, I've never seen my best friend look so broken. "Lilly." The way he says her name is a sucker punch to the gut. He never meant to hurt her, he just doesn't know what he's doing anymore.

"We'll let you guys talk," Ellie offers, kissing the top of Toby's head. "I'm so proud of you for asking for help." Her eyes are red rimmed as she gives him a watery smile.

Toby nods but looks Lilly's way again. I step in front of her, blocking his view, and look down at her. She blinks up at me, her face a mixture of emotions. "Are you okay with talking to him?"

"Will you stay with me?"

"Of course," my response comes out instant and as a hard growl.

She nods her head. "We need to talk. No more secrets." She gives a pointed look at Toby.

"Agreed." I nod. "Outside?"

"Yeah." she answers.

"Give me a moment, we will meet you out there."

"Don't kill him, okay?" she asks, chewing on her bottom lip.

"Can't make any promises." I want to kiss her, but this isn't how I want Toby to find out about us. He's too unstable right now.

She turns around and heads back outside.

Turning around, I walk over to Toby. He finally turns his attention away from Lilly to look at me. He doesn't get a word out before I'm cocking my fist back and driving it into his face. He lets out a grunt as he falls backward off the stool, his ass hitting the ground hard. Grabbing him by the shirt, I pull him to his feet, and shove him against the fridge.

"I deserved that," he groans as he covers his bleeding nose with his hand.

"You deserve a hell of a lot more," I spit, my heart torn over everything that's happened. "I love you, man. You're my best friend, my fucking brother. But the shit you've done to Lilly?" I lower my voice in case people might be around. "Taking her fucking virginity and then running? That's where I draw the fucking line."

"I didn't know she was still a virgin. But that doesn't excuse my behavior, I know. I freaked, man. I was rough with her, I lost control. I thought I hurt her, I thought I was a monster."

"Did Lilly call you any of that?"

"No." He shakes his head.

"Then how about you let her make her own decisions before you assume shit? Do I like how things went down between you two? No. But from what Lilly told me, she enjoyed it, she wanted it. You didn't force her to do anything she didn't want to do. It was your running and breaking her heart, *again*, that crushed her."

"I know, man." He lets out a broken sob. "I didn't want to hurt her. I didn't mean to. I never mean to. It's just... fuck!" I let go of him, and he grabs a handful of his hair. "My head, it's messed up. I don't mean to do the things I do. I fucked up bad, and I hate myself for it. I don't want to be like this anymore, Bishop. I don't want to hurt, to feel so confused, to be in a rage all the fucking time. I'm back on my meds, I took them this morning."

He sniffles, and the back of my eyes burn. I pull him in for a hug, and he grabs onto me, holding me so damn tight.

I hold my best friend while he sobs. The man who's dealt with so much and who continues to do so.

"You need to tell her. Everything. Right now. No more secrets between you two."

"I know," he sighs, pulling back. "Fuck. I got blood all over you."

"It's a black shirt, it's fine." I go over to the sink and grab a clean rag and wet it before handing it over to him.

"Come on. Let's go talk to our girl." When we turn around, Lilly is standing by the back door, tears streaming down her face.

We slowly approach her and when we stop, Lilly launches herself at Toby.

"I'm so fucking sorry, Little Flower. For everything. I don't want to hurt you anymore."

"Then tell me what's going on. Please."

We head outside and Lilly takes a seat on one deck chair, Toby on the one across from her, while I stand back, watching over them as I lean against the pillar.

"Where do I start?" He lets out a heavy, shaky breath. "I have Bipolar Disorder. I was diagnosed around thirteen. I started taking medication for it, and it was almost like I didn't have it. It worked really well, for the most part."

"What?" Lilly sucks in a shock breath. "Toby, that's huge, why didn't you tell me? Why didn't I know?"

"Because I asked our parents not to tell you. I didn't want to risk you seeing me differently." He removes the bloody towel from his nose. I feel a little guilty for hitting him, but also not because he deserved it. "I didn't want you to be afraid of me, to see me as a monster. And before you say you wouldn't have, back then I was conflicted. The more I researched what I had, the more I saw how the knowledge of it could affect people's relationships. And I couldn't risk it. I asked them not to say anything unless I posed a threat to you."

She scrubs her face with her hand. "And this is why you've been the way you have been since I've gotten to school? For the last two years?" Her brows furrow. "Wait, you said thirteen. If it's been that long, what caused all these changes?"

"Fall of senior year, we went to a party."

"Yes, we went to tons of parties," she points out.

"Well, this one, you were dancing with a guy. I got pissed, and I left before I let my anger get the better of me. I was off my meds at the time. With the pressures of school and hockey, the side effects of my meds were getting in the way. I felt like I was failing everyone around me by being tired and feeling sick all the time. So, I stopped taking them. And everything seemed like it was going good. I had more energy, I felt better. I was eating more, focusing more. But it was all an illusion. When I left the party, I went for a walk. On that walk, I ran into Tod."

Her eyes widen. "Tod? Like the one who got arrested for those horrible things he did to that girl?" she asks in a whisper.

"Yeah." Toby's voice goes hard. "That fucking sack of shit." He shakes his head. "He said some things that fucked me up. Some horrible, disgusting things that set me off. I lost it. I beat him so bad he almost... died."

"Oh my god," she gasps, but she doesn't look disgusted like Toby assumed she would. "What did he say to you?"

Toby shakes his head with a pained look. "I'm not ready to talk about that part just yet. Please understand. Please don't be mad that I can't tell you. I promise, I'll tell you everything else, just not that."

"Hey, hey, it's okay. If you're not ready, it's okay."

"Thank you," Toby sighs in relief. "I promise I will, just... not today."

Lilly nods. "Keep going."

"Bishop was there to stop me. We called for help, and he was taken to the hospital." He gives her a guilty look. "There were a lot of legal dealings and a hearing to deal with it."

"Are you kidding me? You all kept that from me too!" Lilly shouts, getting angry. "What else have you been keeping from me? Did you knock up some girl and have Brody pay her off?"

"What?" Toby's brows furrow. "No, no. Nothing like that. That's it, that's everything we kept from you. But, Lilly, we kept that from you because of the details of the event. We didn't want you to live with the knowledge of what that monster said."

"Why? Why would it have affected me so much?"

"Because it was about you," he snarls, anger streaming out of his body. He's not mad at her, just at the memory of the past.

"Oh." She blinks like a deer caught in the headlights.

"The things he said were so vile that it stayed with me, Lilly." Toby looks wrecked.

"The nightmares," she whispers, her tears making a second appearance. "They're about that night, aren't they?"

Toby nods. "Partly. It's a lot more complicated. It's what I'm not ready to talk about."

"This is a lot to take in," she says, letting out a deep breath.

"Do you hate me?" I've never heard Toby sound so small and weak before. Fuck, this is hard to watch, but I'm not going anywhere in case Lilly needs me.

"What?" Her eyes widen.

"Do you hate me? I wouldn't blame you if you did." He gets down on his knees before her, placing his hands on her thighs. "I'm so fucking sorry. I hate myself for all the pain I've caused you. I hate myself for not being a better man for you. I hate myself for keeping secrets and lying to you."

"Stop." Lilly leans down and resting her forehead against his. "I don't hate you, Toby. But I am mad. So fucking mad. I'm hurt and confused, and I'm tired. I'm so tired of it all."

"I'm sorry."

"I know you are." She looks him in the eye. "All of this, it's going to take some time to process. I don't forgive you, not yet. I want you to get back on your meds and work to better yourself. Then you're going to make it up to me. You can decide how because, dude, I'm gonna make you grovel at my fucking feet."

Toby's eyes widen as she glares down at him. I bite the inside of my cheek to keep from laughing. God, this girl. She's fucking amazing.

"I wouldn't have judged you. I wouldn't have hated you. I wish so damn much that you would have trusted me with all of this because you were my everything. You could have been a damn serial killer and I wouldn't have cared. Maybe that says something about me. But, Toby, unless you treat *me* badly, unless you hit *me*, call *me* nasty things, I wouldn't have seen you any other way. But that's the past, and nothing we can say or do now will change it. I need you to not worry about that now. I need you to focus on how you're going to change and move on. How are we going to move on from this?"

"Please, don't give up on me," he whispers again, sounding like a sad little boy.

"If I was going to give up on you, Toby, I would have after the first few months of you not talking to me. You don't give me enough credit."

"I know." He sounds ashamed of that.

"As for what we are becoming to each other and where we go with things? Time is what we need. I love you, Toby. I want to be with you, that hasn't changed. But I need to be able to trust you, and I need you to show me that you're not going to just run at any sign of trouble. Can you do that?" Can you wait for me to be ready?"

"Yes." He nods. "I'll wait a lifetime. I'll spend that lifetime making it up to you. I promise. I'm so sorry."

"Toby." Theo's voice has Toby jumping to his feet. I don't miss the hurt on Lilly's face. I don't think Toby is ashamed of wanting her but there are still things he hasn't told her. I guess that will have to wait. "We need to go. Your appointment is in twenty minutes."

"Okay." He lets out a breath.

"What the hell happened to your nose?"

"He deserved it." I cast Theo a look and shrug.

He shakes his head and leaves. Toby looks down at Lilly. "Talk soon?"

"Yeah," she replies softly.

"I love you, Little Flower."

She just gives him a smile, causing him to deflate a little. She doesn't hug him, doesn't kiss him, and he leaves here with his tail between his legs. I feel a little bad, but he can't expect that just because they talked and he told her the truth that everything will be forgotten.

"I'm so proud of you," I tell her, sitting next to her on the chair.

"For what?" She looks so tired.

"For not giving in and forgiving him even though I can tell you want to."

"He hurt me badly, Bishop. And as much as I want us to get to a good place, to be with him, to love and hold him—I'm not there. He has a lot of making up to do."

"I know."

"I think we should keep this to ourselves, at least when it comes to Toby. I don't want to hide from the world, but I don't think he's ready to hear it."

"I don't think he is either." I kiss the top of her head. "We'll go with what feels right, okay?"

"Okay."

"I do want to tell you something while we're in the moment of spilling truths."

"Okay." She gives me a worried look.

"At the beginning of the year, Toby couldn't stand the idea of you dating." I cringe. "He asked me to use up all your free time so you *couldn't* date."

"What!" she hisses.

"Wait, before you get mad at me. I want you to know that I already planned on trying to use all your free time, but not because I didn't want you to date anyone. Okay, well, yeah, I didn't want that, but it's really because I wanted to get to know you better. I just wanted to be around you more. I was kind of hoping you would end up falling for me." I give her a boyish look, my cheeks heating.

She bursts into giggles. "Okay, that's kind of adorable. And, well, I guess it did work."

"You're not mad?"

"No." She shakes her head. "Anything else I should know?"

"Yes." I grimace. And she looks worried again for a second, her face falling. "Now that you're my girlfriend, I'm going to have to start bringing you home to see my mom. She's going to lose her shit when she finds out. She may pressure me into marrying you because she loves you that much. I'm sorry in advance."

"Oh my god." She giggles harder and everything seems right for the moment. "I love your mom. I'm more than okay with doing that. But the marriage thing... let's put a pin in that." She grins.

"Good idea. But you can be the one to break that news."

She smiles so wide, shaking her head.

"Come on, you. I need to feed my woman."

She gets up, still slightly giggling, and I hang back because her ass looks so damn fine in those sweatpants. They're not just hot on men, you know?

CHAPTER THIRTY-FOUR

LILLIANNA

"BEE. GET YOUR ASS UP NOW!" I SMACK HER WITH A PILLOW.

"Go away. Five more minutes," she grumbles, pulling the blankets up over her head and rolling to the side.

"Fine. I'm going to just leave you here and go buy all the banana chocolate chip muffins from the coffee shop so you have nothing when you go."

"I don't care."

"Ugh," I huff. We have class in less than thirty minutes. We're going to be late because Bee, the little shit, got up and turned off the alarm on my phone because she wanted to sleep in longer. Making it so I wasn't able to get up and get ready. So now I've had to toss on some leggings and Bishop's hoodie. I want to look cute, I'm in that stage when you get a boyfriend and you want to be cute every time you see them.

I don't know why I care, seeing how the man literally washed blood and another man's cum off me. We're never going to talk about that again, but I will forever remember how fucking amazing he was to me that night and continues to be. It's only been a week since that dreadful day, but time has been weighing heavily on me.

B and Jonas asked me about what happened that night, and I told them as much as I felt comfortable with. I'll give them more details later, but right now my head is still a mess.

This is what I know as of right now: Toby's been suffering with something traumatic on top of battling a mental health disorder for years now, and kept it all from me. He says it's because he didn't want me to see him differently or be afraid of him. I understand his reasoning, but I wish he trusted me and our bond enough to know I never would have turned on him like that.

He has been off his meds since I started school, so during most of our interactions lately he was in a depressive state, and then last week he was in a manic state. I'm still learning and doing research to better understand Toby and what he has to live with. But he's wrong. Even in these states, aside from the dry hump then rejection session, and the brawl followed by taking my virginity in the locker room, I wasn't afraid of him. Even with his burst of anger. So, if he just gave me the chance to learn, and help better understand him, he could have avoided a lot of our combined heartache. But I'm not in his head, so I can't try to make him out to be the bad guy. He's not a bad guy, he just did shitty things he needs to make up for.

Ever since that day he told me every heart wrenching thing, he's been respecting my wishes and giving me space. He sends me good morning and goodnight texts. He updates me whenever he does something that betters his health like take his meds or goes to therapy appointments. It's going to take him about a month or so before he levels out, and the meds kick back in, doing their job. So he's asked me to be patient with him, and I will be as much as he is with me.

He's been sending me potted flowers. A new color every day. It makes my pulse race, my belly warm, and my heart ache, in a good way. It's giving me hope that we can move past this. Bee keeps telling me our room is getting too crowded with all of the planters, so I plan on taking them to my parents' house. I can plant them there in my garden behind the pool house. They mean too much and are too pretty to just let them go to waste.

I haven't forgotten or forgiven Toby for the things he's done. He hurt me a lot. But knowing that he didn't do any of those things to me deliberately, I plan on giving him another chance. Some people might think I'm foolish, but screw what everyone thinks. Toby and I have been closer than best friends our whole life. I'm not going to just throw that away. I believe in second chances, if the person proves they deserve it. That's what I've asked of Toby, and he's agreed to it. Only time will tell.

If my mom can forgive my parents for what they did to her, I sure as hell can forgive Toby.

Other things I do know: I'm still in love with him, and I still want to be with him. But I'm also in love with Bishop, and I want to be with him too. I refuse to choose but something tells me that when Toby finds out, he will not be happy about it. That's why Bishop and I agreed to keep it between us and our close friends—meaning Jonas and Bee—and give Toby's meds a chance to take hold before we lay something like this on him.

Bee and Jonas don't know just yet, but we plan on telling them soon, because I don't want to have to keep my hands to myself every time I'm with Bishop. And I know it's hard for him to do the same. We haven't done anything except make out, and it's driving me nuts because I want nothing more than for that man to toss me on the nearest surface and have his way with me. Not to mention I would very much like to lick every inch of his body, tracing each of his tattoos with my tongue.

A knock at the door has me rushing over. Throwing it open, I pout when I see it's not Bishop. "Well, damn, Lills, don't look so happy to see me." Jonas rolls his eyes, smirking playfully.

"Sorry. I am happy to see you." I look at what he has in his hands. "What's that?"

"Coffee for Bee and a muffin. And before you ask why I didn't get you something, your man is on his way up with your drink."

"My man?" I ask, cheeks heating.

"Don't tell me you and Bishop aren't dating." He chuckles. "I'm not stupid."

"Okay, fine, we are. I was going to tell you today, actually." I bite my lower lip.

"He treats you good?"

"Yeah." I smile. "Really good."

"Then, consider him best friend approved. Also, he's the brother of the girl I'm trying to make mine, so I kind of have to like him." He winks, making me giggle.

"Who's at the door?" Bee groans, and Jonas looks over my shoulder.

"Is she okay?" His brow pinches with concern.

"Yeah, just her lady time." My eyes widen. "Shit, you did not hear that from me."

Jonas gives me a blank look. "I've been best friends with you two for years now. Period talk doesn't gross me out. You've done enough of it in my presence in the past. Hell, I'm surprised I don't know when you both start at this point."

"Okay, weirdo." I laugh. "Go on in. Maybe you can get her out of bed. If not, we're going to be late for class." I let Jonas in, and he smiles, looking at the lump on the bed.

"Hey, Bumblebee. Wanna get that sexy ass up? I brought you coffee and a muffin."

"Muffin?" Bee pops up like a jack in the box, her hair messy and all over the place.

Jonas chuckles and looks at Bee like she's the most beautiful girl in the world. *Ugh, they're too damn cute.*

"Is there a party in here that I wasn't invited to?" Bishop's voice has a thrill of excitement shooting through my body. Spinning around, I give him a shy smile. I can't help it. It only lasts a few moments after I see him for the first time of the day, but he does that to me. Makes me feel all ooey-gooey inside. I love it. "Hi." I walk over to him. "No party. Just trying to get Bee up and out of bed."

"How about you let Jonas deal with that lazy-ass and I'll walk you to class?" He chuckles.

"I heard that, asshole," Bee mutters. She gets out of bed, looking like a hot mess but again, Jonas looks at her like he's ready to rip her clothes off as he sits on the edge of my bed.

"For you." Bishop hands me my coffee and leans in to kiss me softly on the lips. I melt on the spot.

"Eww! What the hell," Bee screeches, making my cheeks heat. "Bitch, you didn't tell me you two were official."

"That's right, baby sis." Bishop steps in and wraps his arm around my shoulder, tucking me under his arm. "I've been upgraded from best friend to boyfriend." He flips his sister off and she scowls back, returning the gesture. I giggle because even though these two fight, they love each other like crazy.

"Yeah, well, she lives with me," Bee mutters, going into her closet. "I don't have anything to wear." *That's it?* God, I love my best friend. She's so chill, so supportive. Some friends might lose their mind if their best friend dated their sibling, but not Bee.

"That's all you got to say?" Bishop asks.

"What?" Bee comes stumbling out of the closest with a hoodie and a pair of leggings. "You're dating Lilly. She's literally the best thing that could have ever happened to you. Now, Mom can stop worrying about you knocking up some puck bunny. Also, if you hurt her, I'll kill you." She shrugs.

"Oh, fuck off," Bishop growls, and I glare at my best friend, jealousy hitting me at the idea of him with other women. I know he's had a past, but I still don't like acknowledging he's slept with a lot of the puck bunnies. "But you are right. Lilly is the best thing that's ever happened to me." I grin up at him so he can kiss me on the lips.

"Gag," Bee huffs. "Go be adorable somewhere else so I can die in peace."

"No dying, Bumblebee. Get dressed, we can walk together."

"You." Bishop points at Jonas. "Fuck off. You're not dating my sister."

"Hey!" Bee protests. "I'm not hounding you about dating my best friend, so you have no say."

"So that means you're finally agreeing to be my girl?" Jonas asks, smirking at her.

She swings her gaze to him. "No."

"It's only a matter of time, baby, but I'll wait as long as you need," he chuckles.

"Wait forever. Leave her alone," Bishop throws in.

"Alright, big boy." I laugh, grabbing my bag and phone. "Let's get out of here." I tug at his arm with my free hand that's not holding the delicious, hot goodness.

"Alone in the room? Fuck no," Bishop snarls.

"Alright then. I'll walk all by myself. Maybe some cute guy might offer to walk with me." I sigh dramatically as I let him go and turn to walk down the hallway.

"Fuck that," he growls as he runs after me. "I'll break his fucking hands."

Facing away from him, I grin, loving the alpha male side of him. It's hot.

When we get into the elevator, he pushes me against the wall and crashes his lips against mine. I moan as his tongue sweeps in and over mine, kissing me until I'm a horny little mess for him. "Party tonight?" he asks me. "Toby won't be there. And I want to spend time with my girl without having to worry about keeping my hands to myself."

Biting my lower lip, I nod my head. "Okay."

Toby has been staying at home with our parents and plans on staying there until he's a little more stable. The guys on the team still aren't that happy with him, so he doesn't want to stay at the hockey house. From what Bishop told me, he doesn't want to make me uncomfortable by staying in their dorm since it's across the hall from me.

I feel bad. But having a chance to breathe, to think without worrying I'll run into him all the time has helped a lot.

"Just nothing over the top, okay? You know how these parties can be. Social media is a bitch."

Thankfully, Katie hasn't caused any more issues. Yet. But she has been giving me the stink eye any time she's seen me with Bishop, and she loves to pretend I'm not there when she asks him about Toby. That pisses me off. She acts as if they're friends and she cares about his well-being. I call bullshit. She just wants his dick, and I'll be damned if I ever let that happen.

Toby is mine. Or at least, he will be. Hopefully. *Fuck, I hope so.* Before, I would have jumped at the chance to make things official with Toby, but a lot has changed. I can't, not yet. I've lost a lot of trust in him, especially where my heart is concerned. I need to know he won't shatter it again before I give it to him.

"I just want to hang out with my girl, have a few drinks, and dance a little. Nothing crazy." He quickly kisses me again before the doors open.

He throws his arm over my shoulder as we walk out. I smile, leaning into his warmth. This isn't anything new for him and me. He's been acting like this, all close and whatnot, since the school year started. But since we got together, only I know it's different. I never thought that I'd end up dating Bishop, but I can't think of anything else I want more.

Okay, that's a lie. I'd like to add another best friend to the mix, but I guess we'll just have to wait and see what happens.

CHAPTER THIRTY-FIVE

BISHOP

"This is weird," Lilly tells me as we walk into the hockey house. The party has been going for about an hour now, but Lilly and Bee took forever to get ready. Not that I cared, I was enjoying myself from my spot on her bed as I watched her smile and laugh with my sister.

Who knew seeing Lilly so happy would make me so... happy? Her smile is addicting, her laugh is intoxicating. I'm head over heels for this girl, and it's taking everything in me not to shout it from the rooftops. I've pushed my feelings down for her for so long and now that she's mine, I don't want to anymore.

But she's right and we have to think about Toby. He's in a frail state right now and with how in love and obsessed he is with Lilly, he's going to see me as a threat. And I don't think he's

I'm not out to steal her, but I'm not giving her up either. I am willing to share her, but she's fucking mine now.

"Why's that?"

"I've always gone to these parties with Bee. Now I'm here with you. People are staring," she whispers.

I chuckle. "Let them stare, baby. They should be used to seeing us together by now. I literally spend all my free time with you, and I wouldn't be surprised if everyone already assumed we're together."

"If they do, no one has said anything to Toby because he hasn't killed you yet," she says it as a joke, but I can tell she is worried.

"Hey," I pull her over to the wall. "Everything is going to be okay."

"I hope so." She chews on her lip. *Why is that so damn hot?*

"Let's get some drinks, loosen up a bit."

"Yeah." She lets out a breath. "Good idea."

With my arm around her waist, I guide her to the kitchen. "Grant, hey!" A few of the guys on the team greet me, giving polite smiles to Lilly. I grab her a drink as we stand and chat for a bit. I'm proud of my girl for warming up and talking to the guys, even making a few of the guys laugh. They include her in the conversation and generally seem interested in what she has to say. Yeah, I'm whipped already and I don't even care. This girl could fart and I'd think it's adorable.

"Hey, Bishop!" a puck bunny named Molly calls, coming up to me. Immediately, I cringe. "I've missed you," she purrs, putting her hand on my arm and leaning into me. She looks up at me with half-lidded eyes. "You haven't texted me back in weeks." She pouts. "I thought we had fun. I can't stop thinking about that thing you did with your tongue."

Fucking hell, this girl needs to shut the hell up. "Molly. Look, you're a nice girl, but it was one night and I was drunk at that party. I don't mean to be an ass, but it's not going to happen again. I haven't texted you back because I told you before we did anything it was a one-time-only kind of thing."

"Oh, come on." She pouts harder, and I see Lilly glaring daggers at the side of her head from the corner of my eye.

Grabbing onto Molly's hand, I carefully pry it off my arm and step back. "No. Sorry. I'm off the market now. You can tell all the other girls that too. Bishop Grant is no longer single. I have my eyes on one girl and one girl only. Sorry." I'm not sorry, not at all. It's not that I don't respect the girls I've slept with, but they knew going in that nothing would go further than one night of messing around.

Unfortunately, a lot of the bunnies just take that as a challenge.

"Oh, really?" Molly's face slips from sweet and flirty to pissed. "Who?" she demands, then flicks her eyes over to Lilly. She's not next to me right now but a few feet away talking to Bee and Jonas, although I know she can hear us.

"A girl who is drop-dead gorgeous, who is the best person I've ever met. A girl who I would walk through fire for. Her name isn't any of your business. So, if you don't mind, I'd like to talk to my buddies here." I nod towards John and Peter. They chuckle, listening to the whole thing.

Molly just huffs, flicks her hair, and turns away.

"Damn, Grant. Is that the truth? You got yourself a girl?" Peter taunts.

I look over at Lilly who smiles at me softly. "Yeah, man. I got myself a girl. The best girl in the world." I look back at him.

"Damn. I gotta meet the girl who managed to steal Bishop Grant's heart." John chuckles.

"Soon, my man. Soon." I pat this shoulder.

Lilly slips away from my sister and Jonas, disappearing into the crowd. I excuse myself from the guys and hurry over to them. "Where did Lilly go?"

"She went to pee," Bee says, slurring her words.

My brows jump and I look at Jonas as my sister closes her

eyes, dancing to the music. "Don't worry. I've cut her off. She will sober up pretty quick," he chuckles.

Damn it. I can't even be mad at this guy. "I'm going to find my girl. You, watch my sister."

"With my life." He nods, and shit, I think he means it. *Okay, damn it, I really can't hate him now.*

Weaving my way through the crowd, I look for Lilly by the bathrooms. My body stiffens when I see her standing there talking to Trey, one of the biggest fuckboys on the team.

"You know, I've always thought you were sexy. I wanted to ask you out, but you know, I didn't want to get my ass kicked by your brother," he chuckles.

"Don't have to worry about him," I growl, grabbing his shoulder and pulling him back. "I'll gladly kick your ass myself."

"Grant. Hey, man. No need to be a dick. I was just talking to the pretty girl."

"You were talking to *my* fucking girl. So piss off before I punch you in the face," I snarl.

"Shit." His eyes widen, looking between the two of us. "Really?"

"Say anything to Toby and I'll kill you, got it?"

He swallows hard and nods his head. "Yeah, man. I won't say anything." He stumbles away and down the hall.

"You know, you like to tease me about being jealous, but you're not much better." Lilly giggles. My gaze snaps to her. She's smiling at me, amusement dancing in her eyes.

"Damn right, I'm not. I'm a jealous fucker. You have no idea how many times I had to hold myself back from kicking other guys' asses when we were just friends. And now I don't have to," I growl, wrapping my arm around her waist and pulling her to me.

She looks up at me and licks her lips. "I want you to kiss me," she whispers. "So badly."

I look around, making sure no one is watching, before giving her a quick, heated kiss.

"At some point tonight, I'm getting you alone, *il mio cuore*. There's no way I can keep my hands off you all night."

"Okay," she breathes out, cheeks flushed.

"Let's go dance for a bit." She nods, and I drag her back to the living room. There's some fast-paced music playing, and I pull Lilly's back to my front.

Everyone is too drunk to pay attention to us, so I enjoy the moment. Lilly's ass grinds against my cock, and I groan into the crook of her neck. "Baby, you're making it so fucking hard not to take you right on this dance floor."

The little minx just moans, grinding harder as she moves her hips to the music.

I do my best to keep my hands on her hips and not feel her up like I want to. One song turns into three, and my willpower drains to nothing.

Grabbing Lilly's hand, I tug her through the crowd towards the stairs. But just as I get to the bottom step, my teammate Brad, stops me. "If you are about to go up to your room, I wouldn't man. Ricky just took three chicks in there."

"What!" I growl. "Why didn't he just use his fucking room?"

"No idea." He just shrugs and takes off.

Fuck. Change of plans.

Turning around, tug Lilly through the house and outside. "Where are we going?" She giggles as I continue to lead us around the side of the house.

Once we're cast in darkness, I push her up against the house. She gasps as her eyes widen and then my lips are on hers. She moans as my hands roam her body. "Do you know how fucking sexy you look tonight?" I groan as I kiss and suck at her neck. "You're so fucking tempting. Driving me nuts. I've been wanting to touch you, show the world you're mine."

"Touch me, Bishop," she whimpers. "Please."

Pulling away from her neck, I kiss her lips. She parts them, allowing me to deepen the kiss. Her arms wrap around my neck, sliding her fingers through my hair. She grabs a handful and tugs, making me growl.

I'm so fucking gone for this girl. My cock aches in my jeans, but all I want to do right now is make her feel good. I don't care about me.

"You want me to play with your tight, needy pussy, baby?" I murmur against her lips.

"Yes," she pants, nodding her head.

"When I slip my fingers inside you, will you be dripping for me?" I growl, staring at her with lust-filled eyes.

Her eyes are glazed, bright with desire, her lips wet and swollen from our kiss. If I could see her face better, I know she would have that adorable blush on her cheeks.

She nods slowly as my hand dips under her dress. "Did you wear this for me, baby?" I ask her, bringing my lips to her jaw. I pepper her with kisses as I rub my hand over the sopping wet fabric of her panties. "Shit, baby girl. You're soaked."

"Bishop," she whines, her hips seeking friction.

"Shhh." I kiss her lips softly. "I have you, baby." I waste no more time, knowing we could get caught at any moment, and slip my fingers into her panties. We groan together as I brush over her sensitive clit and into her pussy. "Lilly," I growl.

"Bishop," she whimpers.

Using the heel of my palm, I rub her clit as I fuck her with my fingers. "That's it, baby. Relax. Let me take this ache away for you."

"Oh, god," she moans.

In and out, I thrust my fingers, curling them when I bury them as deep as they can go. The noises leaving her mouth have me nearly blowing in my pants. Not wanting to get caught, I kiss her, swallowing her whimpers and cries.

Her fingers claw at my back, and she grinds against my hand. I want her to cum on my cock, to scream my name as I watch her come apart for me. But I want our first time to mean something, not be outside at a party beside the house.

"Keep doing that, right there," she begs. "Oh, yes, yes, like that."

"You're so fucking sexy right now," I growl, my cock twitching at how crazy she makes me. My mouth waters, and I can't wait to lick my fingers clean when she's finished coating them in her release.

"Bishop," she pants my name in a lusty moan. "Fuck. I'm gonna cum."

Pulling back to look her in the eyes, I find them wide with desire, and my chest swells with primal pride, knowing it's all because of me. "Be a good girl and cum on my fingers, *il mio cuore*," I growl out the command, feeling her cunt quiver around my fingers. My face goes back to her neck, kissing and sucking, not giving a fuck that I'm leaving my mark on her smooth, pale skin.

Pressing my heel down, I crook my finger against her sweet spot, making her orgasm. "Oh, god!" she gasps, and then moans as her pussy grips my fingers.

"Such a good girl. You cum so prettily, Lilly. I love you."

She smiles up at me dreamily but doesn't say the words back. It's okay. She's not there yet.

Now I'm going to go the rest of the night with a fucking hard on.

Totally worth it.

TOBIAS

"Are you staying in tonight?" Dad asks me, stepping in the living room. I look up from the TV.

"Yeah. Nothing else to do."

"Why don't you see if Lilly and Bishop are available?" he suggests, leaning against the door frame.

I huff out a laugh, running a hand through my hair. "I don't think Lilly wants to hang out with me, Dad. I've fucked up a lot, not only the past few weeks but the past two years." The thought of Lilly has my gut twisting. It's going to take a long time before I can get over the image of her face when I left her in that locker room. The pain, the betrayal, the anger, and her telling me she hated me. Each of them stabbed me in the heart like a knife. But I was the one who was at fault. I can't blame anyone but myself.

"I thought you two talked everything out." Not everything, but the big stuff, sure. Telling her about my biggest struggles was the hardest thing I ever had to do. I knew deep down that Lilly wasn't going to toss me to the side because she thought I was broken and not worth it. It's not who she is. Lilly is the sweetest, kindest, most loving person I've ever met. I should have had more trust in her. But it's hard to think logically when you've convinced yourself of something so much you feel it in your heart that it's true, even if it isn't.

"We did. But I fucked up. Big time. I have a lot to make up for. I don't expect her to just forgive me overnight. I need time to get better and work on gaining her trust back." Even if being away from Lilly hurts so fucking much. All I want to do is kiss her, hold her, fuck her. I meant what I said even before I ran. She's mine. And I'm not going anywhere until she tells me to fuck off. Until she tells me there's no chance anything will ever happen between us.

Even then I don't think I could ever truly let her go. She's meant to be mine but I've been too stupid to do anything about it. It's time to man up.

I'm still conflicted though because even if I know she's mine, can we ever actually be together? It doesn't change everything I've been worrying about. But, if I don't want to lose her for good, I'm going to have to try and put my issues aside.

"I'm guessing you're not going to tell me what you did?"

"Nope." I sigh, leaning back against the couch. "I love you, Dad, but that's between her and me." And maybe Rain because I have a feeling Lilly tells her things. More than I would ever share with my parents.

He nods. "Understandable. Things will be okay between you two. You're best friends and have been since the moment you met. She's your sister, she will forgive you. You just need to grovel your ass off," he chuckles.

I really hate that word. "You're right about one thing, I do need to grovel, and I plan to. I've already started. But, Dad, she's *not* my sister." I give him a look.

His brows furrow and I think he's about to argue with me when he nods. He chuckles, but it's kind of sad. I'm not sure why. "I guess you're right. You two have always seemed to have a stronger connection than that."

Dad leaves and I get bored of the TV show I'm watching, so I start to mindlessly scroll on my phone.

Pulling up Instagram, I decide to be a stalker and see if Lilly posted anything new. I smile when I see her newest post from yesterday. She's got her hair up in space buns, her bangs down and curled. Her arm is around Bee, who is kissing her on the cheek while Lilly smiles wide. She looks happy. Good. She deserves to be happy. I've already taken so much of that away from her.

Closing my eyes, I try to block out all the negative thoughts that start to flood my mind. The ones that tell me I'm not good enough for her. That I'm broken and she hates me. My therapist is still working with me on it, but he tells me to try to distract my mind as soon as the thoughts start to flood in.

Opening my eyes again, I see that she's been tagged in some photos, so I click on them. My brows furrow when I see that it's time stamped from ten minutes ago. One is of her, Bee, and Jonas. It's a selfie, and from the looks of the dark background with house lights and people, they look like they're at a party.

Of course, they would be at the hockey house party. Bishop isn't in the dog house with them, I am. And we would be playing tomorrow if it wasn't for me.

I let that fucking asshole on the ice get the better of me, and I let my jealousy of Ryan put me in that mindset in the first place.

I can't help but feel bummed. It's not that I wanna go drink and dance, but I feel like I'm missing out.

My whole newsfeed is full of photos and videos of the party. I get a notification on my phone. Clicking on my inbox, I see that it's from Katie. *Why on earth is she still messaging me?*

Rolling my eyes, I go to delete it when I see another message pop up.

> KATIE
>
> Thought you might want to see this. Some best friend, huh?

My thumb hovers over it. *Best friend?* Fuck, curiosity gets the better of me, and open the message.

The text before says:

> KATIE
>
> I'm so sorry to tell you this, but I think your best friends are hiding something big from you.

THERE'S A VIDEO AND THE THUMBNAIL IS OF TWO GRAINY PEOPLE. Nausea hits me as I press play.

The video starts up, the loud sounds of a party going on in the background. The video is zoomed in on two people dancing. It's Lilly and Bishop. Normally I wouldn't look twice at it. They're best friends, they've been hanging out a lot. It's no big deal.

But the way they're dancing in this video, with his arm wrapped around her waist as he pulls her close to him, and her back pressed against his front. It looks a little too intimate for friends.

Then Katie starts to talk, the voice sounding like it's coming from behind the camera. "No wonder he hasn't been giving any of the puck bunnies attention. He's been fucking the coaches' daughter. I feel so bad for Toby. What kind of best friends do that? He's clearly dealing with a lot already."

My chest starts to rise and fall at a rapid pace. I close my eyes, trying to breathe, to calm down before I let my anger get the better of me. I can't be making rash decisions, I can't jump to conclusions. It's only ever gotten me into trouble.

No, what I need to do is go to this party and see for myself that Katie is lying. That it's all just her being a crazy bitch like she normally is.

Standing up, I shove my phone in my pocket and head to my room. I change into a pair of jeans and a black hoodie, then grab the keys to my car.

"Where are you going?" Rain asks me as I head to the door.

"A party," I tell her.

"You think that's a good idea? Are you going to drink? You know that drinking and taking your meds isn't a good idea?"

I narrow my eyes at her. I don't want to be parented right now. I'm twenty-one.

"I'm going to the hockey house party. It's mostly just the team and some friends. I'll be fine."

I don't give her a chance to question me more before I take off.

The whole car ride there I have to blast music and sing along with it to keep my mind off that video. *They're just friends. Only friends. Everything is fine.*

Parking the car with all the others, I jog into the house. I expect my teammates to start telling me to fuck off and get out, but other than a few looks my way, people pay me no attention. Probably because they're all shit-faced at this point.

The music is loud and the house is packed with bodies grinding against each other. But as I scan all the faces, none of them are Bishop and Lilly.

Going into the kitchen, I see Jonas and Bee looking pretty damn cozy.

"Hey." I nod my head when they look my way. "Have you seen Bishop and Lilly?"

They look at each other and I don't like what I see. It's like they're hiding something. "Ah, yeah, they're around here somewhere." Jonas scratches the back of his head.

I narrow my eyes. "Where?"

"Why do you want to know, Toby?" Bee asks me, arms crossed as she glares daggers at me. "Lilly is having fun. She's smiling and laughing and having a good fucking time. You want to piss all over that? Make her cry some more?"

My jaw is clenched as my fist tightens. She's pissing me the fuck off. I don't care if she's right, she doesn't need to be a bitch about it. "Whatever, I'll find them myself."

"Or you could leave them alone," Bianca adds.

"Is there something you don't want me to see?" I ask her, narrowing my eyes. "Because you sure as hell are determined to keep me from finding her. They're my best friends, Bianca. I want to hang out with them."

"Really?" Her brows rise. "You didn't just casually stroll in here. You saw something that set you off and now you want to see for yourself, don't you?"

"Bee," Jonas says in a warning tone.

Bianca looks up at him, glowering but huffs and walks away, flipping me off as she goes.

"Sorry about her. She's drunk and you know, shark week can be scary as hell," he chuckles before taking off after her.

Feeling pissed off, I fight the urge to grab a fucking bottle of whiskey. I head out back, seeing if I can find them there.

There are some people sitting around the fire drinking, a group of girls gushing over the cute goat, but I don't see them.

"Bishop," a lusty moan has my body going stiff and my blood run cold. "Fuck. I'm gonna cum."

His response makes my stomach twist. "Be a good girl and cum on my fingers, *il mio cuore*."

Time stops and I feel like I'm moving in slow motion as I turn around. Beside the house cloaked in darkness, I see my worst nightmare come true. Bishop has Lilly pushed up against the house, kissing her neck while his hand moves under her dress. Her eyes are shut, her face in pure bliss.

And when she sucks in a gasp then moans, a sound that haunts my dreams, my heart shatters alongside her as she comes apart on his hand.

To be continued. Check out A Game Of Love- Forbidden Game Book Two, to find out what happens next with Lilly, Bishop, and Toby.

ALSO BY THE AUTHOR

ONGOING SERIES

Angelic Academy
Book One: Tainted Wings
Book Two: Tainted Bonds
Book Three: Tainted Hearts
Book Four: Tainted Souls

Black Venom Crew:
Book One: Little Bird
Book Two: Venomous Queen
Book Three: Dark Soldiers
Book Four: Deadliest Throne

Boys Of Kingston Academy:
Tantalizing Kings
Tormented Kings

Boys Of Rose Briar Hill:
Just A Summer Fling (Prequel)
Broken Prince

A Forbidden Game (MFM Stepbrother hockey)
A Game Of Choice

CALLINGWOOD UNIVERSE (ALL STANDALONES)

We Are Worthy- A sweet and steamy omegaverse.
We Are Destiny A steamy poly omegaverse
Wild Child- A steamy poly omegaverse (cowrite)
Knot Going Anywhere- A week reverse harem omegaverse

STANDALONES

If You Go Into The woods- Steamy MF Shifter Novella

CO-WRITES

Solidarity Academy
Knock 'Em Down: Book One
Take 'Em Out: Book Two
Rise 'Em Up: Book Three

Coral Springs University
Hooves & Heartstrings- An MF Monster Romance

Lost Between The Pages
Mad For The Sea Witch

Wild Thorn Ranch
Marshall
Wyatt & Weston

The Sugar River Series
Forbidden Mischief : A MM Step Brother Romance

ANTHOLOGIES

Beach Shots & Monster Knots: A Monster Romance Anthology
For the Love of Villains: Anthology
Autumn Spells: A Charity Anthology
Knotty Holiday Nights: An Omegaverse Holiday Anthology
Snow, Lights, and Monster Nights: A Monster Anthology

SHARED WORLDS

A Night Of Rapture And Pride
Naomi (Dressed to Kill)

THANK YOU

As always, I'm beyond grateful for Jessica, Jennifer, Mylene and Martha. You ladies are family more than anything! Thank you for all the time and energy you put into all my books.

Many thanks to my Beta and ARC teams for your time and efforts to help each of my books be the best they can be!

ABOUT THE AUTHOR

Hello! I'm Alisha Williams. I'm a little weird, very dirty minded and I love to talk. Ice coffee is life and books are my escape from reality.
I write a little bit of everything, but mostly why choose with a LGBTQ+ spin. My books rage from light to dark. I mostly write contemporary but I also write omegaverse and paranormal. But, one thing you can always expect, is spicy content. I live in Alberta, Canada, with my husband and two awesome daughters. Writing has been a lifelong dream of mine. Never did I think I would get to write so many amazing stores, but I'm grateful everyday that this is a possibility.

Wanna see what all my characters look like, hear all the latest gossip about my new books or even get a chance to become a part of one of my teams? Join my readers group on Facebook here - Naughty Queens. Or find my author's page here - Alisha Williams Author
Of course, I also has an Instagram account to show all my graphics, videos, and more book related goodies - alishawilliamsauthor

Sign up for my Newsletter
Got TikTok? Follow alishawilliamsauthor

Printed in Great Britain
by Amazon

37724830R00212